Also Available from Jolly Horror Press

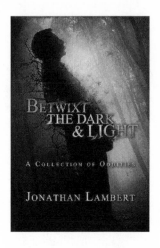

Betwixt the Dark & Light

Don't Cry To Mama

Accursed

A Horror Anthology

Edited by Jonathan Lambert and Lori Titus

Jolly Horror Press

Cover design by Eloise J. Knapp

"The Hands Resist Him" first appeared in "Once Upon a Time, When Things Turned Out Okay" by When the Dead Books ©2019

"Cora's Eyes" first appeared in "Toys in the Attic" by James Ward Kirk Publishing ©2015

"Cursory Review" first appeared in "Pandora's Closet," edited by Jean Rabe and Martin H. Greenberg, DAW Books, Inc. ©2007

CONTENTS

FOREWORD By T.J. Tranchell.. 1

INKED By Angelique Fawns.. 5

THE HANDS RESIST HIM By Michelle Von Eschen 17

THE FAMILY HEIRLOOM By Mya Lairis................................. 37

DIRTY By Jordan Kerns.. 57

MADAM MULANI By Justin Guleserian 61

THE BARTER By J.C. Raye 73

JUDGE NOT By Patsy Pratt-Herzog... 87

RED CAP CHRISTMAS By Jami Baumann 93

1 ARABIAN DAY By Jeannie Warner 111

ATTACHMENT By Sophie Kearing 121

MYSTICAL IMAGE By Jeremy Mays 153

FRIEND OF THE FISHERMAN By Joan C. Guyll 163

UN PERRO SIN PELO By Richard Lau 181

THE CHAIR By Alesha Escobar 191

DO YOU LIKE THE WAY IT BURNS? By Amanda Crum ... 203

TRADITIONAL GOLD WEDDING BAND By Jeff Barker .. 221

THE FORGOTTEN ONES By Natasha Hanova...................... 233

THE RUBY OF LIFE By Sipora Coffelt 241

PERFECTION IN BLACK LACE By Mark McLaughlin 259

WINTER BREAK By M. Guendelsberger 271

THE DENTURES By Judith Baron 287

JAADU By B.D. Prince.. 309

CORA'S EYES By H.R. Boldwood 329

THE TYPEWRITER By Tylor James 341

LITTLE ADVENTURE By Karen Thrower 367

CURSORY REVIEW By Donald J. Bingle 379

ABOUT THE AUTHORS 393

ACKNOWLEDGEMENTS.. 407

FOREWORD

BY T.J. TRANCHELL

When I was a kid, I would stay up late some nights just to see what was on TV. Sometimes I would watch stand-up comedy and other times I would watch the horror shows: *Forever Knight, The First Power, Monsters, Freddy's Nightmares,* and *Friday the 13th: The Series.* Unlike the Krueger show, *Friday the 13th* had absolutely nothing to do with Jason Voorhees, Camp Crystal Lake, or any of the mythology built up by 1987.

What it did have was cursed objects. About 70 of them, one for each episode. There would have been more, but the series was cancelled before the end of the third season.

The thing I loved most about the show was the history and origins of the cursed objects. How each one attracted different people from a variety of backgrounds: rich and poor, the already unlucky, the ones desperate to keep a good luck streak going, and

1

the completely average who walked into a curio shop with money to burn on the wrong day.

In *Accursed*, the second anthology from Jolly Horror Press, you'll find a continuation of those themes. The objects are just as varied as the people who own them, even temporarily.

It makes you think: do we ever really own anything? That sense of ownership over something might in fact contribute to the malicious feelings directed at humans who lord over all creation and force other people, animals, and made things to be subservient.

Indeed, it is the overwhelming desire to own certain things that has caused them to be hexed. How many people have died for every bewitched diamond in history? The need, the desire, to have lordship over an item and the lengths humans go to possess them can become the evil that drives a curse.

Possession is often associated with cursed objects, and the nature of it goes both ways. A person might possess an item, but the item can possess the heart and mind of the owner. Then again, we often think of a cursed object as being possessed.

Case in point: by the time this volume is published, *Annabelle Comes Home*, the latest entry into the Conjuring Universe—films based on the work of demonologists Ed and Lorraine Warren—will have rolled through the theaters and likely be on home video. Every film in the series has an object thought to be a focal point of a haunting or a possession (see? There's that word) which the Warrens then lock in a room in their house. The latest installment purports to unleash every cursed object and the horrors within upon the Warrens and anyone else in their path.

That is what you have in your hands now: a multitude of curses, hexes, possessions, and pure evil at your fingertips. We know you want it. You possess it now.

Keep reading and at least one story here will possess you.

And then we will see who owns what.

T.J. Tranchell
Walla Walla, WA
May 29, 2019

I asked T.J. Tranchell to write the intro to *Accursed* because I knew he would be so serious and academic. He didn't disappoint. What I was thinking when I came up with the concept of *Accursed* was that old Brady Bunch episode in Hawaii. They found that little tiki idol, and Greg almost died in a surfing accident, Peter had a tarantula crawling up his chest, and Alice threw her back out. I don't know why, but I've always remembered that episode. Anyway, as editor, I read all 197 submissions, and these are the tip top. Sometimes curses are funny, sometimes they are horrifying. I hope we have found the balance between the two extremes with this anthology. And I hope you enjoy reading them. Without further ado, here they are.

Jonathan Lambert
King George, VA
October 31, 2019

INKED

BY ANGELIQUE FAWNS

Her entire body was covered in art. Even with her employee discount at Taboo Tattoo, it had cost her a fortune. Hearts seeped rivulets of blood down her soft white arms, roses with sharp thorns decorated sturdy legs, black swans hugged her chest, and snakes slithered down her back. Lily was into bad boys, and thought she'd found her soulmate. He just didn't know it yet. Snake was only interested in her as his tattoo artist. She was losing sleep and going crazy dreaming of the big, heavily-tatted man with hypnotic eyes. There was nothing she wouldn't do to get him, including finding herself in a dodgy part of the city in the wee hours of the morning.

The shop was called Pagan Possibilities. It could only be accessed off an alley strewn with used needles in the Queen Street West area of Toronto. The shop had once been a garage, and still showed signs of it. Paint peeled from the aluminum siding, and a window was blacked out. The smell of cannabis hung in the air like a long dead skunk. Lily clutched the shop's worn flyer in one sweaty hand, trying to summon up the courage to enter. She hoped this was the right place. The literature said the shop was only open from midnight till 3 a.m. on Friday nights, so she had hopped on a streetcar and braved drunks, hookers and junkies to try her luck.

Fingering the stud in her lip, Lily took a deep breath, pushed open the door and walked in. Licorice incense tickled her nostrils. A low glow emanated from crystal lamps and candles and the décor could only be called hoarder-chic. Jars filled with murky liquid, candles, incense holders, garden gnomes, pentacles, hundreds of books, and bedazzled shawls fought for space on every dusty shelf and table. Lily picked up a jar, but quickly put it down again after seeing toad heads floating in the liquid.

"Hmm, there is something you desire. Something you want more than anything in the universe. You think I can help you," said a gravelly voice from the dark.

Lily saw a hunched figure in a dim corner of the garage behind a desk and started squeezing past overflowing tables. As her eyes adjusted to the gloom, she saw the proprietor of Pagan Possibilities wasn't hunch-backed, but wearing a set of wings and a positively stunning black lace gown.

"Hello darling! Look at you! Those are some amazing tattoos, and I positively love the purple hair. I'm Penny and this is my little shop of horrors and wonders," she said, one hand on a slender hip, the other twirling a piece of her long black wig.

Lily looked in astonishment at the store owner. She was gorgeous. A serpent-like body, muscular and sensuous, with soft dark eyes, and only the faint shadow of a beard on her face.

"I was at a summer solstice party with some of my Wiccan friends and found this pamphlet. I'm desperately in love with a man who comes to my tattoo shop and my heart is gonna explode into a million bloody pieces if I can't have him," Lily said, pointing to a tattoo of a shattered heart on her forearm. "Like this."

"Well, you've come to the right place, I have some powerful potions, but if you're a tattoo artist, I have a really extraordinary ink. But let me warn you girl, once you needle this into someone's skin, they will be yours forever. Be sure or beware," Penny said as she reached beneath the desk and brought out a small container of scarlet liquid.

Lily looked in fascination at the iridescent red ink. It slowly swirled and curled in the clear plastic tube.

"It almost looks alive! I'll take it. How much?"

"Three hundred dollars, but make sure this is what you want," Penny cautioned.

Lily was already seducing Snake in her mind, and quickly counted out three hundred dollars in large bills. She handed it to Penny as she tucked the ink into her pocket. Hustling out of there, she went back to her apartment above the tattoo shop to catch a few hours of sleep before her favorite client arrived at noon the next day.

***

When Snake walked into the shop, sweat started to trickle down Lily's armpits. She was wearing her most flattering skull and crossbones mini dress, and had made a special effort to flat iron the long purple hair on the unshaven side of her head.

Six feet tall, with a gym-toned body, long black hair caught back in a man bun, and startling green eyes, he was the most gorgeous human being on Earth. Luckily, he was addicted to ink, and dropped in at least once a month to get a new tat, or add some color to an older one.

"Hi Lily! I'm looking for something special to build up my arm sleeve today. Maybe a dragon? A bloody sword?" Snake said.

He untucked his black t-shirt from his tight Levi's and pulled it off. Lily greedily drank in the wide back, taut muscles, and artistic ink covering the majority of his upper body. She had done most of the work, and a world of castles, dragons, swords and starships already decorated him.

"How about something special today? I designed this just for you," Lily showed him a drawing of a large skull whose teeth clenched a rose dripping blood from the petals.

"That's fantastic. Put it on my tab, and let's do it," he said as he settled into her chair.

Lily knew he was good for the cash so she took out her special tube of scarlet liquid and poured it into the ink cap. It came out in thick globs and looked like it was breathing as it pulsed in the gun. She found a clear place on his forearm and started working on his skin with the tattoo needles. Breathing in his smell of Irish Spring soap and sweat, butterflies started their familiar flapping in her belly. How many nights had she lain awake imagining her thighs wrapped around his motorcycle as she pressed her lips into his back? Then looking into his eyes over a bonfire as they sipped whiskey?

The hum of the machine masked her excited breathing as the black skull with the red rose appeared beneath her fingers. A tattoo of this size took her around four hours, but the minutes flew by. The longer she could be near Snake, the better. She paid special attention to the flower, making sure the ink was extra vibrant. This tattoo was going to be the most important work of her life. After Lily carefully cleaned the reddened skin, she tried to put a bandage on it, but Snake flapped his hand at her.

"You know me baby, I live dangerously. Let it breathe."

Snake pulled his t-shirt back on and studied her for a minute, "You know, you look different today. Really beautiful. There is something...I don't know. Do you wanna go for dinner with me tonight?"

"Yes," Lily gasped, that special ink worked fast. The skull on his arm seemed to wink at her and the blood streaming off the rose looked wet and alive.

"It's four now, what time do you want me to come get you? I almost don't feel like leaving you, I kinda want to just stay here and stare at you."

"Now! I can go now. You're my last client of the day, the benefits of being self-employed," Lily said, "let me grab my purse and we can get some pre-dinner cocktails."

She followed him out, then locked the door behind her, unable to believe her luck. The newly created skull watched her from his arm. She shook her head, it must be an illusion. A tattoo couldn't be alive.

Snake walked down the sidewalk and stopped at a touring bicycle locked to a metal post, with a helmet hanging off the handle bars.

Lily's jaw dropped, "I thought you said you rode a mean bike."

"Yes, this is a top-of-the-line Schwinn. Want me to double you? Or do you have your own wheels?" Snake said, flashing her his devastating grin. "You are gorgeous, those curves and that purple hair. I don't know how I didn't notice before!"

Lily stared at the five-speed, not sure what to say. This put a kink in her *Sons of Anarchy* fantasy.

"Here, climb up on the seat and I'll stand and peddle. I'll take you to my place. I got some beer in the fridge and we can figure out where to go for dinner," he said, looping one long leg over and leaning into the handle bars to make room for her.

She climbed up behind him and tried to enjoy holding onto his broad back as he push-pedaled them down the road. At least the guy was environmentally conscious. Though it was only about a ten-minute ride, her dress got wrinkled and her butt was sore when they showed up outside a small semi-detached brownstone. They both tumbled off the bike.

"Wait till you meet my Mom. You're gonna love her. Hey, maybe she can make us dinner tonight and save me some money?" Snake said, walking quickly up the driveway after dumping his bike onto the lawn.

"You live with your mom still?" Lily asked as she hustled after him. "Aren't you like thirty-years-old?"

"Thirty-five actually. She's divorced and likes the company. Besides, I'm between jobs right now, so it works for me." Snake pushed open the front door.

"How long have you been unemployed?"

"A couple years, but I'm working on an app. Hey Mom, come meet Lily! She's my tattoo artist."

Lily followed him, noticing the photos of a young Snake (he definitely had a dorky, pimply stage), and crocheted art informing guests that "Hookers Do It With One Hand" and "I Crochet Past My Bedtime."

A grey-haired lady stepped out of the kitchen smiling, "Snake, I'm glad you've finally brought a girl home. I was beginning to think you played for the other team."

"Mom, don't embarrass me. I'm taking Lily down to the basement, okay? Maybe you can bring us down some snacks?" Snake turned to descend a narrow set of stairs.

"Nice meeting you," Lily said to the still grinning lady as she awkwardly followed Snake.

Getting to the bottom of the twisty stairs, she took in the *Star Wars* posters, big video game console, ratty couch with a 70's flower pattern and weight set in the corner. The smell of dirty gym socks and mildew was overpowering. Lily felt her heart sink. This wasn't quite how she envisioned her first romantic encounter with the man of her dreams.

Snake was leaning into a beer fridge and pulled out two bottles of Michelob Ultra. "Here you go Lily. Wanna play some *Mario Cart*?" he asked, tossing one to her.

Lily twisted off the top and took a long guzzle. Maybe she could save this.

"Not big into video games, but I hear there's gonna be a rave on the beach tomorrow night. They're bringing in a DJ and everything," she said.

"Tomorrow? I can't. That's my *Dungeons and Dragons* night. You can come play with us if you like," Snake invited.

Lily stared at him. He played fantasy board games? Maybe she couldn't salvage this. He drank his beer in long swallows and the newly inked skull was laughing at her now. She had been picturing dinner in an exotic restaurant on King Street, with candles flickering as they supped oysters—knowing what that would lead to later. Not mom-made snacks in a man-boy's basement. Where were all his sexy friends who gave themselves tough nicknames?

"How did you get the name Snake?" she asked.

"Oh, my name is Stanley, but when I was younger, I was really good at *Snakes & Ladders*," he said, plopping himself down on the filthy torn couch.

"So, Stanley, I'm gonna get going. Sorry to cut this date short."

"Hey, when can I see you again? I go to my cosplay club on Sunday, I bet you'd fit right in." he said, jumping to his feet, "Do you need me to double you back on my bike?"

Lily was already walking up the stairs, but stopped, "Cosplay? What's that?"

"You dress up as really cool characters and act like them, sometimes make mini-plays. I never miss Comic-Con."

Lily blinked. She wouldn't be caught dead dressed up as a comic book character. She continued up the stairs and called over her shoulder, "No need for another bike ride, I'll catch a cab."

She could hear Stanley's mom in the kitchen, but slipped out the door without saying goodbye. Lily was disappointed, how did she read him so wrong? Tears streamed down her face as she walked down the driveway. Snake lived in his parent's basement, was unemployed, and played *Dungeons and Dragons*? And here she thought she was going to be a biker's "old lady." Lily wiped away her tears and started laughing. She stopped walking and had to hold on to a lamppost to keep herself up. She laughed and howled and then sunk to her bum leaning against the pole, completely drained.

After ordering an Uber, she went home and fell into an exhausted sleep. For the first night in a long time, she did not dream of rolling around with a naked Snake.

***

The next day, Sunday, she had a group of five bridesmaids, along with the bride, come in to get matching ankle tattoos of pink butterflies. She was on the third lady when a ruckus broke out on the sidewalk outside the shop.

"Hey! You've gotta see this. It's *Star Wars* out here!" one of the waiting women shrieked.

Lily put down the tattoo machine and rushed to the window. There were seven people dressed head-to-toe in white Storm Trooper outfits doing a dance routine with a portable stereo. A crowd was gathering on the sidewalk.

The performers were carrying big black toy guns and making a huge racket shooting them and doing high kicks.

The tallest one stopped and yelled, "Lily this is for you. Your Snake LOVES you."

Lily wanted to disappear in embarrassment. The

bridesmaids covered their mouths and giggled. Out on the streets a couple of news vans showed up. The local news channels were filming the gathering crowd and the Storm Trooper antics. Taboo Tattoo was supposed to be edgy, dark and mysterious. A group of dancing cosplay Storm Troopers were not helping with that image. Her boss would be furious, and now it was on the news.

She tried to ghost Snake as he sent her text after text that week, ignoring every message. But he didn't give up, instead he showed up outside the shop in various costumes begging her to come over to his place for a *Mario Cart* marathon. One day he was a *Power Ranger*, the next day *The Green Lantern*, and the day after that he showed up as *Deadpool*. The week went by excruciating slow as she waited for Friday to arrive.

Finally, she took the streetcar to Pagan Possibilities in the wee hours of the morning and rushed into the garage as soon as the door was unlocked. If anything, there was even more paraphernalia littering the occult store. Lavender incense was burning.

Penny sat behind the desk, a private little grin on her face. She had seen the dancing Storm Troopers on the news and heard the declarations of love and devotion. Once again, the magic ink had done its job.

"Penny, you have to reverse the power of the ink! Snake is not who I thought he was. This guy lives in his mom's basement and doesn't even have a job," Lily blurted.

"I told you to be sure before you imprinted him with it. You were warned," Penny said, ruffling the green ballroom gown she was wearing.

"I can't live with this. I don't want to spend my

weekends playing fantasy games and traveling by bicycle. Plus, he's scaring off my customers. He shows up wearing cosplay costumes and it's really uncool."

"The special ink is much like regular tattoo ink; it will fade in time and so will its power. You'll just have to be patient. Snake will slowly lose his obsession with you."

"What do I do in the meantime?" Lily asked, leaning over the desk, eyes wide in desperation.

"Join his cosplay club? Learn to love *Dungeons and Dragons*?" Penny chuckled.

THE HANDS RESIST HIM

BY MICHELLE VON ESCHEN

From the outside, the new house looks expensive. It's three stories tall and it has a tower on one corner, like a castle. I try to count the windows, but there are so many that I lose track of which ones have already made the list. Anyone driving up to this seemingly grand estate might assume it's filled with rich people stuff. I can't figure out how Father and Mother afforded it, but my happiness lifts my meager belongings and I up the front steps and carries me across the threshold.

"Peter! Keep your shoes on!" my mother yells.

I step inside and everything makes sense. The floorboards in the entry are giving way to rot. I skirt the edge of an obvious weak spot to keep from falling through. A fairy ring of rusty nails outlines the edge. I grab Sissy's hand and guide her away from the trap to safety at the bottom of the stairs, not because I love her, but I've found her shrill crying

17

completely unbearable. It really is best to avoid setting her off.

Sissy is my little sister. Her name is Anna, but nobody calls her that. She's five and I look after her a lot because I'm already eleven and Father and Mother are busy with things they call 'adult stuff' and things we 'don't have to worry about'. They sure worry a lot.

Father assigned our bedrooms before we arrived and I have complicated directions involving stairs and doors, followed by turns and more doors to guide us to the rooms. The drafts pushing through the thin walls propel us along and I drop Sissy off at her tower room which has windows most of the way around it. Father said that pretty girls deserve pretty views, but when Mother sees the room I know she'll move Sissy somewhere she'll be less likely to fall to her death. I trust the thin panes as much as the rotted floor of the entryway.

The door to my room is next to the door to the attic. They look exactly the same, a dark brown walnut of plain design. Father told me I can remember the difference by reciting 'left is best' for as long as I need until it becomes habit. First, I check behind the door on the right. It certainly doesn't look like a bedroom. The windows are boarded up and the dust has formed snow drifts in the corners where the spiders haven't claimed residency yet. Next, I push the left door open and discover he has stuck me in the other half of the attic, a mirror space to the room behind the door on the right, albeit with better light and far less cobwebs. Later I suggest to Mother that Father might view me as something to be stored away, as he's done with the papers and trunks in the other room. She refutes this statement and claims Father only wants to see me toughen up a bit more and that I'm old enough to start having my privacy. I'm not to think that way again.

While Sissy's room is all windows, I only have two narrow ones across from my bed. They sit upright in the pitch of the roof, creating perfect pockets for me to stand and look out on the yard, which is a mess of brambles and broken garden statues. Mother isn't much of a gardener, so I reckon it'll look that way for at least as long as we're here.

Between the two windows, on the small width of wall there, hangs a painting of a little boy and a doll. They stand in front of large windows made of many smaller panes of glass. Behind the glass, disembodied hands float about. The boy looks angry and focused, his eyes and mouth pursed into tiny slits. The doll grips something with wires and she has only dark holes where her eyes should be. It frightens me and I want to take it to the other attic where it belongs, but Father says I'm not to touch it. "Things of beauty are meant to be observed and respected," he says. "Someone with more money than us thought it was worth owning, so we'll keep it." I stare at it for a bit to appreciate it, but it stays looking like a scary waste of money so I get to work unpacking my things.

I brought very little from our last house, but it's all I had there too. A baseball cap, my mitt, a few shirts and pants. Everything is pockmarked with holes, like the moth-eaten and mildewy quilt that came with the squeaky bed in the middle of my new room. It's better than sleeping naked on a bare floor, I suppose.

Back down the hall, I check on Sissy. She's sitting in the middle of her room, humming a little song, making her raggedy teddy bear dance.

"How do you like your room?"

Teddy stops dancing and Sissy turns to look at me. "It's okay."

We've lived so many places in her short life, I think she's learning to stay detached. Her little pink suitcase leans against the wall beneath one of the windows, unopened, as though she's considered that Father and Mother could move us again tomorrow. I wonder if my hope died as young as hers.

"Do you wanna see my room?" I try to cheer her. Maybe I do love her a little bit.

She beams at me. "Can Teddy come too?"

I shrug. It doesn't matter either way.

She runs by me and as I catch up her hand is turning the knob for the actual attic.

"Ah ah! Left is best, Sissy." I feel powerful and intelligent like Father, possessing this knowledge of the house so soon after moving in.

"The other door?"

"Yes."

She steps into my room and she's immediately drawn to the painting. I wish she'd walk right by it to look out the windows or jump on my bed and make the rusty mattress springs squelch instead of staring at the boy and his doll.

"Wow! I wish I had a dolly that big," she whines. "She's bigger than me even."

I can't blame her for feeling the burn of jealousy. Sissy's getting old enough to realize we don't have much compared to others. She brings a tiny hand up to the bottom of the painting. "Look at her dress, Peter! It's so pretty!"

"Your dress is pretty too, Sissy." In reality, Sissy's dress is too small and tearing at its seams. She doesn't notice my effort to redirect her attention, she's too entranced by the painting. Wondering what all the fuss is about, I take a closer look at it myself.

The painting isn't flat if you view it this close. The brushstrokes crisscross and overlay in specific patterns and directions to create a unique texture for each element of the image. The boy's blue shirt is woven loosely, his shorts a tighter grain. His doll's hair falls in curls so delicate I swear each strand was laid to the canvas individually. The doll's dress is made of larger passes of a brush and pressed smooth somehow, as though it's been freshly ironed.

I can smell the clean, crisp, rich life they represent and his full, glowing face betrays his full belly. Mine grumbles and snaps us out of the hypnotics. Sissy laughs.

"Come on! Let's go play in the garden!"

I follow her out of the house. The boy and his doll are left behind.

From the garden I can see the narrow windows of my room and I half expect to catch a glimpse of the boy staring down at me, but the windows remain empty.

***

My first few weeks are sleepless and even though Father and Mother fight, and the cold creeps through the walls, I blame the painting for my restlessness. The boy stares at me across the darkness of the bedroom, and though I can't see him, I feel his icy glare upon me, judging me for the little I have.

I stand on my tippy toes and hang the ratty quilt over the corners of the frame, but somehow no matter how I place the fabric, he or his doll are peering out at me through one of the holes, so I take it down and search for other options.

***

Last night, desperate for sleep, I dragged the mattress off the bed and propped it up against them. Rolled up in the holey quilt, I shivered on the wood floor. Without their eyes on me, I easily drifted off.

Sometime before the sun came up, before there's any light on the horizon, suffocation shocked me awake. In the dimness of my room I'm convinced the boy has found a way to kill me. I thrash about, but my arms are pinned to the sides of my body, which feels pressure from all angles. I remember the hands in the painting and I know it's them, holding me in place for his wicked plans. My writhing pulls me further from the drowsiness of waking and I realize I'm still wrapped tightly in the quilt. The mattress lies on top of me, having fallen away from the wall.

I struggle out of my makeshift strait jacket and push the mattress to the side. Outside in the dark sky the moon is a crescent, just like in the painting. The windows rattle from an unseen force, stronger than any wind. The mattress feels impossibly heavy as I drag it back to the bedframe and jump on top of it as I throw the quilt on top of me. It makes a terrible hiding place but it's all I have. The holes are so many periscopes, relaying the enemy position and every move he makes.

Because now, against anything I know of the world, the boy in the painting *is* moving.

He sways back and forth, limbering up, reminding his body what it means to act. Sickness creeps up my throat as I watch the boy leave the painting. He sticks out his head and looks around. I lie down and shut my eyes tight before he turns in my direction. When I hear his shoes hit the floorboards, I nearly shriek, but I think it's better to pretend to be sleeping.

He stands beside my bed and bends forward. I can tell his face is nearly touching mine, but I don't feel him breathing, instead I sense a vacuum of space, like I'm being pulled toward the black hole of whatever he is, like all he ever does is take. The sensation passes and I listen to the creak of my bedroom door as he leaves the room.

My eyes flit open just as the doll exits the painting. The hands in the windows behind her are moving too, smashing at the painted glass harder now, in a panic as though they fear being left behind. The doll stumbles to my bedroom floor and shatters into a pile of broken porcelain. I watch as the glass in the painting bursts and flutters in the air like confetti. The hands climb through the empty panes, but they are only hands, I see, as they walk on all their fingers like five-legged spiders. No limbs extend beyond the wrists, no bodies continue after that. They hop to the floor and work at pinching up the doll's pieces and pushing them back into place to rebuild her. When everything is where it should be, the cracks in her ceramic slowly disappear.

She hobbles toward my bedroom door and the hands follow behind her like morbid, fleshy ducks in a row. Neither the leader nor the followers pay any attention to me.

When I am sure they've traveled a ways down the hall, I claw my way out from beneath the webby quilt and swing my feet over the edge of the bed. The springs scream as I lift my weight from them and lower to the floor.

I fear for Sissy, but I find her safe and alone in her room, asleep on the mattress Father found in the basement. The boy and his doll and their gang of hands must have some unknown mission elsewhere in the house. I decide to head back to bed.

In the dark, the doors to the attics are more alike than ever before and as sure as I am about which one is my room, I trust less and less the knowledge as I stare at them. I can't hide in the actual attic. The painted boy will see that I'm missing from my bed. *Left is best, left is best*, my broken mind reminds itself. I remember the coolness of the doorknob as my trembling hand turned it, the emptiness of the painting, and the noise of the mattress accepting my terrified body. Then, I must have passed out due to the fear coursing through me.

The next morning, Sissy and I sit on the bottom step of the big stairs. We're both in our pajamas, our stomachs grumbling for a breakfast we'll never get.

Mother holds up my hands to her face, scrutinizing every depression for some clue. She's already looked over Sissy's.

"Where did you get the paint?" Father asks for the second time, his arms crossed over his chest as though his sternness might remind me of answers I had forgotten.

"What paint?" I ask, because I have no idea what he's talking about.

His untucks a hand from his side and smacks my cheek. "Don't play games."

Mother is talking to herself, recalling some damage she found that they won't let us see. "Tiny handprints in white paint. All over the kitchen. The cupboards are ruined. There's no getting them clean again. What will we do?"

I want to run and look, to understand what they're talking about, but Father won't let us leave the bottom stair. I stare at my hands. Sissy is looking at her own.

"What were you doing in the kitchen last night?" Father demands to know.

"I was in bed. It wasn't me!"

Sissy shakes her head in silent denial. It wasn't her either. I already know it wasn't her. Father and Mother won't believe what I saw though, so I say no more in our defense. Father's face blooms patches of red. I fear he'll throw me into the rotted pit behind him and sell the house with my skeleton beneath the floorboards. "Up to your rooms! No meals!" His voice shakes the windows like the wind last night.

Sissy's cries echo down the hall to my bedroom. The ragged and wet unfairness of it chokes her. In

25

my room, I find the proof I need. The boy and the doll and the hands behind them, all have white paint on their palms, but as I examine it and touch its still wet surface, it disappears, absorbing into their painted flesh, there only long enough for me to see it.

"I hate you!" I scream at the boy on the wall, fully expecting him to hear. He stares at me, lips closed and eyes slim in judgment, the same look as though he hasn't moved at all. I throw the one book I own at his dumb face. I swear his eyes narrow further.

That night, as some cruel joke, the moon is a crescent once again and the children in the painting are free to roam. I shut myself in the closet of my room and sleep against the door. In my nightmares, they start fires and kill Sissy and convince my parents it was me.

"Peter!" Sissy yells through the closet door between poundings of her fist.

I open my eyes and check for daylight coming through the crack under the door. When I believe it's not a dream or the night, I open the door. Sissy beams. She's wearing her best dress. Her Sunday dress. Her Mother-and-Father-will-get-mad-if-they-see-her-in-it-dress.

"The dolly came to see me last night! She's so pretty and nice! She told me all her secrets."

"Did they mess up the kitchen again?"

"Oh no! That was an accident, she says. She says her brother didn't mean to."

I walk to the painting and stare at the boy. He's smirking at me, because Sissy's on their side now. I look at the doll. She's hiding something behind her back.

"Is that Teddy?" I ask Sissy without turning away from the painting.

"The doll asked to play with him."

"Don't give them anything, Sissy! They're up to no good!"

***

I avoid spending time in my room. During the day, the other attic hides me from the boy's endless watch. At night I sleep in Sissy's room, daring the doll to come. Planning in my head a way to shatter her into pieces that can't be reassembled. One night I wake up and Sissy is gone. I run to my room and find her sitting on the floor under the painting.

"Won't you come out to play with me?" she's asking the doll.

I grab her and pull her toward the door. "Sissy, what are you doing in here?"

"The dolly is my friend. I want to play."

"Don't come in here without me! And stay away from that painting!"

***

Knowing I have to be in my room if I'm to protect Sissy from the children, I lie awake in bed, staring at the moon, staying alert to any change in its shape. Despite my efforts to fight it, sleep claims me. When I wake up, the severed hands are carrying me toward the painting. The beginnings of a yell escape my mouth before another hand jumps on top of my face to silence me. The boy stands in the painting with his arms outstretched to the room, awaiting my delivery. He wears my baseball hat. I wriggle and writhe, but the hands have sharpened, claw-like nails that dig into my flesh.

As the boy's hands touch me I grow weak and he hefts me up into the room within the painting. When I'm standing in his place, he jumps out and the barrier closes between us.

He's walking around my room, wearing my clothes, touching my things. I watch as he transforms with each step into an exact replica of me. The boy from the painting hangs my baseball cap on one of the bed posts and sleeps in my place on the bed. His doll is beside me and I can hear her giggling from within her ceramic; a fit of laughter she can't stop as her happiness over my entrapment and the possibility of her freedom consume her.

For the rest of the night, I strain to budge in the dry, tight space inside the painting. I scream until my paper throat feels cut to ribbons. The doll eventually goes quiet, but I sense her presence beside me. In the light of the morning, I am able to look down at my clothes. I'm wearing his shirt and shorts and indeed my belly seems full and my skin and clothes are clean.

The boy from the painting sleeps in so late my father comes into the room to wake him.

"Good morning, Father!" the boy exclaims with more joy than I've ever shown toward the man.

"Father! Father, he's not real!" My screams are useless, muffled by the thick canvas between our worlds.

"Oh, but he is real!" The doll's small voice catches me by surprise.

"You can talk? Who are you? What are you?" I try to turn to look at her, but my movements are limited in the cramped space. The painting is an upright coffin.

She laughs and says no more.

If only Father could smell the oil paint on the boy's skin or notice the stiffness with which he moves. Even his smile gives away that he's an imposter. Father leaves without realizing I'm not in my bed. He never looks up at me in the painting. I pray that Sissy will somehow figure out what has happened.

The boy from the painting makes my bed, pulling the moth-eaten quilt over the lumpy spring mattress on the rickety frame. He caresses the blanket as though it's fine art. Sissy comes in as part of her usual morning routine of bothering me, only I'm not bothered, I'm grateful. I'm screaming and shaking, a boy in a paper and paint straight jacket, losing his mind as he strains to gain the attention of his little sister. The boy who isn't me is also happy to see her and he tells her such. I want her to look in his eyes so she can see he's something else. Something evil.

He asks Sissy if she likes the doll on the wall. She skips over to me and I bellow "RUN!", but my lips stay closed in that forever smirk they've been painted into and anyway, she's looking at the doll instead. The boy stands in front of me, at her side, and for a moment we're a mirror of two different realities.

"Tonight, when the moon is a crescent and the dolly comes out to play, see if she'll show you her room. It's just beyond the edge of the painting there. Don't you want to see her room?"

"I do! I do!"

"Maybe she'll let you wear one of her dresses!"

"Oh I hope so! I can't wait!"

"Now, let's have breakfast with Father and Mother. They're waiting for us."

***

I wait all day, planning a coup of sorts to take my life back, jealous of the time he spends with my family. If the predicament would allow it, I'd be pacing, anticipating the events of the night to come. The sun goes down, the boy from the painting gets into my bed, and shadows fill the room.

"Any moment," the doll hisses, ready to steal Sissy's body.

The room is dark and the boy from the painting is sitting straight up in my bed now, waiting for the crescent moon to appear and the winds to pick up. The hands behind the doll and I begin bashing against the windows. The doll moves and creaks and the boy from the painting gets out of my bed and comes to help her down from the frame. I don't know the magic to move more than an inch in any direction. The canvas is a quicksand in which I slowly tread water.

"You stay there!" The boy laughs and I watch helplessly as they leave my room to get Sissy.

***

"Do you remember the trick?" his saccharine voice questions sometime later. He's in the hallway, talking loud enough for me to hear him as he leads my sweet lamb of a sister to her slaughter.

"Left is best!" Sissy shouts.

I'd give anything for her to realize he isn't me and to instead turn the knob of the door on the right, bury herself in the dust piles, befriend the attic spiders who are far less vile than the boy from the painting masquerading as a friend.

They enter the room in a line. Sissy first, then the doll, and finally the boy.

"It was so nice of you to give her Teddy," he says. "Her dress will fit you perfectly."

***

Somewhere he's found a wooden trunk and he pulls it up to the base of the wall beneath the painting. The doll steps onto it and back into the painting beside me.

"Stand up here, Sissy, and the dolly will help you into her room."

"Don't do this!" I plead with the doll. "She's just a little girl!"

"I was a little girl once." The doll's reply sends shivers down my painted spine.

The doll reaches out an arm and Sissy grabs it and thunder cracks somewhere outside and the doll wobbles back into the painting, tipping back and forth until it centers and I know it, I just know that Sissy is stuck in that doll just like I'm stuck in this boy.

"Sissy! It's a trap!"

"Peter?"

I hear the confusion in her muted voice. She's looking out of the painting at the boy, but his lips aren't moving. The doll hugs Teddy to her chest and she smiles in Sissy's threadbare nightgown. I try to lift my painted arms to claw my way back to our life, but I'm dry and brittle like the fall leaves. There's no substance to me. Sissy stands beside me, dressed in

31

the smock she adored, her lips painted a sharp red. Her hair holds curls like it never would before. I hear her smothered cries beneath the porcelain, as though she's trapped right beneath the fragile outer layer of the doll.

She and I watch the doll learn to walk in Sissy's old body. Her movements are jilted and stiff at first, as though she's only ever dreamed of the limited movements of the partially articulated limbs she's stuck my sister with. In short order she is dancing around my bedroom, full of glee, and celebrating with her accomplice their newfound freedom.

The boy from the painting sticks out his tongue and climbs back in my bed. The doll leaves to Sissy's room. I hope he falls ill beneath the patchwork quilt. I hope she falls out a window.

***

I wait and wait for the crescent moon to arrive and the winds to push the branches against the windows. I wait for my moment to claim my life back and force the boy and his doll into the painting where they belong, but it never happens. There's something more to it that I'm still missing, some magic required to reopen the path between our two worlds. The hands behind us try to scratch and claw at our backs. Day and night we listen to their nails screaming down the glass of the window panes. They too want to escape this prison even if only for a short time.

***

One day the boy packs up my meager belongings and waves in farewell. I can hear the rumble of the moving truck engine down in the driveway. He and the doll are leaving with my parents to somewhere I'll never know. The room is empty for months, maybe years. No one moves in for a while other than spiders and a pigeon who can't find the way back out. It dies in the corner. Sissy and I eventually run out of tears.

***

On another day a young boy moves in and my hope is renewed. It could be that the crescent moon and wind will return and allow me to live in his body. But the new child is not enough. I never see a sibling. No sister for Sissy to inhabit so we can stretch our legs and walk again. It's then I understand that the boy from the painting wasn't judging me for the little I had, he was jealous that I had anything, that I could move about and smile and yell and be heard and loved. I make up my mind to take any chance I get to free myself. Later I could find a little girl and convince the powers to take her in exchange for my Sissy.

The boy grows older. He begins to decorate the walls and I worry because I wouldn't know how to be a teenager if that's the body I'll end up in. Will the hands be strong enough to lift his weight into the painting? Will the hands even help me? He pulls us from the wall and props us in a corner. From there I watch him tack up a poster of a car I've never seen. I've lost all sense of time.

We stay like that for weeks, angled against two walls watching feet pass.

The boy makes friends at a school Sissy and I never attended. One day he brings one of those friends home and up into his room. He is immediately drawn to us.

"What the hell is this creepy shit?"

He picks us up and stares into our unmoving eyes. I plead for him to help. The hands behind us press on the windows and the glass moans under the pressure. Sissy whimpers.

"I don't know. It was here when we moved in. Gotta be worth something. Look at the detail. They look real."

"Nah. You can't bring a chick in here with these weirdo kids staring at you. No way, man."

"It's not weird. It's just a kid and his doll."

"Whatever it is, it's cramping the whole vibe."

"Okay, okay. If you're so scared of it, it's gone."

"Dude, I'm not scared. But, like, their eyes are following me wherever I stand."

I pray he'll put us in the living room downstairs or at least the other side of the attic where there are still windows and sometimes people and at least the spiders will keep us company. He grips the top of our frame and holds us against his leg. The rough jean of his pants scratches my face. He opens the closet door and tucks us between a sled and a suitcase.

Sissy finds more tears and for a moment I commiserate with the last boy in the painting and his doll. Who knows how long they waited for us and the crescent moon and the winds? Who knows how long it took him to figure out the magic to escape the frame of this painted prison? Never did I think I'd turn as hungry for someone else's life as the boy in the painting had before me.

In the darkness, my anger builds by the day, by

the year, until it becomes a force of its own and the strength of it is a window-shaking gale. I can feel that the moon is a crescent in the sky outside the room, beyond the closet, and it no longer matters to me whose life I must ruin to regain my own. Tonight, whoever sleeps on the other side of this door will take my place, if anyone still lives on the other side of this door.

THE FAMILY HEIRLOOM

BY MYA LAIRIS

Cora Sauder was used to looks of praise and respect, especially regarding her cooking. She wasn't a professional chef, but her food was renowned for being delicious and hearty. She ruled her kitchen with a stern authority, her utensils and cookware forbidden to all within her home. One time, she had caught her daughter, Melanie, wearing a colander like a helmet. It was a game that she and her brother Jason were playing—but it was no game to Cora. She scolded her children fiercely, bringing tears to their eyes for their creativity. They were not to touch *anything* in her kitchen other than the food on their plates. She could tell even when a ladle was moved and immediately the act would draw scrutiny. The kitchen was *her* domain and every soul that lived in her home knew it. Others, however, were not so knowledgeable.

"That is such a beautiful bowl. Where did you get it?" Maria Sanchez, her neighbor, asked. Maria was a tall, Hispanic beauty with skin like butterscotch candy and piercing dark eyes. Second-generation Mexican American, she had an outgoing personality that men often perceived as flirtatious. Women often considered it bold.

Cora's first thoughts went down an anger-laced path at the inquiry but swung over to calm when she remembered that her neighbor rarely arrived early for parties, when food was still in the preparation stages. Normally, Cora would have already set food out on the tables by the time Maria sauntered in, but the crowd at the supermarket that day had caused serious delays in her timeline.

She wondered if the wine Maria was drinking was the cause for her near salivating state. To be fair, she was on her fourth glass of Cabernet herself, but that didn't hamper Cora from working her hands into the mixture of ground beef, onions, bread crumbs and herbs.

Maria's dark coal eyes shimmered like hungry obsidian voids yearning for possession as they swept over Cora's mixing bowl.

The bowl was a dark shade of red with flecks of gold. Around the circumference was a labyrinth of shimmering turquoise lines trapped within a black rimmed border. At the north and south of the border were gold faces with tongues distended in a fearful display.

Maria's smile swung from the bowl to Cora's gaze and back down again. Rather than heading outside into the back yard with her husband and the kids, she stood by the kitchen counter watching Cora and waiting for her answer.

What harm could it do to give a reply, Cora figured, her cheeks warmed by the glorious juice of grapes. It wasn't like Maria had dared to ask to borrow it. Withdrawing a hand from her mixture, she grabbed one of two eggs, cracked it over the bowl and tossed the empty shell in the nearby trash. "It's a family heirloom," she said, reaching for the second egg. "It belonged to my mother and my mother's mother before her."

"It looks like an antique. The designs..." Maria set her wine glass down and stretched her hand toward the bowl. She must have seen the way that Cora stiffened in an Olympic worthy shift from buzzed to sober. "They look like—"

"Like a bowl from some long-lost South American civilization?" she offered the question sternly. "Because it is. My grandmother was from Honduras. Slave ships docked there too." Taking up the other egg, Cora deposited the contents into the bowl with the rest of the mixture. She could tell that Maria was shocked, perhaps even regretful for asking. While Maria very clearly looked to be of Hispanic origins with her oil dark hair, she had probably never assumed that Cora would have a similar spice in her lineage. Cora's complexion was a dark mahogany. Her hair was a tightly coiled halo of curls, thick with dominant traits of West Africa but her blood knew several mixtures down the generations.

Brows bowed by a combination of shame and concern, Maria cocked her head to the side. "Oh...I...I didn't mean any offense."

Cora almost felt bad for causing her neighbor to stagger into the pond of cultural assumptions but felt justified in the switch of her attention. Rather than staring at the contours of Cora's mixing bowl, Maria seemed busy trying to shrug off the air of awkwardness filling the kitchen. It really was the better option. "It's all right," Cora said. "My family is just of bunch of ingredients thrown together. This...this bowl," she sighed, "is almost symbolic of the world that created us."

"Well. It's not the tools, it's the artist, when you get right down to it," Maria replied with a faltering attempt at a smile. She slid her well-manicured fingers around the stem of her wine glass and gazed at the meager quarter inch of wine there.

Cora wished that her neighbor would just go out into the backyard for a refill and perhaps a more relaxed atmosphere. There were plenty of appetizers outside and more than enough activity between their husbands and children that could use some monitoring. Cora simply wasn't the one for chit chat, especially when preparing food. So, when Maria turned and took a step toward the sliding glass door off to the side of the kitchen, Cora sighed with relief.

Her response was premature, as right before her neighbor approached the threshold, Maria turned back around. She glanced at the bowl once more.

Cora paused, before looking down suspiciously. She couldn't help but wonder if the bowl was actively trying to seduce her neighbor. After Maria was outside, Cora continued to knead the meatball mixture within the rounded confines. She made sure to press her fingertips down to the hard, ceramic bottom, giving it light caresses.

The thought that the bowl might want a new owner,

called to one even, was absurd. It had been passed on to her and would remain her possession until she passed it on…to the next in line.

***

It was a month later and she was charged with preparing fried chicken for her women's group. Cora was excited for the praise she would surely receive for the tenderness of the meat and her combination of spices. She had grown up among great cooks and had studied the craft intently. Her mother's casseroles were just short of legendary and Cora's grandmother had the most divine recipes for soups. Women in her family cooked like they were beauty pageant contestants, all smiles and good will in front of others but prideful and sure in their accomplishments.

Cora was no different. Just like her mother and her mother before her, she took pleasure in causing full bellies and shudders of epicurean indulgence. There were some things that were hereditary.

She sought her bowl, needing it to house her variety of spices and flour. She kept it on the baker's rack, on the highest shelf next to a distressed collection of succulent plants…however, she could see from the threshold that led into the kitchen that it was not there.

There were few things that could have caused her heart to stagger inside of her chest but seeing that void upon the shelf—processing the absence, was on that short list. Cora staggered into the room to the table and pulled out a chair. She fell into the seat so hard her tailbone ached from the impact. The list of suspects was pitifully small as her husband and children knew that the bowl had been handed down to her like a crown and a title. She had warned them from the first day she had brought it home. Damn it! The decision to have it out in the open was made so that she could always monitor it. No one would have touched it—not even in jest—and yet the bowl was missing.

Perhaps a saner person would have been relieved at the absence of the cursed thing…but then sanity was rarely needed when duty was called for. The bowl was accursed and whoever had taken it, along with their family, would be in danger.

"Diana," Cora yelled out to her eldest child, the one who would inherit the bowl after her and the only one who would understand the true gravity of the loss.

Taller and darker than her mother, Diana came into the kitchen. She wore a headscarf and possessed a dry demeanor, looking much older and certainly wiser than her eighteen years should have dictated. She walked onto the tile floor with firm steps and stopped by her mother's chair like a solider awaiting a command.

When Cora didn't immediately respond, Diana gave her full attention to the state of her mother. "It's gone," she said. "Is…Is that a good thing?"

Her daughter was stoic, perhaps too practical and pessimistic in her ways. Unlike Cora, Diana didn't even make it a point to allow herself to be naïve. Her child knew about things that went bump in the night far earlier than she ever had. "Was Maria in my house?" Cora asked.

"She came yesterday when she dropped off Melanie and Jason after soccer practice. You think she has it?"

Cora shrugged, lifting her chin to stare at the empty space, even as Diana joined her at the table. They had pizza for dinner the night before, perhaps it had disappeared then and she hadn't noticed. Had she grown so complacent with her obligation? She worried.

"Maybe it's time for a change in ownership?"

Shifting her gaze to her child, her future successor, Cora reflected on how she had raised Diana to be stronger than her, smarter and more capable of facing the darkness of the world. She didn't think she had included such a cold nonchalance into Diana's upbringing. "She's not ready to pay that price. No one is," Cora added with a sigh.

"If she's a thief, then she is," Diana replied.

***

Cora waited until she was inside Maria's house and invited into the kitchen for a cup of coffee so she could survey the area. She didn't think Maria would have the bowl out in plain sight but believed there might be some clue upon Maria's features if she possessed it. A tic of the eye, a flinch of the jaw—something would give away her guilt. Cora watched as her neighbor made her a cup of coffee. Looking for tense shoulders or shaking hands as Maria brought her a mug and two creams, Cora broached the true reason for her visit.

Standing over Cora with her mouth ajar, Maria gawked. "You're accusing me of stealing…a bowl?"

The seriousness of what was at stake stiffened Cora's shoulders against the hurt in Maria's eyes. They hadn't been friends that long, but Maria was a helping hand when it came to picking up the kids from events and watching the house when they were on vacation. Their kids played together, and their husbands were tight lawn and sports buddies. Cora was not ignorant of what her questioning risked. "Yes. I'm asking. You seemed really fond of it the last time you were at my house."

Maria's hand went to her hip and she canted her head. "Telling you I thought it was pretty is one thing, but I have plenty of mixing bowls. Hell, if I wanted a really nice one, I could have gone onto Etsy and had one made. Dios mio, I wouldn't have done that to you, Cora. I'm no thief."

The two women stared at each other for a long moment with Cora seeking any chink in her neighbor's armor. Finding none, she questioned her own rationale. Maybe it was someone else. Cora was the first to break away as she found nothing but offense in the language of Maria's body. Her own body language answered back with defeat. "It's missing."

"I'm sorry. It was a glorious piece."

"It was a little more than that," Cora replied, lifting the mug to her lips. Her fingers trembled as she anticipated Maria snatching the offered drink from her hands.

Her neighbor must have taken pity on Cora instead, as she released a long sigh and joined her at the table. Her voice was thick with suppressed irritation. "Right. A family heirloom, if I remember correctly."

Cora shrugged as if it were a simple fact, but she couldn't hold back the true nature of her despair, even if Maria proved to be the best liar she had ever encountered. Cora had to let her know what she was in for. She probably wouldn't believe her, not at first, but over time hopefully the seed would grow and the bowl would mysteriously reappear…if she had it. "It's a *cursed* family heirloom, handed down from mother to daughter for many generations. But it's not what it seems. It's not just a bowl. It's a demon."

Maria inhaled before squeaking out a response. "Excuse me. A what?"

What did she have to lose by telling her the truth? Her neighbor had already borne the brunt of her accusations and surely thought that she was crazy for even insinuating theft. Her last and only recourse was the truth. For if Maria could hear the nightmare's true revelation then perhaps a clue to her guilt might still be revealed. "The bowl—anything prepared in it comes out delicious, made to perfection and a delight to the tongue and the mind," Cora stated. "However, the bowl needs to be appeased. It needs blood to satisfy its appetite. It sits dormant but mindful and should certainly be fed once a month."

The look on Maria's face was one of wide-eyed shock. Her anger seemed to bleed away to an incredulous stare. "You're...you're crazy. You're kidding me, Cora. You have to be."

She did not back down. "It must never be used without a sacrifice. Absolutely not. It doesn't require much, a few ounces of blood only, before any food is prepared. The bowl will absorb it and be sated. Then food can be prepared."

Maria gave a burp of nervous laughter. "You don't actually believe that, do you?"

Cora looked down. There was so much that had to be hidden from everyday life, everyday people. Belief wasn't an issue for her because she knew well what foul things moved in the shadows. It *never* was. But for Maria? "Look, whether you have it, or you don't, you've been warned at least," Cora said. "The bowl—Nouroc'na, if angered, if not appeased, it will take what it wants in the most brutal way. You. Your entire family would be in danger."

Maria's eyes flitted back and forth, her gaze searing Cora with every contact. She seemed to be searching her friend's features for a grin, or a chuckle, anything indicating that she was bluffing.

Crestfallen, Cora didn't know what else to do. There was still no evidence that alerted her to Maria's guilt. For a while they were both in a standoff of sorts, sipping coffee, with the background music of a slow, Latin love tune playing from a radio in the windowsill.

Cora was nearly finished with her cup of coffee when Maria let loose a long sigh.

"I don't have it. I really don't, Cora. And if I did, I wouldn't want something like that in my house, or near it. I would hope that you feel the same."

"Of course...of course," she smiled around the rim of her coffee mug. She tried her damnedest to give Maria the notion that she had been joking. The air lightened between them but not by much. Cora thought their relationship would be damaged forever until Maria offered to spike the next round of java. Once Maria launched into the superstitions her mother and abuelas had, the tension had passed.

There was some laughter for the rest of that morning, but it did little to assuage the dread lying like a weight in Cora's belly.

Could it be that Nouroc'na had sought out another to torment? Had it grown dissatisfied with Cora's lineage and their obedient appeasement over seven generations?

If so, that could be a good thing, she tried to tell herself, but that was something she didn't believe.

***

Watching her husband shepherd her children out of the house, Cora had to wonder about their thoughts. They had been interrogated thoroughly, had witnessed her tearing through closets and cabinets, dressers and garage storage with a fury of intent. She had yelled and cursed as her search for her prisoner ensued. "Are you sure you haven't seen it? Which one of you had company over? You know you're forbidden from touching anything in my kitchen," she had exclaimed to thirteen-year-old Jason and eleven-year-old, Melanie. She had even shot a scrutinizing glare at her husband during her wild search.

All of them had denied the theft, so much so that she had been left with no choice. She had to contact the Council of Binders. She wasn't the only one who was charged with the responsibility of serving as jailer to a cursed object.

They were due to arrive that afternoon, two of the inquisitors and three of the hunters. She knew the inquisitors would certainly query her about every aspect of the mysterious loss. Once they had the information, they would watch the news, read the papers, scour the internet until they caught scent of Nouroc'na and then the hunters' jobs would begin.

They would bring it back, she was certain. But the chaos that it might cause before it was caught worried her.

Diana sat on the couch, both of them waiting for the inevitable knock on the door. Only her firstborn had the right to know and be known by the Council and while Diana may have been worried, she certainly showed little sign of it.

"We'll get it back, Ma." Diana said, steel in her tone. "We'll get it back and we'll lock it up. Get a hutch with glass and a lock this time."

Cora gazed at her daughter from the corners of her eyes. She couldn't help but wonder at her daughter's commitment. While there were those inducted into the darkness who shied away from it, Diana was a scale—able to balance horror and reality like none that Cora had ever encountered. Diana was always looking at the practicalities of a situation, even when demons were concerned, it seemed. Cora wondered if she herself had ever been so casual...but then remembered how easily she had slipped into a treaty with the beast.

The knock on the door was a gentle rap, but it sounded like the rumble of thunder to Cora.

***

She had an awful time getting to sleep that night. As much as her husband's complaints over a simple bowl and the wary gazes of her two children had shamed her that day, Cora's thoughts were only on her missing charge. The Council had been blunt with their questioning and resolved in their intent to help, but the hunters showed the slightest hints of fear as Cora relayed to them the deadly potential of the target that they would need to find. They were tasked with locating Nouroc'na before he consumed too much, before he regained his true strength.

They would contact her at the first clue, she was told. They had even summoned a seeker who was due to arrive in a few days, from Beijing. Her issue was to be dealt with using powerful tools, she was assured, yet Cora's doubt regarding whether she was even fit to guard the bowl kept her awake past midnight.

She had barely closed her eyes when the smell of something absolutely delectable pulled her from the depths of a dreamless void. The scent was also the smell of the biggest well of regret that had ever formed in the chest of a human. The scents of cinnamon, sugar and something foul woke Cora from her sleep with the eagerness of a secret bursting to be revealed. A tear slipped from the corner of her eye as she looked over at her husband. So peacefully he slept, snoring softly, without a care in the world. He knew nothing of the legacy that flowed through her family. And that night she was thankful at least that he would be ignorant in the morning.

Trembling, sluggish, she cast her legs over the edge of the bed and then sat up. She slid her feet into the slippers upon the floor and arose as if her limbs were made from lead. Invisible arms tugged at her limbs as she moved from the bedroom to the hall. She noticed that her eldest daughter's door was open, and Diana stood within the threshold with a look every bit as foreboding and confused as Cora felt. Her child didn't say a word as their eyes met, but when Cora walked by, Diana followed.

Cora walked into the kitchen, the stink of freshly spilled blood and offal assaulting her senses. As she switched on the light, she noted the flour upon the top of the island, the rolling pin and the spices overturned. Cinnamon and nutmeg were scattered amongst the stark white flour. Splashes of bright crimson deceptively looking like some hellish chili powder.

She wanted to focus on the spices and try to discover what kind of cake or muffin was going to be made rather than what she knew had to lie upon the floor behind the stocky fixture, but as Diana moved cautiously to her right, Cora had to swallow her dread and move forward. Somewhere in the back of her shocked brain, she praised her daughter for her bravery. It was an odd thing for Cora to think, when her thoughts were firing like an erratic explosion. "Get back," she ground out in a shaky warning.

Her soldier did as asked, looking to Cora with flaring nostrils and a slightly heaving chest.

Cora took in the readiness for battle that seemed to course through her daughter but knew such offense would be useless. She walked up to where her daughter was standing, just a few feet away from the island and saw the bare brown feet upon the floor.

Cora's trembling went from the tips of her fingers to the top of her head which she could not stop from moving back and forth. She closed her eyes and advanced, until she was able to see what was on the opposite side in its entirety.

Anyone else would have screamed in horror. Cora should have, but the weight of guilt and the anger of shame had taken her voice.

Cora's youngest child, Melanie, lay sprawled upon the floor, face up. Her body was open from breast to groin. Much of the flesh, muscle and organs missing. She was nearly hollowed out. Cora could see sections of her child's spinal column. A quick glimpse at her child's face showed Cora the terror in eyes frozen wide. It magnified her guilt all the more. Her child's body jerked once, and for a fleeting irrational moment Cora thought she might still live. But the clicking sound as Nouroc'na moved his many legs against the floor snapped her back to the reality of the situation.

Ruby red speckled with gold, the demon possessed twenty turquoise eyes layered in clusters. It had six claw arms at the fore with nearly a hundred locomotion claws at the aft like a louse. Its mandibles worked back and forth, grinding and tearing at once, while two of its six claw-like appendages shoved more of the child's meat into its gluttonous form.

The demon shifted every last one of its jewel-like orbs to Cora in a mocking stare, to Diana and then back again to its meal, before scuttling back on its feet as if it could be afraid. It was an act of mockery. Cora knew even before it shook up and down in silent laughter.

"Thaaaaaannnk Yooouu," the demon said, its voice like a grizzly bear moaning in its sleep.

It had been a long time since Cora had seen the demon. Six years before it had clacked its claws, mandibles bubbling with crimson froth, as it glared at a mother giving her daughter an important demonstration. It had been one of many lessons Diana needed to receive but an important one. She had had to starve it to show Diana its true form, to press home the gravity of the responsibility that she would one day inherit.

Just then, Cora said, "It doesn't care if you are a good cook or not. It only cares that it gets what it desires. Never deny it. Never use it without the blood offering...and never starve it. For it is a jealous thing," she instructed her eldest daughter. "The contract is not a bad one, all together. It will give you the pride of being responsible for the well fed, the happy, and the gluttonous and in exchange, you will know that you are sparing the world from its horrors."

"Can it be destroyed?"

Cora told Diana *no* because that was what her own mother had told her. Nouroc'na's shell was impervious to fire, acid, lava or so she had heard. She had never tried any of the techniques herself and could tell from the dry response Diana gave back that she wouldn't be the adventurous one, breaking with tradition either.

The screeching sound of a chair being pulled across the floor caught Cora's attention and she turned to see Diana sitting down at the kitchen table with shoulders hung low. Tears were flowing down her cheeks. Cora looked to her firstborn anticipating the glare of resentment. She deserved it, not her mother or the other matrons of their line. Her. And as Nouroc'na continued his feast, there was nothing more that she could do other than to join Diana at the table.

Cora used to believe that it wasn't worth fighting the dark elements of existence if a balance could be maintained. As she stared at Melanie's corpse and the fiend devouring her, she had to question the sacrifices, the secrets that tied the eldest daughter to the eldest daughter. Had her third child ever stood a chance? Perhaps Melanie had seen the bond between Cora and Diana, the guarded conversations and private lessons. Maybe she had envied her mother's dictatorship in the kitchen, or maybe she just wanted to feel what it was like to be a cook. Pride. Accomplishment. Hope.

The responsibilities of inheriting the bowl, of being a guardian, were meant only for the first-born female, no one else. Her other children were supposed to be spared the duties and the knowledge that came with them. Spared.

The pain of the burden shook her and the barriers

that contained her emotions broke. Sobbing fitfully, Cora barely heard the knock on the door.

Diana got up. It was 4 a.m., a time which no common guest would have visited, but Cora had a strong sense of who the visitor was and there was nothing ordinary about the person at the door.

Her seventy-four-year-old mother came into the house with the tell-tale click of a silver and oak cane. Despite her age and poor health, she had come. She had surely felt something had gone wrong. A gift of hers was to detect tragedies and heartache over distances that nature could never explain. It wasn't precognition. She couldn't tell the future, but she knew damn sure when she was needed.

"I am so sorry, my love. This should have never happened."

Cora could feel the compassion radiating off her mother like a warm embrace.

Esther had warned her daughter about the responsibility of having more than one girl or any children after Diana and for the life of Cora then, she couldn't understand why. She knew now.

Melanie had simply wanted to make something, to perhaps feel the pride of a dish or a dessert served. It was a thrill but at what cost, Cora wondered, breaking down anew.

"We have much to do. Diana, you know the sleep spell," Cora's mother said to her grandchild. It wasn't a question. "Ensure that your brother and father stay under until we have settled the situation."

The next few hours were a blur. Somehow the sun had risen and the birds had begun to sing outside as if it were any other spring day. Cora's mother brewed a pot of coffee and handed out hot cups. They drank the brew, laced with cream and rum, as the demon continued his feast.

Diana rejoined them in the kitchen and had her first taste of the tainted brew as well. They were all at the table, three generations of demon binders, when the grating, sloppy, slurping sounds finally died down.

Diana attempted to get up, but Esther shook her head. Instead it was she that got up and walked over to the island.

Cora could see her mother but not the remains of her daughter. Esther bent down and then rose back up with the fiend in her two hands. It had returned to the non-assuming form of a bowl, albeit much larger with so much substance taken in.

Horrified, Cora got up and rushed to the side of the island to see that there was nothing remaining of her child. No flesh, no bones, no blood. Nothing. It was as if Melanie had never existed. To her husband and her son, the child would be nonexistent soon, their memories wiped free of her with the strongest of spells. Friends, teachers, even official records would be affected once the entirety of the guardian network was alerted. But to have nothing left? Cora wanted to grab the bowl from her mother's hand and throw it against the wall, to take her anger out upon it. But Esther's grip was firm, and she walked past her. "I will take him with me," Esther declared.

"No. No!" Cora demanded. She needed to be the beast's jailer. She needed to be the one who controlled its imprisonment, her decision made from the deepest hatred. "He will remain here. Where I can truly watch him."

Esther looked at her daughter as if to ask if she was sure.

Cora vehemently nodded. "I will notify the Council. They can call off their search for this accursed piece of shit."

The bowl was much too big to fit back on the baker's rack, so Esther placed it upon the center of the kitchen table. Cora instructed Diana to get some fruit and fill the demon's carapace. The demon needed to be controlled and there would be none other who would be as vigilant as she would be for as long as she could. Except, perhaps Diana whose eyes burned with a dark resilience and who hated to cook.

DIRTY

BY JORDAN KERNS

She left Wes on the bed, the crinkled hotel comforter resting lightly on his bare hips. The dimmed light in the room made the floral pattern on the pastel pink and tan blanket look like naked bodies writhing, contorted and ghastly, no eyes, no nose, just gaping mouths and gangly limbs. She ignored the discomfort this image gave her and smiled down at Wes. He didn't snore often, but he sounded like an exhausted puppy when he did. She restrained the urge to kiss his cheek, not wanting to wake him. Tiptoeing around the bed and creaking open the front door, she once again cursed the hotel they had to check into tonight. If only they hadn't left her parent's house early. If only her parents had liked Wes. Now she was in a hotel that smelled like pot grew in the walls and lacked indoor plumbing. She hadn't bothered to put on her shoes—poor decision, really. She avoided shards of brown and green glass on her way to the bathroom: a deadly game of hopscotch.

Glass clinked as she nudged debris away with her toes, yet she never got cut. She grinned, but her triumph faded when she opened the decaying outhouse door. At least it had a lock. Moonlight streamed through the cracks in the ceiling, illuminating the filth covering the floor. She gagged, appalled at her lack of shoes. She sat down, desperate to get her feet off the ground. She held her legs against her chest, hoping more distance meant less chance of filth. She giggled at her position, glad no one could see her like this. Holding her breath, she reminded herself that the sooner she got this over with, the sooner she could leave. She dropped her feet slowly, holding her breath. The wind shrieked through the cracks in the door, and she hadn't realized that the wind wasn't blowing until she entered the outhouse. Once her big toe scraped along the moist ground, monstrous hands broke through the sunken hole she sat on top of, thick claws slicing through her skin and pulling her down so quickly, she didn't have time to scream, to leave a spot of blood, to leave any trace of herself at all.

***

Wes had woken to the sound of Shana softly closing the door. He grinned at her care. Such a sweet girl, so unlike her parents. He waited five minutes for her return. Ten minutes. Twenty. After half an hour, he figured she deserved any teasing she got. He threw the blanket off and stood, grimacing as something embedded in the carpet poked into his sole. He slid his feet into Shana's flip-flops and opened the door to the stagnant night air. He frowned at the glass on the ground, hoping she hadn't stepped on any. He dashed to the outhouse, wanting Shana back inside. Recoiling

58

at the scent emanating from the bathroom, he gently knocked on the door. "Shana? Hello?" Silence. "What did you do, fall in?"

MADAM MULANI

BY JUSTIN GULESERIAN

Karen strolled down the boulevard, arm-in-arm with Hugh, and thought about names. Hermina was an uncommon name, pretty but unusual. Of course, Karen's friend Hermina was an unusual girl. The old cliché about given names determining one's destiny flashed through Karen's mind. She didn't believe in destiny, really. But then why go to a psychic? Because it was a birthday gift, she reminded herself. If she didn't go, Hermina's feelings would be hurt. And Hermina was bound to ask a million questions about the reading, so Karen couldn't fib about having gone.

Still, it was a nice day to be out. The birds flew between the trees along the narrow boulevard, with its little brownstone shops and charmingly faded signs, which had once assaulted the eyes with their gaudy vibrancy. It was quaint, an open stage set for a play in some modest theater of antiquity. Walking down the breezy street, under a clear sky of palest blue, Karen almost felt light on her feet; and Hugh seemed more than relieved to be taking a break from painting the walls of his old den.

Before long, the two of them came to the door of Madam Mulani's. From outside, the place looked wholly unremarkable, a brick front with two curtained windows. A wooden sign, hand painted to depict a cherubic sibyl reaching toward the twinkling astral bodies above her head, hung from an iron arm that extended over the sidewalk. Hugh reached for the door handle, flashed a comic smile at Karen, and opened the door to let his wife pass through. Karen stepped in furtively, half-expecting to trip over some queer gypsy artifact. But this place wasn't cluttered with morbid curiosities. On the contrary, the interior was done tastefully in something like Art Deco—clean white moldings, sleek lines in plaster, curves that gently led the eye down a cool and curious path. Light flooded in through the small windows and was amply reflected by the pristine white ceilings and walls.

As Karen entered the reception room, her gaze was instantly drawn to the nearest wall, covered with photographs of what appeared to be gypsies from a distant past. Interspersed with these photos hung a collection of antique painted advertisements. Among these was a series of ads for the Victor "Talking Machine" phonograph, complete with confused terrier. The trademark, Karen remembered, was taken from a painting titled "His Master's Voice." She also recalled hearing a rumor about the origins of the painting.

According to the rumor, the artist originally depicted the phonograph sitting on his brother's coffin. The terrier "Nipper," who had belonged to the deceased, was painted sitting beside the coffin and staring into the external horn of the phonograph. The implication was that the dog's confusion stemmed from an uncertainty as to whether the sound he heard was actually the voice of his dead master. The artist, being unable to sell such morbid subject matter, had allegedly painted over the coffin in an attempt to make it more commercially acceptable. After the changes had been made, it wasn't long before the image became property of the Victor Talking Machine Company.

Victor, she thought. There's an interesting name.

"May I help you?" asked a flat voice from the center of the room.

Karen abruptly turned from appraising the wall. In the middle of the room stood an old woman, probably in her seventies, wearing a formal blue evening gown, upon which was pinned a large silver broach. Her accent had diminished, but her finely-wrinkled Romanian features sang her origin clearly. She sat at a large oak desk, drinking coffee from a china cup and staring at the couple with apparent indifference.

"I'm sorry," Karen said. "Didn't mean to be rude. Nice collection. Um, I have a gift certificate from a friend. It's my birthday today."

"Many happy returns," said the old woman. "May I see the certificate, dear?"

"Yes, of course."

Karen scrambled through her purse to find it, silently cursing herself. Why was it buried at the bottom? She knew she would be coming here today. Why hadn't she pulled it out before now?

"Have you got it, hon?" asked Hugh.

"Yes, I know it's here. Ah, got it."

Karen produced a small blue slip of paper and promptly handed it to the old woman, whose face instantly tightened.

"Oh! You have the blue certificate. You must be Hermina's friend. You're Karen?"

"Yes, that's right," Karen said. "And this is my husband, Hugh."

"Hello, to both of you. If you haven't already guessed, I am Madam Didikai Mulani. Welcome to my humble ofisa."

The aging gypsy stood and managed a slight bow.

"You know Hermina, Ma'am?" asked Hugh.

"We spoke once, on the occasion of her buying this ticket. She bought a blue one, you see. Not many people buy these. Not many know about them, you see. And of course they are quite costly. I hope it's not in poor taste, my telling you that."

The old woman paused, as if deliberating whether to add anything more. Karen saw the woman's look of consternation but held her tongue. Finally, the Madam spoke.

"Your friend must care for you very much, dear."

"They're very close, ma'am," Hugh said. "I tease my wife that if she hadn't met me first, the two of them would be married by now."

"She worries, though," Karen said. "That's why I'm here. I suppose she thinks I need a kind of spiritual check-up."

"I see. Well, the certificate covers both of you."

"Really?" Hugh asked. He and Karen had promised each other, in the spirit of Hermina's gift, they would try to suspend disbelief. Laughing was out of the question, and even smiling would be frowned upon. But Hugh cracked a slight grin.

"Oh, this should be fun," Karen said. "Hermina reads my cards all the time, but Hugh never had it done."

"The blue ticket is not for a card reading. Hermina didn't explain it to you? I suppose she wanted it to be a surprise. All right, if you two would please follow me."

Madam Mulani took a keyring from her desk and toddled out of the room, waving at the couple to follow. The three made their way into a short hall. They passed an open doorway and Karen peeked in. The open room held a large table with several chairs seated around it. Atop the table sat several decks of cards. At the end of the hall, a second door was closed, secured with three deadbolts. Karen heard muffled and grainy orchestral music coming from behind it.

The old woman worked on the first lock. As the tumblers slid open, the music fell silent. Karen furrowed her brow, as a quiet uneasiness crept over her. What were they going to see that required the protection of three locks? After opening two deadbolts with two keys, Mulani unpinned the broach from her dress. Apparently the broach was a kind of locket, containing a third key. Karen and Hugh exchanged glances. At last, Madam Mulani opened the door. Musty air wafted into the hallway. The old woman shuffled through the doorframe and flicked a switch on the wall, lighting the small room. Karen and Hugh stood, unmoving.

"Please, come along," Mulani said a bit impatiently. "Come in."

The couple crept in and saw that the windowless room was nearly barren save for three objects: a shaded lamp, a small wooden stand, and the antique phonograph that sat atop it. Karen eyed the piece with interest. It had all the look of its years. A thick layer of patina dulled the oak frame. The brass crank and the horn had long ago lost their sheen.

"It's hardly a showroom piece," Mulani said. "But it's in perfect working order, I assure you."

She reached down and picked up a paper sleeve leaning against the legs of the phonograph's stand. From the sleeve, she pulled what appeared to be a blank phonograph record. Lifting the arm of the phonograph, she placed the record on the turntable, gently rested the needle at its outermost edge. She retired to a corner and spoke in a flat, unaffected tone.

"There we are," she said. And then as if reciting a well-worn speech, began. "Each of you, in turn, will approach the phonograph and wind the handle. When this is done, you will hear music. The music that you hear is the sound of your life...your entire life, from start to finish. If the tune is long, your lives will be long. If its end is glad, your lives will end gladly. And so on. Do you have any questions before you begin?"

"Where did you get this thing?" Hugh asked.

"That is the one question I will not answer."

Karen bit her lip. Mulani hadn't spoken of possible dangers or likely outcomes; she spoke of their future lives as if the matter were already settled, a dead language, etched in marble. Something inside her wanted desperately to protest, to shout in outrage. The idea was confining, oppressive. Karen felt a wave of claustrophobia wash over her. She cleared her throat loudly.

"We've never really believed in fate," she said. "Maybe we should go. This probably isn't for us. Hermina would get a lot more out of this than we would, I think." Karen looked to Hugh for agreement but found his eyes fixed on the phonograph.

"Perhaps it is best that you go," said Mulani, quietly. The words didn't sound like a rebuttal. They sounded more like sympathy.

"I want to try it," said Hugh. "You said the certificate covered both of us, is that right, ma'am?"

Madam Mulani nodded.

"Come on, hon," Hugh insisted. "It'll be fun. I've never heard of anything like this."

Karen held out a moment longer.

"You go first then," she said.

"Just turn the handle until you feel it resist," Mulani said.

Hugh approached the phonograph and slowly turned the handle. A deep creaking came from somewhere within the machine's bowels. When it was wound, Hugh kept his hand on the crank and turned to look at Karen.

"Let it go," Mulani said.

Hugh released the handle and rejoined Karen. The handle turned slowly. A sharp crackling sound poured from the brass horn. Hugh cocked his head to one side. Karen couldn't help but think how he resembled the confused terrier on the painted advertisements. His master's voice. His dead master's voice.

The music began, a quiet and gentle air, at first. Rosined bows drew gently across the face of their violins. Soon, the brass rang out, clear and steady, above the rising and falling of the strings. Something in the sound of those horns reminded Karen of Hugh's mother, strong and serene. Karen had to admit, from what Hugh had told her of his uncommonly happy childhood, she couldn't imagine a more appropriate movement to capture it. The music made her feel safe, just like the well-nursed babe her husband had been. Beside her stood Hugh, motionless, silent, looking utterly captivated. It was the same look he wore when enraptured by a strong sense of nostalgia.

After a couple of minutes, the music rose and became bolder. The trumpets surged and were joined by a thundering percussion. Dancing in and out of the central phrases, a lively harpsichord played. Karen wondered what she was hearing. Was this supposed to be Hugh's adolescence, or even his present-day life? Did the harpsichord represent her part in his life? There was no way to tell, of course. She couldn't help but smile to herself for taking the whole thing so seriously as to actually consider stalking out in a huff. No doubt this was some obscure piece of recorded music that the general public wouldn't recognize, played by a stereo from within the phonograph's body. She imagined a small speaker hidden deep inside the horn, and her smile widened. Karen looked over at Madam Mulani and saw that the old woman's face had relaxed a bit. She even fancied that she saw a little smile spreading across Mulani's formerly dour expression. Was this part of the sham? Karen wondered why the old woman's expression so authentically mimicked relief.

Three minutes later, the music slowed, but lacked the serenity of the first movement. There was sadness to it. At one point, the sorrow of the violins rose to an almost wailing pitch before falling again into quiet resignation. Karen looked over at Hugh and saw his look of confusion. No doubt he was trying to identify the music with some former low point in his life. After a while the violins grew quieter still, until they were little more than a muted hum, slowly fading. When the music fell silent, Karen looked over at Madam Mulani and saw that the woman's smile had also faded.

"Was that long?" Karen asked.

"Long enough, dear," Mulani said.

"It sounded kind of sad in the end," Hugh said, frowning.

"Well," Mulani said, "it's hardly uncommon for people to feel a little sad at the end of their lives. I assure you, the ending could have been much worse."

"It was pretty," Karen said.

The three stood in silence for a moment. Finally, the old woman moved to the phonograph and replaced the needle at the beginning of the record. Hugh sighed and turned to Karen with a smile.

"Well, hon, it's your turn."

Karen nodded and crept toward the phonograph. As she wound the handle, her eyes searched the depths of the horn for hidden speakers, scanned the record for a sign of little grooves, and found neither. When she felt the springs resist, she let go of the handle. The crackling sound filled her ears. She quickly returned to Hugh, took his arm, and waited with bated breath.

The sound that poured from the horn was a symphonic aberration. Violins shrieked as if knives had replaced their bows. Trumpets blared sheer cacophony. Bassoons piped up discord and despair. It sounded like riot. It sounded like war. Karen's eyes shot up to Hugh. Hugh's eyes shot to Madam Mulani, who moved as quickly as her arthritic knees would carry her to the machine. She snatched the phonograph's arm from off the vinyl. There was a loud screech and the music stopped. Madam Mulani stood with her back to Karen and Hugh, neither moving nor speaking.

"What the hell is going on here?" Karen demanded.

The old woman continued to stare at the phonograph in silence.

"Listen to me," Karen said, "I don't know if this is some ploy to make me shell out money, but my childhood was happy. I mean, it wasn't Rockwellian or anything, but it was certainly more pleasant than that noise."

The old woman turned slowly toward Karen. The fine wrinkles of her face seemed etched in stone, but the tears welling in her eyes belied her stoicism.

"I'm very sorry, dear," she said, "I don't know exactly why I allow this to continue. I don't know why I haven't smashed this infernal machine into a thousand pieces. I can tell you only that I believe the power behind it to be greater than me, greater than any one life or even a hundred lives. It's not my place to destroy it, nor is it my place to keep it from the world. But what happened here, today, I've seen it happen once before with a girl much like yourself."

"What the hell are you talking about?"

Madam Mulani spoke her next words to the floor.

"That music wasn't yours."

"What?"

"It wasn't for you. It was…"

The old woman dragged her eyes from the floor and fixed her gaze on Karen's protruding belly.

THE BARTER

BY J.C. RAYE

It was not as if they had any sort of agreement between them. At the very start, neither had a choice in the matter.

***

Ianna had simply arrived. Tumbled out of the tree line under a black, soaking sky. Bag and rental key in hand. Desperately fleeing that which was abysmal, now, for the second time in her life. First, it was a country, rent with war, and the soldiers who came by night to have at her. Then it was Dominik, whom she loved. Who'd changed so severely as soon as they arrived in America. Becoming a monster. Coursing with jealous fantasy and wild accusation as if it were a strong fever. Destroying her study books. Making her a prisoner to their home. Holding a blade to her throat whenever he was displeased with how she prepared food, or wore clothing, or breathed in and out. *A woman that is not beaten, is like a room that has not been swept,* he would say. Only two days before he'd brought her out to a cemetery, vowing, with a coarse grin, that *here* was where she'd be making her bed quite soon.

And after that? A blur of pain and haste. A violent thrashing which erupted over a tube of rhubarb lip color, and then his hands on her throat as never before. Selling the precious coin ring and the gold coral earrings her *bunika* had lovingly pressed into Ianna's frightened hands before she and her husband fled Moldova. Finding an agent who could understand her broken tongue, and an owner who would rent for cash to an undocumented. Choosing only what could fit into a worn-out case and bolting for her life. Certainly it was no surprise then, that a sight which might have filled others with immediate remorse, the dilapidated stone cottage, engulfed in drooping branches of pin oak, black shutters with slats torn out as if by the jaws of a many-headed *balaur*, was to Ianna a vision to be savored. And a promise of long awaited well-being.

***

The House had gone through numerous owners and countless renters, employing one calculated method or another, depending on its quarry, and of course, its mood. It turned away as many as would come, in fact. An endless parade of them, over two hundred years. True, some interlopers were more of a challenge than others to drive to wits end, so saturated with pure terror they'd run screaming into the night, leaving possessions and sometimes children behind. But since the House never tired, the time it took to send undesirables packing was of no consequence. The House would not tolerate even one resident, and this woman would be no different.

It knew no other like itself. Though other houses sat within view, barely an acre away to either side and back, there was no exchange between them. The structures offered no movement, no sound, nothing which would convey that they, too, were awake, sentient, like itself. Amusement could emanate only from within; in the creative line of attack or means of scare, followed by a final sensation of genuine fulfillment after a family had been systematically terrorized and off-loaded.

***

Many undertakings Ianna intended for that first night. At the very least, she planned to light the fireplace and sweep out the ungodly accumulation of dust and leaves which partially concealed the pumpkin floor pine. As it was only a little past 9 p.m. when finally, she was able to lock the front door behind her, and squeeze rain from the tangles of her ash brown curls, she considered that there might also be time to disinfect the bath, or perhaps even, investigate rooms above for usable treasures cast aside. Yet, Ianna could not remember a time when she felt more fatigued, when her bones felt so very heavy. The days of stress and physical exertion would now exact a price from her body, and when she momentarily stopped moving her limbs, she could see there would be no returning to it. She was entirely done in. Even unpacking or preparing a bed seemed an impossibly laborious endeavor. So instead, Ianna curled up in a dark corner of a lower room, under the spindly legs of a tall desk, *spiders be damned*, pulled her quilted jacket over her shoulders, and slept as one who was dead.

***

The sooner it was alone, the better, so it did not delay. Moments after the woman put her head to the planks, the House began to *concentrate*, as it had always done, inducing floorboards to creak and glass panes to rattle in their casings, agitations far in excess of any movement the outside storm could produce. This continued, intermittently, for more than a quarter of an hour. But, for all the clatter and judder and effort, the House could not rouse her. It then proceeded to unlock the upper window sashes, so they would fall heavily and heart-stoppingly to their sills, one after the other. Not above the cheap and lackluster, the House eventually pounded on the wall just inches from her sleeping head. Historically sound tactics all, now strangely unsuccessful. Finally, in a spasm of brawn due more to childish frustration than mindful maneuvering, the House blew the front door in with a thunderous crash, separating the wood from one of its hinges. The woman remained still. Her heavy breathing the only indication of life.

***

Before the sun fully rose, Ianna was up and at her work, dusting, washing, scraping, beating, all of the bustle which made a home livable. A home, that would be hers entirely, at least for now. She pushed away thoughts undesirable, such as where she might beg work when the earring-funded subsidy had shriveled up utterly, or how that work would be illegal, some occupation as illegitimate as she was herself, in this country. The agent had spoken very honestly with her, did not *pull punches*, as they said here. Locals would be unsympathetic to Ianna's plight and likely to turn her in to the authorities. Few people knew of the goings on in her homeland, or cared for that matter. *They couldn't find your country on a map if you paid them to.* The agent, an attractive blonde woman with three skinny children, Ianna had seen a photo of them seated around a Santa Claus, cautioned her to stay inside as much as she could.

Ianna hummed as she worked on the house, melodies both modern and from her childhood. This was a true luxury for her, to make a sound without fear. Sometimes she would forget herself while scouring a stain or wringing cloth in water and sing the lyrics out in full voice, strongly resisting the urge to look around, eyes closed, shoulders tightened, expecting the blow which always trailed her little joys. As the day wore on, Ianna became more energized. True, the work was seemingly endless, as the cottage had not seen caring hands in some time. But the freedom. *Oh! the freedom.* To drop a rag to the floor and leave it behind. To cut a slice of bread with prunes and munch on it at any time of day. To sing. To dance with the broom.

She was pleased to discover narrow cabinetry built directly into the walls of the two upstairs bedrooms, and they were packed with unforeseen gems, as she'd hoped. Blankets, sheets, cleaning fluids, rags and bar soaps, some still in their wrapping, their bouquet of citrus and lavender still preserved. Ianna set upright those items apparently toppled by the same intrusive wind which had wrenched open the entranceway while she slept. Though the round top, front door could no longer be locked, with some effort, she could *press* it back into its place. Just enough wiggle room remaining to at least be able to throw one of the bolts. Ianna marveled at the thick iron necking of the piece. She wondered if it was meant for a show of wealth. If not, she giggled to herself, then certainly meant to keep out a behemoth in search of citrus soap.

Ianna also discovered a second fireplace. Part of a summer kitchen hearth, quite similar to the one in her bunika's home back in Jura. As she meticulously scrubbed at the brick, and the thick iron door of the Dutch oven, strong memories of staying with her grandmother, there at the edge of the Dnister River, flooded back to her. She had not seen the woman or any family in more than six years. Tears could have come easily then, thinking of such isolation, thinking of a family one might never again take in one's arms. Yet Ianna didn't cry.

**

The House did not know *pride.* But there was no getting over the small pleasures it garnered as its stairs, floors, walls, and stone were exposed to reveal their true rich color and gleam in a way the House had not known for over a century. While it scrutinized the woman with extreme curiosity, wondering what task would be chosen next, it also schemed, how on this day, tonight in particular, her catalog of chores could be cut short. The displacement of objects, or making them airborne outright, was a skill the House had mastered long ago. But the movement of *people* themselves, was much more difficult for the House, and bound to cause injury beyond the fright. Tonight, it would experiment. It would *indulge.*

**

Much like a willful toddler who avoids bed lest a

moment of life be missed, Ianna sat up late. In the living room by the light of the fire, she was repairing the hole of a crocheted tablecloth found in an upstairs closet. Vigorously dusting on one of the high shelves without the use of a stepstool, the textile had come down upon her head rather pugnaciously. She had screamed to high heaven before realizing her attacker was constructed of tea-stained cotton.

***

It focused on her shoulders. The best place to push. Moving swiftly, just as she leaned forward to break a thread with her teeth, it violently shoved her out of the chair.

A disappointment. The needle did not invade her tongue as the House had hoped but tumbled away from her form to a safe distance. The woman also had the good sense, as if practiced in the art of plummeting, to bend her knees and twist, both waist and shoulders, thus changing the point of impact. She lay there on the floor, sprawled and surprised, but also strangely still. As if thinking. As if working something out. And here became the problem for the House.

***

Her first thought of course was Dominik. That somehow, he had found her, gained entry to the locked home, crept up behind the rocker, silent as the grave. But Ianna knew this was not so. She knew she was alone. Alone as could be. And Ianna had expected it. Not the push to the floor, but...*something.* For the agent had warned her of this one other aspect of the rental; the explanation as to why the house remained empty and available at such a price. With low cast eyes and a sheepish face, the woman had uttered a word: *ghosts.*

But ghosts can only startle, and what was that but a healthy spark of the heart? Spirits had capacity to get underfoot, surely, spilling cups and toppling chairs, even pulling down draperies if they've mind to, but no more than any small child might do. At thirty-years, Ianna still harbored dreams of one day becoming a mother, so it might be good practice after all. Phantoms would not tease her for having a snub nose, or liken her innocence or stupidity with that of a bleating goat. She never heard tell of any ghost putting the hot iron to someone's back or sending them to an emergency clinic with broken bones. *No.* This would not drive her from the home. *So let them come,* she invited, she all but summoned. Spirits, specters, phantasms all. *They're most welcome.* Ianna pushed up onto her hands and knees. She located the needle, recovered the fabric, and resettled into the repair.

***

The House was bewildered. Never in all its years had it witnessed such a *mild* reaction to being flung about as a rag doll. Its mind was disordered, and for once, it lacked direction. Clearly it had not used enough force. The woman thought she had fallen, rather than been pushed. There was no other account for her reaction.

This time, the House gripped her feet. It dragged her down from the rocking chair and halfway across the room. Her head hit hard, first on the seat and then on the pine. And now, though the needle missed her eye, it found cushion in the fleshy part of her right cheek.

***

Ianna lay still for only a moment. She rose to a seated position, there, eye level with the furniture, and gently pulled the needle from her punctured face. She wriggled her nose and jaw as if to appraise muscles for utility. She rubbed at the back of her head, searching for any open wound. And then, sat. For a while. Just there. Thinking. If the house did not want her to return to the rocker, then she wouldn't. She rose and headed upstairs to bed.

***

It regarded her. The evening and next morning passed, and it regarded her still. She was aware of it, the House, aware it was there, and that it could cause her suffering. Yet, the knowledge of it did not impede her chores or mood in the least. In fact, did it not observe further cleaning today with a more *caressing* hand? It noticed the scars and discolorations of old wounds which wound their way along her torso like a creeping vine when she ran the bath or elevated her hair with the long pins. None of these caused by last night's events, but testament to her tolerance for pain and injury. As she toiled away, unperturbed, the House could feel itself *changing.*

In times past, the House would enjoy generating those thuds, clangs and various reverberations throughout, which unnerved and startled. Constant creaks and bangs, though more difficult to sustain, were an amusingly sure-fire means of driving an individual mad. It learned over time that the human mind was very fragile indeed. One such previous owner, in the end, so tortured by lack of sleep, began to see and hear manifestations of his own, ones which far surpassed any terror the House in all its glory could have crafted. But with Ianna, the House *stretched* less, in fact, acting to minimize those sounds within itself which might interrupt her slumber, or cause her to worry unnecessarily about structure or safety. Such was also true of the House's proficiency in transferring energy to objects, once used to crush limbs and upend cribs, now expended, most generously, to seal cracks in walls and pull bricks from where they'd fallen, back up into the hearth.

***

The day Dominick pressed his ruddy face up against the glass of the summer kitchen window, Ianna could not have been more horrified, or more surprised. For it was only with the rental agent she had shared her name. The woman herself had confessed to being a victim of battery in her teens, and so naturally Ianna had assumed a confidentiality in their exchange.

As soon as their eyes locked, his murderous, and hers dire, she threw herself to the ground, as quickly as if her legs had been swept from under her. She had no plan for this. Ianna's tears were immediate, and she unconsciously crawled in circles like an animal trapped within a metal cage.

***

The House *sensed* her terror, momentarily fascinated by a type of human fear for which it was not the cause. Then, it acted. The man smashed at the window with a fallen tree limb, and then attempted to climb through the opening made there. The House, returning the attack, slammed the upper sash down upon his hands, severing one of the fingers. He screamed and fell away from the sill, back into the thorny shrubbery. It stabbed at his face and hands. Shouting from pain, but mostly from shock, he managed to scrambled up onto his feet once more. The House *watched* him look from left to right, calculate his next move, which ended up as a rush on the back door. But it was not a race. The House did not have to travel to meet him there. It only need wait for that perfect moment in time when the bridge of the man's nose would align perfectly with the doorknob. And so it did. And the man fled. Dented face cupped in bloody paws, howling all the way.

***

Over the next few weeks, the two were quite the pair, Ianna and the House. They *did* for each other, and their bond grew, as did their pleasure. Indiscernible in their singular actions perhaps, as a lone vine might be within a dense cluster of creeping ivy, their days were imbued with a nonstop flourish to *outdo* the other in the beautification and function of the House.

Like a great general on a mission of search and destroy, Ianna discovered all of those nooks and crannies which had never been cleaned and tore into them with mad glee. Deep inside clock cases. Between the lines and grooves of the intricate doorknocker in the shape of a mallard's head. In and around the candle cups of every fixture. Enchanted by her tireless charge, the House returned the favor, in abundance. It blocked fall drafts and kept its temperature comfortably even. It produced low vibrations in the bowels of its walls to drive away colonized insects and hairy rodents. As a special treat, and with great industry and practice, the House even reached skyward into a core of outside wire, pulling in unlimited electrical current so she might make use of the lamps she dusted so well. It did not *love* her, but it did get to wondering if any of those frightened away in years past might have lived up to this potential, as a devoted owner, if given more time.

At night, when Ianna had not one more once of strength left, they both would cease in their activities, and simply think about each other, warmly, appreciatively, as the fire crackled and the outside winds heralded the coming of winter.

***

It was on one such peaceful night, four weeks almost to the day of losing a finger, that Dominik returned to the cottage along the Delaware River. And this time, he was not alone. The House knew they were there. Surrounding it. Preparing to enter by force. It heard their whisperings as Dominick directed them about. It saw their torches. The tips of their axe blades which occasionally reflected light. It had no way to warn Ianna, who was seated, in plain sight through the large kitchen window, cutting slices of potato for a soup. All the House could think to do at first was blow out the fire and fastened the locks and catches on all of the windows and doors. But they struck nonetheless.

Ianna fell apart at once, in tears, zig-zagging one way, then another. Helplessly. Hopelessly. She had not seen Dominik's face, yet somehow knew he was the source of all this noise, the chopping, the shouting, and the tearing asunder.

The House panicked as well. It would not allow them to hurt her, create fresh bruising and cuts to her body, as those upon her when she first crossed the threshold. It could also not allow them to *take* her. There was no imagining a life now without her steadfast company. Unfortunately, there was no time for it to think as windows were smashed in and doors kicked through. Concentrating, the House, *moved* her. First, pushing her up the flue of chimney as far as she could be stuffed, no regard whatsoever for the perverse direction of her limbs or collapse of her spine. Then, realizing its foolish error, that the chimney had no door, that the men could reach up and pull her right back down, perhaps with a broom handle or garden implement of some kind, it hurriedly yanked her out again and stowed her away in the Dutch oven. Though this was not without some effort in the jamming, as the space was barely large enough to house a large stew pot. The House was sure they would not look for her there. It slammed the small iron door shut just as they entered the kitchen.

JUDGE NOT

BY PATSY PRATT-HERZOG

Drip...Drip...Drip.

The familiar sound of the leaky tap in the darkroom seemed loud and hostile in the silent studio. Jack wedged himself against the wall in the corner, drawing his knees protectively to his chest. He was still safe. It hadn't found him—yet.

He tried to avoid looking at the pictures scattered around him on the floor, but they pulled at his gaze, unwilling to be ignored. Portraits of powerful men and women dressed in fine clothing posed before raging vortexes of color. Everyone thought the photos were clever creations of art, but it wasn't art—it was *the camera.*

When he'd figured out what the swirling colors in the photographs contained, it was like winning the lottery. Every lie, every act of larceny, adultery, or murder the subject had committed was recorded in those swirling colors. If you enlarged the images, you could read them like a sordid bedtime story.

Jack had made a fortune blackmailing Louisiana's most powerful men and women with their dirty laundry. Best of all, the 'charitable' income from his new benefactors left him more time for his own...hobbies.

When the vintage 60's Kodak came to him, he'd thought the camera and its message a prank from one of his buddies.

The eye of the lens is the eye of judgment.
See only that which you wish to be judged.

In the fishbowl world of social media, everything was judged—every action, every word, every picture—but the camera did far more than judge. One-by-one, his blackmail victims started to vanish. At first, Jack thought they were trying to avoid paying up, but when he'd gone to collect from the Mayor, the camera was already there. He'd watched in horror as it sucked Mayor Townsend into its lens with a writhing mass of hungry black tentacles. One by one, it was collecting them, and he could do nothing to stop it. Jack whimpered and pressed his face against his knees.

He'd burned it, smashed it, and buried it. No matter how many times he tried to destroy the camera, it always came back to him, and they came with it—more and more of them every day.

Jack's head jerked up at the familiar squeak of the wheels on his desk chair. As if pushed by invisible hands, it crept across the floor toward him. The temperature in the room plummeted, sending Jack's frantic breaths out in misty plumes. He pressed his back into the wall, but there was nowhere to go—there was no escape. The seat spun slowly to face him and upon it sat the camera, glaring at him with its one glass eye.

It was growing stronger. Each time he destroyed it, it returned faster to plague him.

Black plastic and tanned leather with little inlays of ivory, lapis lazuli, and moonstone along its casing, it looked perfectly harmless—pretty even.

He laughed, the sound tainted with an edge of hysteria. His laughter quickly turned to sobs as the lens continued to glare, cold and unblinking.

It wasn't alive. He knew it wasn't, yet somehow it was here, and not at the bottom of Lake Pontchartrain where he'd tossed it less than an hour ago.

"Why won't you die?" he screamed.

He kicked the chair across the room where it crashed into storage shelf. The camera clattered on the floor, its unscathed eye glaring relentlessly back at him.

The floor shook and bucked, boards rattled as angry swirls of colored light sprang from the camera's lens and went careening around the room in a dazzling vortex.

Jack ducked as a framed picture jumped off its hook and hurtled toward him, smashing into the wall above his head. Papers and pictures swirled around him in a blinding tornado as file cabinets spat their contents into the air.

Jack scrambled to his feet and stood in the center of the howling maelstrom with clenched fists.

"What do you want?" he screamed.

The pictures and papers slowed their mad dance

and fluttered to the ground forming the letters Y. O. U.

Jack fell to his knees, frantically tossing the papers aside until the word was no longer visible, but he couldn't escape the hovering lights which encircled him, nor the staring eye of the camera.

"This isn't my fault," he told the lights. "I just took your picture. I didn't know what the camera would do to you!"

"Why?" He glared at it, his eyes wide and bloodshot. "Why me?"

The desk beside him cracked open with a sound like a thunderclap and disgorged the contents of his hidden drawers. Pictures of young, naked girls pelted him as they rained to the ground.

He pointed at the camera with a trembling hand. "What right have you to judge me?"

Someone pounded on the studio door.

"Jack Brown, open the door. New Orleans P.D."

Heart pounding, Jack frantically scooped the photographs into a pile.

"Open the door Mr. Brown, or I'll open it for you," the voice threatened.

Jack flicked open his lighter, prepared to set the evidence ablaze, but the colored lights snuffed out the flame as they spiraled back into the lens of the camera. With a splintering thud, the door slammed open and a beautiful woman with ebony skin strode toward him. Jack stared hard at her familiar features, and at the badge and pistol clipped to her belt.

"My, my," she drawled in a Cajun-spiced accent. "What a fine mess." She picked up the camera and held it lovingly in her hands. "What's a matter, Mr. Brown? Aren't you enjoyin' my gift?"

"Your gift?" he croaked.

"You don't rememba me, do you?" She knelt down and picked up a picture of a young girl with ebony skin and frightened eyes. "You used to call me Sweet Adelaide."

Jack felt the color drain from his face. She had been one of his favorites. One of the ones he'd spent 'extra special' time with—until he'd found out her uncle was an Obeah Man. "Adelaide Leveau," he croaked.

"You do rememba. Good." She smiled at him, her brown eyes taking on a scarlet glow. "I thank ya kindly for helping to clean up my town." Adelaide lifted the camera. "But now it's time for you to join all your new friends."

"No," Jack whimpered as she pointed the camera's unblinking eye at him.

"Come now…crying never helped anybody…isn't that what ya used to tell me?" she asked, her scarlet eyes burning with triumph and hate. "Be a good boy and smile pretty for the camera."

"No!" Jack screamed as the eye of judgment opened and its hungry tendrils sucked him in.

RED CAP CHRISTMAS

BY JAMI BAUMANN

Wilhelm Allerton had been running the family antique store for over forty-two years. He followed in the footsteps of his father, collecting rare items. He kept the items he knew to be the most dangerous locked away in his office closet. Wilhelm always kept the closet locked. The key never left the chain around his neck. His three children and seven grandchildren had each tried, one time or another, to break into the closet. Each one received a sound beating when caught trying to pick the lock.

Wilhelm ran his store with military precision. He carefully researched every item. Nothing in the store was over or under priced. Damaged items he found were meticulously reconstructed with his gentle hands. Wilhelm prided himself on the store and its condition. The reason, he thought, he had so many loyal customers.

The store was his life's work. Thus his annoyance at

his heart attack, in October at the age of sixty-five, could only be expected. His children and grandchildren rushed to his side, because for all his quirks, he was a loving and generous man. His irritation became rage when he discovered he would have to spend a month or more recuperating in the outpatient rehabilitation facility.

"My store needs me," he snarled at his oldest daughter, Beatrice.

"Dad, we're more than capable of running the store for you while you recover. Your health is the most important thing." Beatrice sighed. She was just as stubborn as her father. However, she had the doctors on her side.

"Mr. Allerton you've suffered a major cardiac episode. Your heart was badly damaged, and open-heart surgery has left you weak. You'll be here for the rest of this week until you can be safely moved to our outpatient care facility." Dr. Patel had been arguing with Wilhelm for two days.

"You're shipping me off to an old folks' home to rot." Wilhelm pouted.

"No, we're not. It's an outpatient recovery center and trust me; they'll want you gone as quickly as possible." Beatrice rolled her eyes.

"I want to go home." Wilhelm scowled.

Beatrice sighed. "You live two flights of stairs above the store. Besides, we all work. None of us can take care of you full time. It's hard enough getting someone to take care of the shop."

"If your mother was still here..." he trailed off. The guilt he had over the passing of his late wife, Catherine, still haunted him.

Beatrice placed her hand on her hips. She glared at him just like his late wife, "If Mom was still here, she'd tell you to stop being an old fool and do as the doctor tells you. But she's not. So, I'll tell you for her."

"It's for the best, Mr. Allerton. You'll recover and be back to your store soon." Dr. Patel said as he picked up his tablet and excused himself.

Wilhelm glared, then stuck out his tongue at the doctors receding back. If they were going to treat him like a child, he would act like one. His grandson, Bryce, snickered from his seat in the corner. Wilhelm shot the boy a wink. Beatrice groaned, rolling her eyes at the exchange.

Wilhelm turned to his daughter; his voice serious. "The store cannot stay closed for a month. I'll be bankrupt."

"You think I don't know that? Why do you think Bryce is here?" Beatrice beamed at her only son.

"Yes, why are you here? Why aren't you at school?" Wilhelm interrogated his twenty-two-year-old grandson.

Bryce looked around awkwardly. "I'm taking a semester off."

"By choice?" Wilhelm demanded.

A nervous laugh escaped Bryce. "Sure, let's go with that."

"What did you do, boy?"

"Gramps, I'm telling you it really wasn't my fault. A party got a little out of hand. There was a small fire. No one got hurt...well...no one died."

Beatrice glared at Bryce. Her voice came out full of disapproval. "That frat house was a death trap, anyway. Tons of fire code violations." She clucked her tongue. "We settled with the school. After his suspension is over, he can return."

"Cleaning up his messes and not allowing the boy to face consequences again, I see." Wilhelm's voice dripped with disapproval.

"Anyway, it works out for you. Bryce has nothing to do until the next semester starts in January. He can run the store for you." Her voice came out overly cheerful while she braced for his response.

The hospital could hear the roar of outrage throughout. "The fire starter in our family store? Have you gone insane?"

Bryce bit back his sarcastic remarks, afraid his grandfather would kill him from the hospital bed.

"Who else is willing? Maxwell and his family live in Chicago. Jason and I have our own business to run and my girls are still in junior high." Beatrice tossed her hands up in annoyance.

"What about your sister?"

Beatrice gave a very unladylike snort. "Yes, Rachel. Well, Dad, she just quit her job and traveled to Taiwan to find herself. Apparently, your heart attack showed her how fleeting life is."

"She could have told me goodbye." Wilhelm muttered. He often described his youngest daughter as a free spirit, which for Wilhelm was synonymous with disaster.

Bryce snickered from the corner. "I think the very married shrink she ran off with caused that."

Wilhelm gave Beatrice a disappointed look. "Again? See that is why you don't clean up your child's messes all the time. Your mother spoiled her. She never let her clean up her own messes and look what we got? We got a Rachel."

"Yes. I'll keep the parenting advice in mind." The look she gave her father would make a lesser man cry. Wilhelm was immune to his daughter's icy glares. "Well, that just leaves Bryce. He's your only option if you want the store to remain open while you recuperate." Beatrice smiled and patted her son's shoulder.

With a mighty sigh, Wilhelm beckoned his grandson closer. Bryce leaned in only to have his grandfather clutch the front of his shirt. He jerked the boy forward. Their faces were inches apart. "Burn down my shop, boy, and I'll shoot you." Bryce laughed nervously as he removed his grandfather's surprisingly strong grip.

"No worries Gramps."

Wilhelm's body fell back onto the bed. He knew they had defeated him. "The keys are in the cupboard with my clothes."

"Already got them." Bryce smiled as he pulled them from his pocket and dangled them out of his grandfather's reach. "But isn't one missing?"

"The key to the back-closet stays with me. The door remains locked. You must never open it. That includes breaking into it." Wilhelm's tone was serious and strained.

Bryce chuckled as he headed out the door. "I know the rules, Gramps. Get better." He glanced back at the old man in the bed. Wilhelm looked exhausted and frail. It pained Bryce to see his mighty grandfather looking this way. He decided right then that he would be awesome at running the store. He would make the old guy proud.

"Excuse me, Sir?" a pretty nurse stopped Bryce at the elevator.

"Yes?" Bryce grinned, wanting nothing more than her phone number.

"Your mother told me to give this to you." She dropped a key attached to a necklace in his hand. "The ambulance driver found this in the rig after they brought in your grandfather."

Bryce felt a huge wave of disappointment wash over him until he realized the nurse had just handed him the closet key. He gave her a dazzling smile as he pulled the chain over his head. "Thank you." He mumbled as he entered the elevator and pressed the button for the ground floor.

The next day he opened the shop bright and early. His first day was uneventful. He had a few looky-loos but nothing exciting. The second day was the same as the first. He wondered, by day seventeen, how his grandfather hadn't died of boredom.

To fight the monotony, he created a website to bring in more customers. He even created an online shop that would allow people to purchase items that he could ship out.

Days went by before he realized he could no longer fight his curiosity. The key dangled around his neck. He played with it continuously. He debated with himself often. He was trying to convince himself that he didn't want to know what his grandfather hid. It was useless. Discovering what his grandfather was hiding controlled Bryce's every thought, until he had to give in.

November rain was pelting the store window. Bryce had been customer-free for hours. The curiosity eating away at him, combined with the tedium of sitting in the store waiting for someone to come in, left him with no chance. He snatched the key from his neck. He tried to contain his glee knowing he would be the only one in the family to see the inside of the closet. He couldn't.

Once inside the closet, he laughed when he saw what his grandfather had fought so hard to protect. On the floor was a solid trunk and a few wooden boxes. A large ornate mirror hung on one wall across from a bunch of tin pictures. In the middle, random jewelry was hanging on hooks. The big family secret was a bunch of trash his grandfather didn't want to sell. He was disappointed.

Bryce grabbed the top box. It had pictures of little gnomes in red hats painted on it. They were running around a Christmas tree with long silver toys. A little cute if not creepy. Inside were a bunch of gold ornaments. They had thin red and silver beads swirling around in intricate shapes. The handwritten notecard inside said *1931 hand blown Scottish ornaments.* Underneath was the word *Red Caps.*

It was the third week of November. The Christmas antiques had been selling like hotcakes online and even in the store. These should have been laid out after Halloween. "Crazy old man." Bryce muttered under his breath. He put the box of ornaments beneath his arm and relocked the door as he exited the closet. Heading towards the front, he intended to go through the other stuff before his grandfather came back.

He placed the ornaments on the front counter and opened them for display. He started Googling similar items so he could price them correctly. Bryce decided two thousand dollars for a dozen of them seemed fair, especially since he thought including the box with it sweetened the pot.

Bryce didn't need to wait long. After displaying them for a few days, Mrs. Hurst came in looking for more Christmas antiquities for her mansion outside of town. She was his grandfather's richest customer. Wilhelm even considered the fifty-five-year-old widow a close friend. Bryce had always thought his grandfather was a little sweet on her.

The satisfaction he received from running the woman's credit card for two thousand dollars was unimaginable. He couldn't wait until his grandfather arrived that afternoon so he could show him all the money and progress he had made with the store.

About ninety minutes after the sale he heard the tinkle of the front door's overhead bell, followed by the sound of his grandfather's cane. Wilhelm walked up each aisle, examining every item. When he reached the front desk, he looked at Bryce. "You didn't burn it down."

"Missed you too, Gramps."

"The place is clean." Wilhelm commented as he swiped a finger across the glass counter.

"Yes. I also sold quite a few items." Bryce bragged.

"I noticed that. How did you sell so many?"

"You now have a website and a social media account to sell more stuff. *Antique Cache* is on the map." Bryce puffed up his chest with pride.

His grandfather's lips thinned, and he grunted. "I suppose that's useful with all this technology garbage. Now give me the keys. All of them." He held out his gnarled hand. With a sigh, Bryce grabbed the ring of keys from his belt and handed them over. His grandfathers' eyes slipped to Bryce's neck. "All!" Wilhelm growled.

Bryce gave a small frown before removing the closet key from around his neck and adding it to the others.

"I'll be in the back making sure nothing's torched." Wilhelm slowly walked to the back room.

"You're welcome, Gramps. So glad I could help," he yelled after his shuffling grandfather. "It's not like I've kept this place going for you while you were out." Bryce grumbled under his breath. He'd never let his grandfather know how much he enjoyed working here. He closed his laptop and began putting it in his backpack when he heard the startled scream and crashing of boxes.

"Gramps?" Bryce shouted as he started running frantically to the back. His grandfather was on the floor with his back up against the file cabinet. He knelt beside Wilhelm and put his fingers up to the old man's neck. "Gramps, are you okay? Is it your heart?" Wilhelm turned and gave Bryce a wide-eyed stare.

Bryce nearly jumped out of his skin when his grandfather grabbed him around the throat and started strangling him. "Where are the ornaments?" Wilhelm screamed in his face. As his grandfather's grip got tighter, all Bryce could think was that the recovery center had one heck of a gym.

"Sold…them…" was all he managed to say. He kept tapping his grandfather's hand, trying to get him to release his throat.

"You fool. To whom?" Wilhelm tightened his grip.

"Gramps…air…" Bryce gulped.

With a growl, Wilhelm let go of his grandson. Bryce gasped, then fell, sprawling backwards. He rubbed his throat while he sucked in big puffs of air. "Dang, Gramps, you do CrossFit in that rehab?"

"To whom?" His normally gentle grandfather looked murderous.

"Mrs. Hurst. She paid two grand for them." Bryce explained. "Figured you'd be happy. No big deal, we can always get more."

"The big deal is you just killed that woman and her family."

"What?"

"Everything I lock in that closet is cursed or haunted. I hide it away from the world as my father told me to."

"Please, Gramps. Ghosts and curses aren't real."

His grandfather grabbed his cane and struggled to get up. Wilhelm gave a horrified glance at the open closet door. "Lock that back, now!" he pointed as he used the desk for leverage to get to his feet. Bryce did as he asked. When Wilhelm was upright again, he grabbed his cane and headed towards the front of the store. "Where's your car?" he barked.

"Out front. Why? Where are you going?" Bryce called out, following Wilhelm.

"We have to get to her house before it's too late." Wilhelm wheezed as he rushed through the store, his cane tapping rapidly.

"You can't really believe that?"

Wilhelm spun around quickly and rapped his grandson on the top of his head with the handle of his cane. "Doesn't matter what I believe. Doesn't matter what you don't believe. If we arrive at Mrs. Hurst's home and everything is okay, then I'm just a superstitious old man." He turned back around, rushing out the door to Bryce's beat up Jeep Cherokee. Wilhelm climbed in the passenger seat.

Bryce sighed while digging the car keys out of his pocket. "Guess that means I'm driving." He turned and locked the shop door with the secret spare key he had made. His grandfather blared the horn. "I'm coming. Not that you gave me a choice." He muttered as he climbed into the driver's seat.

"Her house is on Sage Trail Place off Route 12," Wilhelm ordered.

"Right." Bryce sighed as he started the engine and signaled to enter traffic. They headed towards the outskirts of town. "What's so bad about these ornaments? Mrs. Hurst will touch them and mysteriously drop dead six years later or some crap like that?"

Wilhelm growled. "If only it were that simple. It was my father, Heinrich, who explained how he came into possession of them. He was there the night they murdered Agnes Kirkland's son and his family."

"They?"

"The Redcaps. Agnes lost her husband in Scotland, so she was forced to move to America with her eldest son. Her son married a woman that Agnes hated. She got the idea to curse her daughter-in-law. Agnes and her friend, a witch, went up to a nearby castle and captured twelve Redcaps in the dozen ornaments. She trapped the angry fairies hoping they would drive the daughter-in-law away."

"Evil fairies?" Bryce started to laugh. "That sounds legit, Gramps."

Wilhelm let loose a small snarl and crossed his arms over his chest. He continued his story. "She gave them to her daughter-in-law as a present on Christmas Eve before Agnes went off to midnight Mass. The witch had given Agnes some bad advice. Redcaps, though mischievous, are also murderous little buggers. The whole reason they are called Redcaps is because they soak their hats in the blood of those they kill. Agnes thought the Redcaps would spoil milk, ruin laundry, and drive her daughter-in-law crazy, so she'd take off."

"Guess that's not what happened?"

"No, it's not. When Agnes returned home, she found her son, daughter-in-law, and all five kids brutally murdered in their beds. The Redcaps were still destroying the house when she ran out into the street screaming."

"Wait...Kirkland? Like, that unsolved case from 1932?" Bryce asked, "I remember that from local high school history. It was crazy; they never caught anyone."

"The same. It wasn't just some unsolved crime. It happened because of the ornaments. There was no mysterious drifter like the papers said. Agnes and the other Kirkland's were our neighbors. My father went back to the house with Agnes before the police got there. Together, they trapped the Redcaps back in their ornaments. When Agnes died, she entrusted the ornaments to my father, and he passed them down to me. They were the very first item in my cursed collection," he explained. Wilhelm started to shift anxiously in his seat, watching the town fade to the woods.

"Okay. Sounds like you don't know if they're cursed or not." Bryce observed. "It's just a story your dad told you."

"I do know it's real because like you I was a young fool who didn't listen to his elders. My father's warnings were just old-world noise. I sold the ornaments back in 1978 to the Smith family. A couple and their two young children. Mrs. Smith called me that night to tell me something was wrong with the ornaments. By the time I got there, they were all dead. I had to break in and trap the creatures before they escaped into the town." Wilhelm's voice was strained and tortured. "I killed four innocent people because I didn't believe in curses. After that, I collected as many cursed items as I could find. It didn't bring that family back, but it saved some others."

"Mrs. Hurst's house is here on the right, Gramps." Bryce didn't know what else to say. Curses weren't real, he thought, but the guilt Wilhelm felt was surely real. They continued up the long gravel driveway to the front door. Bryce motioned to the house as he turned off the car. "I've never seen red and white sheer curtains before. How festive." Bryce mused sarcastically.

"Mrs. Hurst has never had colored curtains in her house. She says anything other than white lace is tacky." Wilhelm said as he grunted and groaned his way from the car.

"That's not funny, Gramps." Bryce called out as the door slammed. He gave a frustrated grumble as he got out of the car to follow.

Wilhelm knocked on the door while he rang the doorbell multiple times. When no one answered, he pulled apart his cane, revealing a sword. His grandfather opened the unlocked door and entered, weapon raised.

Bryce stood there, his mouth gaping in shock. He was wondering if the heart attack had knocked some screws loose. "We're going to jail," Bryce muttered, following Wilhelm inside.

"Kathy?" Wilhelm called out as he slowly crossed the marble entry. "It's Wilhelm. Kathy?"

"Help me!" came a screech from the middle of the house. At the panicked cries, Bryce went running towards them.

"Bryce!" he hissed. "Wait!" his grandfather made a grab for the back of his shirt and missed.

When he caught up, he found Bryce frozen at the living room doorway. "What the hell?"

Mrs. Hurst whimpered from the wooden dining room chair that she was strapped to with tinsel and flashing Christmas lights. The side of her face was covered in bloody deep cuts. Her hair looked like someone had taken a lawn mower to it. Her silk blouse was torn to shreds. Sticking out of her upper thighs were multiple candy canes. She had been stabbed with them.

"Help me," she moaned. Bryce, startled back to reality, rushed forward to untangle her from the lights.

"Mrs. Hurst, what happened?" Bryce asked, while he loosened the first strand. "Were you robbed?"

Her voice was a faint whisper. Her shock was clear. "They came out of the ornaments." She continued to sob. "They killed Harriet and Mr. Fluffernutter."

"Who?" Bryce asked, confused.

"Harriet my housekeeper. They chopped her up and put her in the oven. They cooked her!" Mrs. Hurst's voice was reaching a hysterical high pitch as she cried.

"And my fluffern..." her voice trailed off in a wail. Bryce finally got the first strand free from her ankles and started on the next.

"What came out of the ornaments? Who killed them?" Bryce looked around, terrified. He was expecting giant hulking monsters to attack at any moment.

Wilhelm gently patted Bryce's shoulder and pointed to the ornate fireplace across the room. "Redcaps," he whispered.

Bryce let his hands fall limp as he stood in shock. "What the hell are those?"

On the mantle sat a couple of two-foot-tall giggling creatures. Their scrawny armored legs were swinging back-and-forth, dangling. Long braided beards rose up their faces to meet large bulbous noses. Crimson hats were perched on their heads, dripping with what Bryce could only assume was blood.

A third one was bouncing up and down on the cream-colored settee. It was wearing the severed head of a stuffed bear in an elf hat; like a deformed helmet. As it jumped around, the Redcap took turns between barking and psychotic laughter. The body of the four-foot-tall stuffed bear was sliced to shards and tossed among the presents under the tree.

The Redcap wearing the absurd stuffed helmet started to growl in Mrs. Hurst's direction. It howled with laughter when she starting sobbing again. One of the gnomes on the mantle popped open a bottle of champagne and chugged it. The one next to it growled and started smacking its friend on the head with its long scythe-like axe.

Wilhelm kicked Bryce hard in the back. "Get the

box! Put the ornaments back inside." He whispered fiercely.

With a look of terror, Bryce nodded. He crawled behind the settee to the tree and snagged the discarded box. He glanced around, making sure the things didn't see him as he got the box ready. Only four ornaments were missing from their container. He found them hanging up on the tree. Mrs. Hurst didn't get very far before the little demons attacked. He crawled around the tree as quietly as he could and put the four ornaments back in the box. He scuttled back to his grandfather.

"Why aren't they going away?" Bryce whispered as the two on the mantle continued fighting.

"Give me your hand, boy. It takes blood magic to put them back in the box." Wilhelm used his sword and cut Bryce's palm.

Bryce cried out loudly, more in surprise than pain. The sound, mixed with the scent of fresh blood, got the Redcaps attention. The two on the mantle began snarling, jumped down, and rushed towards them, weapons raised. The one on the settee threw Mr. Fluffernutter's head at them as it growled, grabbing its weapon. Wilhelm seized Bryce's hand and used the blood to draw a cross in it.

"Those of the dark that threaten me in this place. God must banish their evil into the trapping space. Remove their powers until the last trace." Wilhelm cried out repeatedly as he swung his cane sword at the advancing creatures.

With hair raising screeches the Redcaps turned in to gray smoke. The mist was quickly sucked into the ornaments in the box. A fourth swirling cloud of smoke came through a swinging door. It was roaring as it went in the box. Bryce assumed it had been pulled out of the kitchen where it was cooking the housekeeper.

Wilhelm slammed the lid down, trapping them inside. "Still think curses and ghosts aren't real, boy?"

Bryce chuckled awkwardly. "You win, Gramps. The closet is off limits. I'll never go in there again." He went back to untying poor hysterical Mrs. Hurst.

Wilhelm gave a sigh as he handed his sword to Bryce. "Use this, it's quicker."

"Thanks." He used the sword to cut through the rest of the lights and tinsel.

"You know, Bryce." Wilhelm cleared his throat. "Of all my children and grandchildren, I didn't think you would be the one I would groom to take over."

Startled, Bryce handed the sword over to his grandfather as he pulled the cut bindings free. "Take over?"

"Yes, you believe now. I'm an old man and that heart attack proved it. I have to pass on the store and all the items to a new protector." Wilhelm admitted as he helped Mrs. Hurst remove the candy cane daggers from her leg. Once they were out, she leaned heavily against him.

"So, do we tell the cops the truth?" Bryce asked. "We have to call them, right?"

"Yes," his grandfather insisted. "We call them. They won't handle cursed Christmas ornaments better than you did. I'm not about to let those things back out to prove our case."

Mrs. Hurst grabbed Bryce's arm. "Please don't let them out again," she begged.

"It was a crazed intruder, Kathy. We chased him away when we arrived."

"Yes," she wept as she limped towards the front hall. "An intruder."

Bryce took the other side of her waist and helped her to the phone, then sat her on the front porch swing while they waited for the cops to arrive.

"Hey, Gramps," Bryce whispered to his grandfather as the police secured the scene, "What else is in that closet?"

"Many more horrible things. Treasures that are attached to the darkest of the supernatural." Wilhelm whispered back with a smile. "Do you think you can handle running the store permanently and all that includes?"

"I'm your man."

1 ARABIAN DAY

BY JEANNIE WARNER

I climbed into the tower through a small window, and stepped carefully from the ladder over the sill down to the tiled floor. I felt awkward in this invasion, out of my skin. I was devout, and a man of importance. I was not a thief in the night, by Allah! Although, technically, I must be called a thief on this mission to serve my master. I trusted it to no other.

The Simurgh's plume must be returned.

My passing disturbed a few crumbs left for birds on the edge of the window, the faint scratch of them cracking like thunder to my paranoid ears. But no one stirred in the chamber.

Thieves were not expected during the day, in the heat of the afternoon when all sensible people were asleep. Outside, the sun beat down on the brown-packed earth, so hot that the invisible Djinni of the desert were shimmering in their dance, blurring the horizon. I looked back in and around the room, letting my eyes adjust.

The bedchamber was of royal proportions, and for a moment I bowed my head in shame that I was trespassing in this noble palace. But then I lifted my chin and accepted whatever fate would come. I could not allow my Caliph and our lands to be captive to magic any longer. Inward I crept, step by step, the soles of my shoes whispering against fine tiles.

I passed what I took to be a maid lying on a small rug near the window. She was sprawled past the edges of the weaving with her head on a cushion. In the heat, she wore a light covering of cotton over her form for modesty's sake. Less delicate was the soft snore coming from her, but one cannot help these things nor hold them against others.

In the center of the room stood a bed, with stairs on each side leading up to beautifully carved posts holding a canopy of soft pink silk. The canopy was closed against the day's flying bugs. On light feet I searched for signs of writing or drawing.

Ah, there on the other side of the bed; a chair and writing desk, the simplicity of the fine wood embellished with beautiful painted patterns under lacquer, chased with silver scrolling. I am something of a calligrapher when the divine spirit moves—and when my Lord can spare me from his side—and the beauty of this exquisite little piece of furniture caused a rare sort of envy. Following immediately upon the envy was guilt for the sin of feeling it, and I bowed my apology to the name of this Shahryar before starting my search for the Pen which had been stolen.

I had just worked the little drawer open when I heard someone stirring the curtains behind me.

"Who is there?"

It was a woman's voice, her tone nervous. I froze in place, hoping for a moment to be mistaken for the wind, or a mouse.

But it was not to be. I turned as the silks were pushed aside by a slender hand and saw her. Allah bless, for a moment I was any ordinary man struck dumb by the appearance of a woman. Not pretty—she was nothing so commonplace as mere prettiness. She had too much strength in her chin and nose to be called beautiful by the court poets, and far too much intelligence in her eyes. Her shoulders were square, and I glimpsed a body young and lithe, but generous of hip and breast under the thin kaftan.

I averted my eyes back to her face the moment I realized my stare. There was no one feature that called to me, but I have evaluated a thousand horses, camels, goats, and petitioners, both men and women, over the years in service to my Lord. This one's eyes were steady, filled with a depth that comes with life's wisdom. I knew right away that this woman was a pearl, and again I sinned against this ruler for coveting a second possession.

"Are you here to kill me?" my newfound desire asked in a low voice, with a quick glance over her shoulder toward her maid.

I was struck dumb with surprise, and then hastened to shake my head. "No. I am not. I am a thief, not a murderer." I then offered her a salaam, hands pressed together. "I mean you no harm. I am Jafar al-Barmaki, and I beg your pardon for intruding. Especially in your private chambers."

She looked at me for a long moment, measuring,

before rising to approach. My body was tense, torn between desire and regret for the very real possibility that I might need to silence a loud cry or scream.

"You're well-mannered for a thief. And too well dressed to need to steal for food. I think you must be a bit of a liar, but that harms no one here today: Save that by you being here, it means we could both be put to death." I said nothing.

She circled me once, looking me up and down. "A man of good fortune, a man established in life stealing into the King's private chambers? There is a story in it. You must tell me why you are here, for I am in need of a new story." I loved the sound of her voice, for it matched her eyes. Her tones were low and cool, but with a hint of music. She was a storyteller, this much was clear.

I relaxed a fraction, as there seemed less danger of a call for help. The girl sat in the chair and opened the lid to her desk. I realized the desk was hers, for she fit it perfectly. She pulled out a scroll, an ink stone, and a blue-plumed pen that made my heart beat quicker.

"Your pen. Is that ostrich? It is so unusual."

"I think it must be ostrich," the girl hesitated, looking for a moment at the brilliant blue plume in her hand. I lowered my eyes lest she note the flash of manic fear and desperation I felt at the sight. "It was a wedding present of sorts, given to me on the day I married the King." Dark eyes looked up at me, luminous and a trifle sad. "An older woman rushed forward through the crowds, and pressed it into my hand as I passed on my way to the palace in a chair. She said it would help me, and that it came from someone who didn't deserve it. I didn't see what

114

became of her after the soldiers pushed her back. It's beautiful, isn't it?" She ran the plume against her palm, letting the feather tickle her fingers.

I cleared my throat, lest I think too much on those hands and feathers, and the wicked enchantment it brought. "It is. So beautiful that I fear I must steal it. I'm sorry, Lady."

She looked startled, then abruptly frowned. "No, you must not. I think of things when I hold the pen. Wild, wonderful stories swim all around my head. If I couldn't write...I must...N-no. You kill me to say that you will take it."

Her stuttering shocked me, for being so disparate from the character I had already established for her in my mind. "You believe that you will die over a pen? I do not believe a wise and successful ruler such as the Sultan would be so capricious. Were the pen made from the feather of the legendary Simurgh itself; to kill one of his wives for what she could not help? Impossible."

I didn't want to say that if our land's one legend could be believed, the pen was indeed such an exotic and accursed feather. I reached out and tugged the pen loose from her reluctant fingers.

She sagged in her seat as tears sprang up and choked her. "No. He...is sworn to kill me tomorrow morning, and I tell stories so that he will not. I have told every story I know over the past few months, and still he speaks of death. I fear I am running dry, and that will be the end of me and my sister both. Without my pen, how will I write down my ideas? How will I even think of them? I beg of you, in Allah's name, give it back."

The very notion of a Sultan being so irrational was abhorrent to me. "Kill you? For want of a story? Lady, you make no sense." I tucked the curse into my robe and dared to reach out and lay a hand upon her shoulder. I was stealing from the Shahryar, which is death. To touch his wife merely would make the manner of death more unpleasant. "Tell me."

And so she did. Her tale of the Sultan betrayed was a sad one, and I was disturbed that an otherwise capable ruling neighbor to my Lord would be so violently jealous in matters of love.

She kept her voice low and soft, describing the previous months of telling stories by night to her sister to retain her virginity and her life. She explained how it was when she held the pen, she thought of new, wild tales to tell. She spent her days writing down the snippets of dreams the pen inspired, so that she could spin them into stories to tell her husband to spare her life. She spoke of magical words, curses and evil wizards and storylines, hinting at nights of survival won through the lands of the unrighteous Djinni and sorcerers.

I hung on her words, on the shape of her lips, the husky dark warmth of her voice. I fell in love in those moments, a ridiculous fancy for a man of my age and position, and sighed that she belonged to another. She told me how her father was the advisor to the Sultan, who had married her off by her own request to try and end their lord's killing spree. I was struck again by her bravery.

The queen's sister woke in silence during the recitation. She looked more nervous than the young queen but chose not to betray us. Instead, she sat quietly and watched us both, and only rose to light lamps about the room when the sun started to fade away into the western sky.

I cleared my throat as the beauty finished her tale, with the rusty feelings of regret over what I must take and what I must leave behind. "Perhaps I have one more story for you, to spin out for your revenge-maddened husband. I give it to you because you have held magic in your hand, and it has played you true, even as it curses my land and my King.

"I have the great honor to be the Vizir of a wise and noble Caliph, in lands far up the river near the mountains by your northern border. My son, by turns a trial and blessing to me, is engaged to the only daughter of my Lord. This daughter, of whom the poets sing, is known far and wide for her fair face and pleasant nature."

I thought of the vapid princess, and my tone dried to match my expression. "Yes. She is very pretty. These two are to wed, as they have been betrothed since childhood. The Caliph changed the very law to ennoble her future husband-to-be, and tutored my son for hours in statecraft. It is widely seen and applauded as a good match for them both."

A cooler breeze blew in through the window as night fell. I continued, "Two years ago, all manner of strange things began to happen. Impossible dark magic in a civilized time where magic ought to be long buried under the sand. My son departed to the Caspian Sea with a crew, calling himself a Prince. 'Sinbad', he said we must call him." My frustration mounted at the thought, and I rose to pace. The women followed me with their gazes. "I've not heard from him in weeks.

"Meanwhile the princess has fallen in with a Chinese beggar she met in the market place. The strange boy has an acrobat's skill, and a silver liar's tongue with his promises. He has gold from we know not whence, that he had none of before—according to the women of the wells. Now the princess wants to marry him instead of my son. Her father said that I should marry her to my son by proxy if he is away, but I pray it doesn't come to that."

She bit her lip, and I turned to look into her suddenly thoughtful face. "Does any of this sound familiar, my Lady? Like one or more of your stories, perhaps? I went to a fakir who is able to see what is unseen. He told me that a wife my Lord had divorced for being barren had grown embittered and stolen the cursed feather from his treasure. The barren consort had it made into a pen, he said."

I sighed. "That feather was the only object ever rumored to be magic in our land, as it happens, and I had not even believed in magic or curses. The fakir prophesized that the one who holds the pen would destroy my kingdom and its future." I couldn't help my fists clenching. "When I found and questioned her, the consort said she'd visited her cousin far away, and given it to a foreign king's new bride. This is the cursed feather. I must have it back."

The young queen drew her breath in sharply. She was too honest to hide the emotions that rose in her eyes, so near the surface from so many days and nights living in fear. "I never meant—oh my good sir. What have I done? You...must take it back. It is only right." But her tone was broken, and her sister hastened to wrap an arm around her shoulder to hide her face with a veil.

I pulled the feather out again and turned it in my fingers. "Lady," I said at last. "I do not think you need a magic pen to tell your stories. I think you have a magic all your own. You've started so many tales, and spun webs that have lured your husband into staying his hand to listen."

I waved her sister away and knelt beside her chair to take her chin in my hand to look into her eyes. "You have bewitched me, and I have heard your voice for but a short time. In my youth, I might have cast aside my family and responsibilities and tried to convince you to run away that we might find our own fortune." I sighed, letting go. "But I am old, and have the future of my people and my Caliph to think on. I am taking this pen, because it was stolen and must be returned to be locked away so that it can cause no further harm. But I will wait and watch your window for three days."

I turned to look at her sister. "If you judge that the Sultan's interest wanes, and that your sister is in danger in the morning, put a lamp in the window. By day or night, I will do what I can." Which was more of a promise than I think she could know. I do not promise lightly.

I heard the sound of footsteps approaching outside the chamber door and judged it a prudent moment to retire in haste. My eyes returned to the Lady, and I smiled as gently as I could as I backed toward the window. "I do not think I will see a lamp. I think you will live a long and prosperous life. As your husband grows in sense, he will come to share his thoughts and life with you more fully, and I think it will benefit your kingdom."

With that I hoped over the sill and slid down the ladder to flee the grounds. I did not believe the ladies would call for help or raise an alarm, and true to my evaluation, they did not. Nor did I see a lamp in the following three days and nights.

I returned back to our lands with the cursed feather and the sad weight of regret. My lord the Caliph was a righteous man, who locked the thing away so that it would never be used against us again. Nor did he think it wise we should try to use it to benefit, for he did not believe in usurping the will of Allah.

My son never returned, and I married the Princess. Alas. I still dream of dark eyes, and a voice telling tales in the night by lamplight.

ATTACHMENT

BY SOPHIE KEARING

I'm at home even though I'm supposed to be in my second class of the day. I just can't be around other people when I feel like this. You see, after Religion and Revolution 301, I stopped by Professor Moriarty's basement office for our twice-weekly "mentoring session." Instead of having one of our long and satisfying encounters, however, she broke things off with me. I sure didn't see *that* coming.

I always told myself that I could be light and breezy with Mori—that I'd detachedly enjoy her worship at the altar that is my nubile body, then let her down easy before winter break. Apparently, she had the exact same idea, only she beat me to the punch. Now, if I thought she was dumping me so she could focus on her husband and kids, it wouldn't be such a big deal. I know this woman, though, and the only reason she'd give up our scheduled trysts is so, come January, she can select a new student to entice into her lair of

Sapphic delights. And I am fucking incensed. I am *vi*brating with rage. I can hardly believe the impact this stupid little break-up is having on me.

I storm into the upstairs bathroom and lock the door. I come down on the toilet with such poorly-contained fury that the wooden seat gets displaced. I stand, kick the tub's white belly, and unleash a string of obscenities. I cross my arms and press my back into the wall.

I pray.

But don't go thinking that I believe in God. God is for children and weaklings. I know this attitude would come as quite a shock to most people, considering my major: Comparative Religion. A *lot* of things would come as a shock about this college's members, very few of which abstain from drugs, casual sex, or atheism. So please don't think that I'm praying to God. No, I pray to the ether, to the void, to whatever out there that's *real*.

"Please help me," I whisper. "I don't want to be this fucking pathetic. I want to feel strong again. Please."

Nothing changes.

I stay against the wall, crying silently. Eventually, I cool down, but it's only due to the passage of time. Nothing outside of myself has granted me succor, trust me. This is just evidence item number 2,036,591 that there really and truly is no God. I splash some water on my face, rinse out my mouth, and turn off the squeaky faucet. I gaze into the basin. Ugh. There are black flakes that won't fit down the drain. And I know exactly who put them there.

I head straight to Amity's room. Oddly, I'm relieved to find her door closed. Maybe she'll have her headphones on blast and won't hear me knock. Then I can just stomp downstairs and bang around in the kitchen until Craig asks me what's wrong and we can bitch about our clueless roommate for a while. But who am I kidding? The huge, expensive headphones I bought Amity last Christmas are always in the same place—the cubby above her desk, covered in a fine layer of dust, thick cord coiled around the liberally padded earpieces—and the only thing that's ever on blast in this house is her formidable set of speakers. The very thought of them reignites my anger. Why should I retreat to my habit of kettle slamming and bitter complaining when I can unleash my ire on my deserving roommate? My knuckles connect with the dark, polished surface of Amity's door.

Too quickly, she calls, "Yeah?"

Oh, Christ. She's in the mood for attention. Forget it. I can't fight with her when she's like this. I turn, trying to decide if I should make an attempt for the stairs or play it safe and run into my room. My calculations aren't quick enough, and Amity's door whooshes open.

"Oh, hey," she says, all white teeth and perfect skin.

"Hey. I don't mean to be a dick, but you said you'd be better about the bathroom."

"What're you talking about?"

"There are eyeliner shavings in the sink. Again."

"Well, they must be yours or Craig's."

"Stop it, Amity. I only use twist-up liner. And Craig is a neat freak."

"*Craig's* the neat freak, huh?"

"CASE IN *POINT*," I boom, "THE MESS *MUST* BE YOURS!"

"Whoa, whoa, whoa!" My roommate takes a step backward. "Serena, look at me. Look at my face. I'm not wearing any makeup, and I haven't all week. I haven't left the house, even for classes. I've done nothing but work on my term paper. I'm busting my ass to get it done before the end of the semester. I am *not* spending winter break explaining an incomplete in Theology to my fucking dad. That is, if he actually separates himself from that goddamn dig long enough to fly home for the hol—"

If I hear one more syllable of Amity's vacuous rambling, I might seriously choke her. In my mind's eye, I can see my fingers curving around her slender, lily-white neck, and I can practically feel her pulse slowing to a stop. "Fine. So the shavings in the sink are days old. Like that's better or something. It just shows what a long-term pig you are, Amity." I turn and walk away.

My roommate scampers into the bathroom.

"Um, I don't know what those are, but they're not kohl shavings, Serena."

I start down the stairs, smiling because I know that the one thing I can do to really get under Amity's skin is ignore her.

"Do you hear me, Serena? That's not my makeup in the sink. You owe me a fucking apology!"

***

Craig is at the kitchen table. He smirks and snaps the campus newspaper. "Too bad we need her, huh?"

Amity's mother bought this house mere months into her freshman year. She wanted to put some quick distance between her daughter and all those "dreadful fraternity houses on campus." Craig and I were the only ones who responded to an ad (in the very publication that he is currently perusing) for two "quiet students in the College of Religious and Esoteric Studies who would appreciate living in a charming Victorian house away from distractions." Well, Craig and I really *do* appreciate it:

He grew up in a happy, beautifully wallpapered home much like this one and will always want to live in an old house.

I was raised by two emotionless minimalists who I can't stand, and I wanted to live somewhere as different from my childhood home as I could get.

Craig and I love these creaky floors, the smell of old wood, and the fact that we have a circular sun room up in the turret. Yes, we have a turret—a *tow*er, for God's sake. Best of all, we live here for a pittance.

"Yup." I fill the kettle with water. "So...is our horoscope any good this month?"

"Nope. All doom and gloom."

"Ugh," I say, clanging around at the stove. It's a gorgeous, two-tone Peninsular oven, converted from wood-burning to gas. I flick my head toward an open box on the table. "What's that?"

"Another package from *Dr.* Fleming," Craig says in a deep voice, mocking the hilarious self-importance that is Amity's father.

I peek into the box, which contains the usual collection of useless tchotchkes sourced from the local village close to his dig site. It's hard to believe that just a few months ago, Amity had skipped into my room with a box just like this. We'd picked through the items and giggled at the things her father considered so precious. Whenever one of us would unwrap something that wasn't junk, we'd squabble over who should keep it. I'm a big proponent of finders-keepers, so I managed to claim a few silly little trinkets for my dresser. Today, however, I cringe at the memory of Amity sitting on my bed, rubbing my nose in the treasures that come to obedient Daddy's girls.

I frown and ask Craig, "Why does one of the flaps have a triangle drawn on it?"

"No clue."

"Organic Peppermint or Yogi Detox?"

"Detox so I can re-tox, baby!" Craig sings

I lean against the counter and gnaw at a cuticle. "Is it so damn hard for her to just take her package up to her room?"

"Apparently," Craig says. "And don't you dare take it up to her. She needs to do it herself."

"Oh, trust me, I'm not here to be Amity Fleming's personal assistant. But I shouldn't have to eat my breakfast and drink my tea right next to her pile of junk every morning."

"Should I take a dump in it and put it on her desk?"

Craig and I erupt into the laughter of familiar commiseration. I bring our mugs to the table, fragrant steam trailing.

"Gamma Zeta tonight?" he asks. "Last party before exams. After that, everyone's gone for Christmas break."

I scoff. "*I'm* not going *any*where after exams. I'm staying right here. I might put up a tabletop tree, but...that's about it."

"*What*? That's no way to spend the holiday."

"Stop." I blow on my tea. "You know I'm a Grinch."

"Serena...when was the last time you went home?"

"*This* is my home."

Craig lets his mug clunk down on the table theatrically. "By God, I'm staying back with you this year."

"No, you're not. I won't let you. You love Christmas and you'll miss your fam—"

"*You're* my family," he says cheesily, pulling me into his arms.

***

After having way too much keg beer and the perfect amount of fun, Craig and I take an Uber home. We pour ourselves from the car and cackle all the way through the front door.

Amity's in the living room, an assortment of friends fanned out around her. She's nursing a glass of red wine and trying not to look bothered by us. I know she's rich and popular and I should be jealous. But the sight of Amity—with her twisted mouth and pink silk pajamas, trying to ignore how blissfully intoxicated her roommates are—only makes me pity her.

Upstairs, I sit on the edge of my bed, pull off my booties, and toss them into my closet. I remove my socks and finagle little black bits from between my toes. Dark pigment transfers onto my fingers. "Gross."

"What's wrong?" Craig asks.

"My feet got so sweaty that my toe jam is, like, dying my hands. Ugh, I'm disgusting."

"That *does* sound disgusting," he says breezily, unburdening himself of his sweater and t-shirt. "To the clawfoot!"

Somehow, we both fit in the tub along with the bubbly water that I consider the ideal temperature but that Craig condemns as way too hot.

"Serena, get clean. I'm literally about to pass out."

My laughter reverberates in the tiled room and I take up a bar of soap. After I'm thoroughly scrubbed, I look at Craig. His eyeliner is smudged and his hair is slightly wet. I climb on top of him. I'm not surprised to find him ready. He kisses me, and I begin to move.

***

I wake to the sound of Amity pounding on my bedroom door.

"Serena, you get out here right now!"

I'm disoriented and parched, but I still manage to yank my door open aggressively. "Amity, are you fucking kidding me? It's not even seven!"

"After your big goddamn show about keeping the sink spotless, you've got the nerve to leave the bathtub looking like *that*? It's revolting, Serena!"

Did I leave a mess behind? I don't usually see debris in the tub after I drain my bathwater. This must be because I had Craig in there last night. "It's too early for this, Amity. Just use the bathroom downstairs."

"We need *both* showers, you idiot! There're five of us."

I sigh and pad into the bathroom. Amity follows me. She's already set out a can of cleaning powder and a scrub brush. I peek into the bathtub, expecting to see a few footprints or a clump of hair. I gasp. The ivory porcelain has been marred with intensely black crumbles. At first I wonder if this is the stuff that was between my toes last night, but those dark fragments were smaller and would've made it down the drain easily.

"What the..."

"Mmm hmm." Amity stands with her arms folded

tightly over her chest. "That's what *I* said. And after all your preaching yesterday. Clean it up."

I run the water and scrub. For a long time, it seems like all I'm doing is spreading the mess around. The best I'm able to do is leave the tub floor with a dull grey film. Amity, embarrassed, sends her pals home.

I take the scrub brush down to the kitchen and soak it in a bowl of diluted bleach. I glance at Craig's door. There's no way the commotion didn't wake him, but he certainly wasn't at the brunt of Amity's self-righteous tirade. It seems unfair, since whatever that crap was had to have been his. I should check his shower for weird black stuff…maybe show it to Amity and clear my name. Instead, I pull a small container of kale crunch salad from the fridge, fix some hot water with lemon, and plop down in my chair. The package is still sitting here. I'd love to rip Amity a new one over this, but unfortunately, after this morning's sanitation crisis, I'm in no position to complain.

Later in the morning, I gather my toppled booties from my closet. I'm shocked to find dark speckles on the closet wall and adjoining floor, where all my shoes are lined up. Before I can stop myself, I swipe my fingers across the wall. An unpleasant, earthy odor transfers onto my hand. This closet is on a wet wall, and this must be mold. Now all the black stuff sprouting up everywhere makes sense.

The next day, Amity's mother is here with a team of people who are wearing face masks and toting supply bags. After an hour of swabbing my closet, searching the basement, poking at the insulation in the attic, inspecting behind the wallpaper, and shining flashlights under the sinks, the head honcho of the operation uses a somber tone to deliver the news: "Well, Mrs. Fleming, there's no question you've got mold. I've never seen anything exactly like this. We can't say whether it's Stachybotrys until we have these samples analyzed at the lab. Regardless of what strain it is, though, this house isn't exactly a healthy environment."

"Quite right," Mrs. Fleming sniffs. She gives me and Craig until the end of the day to tie up loose ends and vacate. "I'll cover your homeward expenses, of course, or you can simply accompany me and Amity to Fifths. No one should have to be alone on the holidays." Her gaze flickers toward me. "And our Christmas parties are legendary."

Mrs. Fleming explains this "grave emergency" to the dean and gets us excused from our exams. Craig and I decide that it's only right to be nice to Amity on the plane. We include her in our impromptu sky games, which utilize our tiny bottles of booze, peanuts, and barf bags.

When she leaves to use the rest room, I lean into Craig. "You shouldn't be coming with us, you know. Your parents'll be so—"

"My parents have more kids than they know what to do with. Trust me, my absence won't decimate their Christmas. And I can't possibly miss the chance to be a guest at—" Craig elongates his neck and uses a haughty British accent. "—*Fifths Manah.*"

***

Fifths Manor is sprawling, grand, and all made possible by the wealth of Mrs. Fleming's family. It's odd that a place like this is merely a sporadic landing pad for Dr. Fleming, his preferred accommodations being the Spartan offerings of his faraway work site. Amity and her mom spend their time fussing over holiday decorations while Craig and I explore the library. We also help ourselves to—incredibly—one of three bottles of 1900 Bordeaux that we find in the wine cellar. We enjoy the vintage nectar while wading around in the heated swimming pool, which is located in a solarium that's clearly an extension off the original house. Afterwards, wrapped in plush, over-bleached robes, Craig and I scuttle up the main corridor. We come to a stop in front of a small elevator. Its antique door sighs open to reveal an impeccably groomed man that I'd guess was about twenty-five or twenty-six.

"Oh my," Craig murmurs.

I give his shoulder the back of my hand and smooth my hair.

"Oh, hello," the man says, hand outstretched. "You must be Amity's schoolmates. I'm Gerald, her brother. Welcome to Fifths. I hope the place is treating you well. So sorry I don't have more time to visit; afraid I've got a full schedule today. Well then, do enjoy your stay." He bustles off.

"'Enjoy your stay?'" I whisper snidely.

"I know, right? Is he her brother or a hotel concierge?"

Sunset finds us primping in my suite. At Fifths, you don't just microwave something and stand at the counter stuffing your face. You "freshen up for the evening meal." Then you take a seat in the dining room, where I'm pleased to find an intimate round table rather than a long, rectangular affair that provides nothing but distance and strained interactions. I'm surprised when, halfway through pre-dinner drinks, none other than Dr. Fleming rushes into the room.

He pecks his wife on the cheek. "I'm not late for the first course, am I?"

"I'm so glad you're here, Daddy!" Amity squeals, rising to embrace her father.

Dr. Fleming introduces himself to us even though we've already met him twice. Then he asks, "Where's Gerald?"

Mrs. Fleming waves her hand around limply. "Somewhere or another."

Gerald gets home in time for dessert.

After dessert, the Flemings migrate to their "parlor," where the staff already has a fire roaring and faux fur blankets laid out. Before joining them, Craig and I stop in my suite to use the bathroom. I pee, then stand at the mirror brushing my teeth.

"Is that oral hygiene I hear?" Craig teases from the overstuffed armchair in my sitting room.

My answer comes in the form of a muffled grunt. I pull my toothbrush from my mouth and spit into the sink. I grimace at the food fragments now marring the otherwise pristine porcelain. This reminds me of when I've eaten blueberries, gargled shortly afterward, and had to wash lingering shreds of fruit skin down the drain. But I haven't had blueberries in weeks. And at dinner, I partook only in the tomato bisque soup, warm sourdough, and a little vanilla gelato. So these dark, fleshy bits in the sink must be from breakfast. I poke at one of the offending pieces, and I'm left with a black mark. I wash my hands, satisfied that my finger is clean only after assaulting it with a pumice stone. I'm so angry at myself. I don't want to be some unkempt freak who has 12-hour-old food in her mouth, least of all on a day she's keeping the company of Gerald Fleming.

Craig appears in the doorway. "I wouldn't bother getting too spruced up, Serena. A guy like Gerald probably has a girlfriend already."

"Or a boyfriend," I retort, loitering in front of the sink so he won't spy my mess. I use the mirror to regard him with a twisted smile. "Don't try to discourage me, sweetie, and I won't try to discourage you. There's nothing wrong with a little friendly competition."

"Be careful what you wish for," Craig warns playfully.

***

Both of us end up feeling stupid we ever thought we'd be so much as blips on Gerald's radar. He does nothing but listen avidly to his father's stories of unearthing ancient relics and faithfully patronizing the commerce tents in the local village.

"He's too good for me," Craig whispers, and we share a soft chuckle. "I'm gonna go back to the library to look through a few of those books. You wait a few minutes before leaving. I don't want them speculating as to why we left together."

"Who says I'm leaving?" I grin cheekily.

Craig's face falls a little, but then bounces back into one of his good-natured smiles. "Good luck, Serena." He squeezes my hand, then excuses himself from the group.

His gesture of preemptive forgiveness would normally play on my heartstrings and incite me to leave the parlor and meet him in the library. Instead, I accept a "nightcap" from the butler and pay closer attention to Mr. Fleming's enthusiastic tales. He and his team are in the midst of excavating the site of a church, monastery, and convent from the 1800s. Considering the fact that such institutions are known to be quite minimalist, the grounds are yielding a good amount of astoundingly well-preserved pieces.

When Dr. and Mrs. Fleming retire to their suite, Gerald comments, "You seemed quite taken with my father's work."

"I was. I—I am."

Amity sucks her teeth and rises from her nest of blankets by the fireplace. "Good night, you two."

I watch my roommate leave, then cast a confused look at her brother. "Okay…I guess I said something to offend your sister."

"Don't worry about her. She's still a virgin and can't stand it when I'm about to get laid."

In the most clichéd moment I've ever lived, I choke on my Grand Marnier.

Gerald's laughter is rich.

I wipe my lips with the back of my hand. "That's a bit presumptuous of you."

But when Gerald reaches up the back of my sweater and lets his hand linger on my lower back, it's clear to me that his presumptions have always served him well and will continue to do so on this surprising, visceral night. Everything flows as if we've been together before, yet it grants the electricity of a first encounter. The cozy afterglow is ruined by the upheaval that ensues when we realize my inner thighs are covered with speckles.

"Oh!" Gerald yelps when he sees that his genitals

are coated with something dark. "Why didn't you tell me you were menstruating? Goodness, Serena. My mother won't take kindly to blood all over her furniture."

"It must've just started. Oh God, I am *so* sorry, I—"

"Don't apologize. I suppose these things can't be helped. But I *am* squeamish around blood and I need to get cleaned up. I'll send one of the maids to—"

"No! No, no. Nothing's gotten on the furniture," I say without even checking. "Please, I'm embarrassed. Don't send anyone, okay? I'll see to everything myself."

Gerald looks doubtful, but gives me a quick kiss and departs.

Thankfully, the couch is indeed unblemished, and I scurry to my bathroom. I sit on the toilet and pee, then wipe. The paper doesn't reveal a bright red smear, but one of terrifying blackness. Trembling, I put a bed of toilet paper between me and my underwear, pull up my leggings, and slip down to the cool marble floor. Oh my God. It's *me*. The "kohl shavings" that I accused Amity of leaving behind. That nasty "toe jam." The black flakes in the tub at home and in the sink here at Fifths. Even the weird stuff on my closet wall and floor probably came out of my booties when I tossed them in there. It's all me. What the...what the fuck is *wrong* with me? Do I have some kind of fungus? Confused, disgusted, and rattled, I raise the toilet lid and heave up a burning torrent. The black shards that bobble alongside my half-digested dinner cause me to vomit again, then again. I groan, flush, and make my way to the vanity. I rinse with mouthwash. I spray myself down with perfume, terrified that I reek of mold. I scurry down the hallway toward Craig's room.

I hear voices. I retreat into a shadowy alcove just in time to prevent Gerald from seeing me as he emerges from Craig's suite. I'm seized by bewilderment for mere seconds before I'm filled with icy rage. Is *this* why Gerald was so eager to leave me? So he could head over to Craig's room for his third helping of dessert in one evening? Worse—is *this* why Craig was acting like such a goddamn good sport? Because he knew he'd win in the end?

Gerald can't seem to get away from Craig's room fast enough. He makes a turn onto the main corridor and vanishes from sight. Well, I suppose he wouldn't want to get caught, would he? Those two've known each other for a matter of hours and they've already teamed up to make an absolute fool out of me. Thinking of Craig—the one person I'm closer to than anyone else—betraying me sends my inner torment to astronomical heights. My hands turn into fists, knuckles scraping against the textured wallpaper. I'm startled when I see Craig exit his room, but not too startled to make my move. In an instant I have him shoved up against the wall, the element of surprise no doubt instrumental in my ability to move someone so much bigger than me so quickly.

At first he looks stunned, his body tense under my fervent clutch, but then he lets out a laugh that sounds both bitter and amused. "What, you want it *here*? The hallway is a little too public for me, Serena, and even *I'm* not so desperate as to want Gerald's leftovers."

I slap him across the face. "You wanna talk about desperate, huh? It's *you* who just had *my* leftovers!"

"Jesus *Christ*, Serena. How much did you have to

drink?"

"This isn't about how much I drank. This is about you acting buddy-buddy with me, when all the while you knew Gerald would end up in your room. When the hell did you two plan *that*?"

"What the fuck are you talking about?" Craig demands. "All he did was ask me to make sure you were alright and see if you needed any help with... your accident. He told me you were embarrassed around him but that maybe you wouldn't be embarrassed around me." Suddenly, he looks like a lightbulb has turned on in his mind. "Oh, *that's* why you're like this. Your period."

"I'm not on my fucking period," I snap. "He'll see when he gets to his room that it's not blood. It's...it's something else."

"Something *else*? Are you okay?"

I drag Craig into my room and apologize for freaking out on him. Tearfully, I relay the bizarre events of the last two days.

"Hey, hey, hey," he coos. He pulls me to him and smooths my hair. "I hate seeing you like this. Why don't we get you into bed, and we can figure this out in the morning. I'll get a tampon from Amity, and we'll just wait and see what they say about the strain of mold in the house—"

"Didn't you hear a word I just said? It's not the house! It's *me*!" I pull the wad of toilet paper out of my underwear and show him the fetid sludge.

"Whoa, come on, Serena!" Craig says irritably. But then he accepts the specimen and studies it from different angles. "Serena, this is not good. First thing in the morning, we'll schedule you a doctor's appointment." His brow furrows. "This smell…it's like mushrooms gone off, isn't it? But with a dash of something else."

"Yeah. I couldn't put my finger on it before, but there's definitely something rotten about it."

"Christ, is this synchronicity or what?"

"What are you talking about?"

"Well, the book I was just reading mentions this strange, earthy smell that can sometimes accompany people with certain afflictions."

"What kinds of afflictions?" I follow Craig to the library. We sidle up to a table strewn with books, both old and contemporary: *Unexplained Paranormal Phenomenon of the Eighteenth Century, Dark Spirits and Demonic Entities, The Earthbound Attachment, Astral Body Healing,* and others. "Um, this looks like you're researching for Father Riley's class or something. Where're the *med*ical books you mentioned?"

"I never mentioned any medical books, hon. Amity's dad isn't a medical doctor. He's an anthropological archaeologist with a specialty in Religious Studies. The afflictions I read about were spiritual."

A derisive laugh escapes my lips. "Okay, Craig. Good luck with all these. Look, I'm gonna go to bed. We can talk about this in the morning."

"Look at this," he says, thrusting an open book at me.

It's a vintage tome that has basic line drawings of people with dark bits on their tongues and feet, as well as shirtless men with coated armpits. There are even babies with black scaling on their scalps in lieu of cradle cap. I'm sure it would've been considered indecent back then to feature women with smeared underwear.

Craig stands behind me and reads over my shoulder. "'The strength of the odor varied from subject to subject, with some individuals experiencing the strong stink of rotten mushrooms only in their bodily excretions, some experiencing a light, mildly unpleasant vegetal scent radiating from their skin, and others emitting fiery or sulfuric smells of moderate sillage.'"

"Sulfuric? That's classic Satan lore. I gotta say, I'm pretty flattered that the Prince of Darkness wants to possess little old me."

Craig takes a whiff of my neck. "Well, I can tell you've got perfume on." He presses his nose into me. "I'm really not getting anything unpleasant from your skin. I'd say you're in the first category."

"Great."

Craig tosses the book on the table and grabs a modern energy healing text. "That's how it is when things are only in the first stage."

"So there are stages. Apparently, it's just like cancer."

Craig ignores me. "When the dark entity is trying to make your body a little more habitable for itself, it gradually starts changing things, like your willingness to compromise and your ability to trust others. It makes you selfish, so you'll spend more time feeding it and less time accommodating others."

I give an embarrassed chuckle. "Craig, I can't tell if you're serious or not."

He glares at me.

"Okay." I cross my arms. "Let's say it's true. That

some entity is taking me over. How the hell did it get in me?"

Craig flips a few pages. "I guess it's first able to enter through your astral body, then it slowly seeps through your aura, your mental, emotional, etheric, and physical body. It burns up all the positive stuff until you're left with little more than this base, primitive energy that makes you a comfy home for a dark being."

"A *dark* being? Craig, I don't have a freakin' demon inside me, okay? I'm tired and I'm not in the mood for these stupid, hokey books."

"As an Esoteric Studies major, I take offense to that."

***

The next morning, Craig and I sit at breakfast just long enough for Craig to shovel some scrambled eggs and sliced melon into his gourd and for me to have a scone and some tea.

Mrs. Fleming frowns. "You two are leaving already?"

"Serena's coming down with a little something, so we made a doctor's appointment," Craig says. "Sometimes they can give you pills that help you get over a cold faster."

"Goodness, why is everyone running off to the doctor's this morning? Gerald left after only a few sips of coffee, and looking healthy as a horse, at that!"

Dr. Fleming peers over the top of his newspaper but says nothing.

Amity rests her fork on her plate. She wears a look of distaste.

Craig and I go back to my suite to collect our coats and my purse. When I look up from zipping my coat and find Dr. Fleming in the doorway, I give a start. My reaction seems to amuse him.

"You think it's funny to scare people like that?" I ask. "What the hell is wrong with you?"

"Se*re*na," Craig admonishes.

Dr. Fleming enters the room and closes the door behind him. "It feeds off your negative emotions, Ms. Sellers. Amplifies them to make sure you don't have close relationships in your life. And you would never know it. You would never know because that fire and reactivity actually feels better than what you were no doubt feeling before it got into you: Alone. Powerless. Pathetic."

Pathetic. The last time I said that word, I was in my bathroom at home. Crying over Mori.

"Try to pinpoint the time when you started snapping at people more, getting into heated arguments...then realize that this entity started casing you way before then. Subtly influencing your choices, seeing if you'd be a good conduit for the lower delights of this realm: booze, meaningless sex, constant drama."

I think of Amity and how I've relished hating her for the last few months when I'd previously considered her nothing more than a sporadic nuisance. I think of Professor Moriarty, Craig, and Gerald; I guess I hadn't stopped to think that I'd gone from occasionally sleeping with Craig to adding my professor and Amity's brother to my repertoire. I think of guzzling cheap beer at Gamma Zeta even though normally I'd arrive at a party with my own six pack of craft beer. Still, I scoff and say, "So let me get this straight: The devil needs me so he can have a cold one, get laid, and eat people's anxiety?"

"The *de*vil? Goodness gracious, Ms. Sellers, let's not lose our heads. We're talking about an earthbound attachment here. A person who died and, for whatever reason, chose not to cross over. Some say it's because they fear judgement, and some say it's because they're simply *that* addicted to earthly pleasures. This entity needs a vehicle, needs *sustenance*. And in this case, that vehicle is you. That sustenance was acquired through all your squabbling with my daughter, your after-dinner drinks, and your, eh, rendezvous with my son."

Instantly, I am mortified. But I hide it with a snarky retort. "Wow, father-son locker room talk. In a mansion. Super classy."

"I assure you that last night was the first time Gerald has ever spoken to me of such things, Ms. Sellers. He was terrified, you see, of the substance you left on him."

Wow. Just when I thought I could *not* be more humiliated.

Craig steps forward. "Serena was scared, too, Mr. Fleming. She had no clue that she was being…infiltrated."

"Yes, well, infiltration aside, I sent Gerald off to the doctor as a precaution, and you should go as well. You'll find you have a clean bill of health, however, and then you'll be ready to take me seriously."

***

The old man ends up being right. The gyno doesn't find so much as one black speck inside me, and suggests that I could've just had some mid-cycle spotting. "Spotting can sometimes be quite dark," she explains.

142

Craig and I leave the medical building.

"Apparently this thing can hide its own symptoms," I say bitterly.

"I guess it temporarily stopped its 'burning' process. I read about that, and it makes sense. If doctors were to discover there's something wrong with you, all the poking and prodding would definitely make for an uncomfortable stay."

"You say that as if I'm a motel room soon to be vacated." My voice catches, and I can feel my face contort hideously in the winter sunlight. "But I'm more like a disgusting, moldy house that some ghost will haunt till it collapses."

"Hey." Craig holds me tightly. "Don't you compare yourself to our off-campus Victorian. We'll get you clear of this. Amity's dad'll help us."

***

The old man "helps" us by bringing us to the isolated village that stands thirty miles away from his archeological dig. There are no barf bag Olympics on the commercial plane or on the smaller charter. There's only my hyperawareness of the black smegma that I now seem to be producing at an alarming catch-up rate.

Upon arrival, Craig is taken to the men's living quarters and I'm showed to a room on the women's side. A female attendant brings me a tray for lunch. I accept it gratefully. As I'm devouring my food, I hear her flip a lock on the outside of the door.

"Hey!" I shout, springing from my bed to test the door handle.

I spend the rest of my afternoon calling for help and banging on the door. No one comes, and the door doesn't budge. In the evening, someone slides a dinner tray into my room using the narrow flap at the foot of my door. This is when I'm hit with the highest wave of panic: I've been imprisoned.

The next few days bring me only increasingly bland food. I try to smash the windows, which I discover are comprised not of glass but of some indestructible material. On the fourth day, Dr. Fleming steps into my room and hurriedly closes the door behind him. I hear the lock engage from the outside.

"What in the *fuck* is going on?" I scream. "You said you would cure me, but instead you PUT ME IN JAIL!"

"Serena, this *is* the cure. The only reason I didn't tell you before is that you never would've agreed to it. We need to withhold all the earthly delights this thing is using you for."

"I COULD'VE DONE THAT AT *HOME*, YOU ASSHOLE!"

"No, you couldn't," Dr. Fleming says quietly. "It's not only the obvious things, Serena. If need be, this thing could probably scrape by for years on the small pleasure of you watching TV or merely holding hands with Craig. Even this very interaction, this emotional spike you're feeling, is helping to keep it alive. The only reason I'm in here is so I can examine you."

I'm incensed and shaking, but I allow him to swab my inner cheek, nostril, and toes.

"I do also need..." He clears his throat and opens a Ziploc bag. "...that underwear you have on."

I remove my pants and panties, suddenly overcome by libidinous thirst. I don't care if sex would feed this entity. Who knows if any of this "earthbound attachment" crap is even true. I approach Dr. Fleming as if to simply hand him his sample, but in no time I'm pressed against his body.

"Ms. Sellers!" he barks. But he doesn't extricate himself right away.

In fact, I can feel that he's hard. "Wow. I guess you're not so old after all."

My words snap him into action. He pounds on the door and somehow slithers out of the room without allowing me to escape.

The next few weeks are absolute hell. I develop large bruises all over my body from throwing myself against the windows and door. I lose fifteen pounds eating only gruel and water. I grow so lethargic that I don't even masturbate anymore. The only items in here to occupy my time are a bible and a friendly plant to whom I can complain. It has one of those big self-watering bulbs plunged into its soil. One day I get the urge to nestle my fingers into that moist dirt. Its fragrance is intoxicating to me, and I find myself licking my fingers. I scoop more soil from the pot and smash it into my mouth, both horrified and pleased by my behavior. When I reach in again, my fingertips connect with something pen-like. I inspect the object, which seems to be a surveillance camera that's been painted dark green. If I would've found this days ago, I would've made damn sure to destroy it as violently as possible. But all I do now is tuck it between the mattress and box spring, then lie back down. My favorite thing to do in here is count the cracks in the ceiling; I don't even have to get out of bed for that.

The next time Amity's father enters my room, he determines that I'm fit to leave. Words can't convey my elation when I rush into the muggy but blissfully open outdoors. When we leave, I take a final look at the women's camp. There's an upside-down triangle painted onto the banner above the gate.

My reunion with Craig is sweet. He holds me close. From over his shoulder I can see that there's a banner topping the men's gate, and on it: a solid, vertical line.

When Craig and I finally return home, we're surprised to hear music blasting from upstairs.

"What the fuck is *she* doing here?" Craig says. "There's still a week of winter break. She should be at Fifths!"

Normally, I'd be thrilled to get back into our us-against-her mentality, especially at Craig's initiation. But today, I just don't feel like it. "No worries. I'll run up and tell her to turn it down."

"'No worries,'" he mocks, hanging his scarf up on a hook.

I giggle at his grouchy mumblings and climb the stairs two at a time. I rap on Amity's doorframe. "Hi, Am. I'm back."

"Serena!" Amity leaps out of her desk chair, clearly relieved to see that I'm alive and well. But she doesn't launch herself at me as she once would have.

"Sorry. My dad said to give you some space for a while."

"No offense taken. But, uh, can you turn the music down? Craig has a headache."

"Oh! Sure!" she says, happy to do me a favor in lieu of touching me.

***

The next day, Craig and I are eating bagels and flipping through magazines on the couch when Amity starts clomping around her room in high heels.

Craig glares up at the ceiling. "*Really?*"

"Who does that?" I say, mostly just to show Craig my support; we both know that Amity Fleming "does that." "Seriously—*so* annoying."

I make my way up to the second floor. I'm five feet from Amity's room when her phone rings. She stops teetering around and paces slowly, the click of her heels softer now. I decide I'm in the mood to eavesdrop. I used to do this all the time when I was a kid, and I'm feeling spry.

"Oh, hi, Dad." There's a pause while she listens, then she speaks at a lower volume: "Yup, Serena's back to her old self and Craig is...mean, I guess."

I frown. Without moving, I bark, "Amity! No heels in the house, remember?"

"Ugh!" she grunts, kicking her shoes off. "Actually, Daddy, Serena is still super bitchy." She falls silent for a few seconds then says, "I don't know. I don't know, Dad!" She sighs and listens quietly again. "Fine, I guess she's a two-and-a-half now and a four-and-a-half before her treatment?"

Jesus. Have I just been rated on a five-point Bitch Scale? I mean, I'd love to think that Dr. Fleming's just following up to see how I'm doing, but he could've called me directly if that was the case. And why is the old man asking after Craig? Something's not right here. As I descend the stairs, I realize that I'm nervous to tell my pal about Amity's phone conversation. He'll probably fly off the handle.

Fly off the handle is not what he does. Before I can even get halfway through my story, his mouth is on mine and his hand is down the front of my sweatpants. It isn't until we're done that I realize this is the first time we've had sober sex.

He gives me a kiss and eases off me. "Wanna order some Thai?"

"Um, we just had bagels, you heifer," I jibe.

He scoffs and shuffles into the kitchen. "No offense, Serena, but I have a lot less body fat than you do. So if either of us is a heifer…Goddamn it. Do *not* tell me all the menus are in Amity's room again!"

When Craig thunders up the stairs, which I've never seen him do before, I have to admit something to myself: He has been a *terr*or since we got home. And it's not because he's tired from all the traveling. It's something else.

In search of answers, I finally do something I've been meaning to do since Craig and I got back. I go down into the basement, where we keep our recycling bins until it's time to set them out for pick-up, which is once every six weeks. I rifle through all the broken-down cardboard boxes until I find exactly what I knew I'd find: a box with a vertical line on its flap. I rush the flattened cardboard up to the living room.

"There you are," Craig says. "Hurry up and look through this menu."

"You used to be such a picky eater, and before today, we never hooked up unless we were drunk."

Craig puts down the menu. "Is this your way of saying you want it again?"

"Now you're ravenous all the time—for food *and* for sex. With me it was booze and sex. The one that's got you has different tastes, I guess."

"Wait, what?"

"Have you ever poked through one of the boxes Amity's dad sends?"

"Hell no. It's all just junk. And it stinks."

"But she's tried to get you interested, hasn't she? She's tried to show you the packages that have the line on the flap?" I show him the cardboard I brought up.

"Yeah, she *tries* to show me. But I don't wanna get pulled into an hour-long boredom sesh, so I just tell her I have to write a paper or something," he says, smirking. "I don't give in like you do, Serena. I'm not as nice as you."

"Oh my God. Was that a complement, Craig?"

"Not if you really think about it."

"Ouch. You've been a real cockbag since we got back, you know that?"

"I just call it how I see it, girl." He looks pensive for a moment. "Actually, while I was at the men's camp back in that village, they tried to get me interested in all their foul little trinkets, too."

"They did?"

"Yeah. At least once a day they would draw my attention to this weird little urn-looking thing. Finally, I took it to my room just to shut them up about it. I know they have pride in the few items they make there, but Jesus Christ."

"An urn-looking thing?" I take his hand and drag him upstairs, the open Thai menu flapping in his other hand. I pluck up a golden lidded pot from my dresser. "Was it like this?"

"Yeah, sorta. Look, I'm gonna call in my order. You want anything?"

"Nope. I wouldn't wanna add to my body fat."

"Hey, come on, Serena." He pecks me on the mouth, then reaches for my phone. "I wasn't complaining. I love a little junk in the trunk."

I roll my eyes and fire up my laptop. I do a search and end up on a site that features scanned pages from an old book about different forms of spirit possession. A section about qualities that make a person more prone to being targeted by "lost souls" mentions being "without clan" and "born of the Earth element."

Craig places his order, then plops down beside me.

"'Without *clan*?'" I mutter. "Is that supposed to mean family? I mean, I may not be close to mine, but you're certainly close to yours. And even though you weren't with them for Christmas, you were with me. I mean, the closeness we have is much more important than blood or last names."

"Well, I wouldn't exactly say I was feeling 'close' to you while I was over there, Serena. Not after they showed me footage of you throwing yourself at the old man."

I don't know which is worse: my anger at Amity's dad and those village assholes for surveilling me, or my embarrassment that Craig saw me trying (and failing) to seduce Dr. Fleming. "Craig..." I take his hand in mine. "It wasn't *me* doing that stuff. And it isn't *you* that constantly wants to eat and have sex. There was something in me when I was locked up, and now there's something in you. And those fuckers *put* these entities in us on purpose. I'm sure those goddamn urns are the vessels they use to house the entities, and to 'infect' the people they consider most susceptible." I look back at my computer screen. "Now, this 'clan' thing. I guess I can see how both of us were feeling super isolated and 'without clan' when we were infected. But this 'born of the Earth' crap...I mean, *all* humans are 'born of the Earth.'"

"Not 'of the Earth.'" Craig points at my screen. "'Of the Earth *el*ement.' The only thing I know that sounds similar to that is the Earth signs in astrology. And we're both Virgos."

I bite my lip. "Well, I'm not sure if this book is referring to astr*o*logy, Craig."

"Well, *I'm* not sure why anyone would purposely infect a pair of college kids with earthbound attachments, Ser*e*na."

"Maybe to study us or something? To see exactly what it takes to infect us, see what we do when we're infected, and see how long it takes to cure us?"

Craig sighs, his head tipped back dramatically. "Maybe. I mean, how the hell can they even capture lost souls like that?"

"Keep it down. We don't want Amity to hear that we're onto her. Ugh. I can't believe that shady bitch was in on all this."

"Don't worry. Amity can't hear shit at the moment."

"Oh my God. Is she *finally* wearing the headphones I got her?" I walk over to Amity's doorway, smiling.

The headphones are still laying uselessly in their cubby. Amity is sleeping, head down on her desk.

"Am?" I shake her shoulder.

She falls to the floor. I hear wheezy laughter behind me and turn to find Craig, arms crossed, shoulder pressed into the doorframe.

I giggle. "Oh my God. Is Little Miss Perfect inebriated? In the middle of the day?"

Craig giggles snidely.

I pivot back toward Amity and hook my hands under her armpits. "Come on, Am. Let's get you into—" I've never felt such complete limpness in a human being. Amity's head lolls grotesquely, and I drop her. "Oh my *God*! I think she's—I think she's *dead*!"

Ladies and gentlemen, we've got a real Sherlock Holmes here!"

"Shut *up*, Craig! I'm serious! How did this—What the fuck happened?!"

"Nothing too bad. I choked her is all."

"You *what*?" I collapse against the dresser. "Oh, no...no, *no*."

The doorbell rings.

"*Yes*! Food's here. Damn, that was fast! Splash some cold water on your face and come downstairs. I'll get the plates out and see what's on Netflix."

MYSTICAL IMAGE

BY JEREMY MAYS

Eric yawned as he sat down in front of his computer screen and booted up. The fluorescent glow was soothing to him. The internet, after all, was one of the only friends he had in his boring adult life. He had never been popular in school. Not a fit with the brainy or athletic cliques and unfortunately, that seemed to carry over as he moved on into the workforce. He adjusted to this reality by living behind a monitor and keyboard, surfing the wide world of the internet.

He took a quick sip from his Yoda mug. Another morning at his computer. Mornings had become ritual. Coffee and the news. He clicked on an icon in the upper right-hand corner and headed to the *Evening Sentinel* website. Though Eric still preferred most of his text in tangible format, the daily news came from online sources.

The *Evening Sentinel* web page displayed a gleaming sun with a smiley face in the center, the *Sentinel* trademark. Eric thought it was the cheesiest thing he'd ever seen, but the *Sentinel* always provided the best local news on the net.

He previewed the latest stories. One was about two local teenagers that were found dead after some bizarre deer hunting incident. *Cool. Southern Illinois at its finest*, Eric thought. He grabbed the mouse and was about to click on the headline when something farther down caught his eye. *Famous Artist Dies in Mysterious Fire*.

Before he could get into the story, his front door flew open and a scrawny figure burst into the room. Eric knew who it was without even looking up. His one *real* friend, Ben Teriet. Eric had met him a few years ago at the local book store which had the only version of an internet café in town. Both seemed to click with the group of misfits that clung to the computers, bookshelves, and gaming rooms at the establishment. He latched onto Ben quickly, happy to find a friend outside of social media. Ben suffered from the same ailment of social awkwardness and was eager to make a real friend too.

Ben, didn't waste any time on greetings and salutations; he hopped over the clothes scattered across the room and threw a newspaper in Eric's lap. "Did you see this?"

Eric looked down to see a copy of the *Sentinel*, the same one he had on his computer screen. He directed Ben's attention toward his computer. Ben looked up and frowned. "Oh, so you've already read about it?"

"No. I pulled it up, but I was just starting to read it when you barged in. What's so thrilling?"

Ben began to shake with excitement and pointed at

the story. "Read it."

Eric glanced over the article. He looked up at Ben, puzzled.

"I don't get it, who was this guy?"

"Jonathan Roberts! He's only my idol!"

"I'm disappointed," Eric quipped, "I thought *I* was your idol."

"My real idol, asshole. You know, the Mystical Image guy!"

Eric suddenly made the connection. Jonathan Roberts was an artist who had made a killing on the 3-D art that lined the walls of numerous offices and bedrooms all over the country. Ben loved them. Different swirls and designs graced the pages, and somewhere deep within the patterns, an image was hidden. The image could be seen by the onlooker if they tilted their head just right, crossed their eyes, or stood on their head. Whatever worked.

Ben had a large collection and could see the figures in all of them. Eric, on the other hand, hated the stupid things. As far as he was concerned, there were no images. No eagles or bears, no American flags or sunsets. They were a complete waste of time and energy, as he had learned through experience, after hours of staring at them until he was more confused than when he started. Ben could look at any of the pictures for ten seconds and tell there was a dinosaur or elephant or whatever was supposed to be there. All Eric saw was a bunch of colors and lines.

"Oh," Eric said, showing his lack of enthusiasm for the entire situation.

"Roberts died in a fire last week at his home in St. Louis. They're auctioning off his last work tomorrow, and no one has ever laid eyes upon it except for Roberts himself. Mom said she'd get it for me!"

Twenty-five-years-old, Ben still resided in his mother's basement. And why not? He had no bills, his mother paid for everything. She provided him with a home, car, phone, food, and every other amenity one needed, all for absolutely nothing in return.

Eric tried his best to ignore the comment and looked at the story in front of him. One detail caught his eye. "Suicide?"

"Yeah, he set fire to his own house. Dude hadn't been right for a while, terminal cancer or something. His career was going to shit anyway. All the knock-offs, you know? His last few works were really morbid too. Freaked people out. His close friends thought he was involved in black magic and Ouija boards, contacting the spirit world kinda stuff."

Eric chuckled as he got up from his desk and handed Ben's newspaper back. "Spirit world? Black magic? Come on, Ben, really? You can't actually believe all that shit."

Ben's face turned crimson as he looked down. "There's something else."

"What? No, let me guess. He was also pregnant with an alien's baby?"

"No smart ass," Ben's expression suddenly became void of all emotion. "They never found his body."

***

Eric didn't sleep well that night. His dreams were plagued with images of Jonathan Roberts burning up in his home, of darkness and shadows, and of Ben. He woke in the morning, drenched in sweat, and remembered everything from his dreams except for the part about Ben. What did that signify?

He performed his morning routine and headed off to work. He sent Ben a quick text on the way and another during his lunch break, but got no reply. Eric wasn't concerned at first. Ben was known for staying up until the wee hours of the morning, gaming against people from all over the world. He often slept well into the afternoon.

It wasn't until after work, when Eric stopped by the bookstore, that he began to worry. No Ben in sight, which was very unlike his friend. On a normal weekday, Ben would have already staked his claim to a computer in the store, headset on, playing away. Eric figured it was probably nothing, but with the dreams he had last night, Ben's absence troubled him. After another text and phone call with no response, Eric decided to stop by Ben's house and check on him.

When he arrived, he breathed a sigh of relief when he saw at least one vehicle in the driveway, Ben's. Eric didn't bother to knock. He made a Ben style entrance and burst into the house. There, in the front room, was Ben, sitting cross legged on the floor, staring at a picture propped up against the couch. He didn't move or show any sign that he was aware Eric was present, he just stared straight forward.

"Ben?" Eric said as he turned to shut the front door. "Ben!"

Ben dropped his head in defeat. He turned and looked at Eric. Bags bulged out under his glassy eyes. He looked like an addict who'd been strung out for a week. He stared straight through Eric. A shiver ran down Eric's spine as he took a step backwards.

"Damn it, Eric!" his voice hissed with an inhuman

tone. "I almost had it! I almost had it and you screwed it up!"

Eric was lost. Almost had what? What was wrong? Then, as he saw Ben turn his attention back towards the couch, Eric put it together.

He walked behind Ben and stopped. He looked at the object that imprisoned Ben's gaze and attention. It was an image as big as the others that graced the walls in the room. Yet this one was different. Looked different. Felt different.

There were no colors, only swirls of gray and black. They infested the picture, covering the entire canvas. The hairs on Eric's arm stood up. He wanted to try too. Stare and not look away. But that wasn't all. Was that a voice he was hearing? Someone or something was whispering from behind the artwork. Muttering his name. Beckoning him to come closer and stare.

Eric shook his head and turned aside. A blinding pain shot through his skull. He stepped away from Ben and sat on the chair behind him. Ben was still engulfed in the picture before him.

"Ben?" Eric asked as he rubbed his temple. "Ben!"

Ben cocked his head sideways, signaling he heard Eric, but never took his eyes off the image. "Yeah?"

"What's in it? I mean, what's it of?"

"I dunno yet."

The answer shocked Eric. He didn't know? This was the guy who could see into all of these things in a matter of seconds, and describe every inch of detail. He couldn't see this one? Why?

"You mean you don't understand the image, right?"

"No, damn it!" Ben screamed. "I can't see the image. I can't see anything! Every time I start to get it, I lose it because of some idiot like you interrupting my concentration. First, it was my damn mother who wouldn't back the hell off and now you, you son of a bitch!"

After the uncharacteristic outburst, Eric decided it was best to make himself scarce. To give his friend some space and time to cool off. He didn't like seeing Ben so frustrated. Sure, Ben had been obsessive in the past with these images, but this was going a bit too far.

"How much did your mom pay for it?"

Ben didn't respond at first, but as Eric stared at the back of his head, the reply came. "Nothing."

Eric was startled. "Nothing? I thought it was a collector's item? I mean, a famous artist's last work and you got it for nothing?"

"No one wanted it. They begged my mother to take it. It was like they were afraid of it or something," Ben's voice was a dead monotone.

Suddenly Eric was afraid too. Terrified. This was way too weird for him. He wanted to go home. "Uh, Ben? I'll leave you and your picture alone now. I'll call you later."

He got up and headed for the door. He paused, feeling guilty for leaving his friend. Maybe Ben *shouldn't* be left alone. He glanced back at him, but Ben never even turned his head.

"Don't bother."

With that final statement, Eric opened the front door and slipped out.

He was plagued with nightmares again, the same as before. They were darker images this time, more threatening and ominous. This time, it was Ben who burned in the house fire.

***

Eric woke up early, more exhausted than when he'd gone to bed. Though worn out, he was too worried about Ben to lounge around. He'd forgotten to call him before he fell asleep. His heart started racing.

He jumped up, threw on some clothes, and grabbed his phone. The screen was blank, no new messages from Ben. He shot him a quick text and waited for a response. Nothing. He grabbed his keys and headed out.

Eric arrived at the Teriet residence in no time. He bounded out of his car, nearly forgetting to shut the vehicle off. He raced towards the front door and was greeted by Ben's mother.

"Hey, Eric. Up early on a Saturday, aren't we?" Ben's mother reached down and picked up the newspaper that lay at Eric's feet.

"Yes ma'am. Is Ben up?"

"Yeah, he's been up in his room all night. I think he's still staring at that stupid image. Had to nearly drag him and that silly thing to his room last night. Did he tell you I got it for free?"

Eric didn't bother asking permission to enter. He shoved past Ben's mother and rushed to his friend's bedroom. He threw the door open and stepped inside.

The room was dark, except for a small stream of light that penetrated the cracks of the drawn shades. The bed in the center of the room was still made, showing no sign that anyone had slept in it. Eric looked around, but saw no signs of Ben. He wondered where he could be. Then he saw it.

The image hung on the wall next to Ben's desk. Eric looked at it from across the room. Had it gotten bigger since he'd last seen it? He could swear it had almost doubled in size. Impossible. He turned and closed the door behind him.

He approached the image slowly. The dark swirls of black and gray caught his attention and he ran his hand over the picture. He jerked it back quickly. It was vibrating. Almost like a heartbeat.

His ears caught a sound, muffled in pitch. At first, he thought it was the TV coming from the Teriet living room, but he soon dismissed that idea. To his horror, he determined the sounds origin. It was coming from the image. A faint, quiet voice, calling out to him. Calling his name.

Eric, though frightened, did not run. He took a step back from the canvas to get a better perspective. The colors seemed to come to life as they swirled around in front of him. Both terrified and curious, he couldn't turn away. He just stared, transfixed by the tornadoes of hue spinning before him. Intoxication came over him and he realized how Ben must have felt. Why he had been so hypnotically driven to this image. Then, as quickly as the sensation started, it changed.

His eyes were drawn to two small dark spots forming in the center of the canvas. They began to grow, shutting out the gray color scheme and dominating the entire work. The two dark splotches began to take forms of people. Sheer terror overwhelmed Eric's body. He couldn't turn to run; all he could do was stare in disbelief. Then one of the figures took on familiar features. Its mouth formed a sinister grin as its yellow eyes glared at him. Eric's lips opened in a silent scream as the familiar figure and its newly found master reached out of the image for him.

***

"Ungrateful kid," Martha said as she picked up the art she'd driven all the way to St. Louis for. It was lying face down on the floor, as if it had fallen from the wall. "When will they ever learn to respect things? Ran off without even telling me where he was going, and left the room a disaster. That Paulson kid is a bad influence. "

Martha hung the image back on the wall. She didn't remember it being so heavy. She turned to the living room to finish reading the paper. As she left the bedroom, she heard something. A distant voice, maybe. She stopped, cocked her head to one side, and listened again. Yes, she did hear something. Curious, she turned and walked back up to the image, the source of the noise. She looked at it again.

"Waste of trees. Nothing in these stupid things anyway. Just a bunch of lines and colors. And not even any color in this one." Martha laughed. She, too, saw nothing at first.

Though, the longer she looked, the more she noticed a change. She saw the colors begin to swirl, to move. Twisting and turning, undulating. Then she saw three distinct, dark forms begin to appear in the center.

Martha stared forward.

And waited to see the image…

FRIEND OF THE FISHERMAN

BY JOAN C. GUYLL

When Ross was posted out to Singapore to head the regional sales department of his multinational company, I was delighted. The expatriate perks that came with the job, plus the additional 'hardship' pay, made it worthwhile to relocate ourselves to the Far East.

As an expat wife, I quickly grew accustomed to the maid who cleaned the house, the cook, the gardener and the chauffeur. All these extras came with the job. The only downside was that Ross's daily commute to his office also included flying to other branches around the region such as Jakarta, Bangkok and Kuala Lumpur. After the first couple of years, I got used to his regular absences. Left on my own, I soon found a place in the expat wives' social group at the American Club. Our main activities involved gossiping, planning Christmas parties, trying out new restaurants and looking after the kids. In my case, Amy, our only daughter, was already in her late teens and needed little parenting. Life, as a rule, was very laid-back and enjoyable.

Whenever Ross was not 'outstation' (the local lingo for husbands who flew overseas as part of their work), my social activities were scaled down to accommodate him. Playing the dutiful wife, I made sure that his dinner would be ready and served hot at the table as soon as he got home. He'd then adjourn to the living room, settle into his favorite chair and peruse the regional newspapers. Once he was finished reading, he'd put his feet up on the coffee table, turn on the TV and channel surf before falling asleep in the chair.

Thirteen years in Singapore passed in a flash. We hardly spoke, like many married couples who'd been together too long, we had nothing to say to each other. Amy had by then returned to Texas, graduated college, and married a nice Pentecostal Pastor named Robert. Ross, who was due to retire that year, surprised me one night when he turned to me instead of the TV and said, "You need to come to Bali with me next week."

"Bali?" the proposal was so unexpected I didn't know how to react.

"A new branch has to be inaugurated. They need someone to cut the ribbon. Lionel's wife usually does the honors but she's back in the States helping their son settle into Yale and Lionel suggested I ask you."

Lionel was Ross's managing director. I had never been to Bali. My holiday preferences were Australia for events at the Sydney Opera House or Texas to visit Amy. Third world countries never appealed to my fastidious nature. However, I had been summoned to do my duty and it was a small price to pay for thirteen years of comfort and luxury, so I agreed.

We flew to Bali. I did my ribbon-cutting duty and met some of Ross's Indonesian colleagues. They were all very polite and friendly, especially his local secretary Haslina, who followed him around like a shadow. She reminded me of our maid back in Singapore: young, petite and pretty, and also Indonesian. By late afternoon, I was scheduled to fly back home alone as Ross had some 'loose ends' to tie up at the office.

"I'll catch the late afternoon flight tomorrow, Peg," he said as he gave me a quick kiss on the cheek and closed the door of the taxi.

Looking back at him as he stood by the curb, I remembered seeing his gaunt face and thinking, *Poor Ross. He's working too hard. Certainly deserves his retirement.* Upon my arrival at the flight counter, however, I was told that my flight had been cancelled. The next flight was the same as the one Ross was booked on the next day. I tried contacting Ross at his office but was informed he had gone to Ubud. As I left the airport, taxi-drivers accosted me, eager to get a fare. One of them shouted "Ubud shopping Madam?" and I stopped. *Maybe I could catch Ross there? Ubud was probably a small place.*

My impromptu taxi-driver was a wealth of information. Ubud was a village in the Balinese foothills where local craftsmen abound and where I could, if I wished, shop for souvenirs. *Even if I don't find Ross, at least I can do some shopping* I thought, as the cab drove past cotton bedspreads, painted wind-chimes and wooden carving stalls on the roadside leading into Ubud. I was enthralled and thought of friends back home who might appreciate a souvenir. Just as the taxi pulled to a stop, I saw Ross walking along the street, holding Haslina's hand. Before I could get out of the taxi to hail them, I saw Haslina dragging him into a narrow alleyway where they disappeared.

My heart began pounding in my ears as I hurried after them. *Had I inadvertently stumbled upon my husband's secret? Would I find them in a love-nest somewhere?* An old shop house stood at the end of the alley. There were wood carvings outside the partially open door. Through it, I saw Ross examining a rather curious object. It was at least five feet tall and wrapped in black cloth. Haslina was nowhere to be seen. I pushed the door further ajar and stumbled into a rustic woodcarving workshop. *Not a love-nest then. Silly me.*

"Ross," my voice faltered, unsure of the reaction I would get.

"Peggy!" He turned and for a fleeting second, his face reminded me of a little boy caught with his hand in a cookie jar. And then it was gone and there was annoyance instead. "Aren't you supposed to be on your way home?" his voice sounded brittle.

"My flight got cancelled. They put me on the same flight as yours tomorrow and I was heading to your hotel but the taxi driver told me Ubud is a great place to shop for souvenirs. Didn't actually think I'd see you. Small world isn't it? So what are you doing here?" My mind was reeling back to that moment I saw him being pulled into the alleyway by Haslina.

"Ah…the office lads organized a going away gift for me. Haslina had to drag me here to surprise me with it." He laughed. It was hollow and tremulous. His emphasis on the word 'drag' was not lost on me.

Whether or not I'd seen him holding hands with his secretary, he'd now managed to explain it away. *Clever, very clever!*

In our forty years of marriage, Ross had never once caused me to doubt his fidelity. I was not a suspicious person by nature. Besides, I knew Ross was well liked by his staff. The ladies, especially, were envious that I had such a 'strong and silent' husband. I decided to give him the benefit of the doubt.

Turning back to the object, he said to me, "Would you like to undo the knot?"

"Oh, this is the surprise then?" my voice betrayed my sarcasm and before I could reach out to pull the knot, Ross undid it in a huff and whipped the black sheet off to reveal a life-sized sculpture of an old fisherman.

I knew my husband entertained the idea that on his retirement, we would return to USA and he'd spend his days fishing largemouth bass in the lakes. Perhaps the statue evoked in him a sense of fulfillment—this was how he wished to see himself. At least that was how I reconciled my mind to the obvious delight shining in his eyes, whilst admiring the grotesque figure.

Carved out of a black wood, it badly needed cleaning. Cobwebs hung over its hat and face. I had seen better carvings in my years of living in the Far East and was unimpressed with this old monstrosity. To my surprise, Ross took out his clean white handkerchief and brushed the webs off the hat and began wiping the wooden face. It might have been the way the light fell on it but I swear I saw the fisherman's eyes gleaming and a shiver went down my spine.

Just then, Haslina stepped out of the shadows with an old man. "This is my grandfather, he carved it. He's happy to give it to you, *sayang*." When she saw me, she started, her face turning red.

Ross stepped in front of me and thanked the old man in the local lingo for his gift. "*Terima Kasih*," he said over and over again. The ambience was awkward to say the least as I stood like a sore thumb, waiting to be introduced. When Ross finally responded to my prodding in his back, he stepped aside and I gasped when I saw the old man's face. The aged lines, the gleaming eyes, it was the face of the wooden fisherman. Ross, on the other hand, appeared oblivious to the uncanny resemblance. The old carver's smile did not reach his eyes as he pried me away from Ross and led me to his more touristy works. While I stood chatting with the old man, I caught Ross grinning at his secretary like a schoolboy, while she simpered. *She certainly knows how to make the old boy happy. And what was that she called him? Sayang...isn't that darling in Indonesian? Some kind of mid-life crisis?*

A week after we returned to Singapore, the statue followed. It took three men to carry it into our home. Ross fussed over it like a mother hen. I had never seen him so worked up about anything we'd ever owned. He made sure the fisherman took center-stage in our entrance hall. When the maid tried to clean the statue, he waved her away. Ross took it upon himself to rummage for wax polish and a new piece of chamois. Then to our astonishment, he spent the next hour working on the fisherman, making the teak shine like black marble.

Albert Camus once wrote, "After awhile, you could

get used to anything." But I must admit that I didn't take to the fisherman at all. It sat like The Hulk, hunched over, with malevolent eyes peering out from under his hat. I was extremely uneasy. And I wasn't the only one who felt that way. Our maid refused to go near it. The dog would sit a few feet away, bark at it, then crawled off whimpering and cowering in fear. Ross, however, was totally enchanted by it. He developed a maniacal cleaning fetish for the wooden fixture. Instead of the usual routine of dinner, newspapers then TV, it became dinner, wax and polish. Around this time, Ross's outstation trips increased as well.

"Aren't you supposed to be scaling down and retiring, Ross?" I enquired one day when he informed me that he'd be away for another week in Bali. It crossed my mind that there might be other reasons why he was attracted to Bali, remembering that little fiasco in Ubud with Haslina. However, Ross had always been such an old stick-in-the-mud, I couldn't imagine him daring to even *contemplate* an office romance, let alone with someone half his age and from a different culture.

"Still a lot of loose ends to tie up. I can't be expected to let go so easily, you know?" He sounded annoyed, a fairly regular occurrence lately, which I put down to the pressure of his imminent retirement, so I didn't pursue the matter further.

When he left for his trip, I wrapped a pink bedspread around the fisherman. I'd had enough of its eyes following me when I walked within sight of it. Ross flew back from Bali earlier than expected. I had been to the club for a farewell lunch that went on well into dinner and was quite inebriated when I got home. The moment I stepped into the hall, I sensed something was amiss. The fisherman was uncovered, his eyes gloated at me. Ross sat by his prized possession, spraying wax and polishing vigorously.

My cheerful, "Hello darling, you're back!" was cut off in mid-sentence when Ross whipped around to face me and hissed, "How dare you do that to him!"

My throat went dry. I had never seen him so furious. He must have seen the fear on my face but that didn't deter him from picking up the bundled pink bedspread and throwing it at me. "Don't you *ever* treat him with such contempt again!"

Shocked at his sudden uncharacteristic outburst, I rushed into our bedroom and slammed the door. Ross slept on the sofa that night, watched over by his friend, the fisherman.

I lay in my bed, unable to fall asleep, thinking of all our years together. We married young and life had been good to us. Sex was regular at first. However, as Ross took on more responsibility, our sex life diminished and for the past thirteen years, it was virtually non-existent. I wondered if that was why we'd grown apart in our old age. Perhaps I should go out and buy a fishing rod to get him to caress me and massage my wrinkled skin with lotions and oils. At that ridiculous thought, I fell into a troubled sleep where statues raged like zombies and chased me down narrow alleyways. The next morning, I woke up with a pounding headache. It didn't help that the maid was also banging on my bedroom door.

"Telephone Ma'am!"

I rolled over and picked up the extension. It was

Lionel. I was instantly awake.

"Ross had a heart attack and is on his way to Gleneagles hospital."

I didn't wait to hear the rest. I rushed to the hospital to be by his side. As I sat watching him, his face pale against the light blue pillows of the ICU, his eyes opened and focused on me.

"I need to confess..." his voice was thin and weak.

Leaning forward to catch his words, I patted his hand and whispered, "Take it easy darling. The doctor says you're lucky to be alive. But you need rest. Whatever you have to say can wait till you get better."

Ross shook his head, his hand gripped mine as he stammered, "I must confess...I...I've done a great wrong."

I thought he was worried about his collapse in the office and I tried to soothe him. "Ross, darling, whatever you've done wrong can be corrected in time. You need to rest now."

His grip tightened until my hand hurt and something I saw in his eyes made my heart sink. Our eyes locked. I was so close I could smell his stale breath as he whispered, "Haslina has a baby. My son."

He slumped back onto his pillow and relaxed, as if a heavy load had slipped off his shoulders. I felt the weight of his burden on my heart and snatched my hand from his. Reeling back from this grey and sickened man, my head began to pound with the impact of those words. *Haslina! His secretary—the one I met in Bali.* My mind wound back to that trip. His schoolboy grin; her smug little smile. *Was she already with child then? Why did it have to be a boy? A boy, whom I had been unable to give him from my womb!*

I staggered out of the ICU, shattered by Ross's betrayal. Onlookers must have thought my husband had died by the way I was weeping. Just then, my phone vibrated.

"Mum, Lionel phoned us about Dad. Robert and I will fly over on the next plane." Amy sounded so far away and I felt a sudden pang of nostalgia. I wished she was here and fifteen again. I wished we were all back in Texas and had never come to Singapore.

I decided to go home. The doctors told me that although Ross wasn't out of danger, his vital signs had stabilized. I needed time to process what he told me. As I entered our home, the fisherman glared at me again, this time with what I perceived as a strange smirk. I'd never noticed that smirk before; perhaps it was the amount of waxing and polishing Ross had plied it with, which had altered the tired face, making it look alive and smug. I walked straight up to it and shouted, "I will fix you! Bastard."

The maid and the cook must have thought I'd lost my mind, yelling at the statue as I did. I gathered all the household servants to help me move the fisherman outside, to the far end of the garden. I heard them whispering. They were concerned for my sanity. I grabbed a kitchen cleaver and rushed out to the figure, now lying tipped over in the compost heap. Raising it over my head, I brought it down on the face of the fisherman. I missed and hit the hat instead. Perhaps it was the angle of swing. Whatever it was, the cleaver glanced off the curve of the hat and flew out of my hands. The hat wasn't even scratched. The servants were holding me back now.

"Black magic ma'am. You can't destroy it!" shouted

the cook.

"Nonsense! It's made of hardwood teak. Give me an axe. I'll try again," I raved.

"No Ma'am, please. I know our island magic. This thing is too strong for you," cried the maid.

I tore around to the garden shed, found an axe and tried hacking at the statue again. Perhaps I was weeping too hard from my anger at Ross's betrayal and my strength was spent. But there wasn't even a nick on that pristine face. I hated it even more.

Monsoon season was upon us then and dark storm clouds had gathered overhead as I battled the statue. A mighty clash from the Heavens opened up the rains and I was dragged back to the safety of the house before I could think of another way to destroy the fisherman.

As I sat in the living room, looking out into my garden, each lightning flash lit up the fisherman's eyes. It got so bad that when I closed my own eyes, I could still see two spots of that devilish gleam. It unnerved me but I refused to go to bed. Quitting seemed like admitting defeat and there was no way I was going to be defeated by a block of wood.

Amy flew into my arms when she arrived home with Robert following close behind. My vigil must have made me look a wreck because she insisted I go to bed immediately and took control of the household.

"Go see your father Amy. I'm sure he'd want to see you," I spoke from my bed.

When they had gone, I got up again and crept out to the garden. The rains had ceased by then, although the grass and trees were still dripping wet. In the garden shed, I found a can of kerosene. Pouring it on the statue, I tried to start a fire but it wouldn't burn.

"Damn you!" I cursed. Then I had an idea. I ran back to the house, grabbed the pink bedspread, the very one which Ross had thrown at me, and dunked it in the kerosene. I threw it over the fisherman, followed by a lighted match. The bedspread burst into flames and I whooped with joy.

That brought the staff running out of the house to grab me, thinking I was going to throw myself into the fire. As they brought me back into the house, we heard the phone ringing. I picked it up. It was Amy.

"Mum, you'd better come quick. Dad's taken a turn for the worse. He's delirious and keeps yelling for his fisherman friend."

When I reached the hospital, I stood looking down at my husband, a man I married for better or for worse so long ago. In his fevered state, he shook his head from side to side mumbling some incantations as if he was fighting demons in his own head. Looking at him through my tears, his face transformed into that of the fisherman and I turned away in shock. Amy and Robert were outside consulting with the doctor over Ross's prognosis and as they re-entered the room, both saw my distress and rushed over to hug me. When I looked back, he was just Ross again. My husband seemed to have aged overnight, however, and my thoughts went back to the fisherman.

Let go of him you bastard. This man belongs to me. My mind challenged the fisherman, who changed my husband from a quiet man to an obsessed tyrant. From the moment Ross set eyes on the carving, he abandoned our safe and secure marriage, set aside his high moral standards to jeopardize his entire career

174

and retirement pension. If Lionel, a devout Catholic, found out about Ross's affair with his secretary, the golden parachute promised to Ross would be withdrawn as a breach of contract. We would lose all we worked for and return to the States in disgrace. I couldn't allow that to happen and was glad that I had destroyed the statue before I left the house. I turned to Amy and Robert and told them to go home and rest while I kept watch over Ross.

"Robert wants to meet up with his old varsity friend, Pastor Wong. I'm going home to catch up on my sleep." Amy yawned.

Later that evening, the rains started again. Ross's fever subsided and I wondered if the spell had been broken by my burning of the fisherman. My hopes were dashed the moment I stepped into my house. There, crouching in the entrance hall, was the fisherman. His smile had widened, his tanned wooden surface unscathed by fire.

"Who moved it back?" I shouted for the maid, shaking with fury and fear. In my thoughts, I was beginning to believe it was indestructible. Perhaps the cook was right.

"Miss Amy came home and saw it lying in the garden. We tried to tell her, but she didn't understand. She said it was her father's favorite and no one should have touched it. She scolded us Ma'am." The maid was almost in tears.

Woken by the commotion, Amy walked into the lounge rubbing sleep from her eyes. "What's the matter Mum?"

Just then Robert came back from his meeting and as he stepped into the hall, he froze. "What's this monstrosity?" He eyed the statue.

Amy laughed and said, "That's my father's pride and joy. And guess what? I found it at the end of the garden, completely covered in soot. Dad would throw a fit if he saw…"

"Amy, that thing is evil," Robert interrupted.

All the hairs on my arms stood up as Robert confirmed my deepest fears. In that instant, I also relaxed a little. I *wasn't* going mad. This statue was evil and had taken over our lives.

I sat them both down and told them the whole story, from the moment Ross first saw the fisherman and its carver, the uncanny resemblance, the connection with Haslina and Ross's confession.

Amy hugged me tightly when I finished. "I'm so sorry Mum. I didn't know."

"My world's been turned upside down in the past year. I thought I was going mad." My voice shook with barely controlled emotion.

Robert explained how he had been studying Eastern beliefs and superstitions in preparation for a new posting to Indonesia. "The locals believe in black magic and love charms. I guess Haslina must have colluded with her grandfather to work something on Ross, and the statue is the key. It certainly drove a wedge between you and Ross."

"How do we destroy it? And if we do, will it affect Dad?" Amy asked.

"I'll have to ask Pastor Wong. He has a team dedicated to exorcism." Robert picked up the phone as he spoke.

None of us slept well that night. The next morning, Pastor Wong arrived with his team of seven. They lifted the fisherman onto a truck, heading to a saw mill owned by one of his parishioners. Robert and Amy accompanied them. I made my way back to Ross's bedside, promising Amy that I would keep updating her on her dad's condition as she updated me on the destruction of the statue.

When they reached the saw mill, the owner was aghast when he heard what they proposed to do.

"Please use another mill. This sculpture is too life-like. I dare not anger the spirits and bring bad luck to my factory," he pleaded.

Pastor Wong was not so easily deterred. After an hour of intense prayer as the group surrounded the statue, where he impressed on the mill owner the power of Christ, they set to work, placing the statue on a conveyor belt that drove logs through gigantic circular saws. The grinding and screeching of the huge blade, swirling round at high speed, was deafening. As the statue reached the saw, the tone amplified. Yet nothing happened. The statue appeared stuck and unable to move forward.

During this time, Ross began rocking from side to side. My hand rested on my vibrating mobile phone. I thought of his betrayal and my heart squeezed with pain. I couldn't bring myself to touch him. But I did talk to him. I told him of Robert's discovery and the attempt to burn the fisherman. I asked him if he agreed with my decision to destroy the statue. He was too weak to talk but continued shaking his head, his eyes closed. I noticed a tear rolling down his cheek, dropping onto the pale blue pillow. I did not convey this to Amy.

Back at the mill, efforts increased. The machinery

was stopped, heavily oiled, and started up again. The prayers of the group rose in a crescendo as the wail of the blade sliced into the fisherman. Splinters of wood and flecks of red flew out. Amy felt the grip on her hands tighten in their prayer circle, each one thinking one thought. 'The fisherman is bleeding!'

As they decimated the statue, Ross began writhing and screaming in pain. Doctors rushed in to work on him, trying to plug him into various life-resuscitation machines. I was ushered out, only able to look in through the glass window at my husband, whose life was slowly ebbing away. Amy kept me updated.

"How's Dad?" She asked anxiously.

I hesitated only for a second and replied, "Tell Pastor Wong to carry on, everything is under control here."

When the statue was finally reduced to sawdust, Pastor Wong and his team set it alight in a kiln. The heat of the blaze was so strong, the wall of the kiln glowed and Amy swore she could see shadows dancing in the light. The moment the last ember waned into blackness, Ross died.

After his funeral, I had plenty of time to contemplate what would have happened if Ross survived. Would he have had the heart to leave Haslina to her fate with their son? Or would the statue succeed in exerting its power and make Ross abandon me instead. I knew my life would never be the same again if the truth came out to our circle of friends. We'd have been the *plat du jour* gossiped throughout the expat community till kingdom come. At least this way, our dignity had been saved. His secret was still intact as I flew home with his ashes in a jar. I looked forward to a life of comfort and luxury with the generous work insurance pay-out Lionel had helped to expedite. After all, it was the life I had become accustomed to after forty years of marriage.

UN PERRO SIN PELO

BY RICHARD LAU

"Curse of the Wolfman?" Hah!

Anyone who believes that knows nothing of curses, wolves, or men.

Tell me, what hombre wouldn't want to grow more hair? A manly, hairy chest? Even for only one night a month during a full moon.

What man wouldn't want to feel feral power coursing through his veins? To release a good, loud and proud howl, not caring who hears and hoping someone does? To go on a good rampage, once in a while? Every vato knows some cabrón who deserves a good ripping. Es muy macho.

A curse? I say with much sarcasm, yeah, right. A blessing is more like it.

You want to know what a curse is? A real curse? Put yourself in my shoes, amigo.

Every full moon, my hair starts falling out. Not just on my head, but my face, arms, legs, chest, and, sí, everywhere else. Stubble, with the accompanying itchiness and roughness, is certainly a curse.

I've considered keeping my head and face shaved, but my hair grows back too quickly. It's not worth the effort. Plus, people think it's cool that I keep changing my hair style and appearance. If they only knew.

Not only do I lose my hair, but muscle and mass, too. The only thing that stays the same are my dark brown eyes.

The result of my transformation? A very small dog without hair. That's right, un perro sin pelo. I believe the breed is known as the Xoloitzcuintli, or for those of you who shudder from Aztec tongue-twisters, simply the Mexican Hairless Dog. The members of my family have other names for it, words not polite in English, Nahuatl, or Spanish.

Every full moon, instead of a mighty howl of protest at my dire fate, I yip my dismay, like an angry squeaky toy.

All the men in my family suffer from this. Our homes become kennels. The toughest and bravest among us find themselves easily lifted and ingloriously placed in locations where we won't be any inconvenience to the womenfolk. Now that, my friend, is a curse.

According to la historia de mi familia, there was an ancestor now called Uncle Hector, though his real name and relationship has been long forgotten.

This tio Hector is said to have come over to the Americas with the conquistadores and led his men in the uncharitable slaughter of a group of Mayans. It's said that before she died, a Mayan witch told him, "A cowardly dog you are; a hairless dog you shall be!"

Hector laughed, until the next full moon. Then he went missing. All his fellow soldiers found were his armor, weapons, and clothes, guarded by a small, yapping dog. You already know who that was.

The soldiers figured Hector had either "gone native" or deserted his post or both. How else could they explain the evidence at their feet? With a dismayed yowl, the furless little dog added an additional pile to what was on the ground before them, and in disgust, the comandante kicked the annoying animal.

The next day, Hector stumbled into camp and was immediately accused of desertion. He was thought to have shaved off his beard and hair in a misguided attempt at disguise. Not recognizing his own distorted bootprint on my uncle's abdomen, the comandante concluded that Hector had somehow hurt his ribs during his desertion, and the injury forced him to return for aid.

Not thirty days later, Hector escaped a cage built to hold a man, not a much smaller dog.

Knowing he could never hide his condition on a long shipboard journey back to Spain, he settled in the New World, running from discovery, capture, or worse.

And today, we still run.

One night, I was coming home from college, and a scheduled bus didn't show. The one-hour delay until the next bus meant my transformation would occur before I got home. After veintidós años of this crap, I had enough experience to find, in advance, safe refuges on my route wherever I was going on that "special" day.

I called mi madre and told her where I'd be hiding. With both concern and relief in her voice, she said, "I'll be there as soon as I get off work. Take care, mijo."

The closest hideaway was an apartment trash dumpster surrounded on three sides by six-foot high cement walls and a slotted wooden gate on the fourth side. I ducked behind the metal blue bin, leaving the gate partially open so I wouldn't be trapped, and settled down for the inevitable. If I was lucky, no one would take my clothes or my backpack. I would guard them the best I could.

Time passed, but I didn't mind after the sun had set and the moon came out. I was used to the process, so the shrinkage and alopecia went quickly. Mostly, I just noticed the change of colors in my vision and a sharp increase in my sensitivity to the smells around me.

As a dog, all of the scents were interesting, though in my tiny form, I had little access to the objects in the metal container that were producing the majority of them.

I checked around the base of the bin for marking messages, as we dogs call them. I found nada, except for a few weeds springing out of pavement cracks and a few pebbles.

Then I saw it: a set of keys on a bronze metal ring, hugging one of the dumpster's rear wheels. Even among the other odors, the key ring and its cactus-shaped leather fob gave off a faint scent of jasmine. I don't know why I didn't notice it before.

Suddenly, the scent grew stronger, and I heard scraping as the gate opened wider. A spot of light moved in circles along the walls and ground.

Oh no! What to do, what to do?

A pale, fleshy spider with ringed legs dropped, crawled, and pounced on the set of keys.

"Aha!" I heard a feminine voice say. "I thought I dropped them here."

Then a shadowy shape curled around the edge of the bin and blinded me with the beam of light.

"Think rat! Un raton rabioso!" I encouraged myself, chanting the words like a spell. I backed into a corner, baring my teeth. My growl sounded as dangerous as the motor of one those hand-held, battery-powered fans.

"Oh! You poor, frightened thing," exclaimed the voice, high pitched either from surprise or trying to entice me with cuteness. Needless to say, this was not the effect I was going for. "Are you lost, little one?"

"No!" I shouted, but it came out as a sad, affirmative-sounding yip.

A sweater that smelled like a flower garden was wrapped around me, leaving only my head poking out to one side. I felt the ground fall away from beneath my paws. I struggled with the ferociousness of a hundred wet dachshunds and bit, but all I managed to do was pull a muscle, gain a mouthful of chewable cloth, and drool all over myself.

Completely a captive, I could only note the number of the apartment we entered.

Once we were inside, the cloud of the sweater dispersed, and I was plopped unceremoniously down on a tiled kitchen floor. I prepared to make a break for it, when I saw the white ceramic bowl of kibble on the floor in front of me, as if I had been expected.

Not sure whether it was the stomach of the dog that overruled the brain of the man or vice-versa, for I had skipped lunch and missed dinner, but all thoughts of escape vanished, replaced by a new single focus: "Food!"

The kibble tasted oddly fishy, but I still gobbled it down.

"My, aren't you hungry!" said the woman in a purple sweatsuit, kneeling down and stroking my back. Her warm fingers on my skin felt very nice.

"I was downstairs hoping to find my keys, but I didn't expect to find you." She sounded a little lonely.

I looked up at her, as I continued gobbling. Curly hair, as dark as a moonless night, swaddled a kind, smooth, brown face that was shaped like an inverted pear. Her lips were absolutely kissable...or lickable. I get confused during these times of transformation.

Even with my canine senses, I could tell she was beautiful, muy hermosa. I put on my best pathetic puppy look, which isn't hard when you looked like I did in my dog form.

As she added more food to the bowl, I nuzzled her chin, and she scratched mine.

"Now who do you belong to?" she asked. She could tell that I had no collar hidden by fur I also didn't have. "You look healthy, except for smelling a little like a trash bin."

After I had finished eating, which took some time, she gave me a damp towel wipe-down. At first, I protested, but she gave me the sweetest smile and said, "You're going to have to clean up a bit if you're going to stay here tonight."

Mi corazón!

"That's much better!" she said, after I was cleaner and had regained my natural scent. I licked her hand con muchas gracias.

"How sweet!" my rescuer exclaimed. "What else can you do?"

I answered with a sharp series of barks, which meant "Toco mi nariz asi" as I put my paw on top of my muzzle, which I had been told was my most adorable move.

She burst into laughter, and I felt muy feliz that I also made her very happy.

We curled up on the couch, enjoying the comforting softness of the cushions and the ball formed by the two of us. We gazed into each other's eyes until we fell asleep. I can't remember a more peaceful night. I was so relaxed in her arms that I didn't think about how I would get out again in the middle of the night unless she had a doggy door.

And so, the next morning, as the sun rose, the apartment contained one anxious naked man and one equally surprised, hissing cat. It was probably ticked off because I had eaten all its food. Ugh. Tuna or salmon morning breath. Both the cat and I regretted my gluttonous decision the previous evening.

Funny, though, I hadn't noticed the cat the night before. Maybe it was hiding in a closet and hunger had given it the bravery to come out for breakfast. It was a large cat, about twenty pounds, and the way it moved, I could tell it was muscle, not fat, rippling under its coffee and tan fur. I was glad I was in human form again, and towered over it. The cat didn't seem to notice or care, so I stomped my unshod foot at it.

The cat flattened its ears against its head, bared its teeth, did an excellent impression of a hissing cobra, and swiped at my naked leg. Though the paw moved too fast for me to actually see the claws, I was pretty sure they were extended, which gave me an additional reason to get dressed.

At first, I was relieved that the nice woman must have left before I reverted back to my human form. But how to get down to the dumpster to get my clothes? I have a slight build, so maybe something in her closet would fit, but what if she returned and caught me in her clothes? Or out of them? Which was worse?

I looked around for a landline phone. Luckily, there was one. And luckily, there was someone at my home to answer my call.

"Letty? This is Javier. I need you to bring me a set of clothes."

"Where have you been?" Letty demanded, preferring, like any older sister, to argue rather than help. "Don't you know Mama's been worried sick about you? She found the dumpster, and she found your clothes. She found your phone. But you were nowhere in sight."

"I managed to make it into one of the apartments," I said, trying to hold back the embarrassing detail of being carried inside.

"Did you ever think that when Mama arrived, it was too late at night to go knocking on doors?"

"I didn't have much choice," I muttered, still trying to keep the details vague. "Look, I really need your help, Letty. I'm stuck in a woman's apartment without any clothes on, and I don't know when she'll be back."

"Men!" said mi hermana in disgust, though I couldn't tell if she meant men in general or the cursed ones in our family line. "It sounds like you had a lovely evening. Mama had me calling hospitals and animal shelters all night."

When she paused for breath, I told her approximately where I was on my route home, a description of the apartment building, and the number of the apartment I was in. Having vented her frustration, my sister said she'd be right over with clothes. As I said, the women in my family have lots of experience dealing with loco situations like this.

While I waited, I poked through the kitchen cabinets and refilled the bowl with kibble. The cat was interested but also had more self-control than I did. It just kept its distance and kept its stony stare focused on me.

My sister arrived before the lady got back, and as I dressed, I told her what had happened.

"Estúpido!" she said. "You should have crawled under the dumpster and hid. Or ran around to the other side and out the open gate. Mama said she would come pick you up." I had to admit she had a point, but she was analyzing my predicament as a full-grown woman sitting calmly on a couch, not as a purse-sized puppy trying to think on the fly.

I gave the apartment one last longing look, wishing I had some flowers to leave behind as a thank-you, but then I realized that a dog wouldn't and couldn't do that. We left, locking the door behind us.

Two nights later, I still couldn't get the face of the bella dama out of my head. I was trying to think of a way to go back over to her apartment and introduce myself. Would she like me as a man? Or should I wait until the next full moon and go pawing at her door?

Then the phone rang. Letty said it was a woman asking for me. "Should I tell her that you're out fetching a paper?" Dumb sister joke. I must remember to pay one of her expensive shoes a visit next month.

I grabbed the phone from her.

"Hello, Javier. This is Lucille," a woman's voice said. "I believe you were over at my place the other night?"

I was speechless, so fortunately, she continued. "I've been working up the nerve to call you, especially after you didn't come back."

It turns out that Lucille used the re-dial feature on her landline to call me. But how did she know my name?

She explained that she had overheard me when I was calling my sister. You see, Lucille is also cursed. She only attains human form after sundown. During the day, you can say she's "feline fine."

We all have our curses and blessings. The goal is to find someone who loves us for them. And Lucille and I certainly do.

THE CHAIR

BY ALESHA ESCOBAR

"What is *that*?"

I watch Jordan's shoulder blades retract and hear him grunt as he pulls a brown leather recliner through the front door. He never cared about decorating and had always left it up to me, so I couldn't help but stare at the monstrosity that clashed with the grey-black-and-white color scheme of the living room.

He heaves a sigh as he throws his thick arms around the chair and lifts it, carrying it over to the little nook area with a small bookshelf. "You remember my uncle, Edward?"

How could I not remember him? He was the liveliest person at our wedding, and he doted on me as if I were his own daughter. Uncle Edward with his salt-and-pepper hair and infectious laugh is unforgettable. I tentatively nod and rush over to shut the front door. "I thought he moved to Vegas this week."

Jordan wipes the sweat from his brow. A dark stain

191

travels down the front of his thin beige t-shirt. "Yeah, and he didn't want to take this, so, I figure it's still good and we could use it."

I press my lips into a thin line. "Babe," I try to hide my grimace as he plops into the recliner and rocks back and forth, nearly hitting my bookshelf. "It's ugly and doesn't match. And it's taking up space."

He motions toward the direction of the guest room. "I'll put it in there. I promise it will be out of the way."

I arch an eyebrow and approach him. "Really?"

He leans forward and pulls me into his lap. Just as our lips brush, his phone rings. With an apologetic look, he pulls it out and answers. "Hey, Wendell...you got him? Yeah, I can do that. I'll be right down."

I feign a saddened expression and sneak in a quick kiss. "What does Wendell want?"

"Needs my help. I've got to go."

I push myself to my feet and allow him to get up. He plants a kiss on my cheek as he heads over to the door leading to the garage. After sliding his gun into his holster and grabbing his badge, he grabs his keys and gives me a wink. "I'll try to be back by dinner. What do you wanna eat?"

I shrug. "Chinese. Do you need me to grab you a change of clothes?"

He shakes his head. "Got some in the locker down at the precinct. See you tonight."

"Be safe."

He's through the door and headed out, and I'm left alone with the ugly chair. As the day passes and turns into evening, I run some errands, then return and move from one chore to the next until I finally settle my gaze on the recliner chair. I grab a rag from beneath the kitchen sink and gently wipe it down. Why Uncle Edward would take everything in his home and not this chair baffles me. Why the hell Jordan agreed to take it is even more of a mystery.

I turn on the television and check my watch—it's 7 p.m. and Jordan hasn't even checked in with me. There have been other nights like this. I'd sit around waiting, fearing Wendell or someone would call me to tell me some punk took him out. Then, after the first three years of our marriage, I got used to it. I still fear for him from time to time, but usually a late night means he's doing good work.

Nevertheless, I head into the kitchen with a pang of disappointment and pull out some leftover spaghetti, making sure to save some for him when he gets in. So much for Chinese.

I decide to try out the chair. If it's comfy enough, maybe I'll keep it in the guest room and not force it into the garage. It squeaks a little as I rock back in it and cradle my bowl of hot spaghetti. I drape a red blanket across my lap from a nearby storage ottoman.

Not so bad...

I pass the time watching "Kitchen Nightmares" and scarfing down my sad dinner. My eyelids grow heavy and my muscles relax as I give into sleep. At some point my eyes pop open and I'm in the darkness of the living room, the soft glow of the television with the words "Are You Still Watching?" prompting me to hit the continue option.

I hear footsteps behind me, slowly approaching.

Finally, he's here.

I try to make a move to get up so I can greet him, except my body is frozen in place and my limbs refuse to obey me. It's like some invisible force is holding me in place. A chill creeps down my spine. The hairs on my arms raise as I realize that whoever is approaching is not Jordan. The sound of the footfalls are not his, and he never enters the house without greeting me or calling out to me.

"Jordan?" My voice cracks and my heart pounds in my chest. I gasp as the chair slides backward.

It suddenly halts. The sound of footsteps falls silent, and the only things I hear are the throbbing in my ears and the steady breathing of the person behind me. As soon as I see in my peripheral vision a coal-black hand reach out toward my face, I squint my eyes shut and holler.

Everything goes dark and there's a crash.

I open my eyes and see Jordan kneeling, carefully picking up the broken pieces of porcelain from my empty spaghetti bowl. I must've fallen asleep with it in my lap.

"What time is it?" I ask in a weak voice, glancing around the living room to ensure I'm not dreaming or in some sort of haze. The chair is back in its original position, though I *know* I felt it slide backward several feet.

Jordan gives me a half-smile, the bags beneath his eyes testify to the long evening he must've had. "Sorry about dinner, I'll make it up to you. I didn't want to disturb you. You looked comfortable."

I watch him take the pieces over to the garbage pail and dispose of them. I hop out of the chair and approach him, letting him wrap his arms around me. The warmth and security of his embrace is way better than anything my blanket could offer.

"I left you some spaghetti."

He plants a kiss on the top of my head. "Thanks."

"You said I was asleep when you came in?"

He nods and opens the fridge. "I came over and saw the pieces on the floor. I would've let you keep sleeping, but at that point your eyes just popped open."

Ugh. I shudder at the idea of sleeping in that chair all night. Maybe I subconsciously sensed Jordan come in and it manifested in my dream?

"I'm a little tired." I wrap my blanket around me. "I'll see you upstairs."

"Love you, Lexi."

"Love you."

I waste no time getting upstairs and into bed. I'll have to convince him to get rid of that chair tomorrow. I never wanted it anyway, and after that weird dream, which felt all too real, I want it out of my house.

Morning arrives and Jordan's already in the kitchen making breakfast. My stomach rumbles as I take in a whiff of dark roast coffee, bacon, and some fruit and pastries sitting on the table.

"Thought I'd make up for last night," he said, pouring some pancake batter into a hot pan. "How'd you sleep?"

"Okay." I glance at the chair. The same sense of dread I felt at that pitch-black hand reaching toward my face began gripping my chest. My throat tightens, but I manage a faux smile as I sit at the table. "Did you try out the chair last night?"

Jordan brings over a heap of pancakes and settles across from me. "Yeah, it's comfortable. Watched some TV, ate that spaghetti and had a beer. It looked like you were cozy in it too."

Hardly.

"You didn't feel anything weird, or see anything out of place?" I poke a slice of banana with my fork.

He stares at me as if I have a second head. "I sat there, ate, then came up to bed. You were out cold."

Ah-ha! He didn't sleep in it like I did. Maybe that's it.

I try to convince him we don't need it, but it's not working. He promises that he'll move it into the guest room, but then Wendell calls again and Jordan's off to help his partner. Screw it. I'll put it into the other room myself. At least I can shut the door and not have to look at it.

Jordan would laugh his ass off seeing my petite five-foot frame struggling with the recliner. I push it across the living room, grunting and cursing all the way. I pause when one of the creaks from the chair sounds like a groan. Goosebumps form on my arms, and my throat tightens again. A nightmarish image of the chair coming to life and devouring me flashes through my mind as I desperately slide it across the threshold into the guest room. The damn thing feels like it's getting heavier, as if actually protesting its relocation.

Screw you, Chair.

I wipe my hands on my knees and shut the door. Good riddance.

I go into the kitchen and grab Uncle Edward's number. I dial it and stare at the closed guest room door. He picks up after a few rings.

"Hey, Lexi! How's it going, sweetheart?"

"Good. How's your move? Are you all settled in?"

"I sure am. How's my nephew doing?"

"Great. He just left for work a little while ago."

"That's nice to hear," he says in a warm tone. "I'm so glad he found you, he's a thousand times better because of you."

I chuckle and utter a "thank you." But then I remember he dropped a damn haunted chair on us, and I frown. "Uncle Edward, Jordan brought home that chair yesterday. Did you really mean for him to have it?"

Duh. Because people accidentally give away furniture all the time.

"Oh, you mean that old recliner?"

"Yep. That's the one."

"It's been in the family for years. My mom used to sit in it a lot, it was her favorite chair. I decided not to take it. You know, have a fresh start in a new home."

I roll my eyes, not buying his excuse. "Have you ever fallen asleep in that chair?"

He pauses for so long that I repeat my question. He finally answers. "Yeah. Once or twice."

"This is going to sound weird, but I fell asleep in the recliner last night and had a terrible dream. It felt so real. That recliner is weird, and it gives me these bad vibes. I don't know how to explain it. Did that happen to you?"

"I'm sorry, Lexi. I thought it was just me."

"Then I'm not crazy?"

"No."

"So the shadow man, the moving backward, all of that…"

"Among other things."

"Why did you give it to us?"

"I thought maybe it was attached to me, because I

was in a dark place after my mother died. I told myself that it was some type of negative energy from the old house. I figured if the chair found a new home, that all of that would go away."

"Great, so we inherited a cursed chair." I don't even want to ask if Jordan's grandmother died in the damn thing.

"I'm sorry, Lexi."

"Well, we're going to get rid of it. We can send it to a junkyard or something."

"Okay, call me if you need anything."

"Bye."

I console myself with the fact that the chair is shut away in the other room, and even if I have to cry and plead, I will get Jordan to trash it. I leave the house for shopping and a lite lunch, get back and settle on my plush grey couch. My phone dings with an alert; looks like Jordan will be getting in late again. He and Wendell caught a murderer.

The evening sky swallows up the remaining daylight, and I'm once again wrapped in my blanket watching television. This time I opt for chocolate and popcorn, with a tall glass of wine. I drift into sleep again, thankful for the peaceful quiet. Time seems to no longer exist as my mind falls into blissful rest. After a while, I'm stirred from sleep by a gentle hand on my shoulder. My body coils with tension and I open my eyes, but I relax when I see Jordan's hand, with his silver watch on his wrist, standing behind me and gently massaging my arm.

My eyes close again, but I try to make small talk. "Hey, how'd it go?"

His fingers make a seductive swirling motion up

and down my arm and across my shoulder. His thumb brushes my lips, and I'm roused from my fogginess. Then, I freeze. Because I realize I'm back in the recliner and not on the couch. What the hell is going on?

Jordan suddenly squeezes my chin with a savageness I've never known from him. I'm afraid that if I don't fight back, he'll rip half my face off. I let out a screech. I claw at his wrist and try to pull his hand down as he's trying to cover my nose and mouth with his huge hand. I manage to look up at the figure towering over me from behind, and he *looks* like Jordan, but his eyes are hollowed out and completely black, and the row of teeth peeking beneath his snarl looks like it belongs on a predatory animal.

I buck against the chair, still tearing at his arm and screaming into his hand.

"Shhhh," the fake Jordan says to me in a serpentine voice.

I drop my hands and grow rigid. Tears sting my eyes. Is this another bad dream?

"Do you hear it?" he asks.

I slowly shake my head.

He leans in closer, his hot rancid breath on my cheek. "The Devil is here."

I screech again and start clawing and swinging with every bit of ferocity that the adrenaline in my system would allow. I feel a pair of arms trying to restrain me, but I manage to slide downward and roll onto the floor. I scream and kick, uttering incoherent half-prayers and calling out for the real Jordan to come help me.

Suddenly everything goes black and I wake up. I'm on the recliner, and Jordan, *my* Jordan, is on the grey couch wolfing down a slice of pizza and watching a show. He looks over at me with affection.

"I think you like that chair more than you're letting on." He smiles.

I jump out of the chair and join him on the couch, making sure to sit on his right side, so that he's between me and that godforsaken piece of furniture. I jab an accusatory finger at the recliner. "I pushed that chair into the guest room earlier today and I was sitting on *this* couch when I fell asleep."

He wipes his mouth with the back of his hand and gives me an incredulous glance. "Uh...you were asleep in the recliner when I got here. That's why I'm here on the couch. I'll move it to the guest room tonight before I go to bed, remember I told you?"

I pull my legs up and cross my arms over them, eyeing the chair. "You're not listening. I *already* put it in the other room. Now it's here again. By itself!"

He lets out a chuckle. "Come on, Lexi. Stop playing around."

"I talked to Uncle Edward today and he said the same thing happened to him. That chair is cursed. I want it out of here."

Jordan narrows his eyes at me. "It was my grandma's, and I said I'd move it. You actually called Edward? You know he's crazy, right?"

The back of my neck burned with anger, and my jaw tightened. I motioned toward the chair. "Then you sleep in that thing."

He looks over at it, then back at me. "Are you kidding me?"

"See for yourself."

"I'm not going to sleep in a recliner, Lexi."

"You don't believe anything's wrong with it. You think I'm crazy? Do it, unless you're afraid."

He waved a dismissive hand through the air. "It's just a chair."

"Then sleep in it tonight. I dare you."

His eyes widen. He turns and looks at the chair and then back at me. "You're serious. You're actually scared of it?"

"You'd be too, if you saw what I saw. If you felt what I did."

"Me? No. I'm the guy who just helped put away a murderer, who took down the 16th Street gang...and remember that weird cult leader from last year? *Those* guys were scary. That is just a chair."

"Then sleep in it!"

He shrugs. "Fine. I'll sleep in it tonight."

I give him a curt nod. "Good. Then you'll see."

He grumbles as I hand him my blanket. "You know, husbands actually have to do something shitty to end up on the couch, or in this case, a recliner."

I march toward the staircase and then turn to face him. "Bringing a possessed chair into my house *is* shitty."

I head upstairs and retreat to the comfort and safety of our bed. Although my sleep is shallow, I'm grateful it's uneventful. As soon as the sun's rays peek through my sheer white curtains, I rise out of bed, ready to find out how Jordan fared. Knowing him and his pride, he'll probably still be in it and then insist it's the best sleep he's ever had. My cell phone rings and I answer. It's Uncle Edward.

"Good morning, Lexi."

"Hey, how are you?" I head downstairs.

"I feel bad about the chair. If you want, I can send some guys to come pick it up."

I make it into the living room and the recliner is gone. The sliding glass door is open, and I can see Jordan in the backyard, hacking away at the chair with an axe. "Actually, that won't be necessary. Jordan's got it handled."

"Are you sure?"

"Yeah. Talk to you later."

I smile. I hope he breaks it down into a thousand pieces and then burn them to ash.

Just in case, I pull up the browser on my phone and Google "How to Dispose of a Cursed Item."

For a moment, Jordan's gaze meets mine, and we both stare at each other. The look in his tired eyes tell me that he's sorry. He resumes breaking down the cursed chair.

"Breakfast and coffee?" I call out.

He nods before delivering another blow.

I turn and head into the kitchen. I can't help but wonder if there are any weird heirlooms lurking around in my family. If my parents or a relative leaves me some item, I'm definitely going to turn it down. Especially if it's a chair.

DO YOU LIKE THE WAY IT BURNS?

BY AMANDA CRUM

I was raised in a trailer park in one of those Kentucky towns that looks like a hundred other Kentucky towns. Small, threaded with farmland and fast-food joints and one cemetery that delves for acres into the woods, keeping the secrets of all the folks who have ever taken their last breath inside the county line. It's a medium-good place to live, but for all the ghosts. My hometown is ripe with them.

On the day I met Josie I hadn't slept in forty hours or so and was nodding off during orientation at my most recent place of work, a call center crammed into an old Wal-Mart. My job would be troubleshooting computer issues, but on no sleep and with the remnants of the gin I kept in my closet still sloshing around in my brain, I wasn't good for much. I felt like a child's hurried drawing, all sharp points and dark eyes. The man in charge of our orientation was relentlessly excitable, exuberant as a puppy. I wanted to punch him in the dick.

"What if we're in Hell?" the little blonde on my right whispered. She was past petite, edging into tiny territory, beautiful, and her hair looked like spun gold even in the headache-light of the conference room.

"Hmm?" I murmured.

"What if this guy never stops talking and this is our eternal punishment for masturbating to that Nine Inch Nails video in high school?"

I snickered. "That makes sense, given the state of this coffee."

Tiny Blonde laughed, making the silver fairy at her throat wink in the fluorescents. "I'm Josie."

"Amy," I said, sticking out my hand.

It was a strange feeling, forging a friendship with another female. I didn't have many of them in my life, never had. Best friends had come and gone throughout childhood and my teen years, but they always seemed to tire of me quickly. My moodiness, the way the boys looked at my breasts. I have never been a girl in the sense that most are. I never cared about makeup or flirting and never learned how to do either. Living with my father made me sullen and impetuous, always ready to run wherever my long legs would take me, always the quiet girl in the back of the room. Everyone thought I was shy; I just hated all of them and didn't care to make conversation. Josie was the first girl to initiate a conversation with me in years, too pretty to care about the shape of my tits or the way my red hair drew gazes. She wasn't that sort.

After, I had nowhere to go but home. It was rainy, the kind of slick October rain that peels leaves off the trees and sticks them to the asphalt, and my car's tires were too shitty to drive around in that. I stopped at McDonald's and ate my cheeseburger as I drove through the blue evening, windshield wipers overpowering the music. I didn't care. It reminded me of being a kid and falling asleep in the backseat.

It was hard to escape memories driving through town. I'd gotten out after high school and moved to the closest big city for a while, where I met a man in a band who liked to use his fists. After he gave me a ring, a tiny gold circle with a diamond chip, I had a vision of the next five years spent drowning, wearing long sleeves, taking showers in the dark. I threw as many of my things as I could fit into my Ford Escort and left; months later, I pawned the ring. Got seven dollars for it.

But the place where you grew up holds a special kind of sadness, even more than what happened to you at the hands of a madman. There are all the places you ate with your mom, the public library, the smell of shorn grass, all the changes and new buildings that make you think of an old friend who's had facial reconstruction surgery. It's enough to make a person drink.

My father lived in a modest house in a quiet cul-de-sac, miles away from the trailer I grew up in. His second wife remarried years ago, leaving him to stew in bourbon and his own self-hatred. I had nowhere else to go.

He was asleep in his chair, a relief to me as I slid past in the darkened living room. "Bonanza" blared from the TV. He was probably down for the night. I grabbed a fresh pack of cigarettes from the carton on the kitchen table and headed downstairs to my room in the basement. It was freezing in the winter and drew silverfish in summer, but my father never left the first floor because of his hip, so it was mine. I did all the laundry and he let me stay for free. A decent trade.

That night I finished the gin from my closet, peeled off my clothes, and lay naked under the ceiling fan. Even with the booze in my veins, it didn't take long for my skin to cool and then freeze like marble. I welcomed it. I counted the scars on my body and tried to remember when each one had marked me, if they were old or new. I fell asleep still counting.

***

Josie and I began hanging out on our lunch hour every day, sometimes smoking a joint in her car, sometimes just sitting in the courtyard out back and listening to music. She didn't feel the need to fill up the space with chatter, which I appreciated, but it made getting to know her difficult. Still, she was a mellow girl, down for anything, and since I didn't aspire to do much outside of shutting down my anxiety with one substance or another, we got along just fine.

Halloween dawned stormy and full of wind; we sat in her car at lunch, eating spicy chicken sandwiches from Checkers and chasing them with cream soda. We were deliciously high, ravenous, licking the mayo from our fingers when we were done. Across the parking lot, the windows of the office building were covered in dollar-store skeletons and mummies, bursts of orange and black dotting the horizon. I found it violently unfair that we still had five hours of work to go.

"We should have a party tonight," Josie said suddenly. "Get properly wasted."

"At your place?" My father certainly wouldn't allow

company.

She shrugged. "Sure. My roommate is working late tonight and rent's not due 'til next week. We can stop by Andre's, he'll hook us up with more smoke."

"It's kind of short notice. Do you think anyone will come?" In truth, it didn't matter to me one way or the other. I'd never been to Josie's house and I was curious about where this tiny enigma lived.

"Don't know. But if no one shows up, we'll have a shitload of weed and beer to ourselves."

I couldn't argue with that logic.

The storm cranked up again just as we finished lugging our treasures into her house. It was a huge old Victorian on a crumbling side street, the top half of which she shared with her roommate. The bottom half was rented by a married couple, Josie said, but they were cool. The woman was a nurse who sometimes came upstairs to smoke with them after a long shift.

To get to Josie's place, we took a narrow enclosed staircase on the far side of the house, a corridor hardly wider than a throat that was sandwiched between the heavy outer door and a smaller, beveled-glass one at the top. At 6:30 p.m., it was already pretty dark outside; the clouds had obscured the moon, leaving us bathed in the warm light that poured through the glass door. We teetered up the steps with our arms full of beer and bags laden with enough junk food for several days, plus a smaller bag stuffed deep down into Josie's purse.

"MICHELLE!" Josie called after she got the door open. "You parked in my spot again!"

"That's not your spot, bitch," came the amiable-enough reply from down the hall. A slender brunette appeared, her hair in rollers. She pulled a pack of cigarettes and a lighter from the pocket of her apron, which read *76 Truck Stop* across the front. "As long as I'm paying rent here, I'll park wherever I want."

She looked me up and down. I suddenly regretted not caring what the wind was doing to my hair as we unloaded the car. "You the new bestie?"

"Um...." I began. Was that what I was? Had Josie been talking about me?

"This is Amy," Josie said, rolling her eyes at me. "Be nice to her."

"I'm super fucking nice," Michelle said with a little smile. "Until it's time to not be nice."

"Come on, you can bring that stuff into the kitchen," Josie said to me.

"What is all that?" Michelle asked.

"We're having a party," Josie said over her shoulder.

"You didn't tell her?" I whispered.

"She won't even be here," Josie whispered back. "Fuck her."

I sat my bags down on the kitchen table and looked around. The room was sparse other than the appliances, plus a postage-stamp-sized table and four chairs. A small black cat lounged on one, looking up sleepily at me before deciding I wasn't worth checking out.

"Josie? Can I talk to you for a minute?" Michelle asked. She was still standing in the hallway. I could smell another storm coming.

Josie left the room and I heard a door slam somewhere. The cat regarded me solemnly as I sat down across from him and listened with half an ear to their conversation; they must have been in the room directly behind the kitchen. Every other word Michelle said was punctuated by small thuds that must have been the rollers she was pulling out of her hair.

"...Told you (thud) don't (thud) deal with (thud) shit anymore..."

Josie's words were muffled, but I could tell she was trying to calm Michelle down. I had never felt so out of place. I scratched the back of my calf with the toe of my shoe and thought about the new bottle of gin in my bedroom, waiting to be cracked open.

After a little while, the girls emerged. Josie came into the kitchen smoking a cigarette; Michelle left without saying goodbye.

"I'm sorry about her," Josie said. "We've kind of been rubbing each other the wrong way lately."

"Maybe we shouldn't have a party," I said. "I don't want to cause problems."

"Fuck her!" Josie said again. "She'll be at work until 2 a.m. and I'll have this whole place cleaned up by then. We've already invited people, anyway. Come on, I want to show you my bedroom. I just redecorated it."

She picked up the cat, who went without complaint, and led me to the other end of the house. Beyond the door lay a huge bedroom dominated by a mahogany four-poster bed and a fireplace with a carved mantel. The walls were dark blue and accented with hanging gold stars and moons; the duvet on her bed matched. A small television sat on a table in the corner, along with an ashtray and several soda cans. Jewelry was hung neatly on the wall across a row of nails, creating a sparkly tableau in the dim light of her bedside lamp. Books lined the mantel; everything from Stephen King to Hemingway, I noted with approval.

"It's beautiful," I murmured, and I meant it. It was the way I would have done my room if I'd ever cared enough.

"Thanks. I have the softest bed ever," she said, jumping up onto it and patting the mattress for me to do the same. "Come and have a smoke with me."

She produced the baggie she'd gotten from Andre and began expertly rolling a joint on top of a book. I kicked off my shoes and jumped up, sinking immediately into the softest pillows I'd ever felt.

"Oh my God," I said, "This is heavenly."

"Wait until you get nice and high," she giggled.

She was right. Andre's weed was strong and I felt myself going lower, easing into the mattress with each draw. My arms and legs felt heavy and I began to drift, sailing down a strange current filled with blue stars. As I dozed, I fell immediately into a dream.

Metallica played gently somewhere, pleading to the Sandman as I walked through Josie's house. Each room was dimly lit, but I navigated them easily. No one was around. I could smell something burning, something sweet. Lights flickered in the kitchen, beckoning me forward.

The madman in the corner was naked, crouching with a knife between his teeth. Dirty, lank hair fell onto his shoulders and obscured his features, but I could hear him making tiny mewling sounds, like a kitten in distress. He pulled the knife from his mouth and turned it in his hands, inspecting it.

I began slowly backing away, gripping the door frame for support.

"I found it in the closet," the man said without

looking up. "Do you like it? Do you like the way it burns?"

I turned away from the kitchen, ready to go back down the hall, and woke up in Josie's bed with flames licking at my fingertips.

"Jesus!" Josie screamed, flapping at the fire with a pillow until it was extinguished.

I pushed myself up into a sitting position, plunging two fingers into my mouth to curb the sting. The room reeked of smoke and burnt cloth; a jagged line of blackened cotton ran the length of the comforter where I had lain.

"How the hell did that happen?" Josie panted, sitting back on her heels to look at me in concern.

I pulled my fingers from my mouth, expecting to see the skin dangling from them in scarlet ribbons, but they were only slightly reddened. "I don't know, I passed out and had this fucked up dream, and I woke up on fire."

"Is that your lighter?"

I looked down at the silver Zippo lying beside me on the bed. "No. I used it earlier to light a cigarette, but I put it back on your dresser where I found it."

Josie shook her head. "It's not mine."

"Maybe it's Michelle's?"

Josie shrugged. We were way too high to deal with it all.

"Are you okay?" she asked.

"Yeah. Kinda freaked. Really thirsty."

She laughed, and then I started laughing, and we couldn't stop. It was so absurd, the entire situation. She grabbed my hand and pulled me toward the kitchen.

"Come on, let's get some white grape juice. It's

incredible when you're high."

***

A week later, Josie came to work looking like she hadn't slept in days. Purple half-moons circled her eyes; she looked depleted.

"Hey. What's going on? You look like shit," I said.

"Michelle moved out. We had a huge fight last night."

"Fuck. I'm sorry."

"It's been coming for a long time," Josie said dismissively. Then, "Do you wanna move in with me?"

***

My father put up a weak fight when I told him I was moving out. It took a promise to come by and help him with the housework twice a week to get him on board, something I was happy to do if it meant I could have a place of my own.

Michelle's old room was spacious, with an ancient fireplace and a deep closet. All the better to hide my gin in.

Josie helped me haul my stuff upstairs, and even gave me a set of brass stars of my own to hang from the ceiling. I set up my bed—a cheap, simple frame that was put to shame by Josie's four-poster beauty—and we celebrated with cold beers while the season's first snow fell outside the window.

I only thought about the dream a few times that night.

The next day, I met one of our downstairs neighbors: Lisa, the nurse who promised she would be up for a smoke soon. She was a tiny woman with a cloud of dark hair and kind brown eyes. She looked exhausted but seemed nice enough, apologizing for her husband's absence.

"He's a truck driver, so he's not home much," Lisa explained.

Her half of the house was tidy but crowded, stuffed full of furniture and books. Every wall held framed photos, but I didn't step too far over the threshold to check them out; the entire place held the eye-watering stink of a hospital. Lisa herself was still wearing her scrubs, which, I noted with an inner gag, were streaked with blood near the hip.

Josie also gave me a tour of the home's attic and basement. The house was elderly, with an old-fashioned trash chute connecting our apartment to Lisa's. The opening was in a small mudroom off the kitchen, and it led all the way down to the basement, where the trash bags dropped into a massive receptacle on wheels. I'd never seen anything like it.

"Just make sure you don't put any liquid into the trash," Josie warned me that first day. "Michelle threw away half a soda and it leaked all over the basement and the landlord had to call an exterminator out here. Made us pay for it, too, the bastard."

I promised I would be careful and made a mental note never to go into the basement alone. It was the creepiest room I'd ever been in, with stone walls and a hard-packed dirt floor. A lone, tiny window filtered in watery light, which barely reached more than a foot into the room. I shuddered, picturing the man from my dream crouching in a darkened corner. It would be all too easy to imagine him there every time I came down.

***

When the fire started in the kitchen, Josie and I were both asleep.

Smoke alarms pierced the night, yanking me into a sitting position before my eyes were even fully open. I had been dreaming about Halloween, a nightmare that combined the naked man and a burning bed, and it felt stuck to me like gum to the bottom of a shoe.

Josie was already banging on my door, screaming something unintelligible. By the time I stumbled out into the hallway, she was in the kitchen, digging around for a fire extinguisher beneath the sink. Smoke billowed out from under the door to the mudroom.

I covered my nose and mouth with my t-shirt and dove in, grabbing a dish towel to douse in water. Using it to protect my hand from the door knob, I shoved the door open and fell back as Josie sprayed the extinguisher blindly in front of her.

It seemed to take forever. Both of us nearly collapsed into coughing fits, but the chemical spray did the trick, covering the entire floor of the mudroom in white foam. Lying in a smoking heap sat a thick book.

"What the fuck?" Josie whispered, panting.

"You took the words right out of my mouth," I sputtered. My lungs felt like they were on fire.

We gingerly stepped through the foam, watching the book as if it might suddenly sprout legs and run away. Josie nudged it with her foot until it flipped over, exposing a black leatherette cover. The Bible.

Do you like the way it burns? the naked man had asked in my dream.

"Does Michelle still have a key?" I asked. I hadn't seen her since Halloween, but Josie made it sound like the two of them really had a knock-down-drag-out fight. Maybe she was still pissed.

"She gave it to me when she came to get the last of

her stuff, but I guess she could have made another one. But why would she do this? It's extreme, even for her."

"I don't know," I said, bending down to inspect a gleaming silver Zippo within the mess, "But I think you'd better call her."

***

Michelle had gone home to live with her mom, but she wasn't there when Josie called.

"She's in Cincinnati for the weekend with her boyfriend," Josie said, hanging up the phone.

I twirled the Zippo around on the kitchen table so that it caught the morning sunlight in mesmerizing flashes of gold. Neither of us had been able to go back to sleep after the fire and reality was quickly getting away from me.

"Who else would have access to the apartment? Could Lisa get up here somehow?"

Josie shook her head. "Even if she did...why? I've known her for four years and all of a sudden she decides to burn a bible in my mudroom?"

"I still think Michelle had something to do with it. This is the same lighter that started the fire on your bed."

Josie lit a cigarette and paced the kitchen as it streamed between her fingers. She stopped abruptly and looked at me curiously.

"What?" I asked, sitting up straight in my chair.

"It just occurred to me that I don't know a whole lot about you."

"You think I did this?" I asked incredulously. "You really believe I set myself on fire? Or that I started the one in the mudroom and then ran back to my bedroom to pretend to be asleep?"

Josie shook her head again. "I'm always doing this. I'm always doing impetuous things."

Like asking me to move in with her. I stood up and grabbed the lighter. "If you want me to leave, just say so. But I didn't do anything wrong. Ow, fuck!"

The Zippo clattered to the floor and I brought my injured hand up to inspect it. A gash had been cut across the fleshy part of my palm, just below the thumb.

"Shit," Josie whispered.

She grabbed a towel and tossed it to me. Even wrapped three times around my hand, the white cotton bloomed with blood immediately.

"There's nothing sharp on that fucking thing," I said. My voice shook, but whether from fear or anger, I couldn't tell.

Josie tamped her cigarette out in the sink, stabbing it against the steel basin angrily.

"Come on. Let's see if Lisa's home. She can sew you up."

***

Josie stood in the doorway of Lisa's kitchen, biting her thumbnail. She was making me nervous, but I sat as still as I could while Lisa cleaned my wound and prepared to stitch it.

"We're really sorry to bother you," I said, looking everywhere but at my own hand. The smell of blood was overpowering in the cramped kitchen.

"No worries, girl," Lisa said. *Worries* came out *worriesh* and I wondered if she'd been smoking before we came down. Too late to back out. "How'd this happen, anyway?"

"She was cutting an apple and the knife slipped,"

Josie said.

I shot her a look, but she wasn't paying attention to me.

"Here we go," Lisa said, holding up the hooked needle. "You ready?"

I nodded and steeled myself, clutching my jean-clad knee. A wink of gold caught my eye and I followed it to Lisa's neck, where a coin-like pendant hung. Etched onto the surface was an image of Mary and her crown of stars.

"Are you Catholic?" I asked. My father was, but we hadn't been to church in years. I used to love the hushed reverence of the nave, the smell of candle wax and incense. Comfort.

"Used to be," Lisa said, squinting while she worked on my hand. "My husband never liked it. Raised a Baptist and always said he'd die one, too."

"Where is Roy?" Josie asked. "I haven't seen him in a while."

"Still on a run," Lisa said. "Company's got him working like a dog. He had to go all the way to Canada this time."

"What did you mean, "used to be"?" Josie asked.

Lisa paused her sewing. "I never was the best Catholic. I tried, though. I tried to be good."

"But you still wear the medal?"

"Mhmm. Comforting, I guess."

The feel of the needle moving in and out of my hand was making me nauseous.

"Are you almost done?" I asked, keeping my eyes averted from my hand.

"Christ, you two ask a lot of questions," Lisa said harshly, cutting the thread with a jabbing motion. It pulled my skin and I hissed in pain, yanking my hand away.

"Sorry," I said, cutting a glance at Josie.

"Sit tight," Lisa said with a sigh. "I forgot to grab tape for the gauze."

"What the fuck?" I whispered to Josie when Lisa left the room.

Josie shook her head. "I've never seen her act that way."

I could hear Lisa moving things around in the back of the apartment as she searched for tape. "Maybe we should just go."

"Let her wrap your hand. You don't want it to get infected, do you?"

I sighed shakily and stood up, aware for the first time of how strongly the place still smelled of disinfectant. It cut through the air as I moved from the kitchen into the hallway with Josie in tow.

"Lisa?" I called. "It's okay if you can't find the tape. I can run down to the pharmacy and grab some."

No reply. A grunt, then a sigh. A sound like boxes shifting.

"That's a shitload of pictures," Josie said.

I followed her gaze to the wall, where dozens of framed photos were hung nearly floor-to-ceiling. Lisa as a teenager, standing outside an ice cream shop with a blonde kid; Lisa as a new bride, holding a bouquet over her head as she stood in a patch of sunlit grass. Another of her with the groom, the truck driver.

The man from my dream.

I moved closer to the frame, unsure of what I was seeing. His hair was shorter and he was ten years younger, but it was him. The naked, crouching man with a knife between his teeth.

"He was handsome, wasn't he?" Lisa asked. She was right behind me in the darkened hallway.

I jumped backward and hit Josie, who pulled me away from Lisa by my shirt.

"That's your husband?" I asked. My voice sounded like it was underwater.

"That's my Roy. He's a truck driver, so he's hardly home."

"Yeah, you said already," I said. I could feel Josie's fingers digging into the soft flesh of my side; she was slowly backing up and was pulling me with her.

"I feel bad about the last time I saw him," Lisa said with a manic little laugh. "We had a fight about him doing so many drugs on the road. He took a lot of speed to stay awake, you know?"

I nodded.

"All I said was that I didn't want him to kill himself with that stuff, but he turned it around and said I was one to talk. Called me "high and mighty" for someone who smoked so much. But God created marijuana. Man made those pills. That's what I told him."

Josie and I were at the end of the carpeted hallway. I could see the front door to my right; the kitchen was on the left. My hand was throbbing, my stomach rolling. The hospital stench was overpowering in the state I was in, especially mixed with the blood smell.

"I told him if he killed himself, even on accident, that he'd go to Hell. He was lighting his cigarette when I said it, and I smacked the lighter out of his hand. I can get real salty when I'm pissed off, you know. I smacked it, and it was still lit when it fell on his arm. I thought it was pretty ironic, considering we were talking about

Hell. I said, "Do you like the way it burns? Because that's what you'll feel when you meet the devil."

Do you like the way it burns?

"I'm sure he's not mad anymore," Josie said. Her voice was shivering, a breath in the woods on a November evening. "We should probably get going, though. Thanks for everything."

"You really think he's not mad anymore? Because I've been real worried about it. It was the last thing I said to him," Lisa said, and as she stepped out of the shadows of the hallway, I saw what Josie had already spotted: the wickedly sharp surgical scissors, still in Lisa's hand and pointed directly at us.

Something hard pressed against the top of my thigh. It began to tingle, burning a cold rectangle against my skin. I reached discreetly into my pocket and wrapped my fingers around it. The Zippo. Maybe I'd put it there before we came downstairs; maybe I hadn't. What mattered was that it was there. I held it tight in my fist, the cursed piece of flint and steel that held the specter of Roy and the memory of his violent death. How long had he burned before Lisa put him out of his misery? How much of him was scorched into this house? Enough to send us a warning in the form of a burning bible. Enough to infiltrate my dreams.

"Do you girls go to church?" Lisa asked, and in the light her kind brown eyes were a murky red, the color of Hell. The color of flames. She looked like a demon come to life.

"Yes," I said, pulling out the lighter. "Let me show you my medal."

TRADITIONAL GOLD WEDDING BAND

BY JEFF BARKER

It starts with the ring, a wedding band actually. Men parade around her flaunting left hands gripping beer bottles. Many ring fingers are empty. Some finger pads are compressed and gaunt where a ring was conveniently removed and slipped into a pickup's center console. Those people are no good to her. Some men are more brazen with their chic materials: titanium, tungsten, cobalt, even ceramic. Those men are also no good to her.

They are like flies buzzing about, offering to buy her drinks, prompting her with generic questions, reciting lines that have turned the heads of lesser women.

"What's a girl like you doing in here?" or "My God, look at you."

Leave me, she says, and waves her hand past her face.

The men, mostly in groups, laugh with each other, hoping to be included on an inside joke they fear they've missed.

No. She buys her own drinks and does not barter her time for senseless attention. Instead Morgen sits in silence and waits to spot a thin gold wedding band. That's the routine.

She grows bored, leaning into the bar, and begins swiveling in her barstool. Her playful hips roll back and forth with the enthusiasm of a preteen girl. The movement looks out of place on such a polished woman. More men crowd around her; this new group guarded with apprehension after they watched the previous lot shooed away with the flip of her wrist.

"My name's Rick." The voice comes from over her right shoulder. "You're giving everyone a heart attack in here."

Morgen can smell the faintest scent of fear on him as he chuckles to himself and takes a quick drag off his beer bottle. She runs her fingers through her hair, gathering them into a bunch behind her neck. When she slides a green hair tie from her wrist, along her hand and onto her hair, she imagines Rick picturing a thin condom rolling down the base of his penis. The scent of his fear grows tart. She sniffs it in, letting it engulf the back of her throat, and then turns to look at him.

Rick's head is tilted with a sideways smile just above a loosened neck tie. His look, that of a frat boy who was just beginning to be worn down by the redundancy of adult life, has probably succeeded in scraping a weaker woman from that very barstool.

Morgen lowers her eyes down his left arm, past a gold watch, to his hand. It is buried into the front pocket of his jeans.

"Let me see your hand," she motions her chin toward the one shoved in his pants. He lifts it out and presents it to her, absent of a ring.

She turns back to the bar and flicks her wrist, dismissing him.

"Oh, I see," he says. "My watch isn't good enough. Well, best of luck finding a Rolex in this place."

She can feel him standing there, either waiting for her to laugh at the joke or too embarrassed to walk back to his friends. She swivels back to face him and sniffs toward his chest. The smell of fear around him has dissipated. Morgen slams her palms together less than an inch from his nose. The bang clatters off of the dark space around them. He flinches, backs away, and then is gone.

Morgen turns back in her seat and finds the bartender standing across from her, mouth hanging open, with a piece of white gum resting next to a tongue ring. She wears a t-shirt that has been modified with a pair of scissors to insinuate her pushed together breasts. Morgen taps the empty glass and the bartender's trance is broken.

"That's one way to get rid of 'em," she says, scooping ice into a new glass. The bartender's eyes are averted; her smile uneasy. Morgen notices a pentagram on her wrist while she pours vodka over ice. She asks to see her tattoo, and the woman leans onto the bar and presents her wrist.

Morgen pulls the pentagram to her face then looks up at the woman. "May I?"

"Um, depends on what you plan on doing."

She presses her nose against the bartender's wrist and snorts a long slow inhale. The woman does not pull away, but makes eye contact with a mustached man two seats over who gives her a wink of encouragement.

Morgen can smell the rot of regret and sees an image of the woman's sister floating face down in a backyard pool, her brown hair fanned out around her head like a blossoming flower. The bartender, much younger, stands at the edge of pool screaming and pointing, too afraid to jump in the water.

Morgen releases the woman's wrist. "You're not a witch."

The bartender leans back to her side of the bar. "Of course not," she says, clearing her throat and pulling on her t-shirt. "Oh, the pentagram? I just got that to fuck with all the crazy Christians around here."

"Does it work?"

"They ignore me, so I guess it does." She moves to the mustached man and asks him if he's ready for another beer.

Morgen picks up her drink and swivels her chair around to face the dim space behind her. There are a couple dozen people standing around high top tables, shouting at each other over the music; overdramatic facial expressions to match their words, conversations bathed in the significance of the moment. They pulse with the joy of possibility, the freedom granted them by their temporary inhibitions.

Morgen stands and begins to walk toward a dartboard in the back of the room where three women congregate in a circle, each of them leaning on one foot, hand on a hip, unaware of how they mirror each other. They look like an interesting group and she wonders what she might smell in the middle of their circle, so she heads their way. She lets her eyes wander to left hands in the room as she strolls.

Then she sees it. The thin gold wedding band is on the ring finger of a broad shouldered man, sharp nose, gray hair around his ears, late forties, twice her age. He is still wearing a leather jacket, despite the overcompensating heater which makes beer bottles sweat and mingles each person's scent making it difficult to distinguish one from the other.

The man sits at a table across from another man wearing a Saints hat. They shake their heads at their bottles, agreeing on the seriousness of the comments just shared. She approaches the table. "Hello. I'm Morgen." She offers her hand and he shakes it. She pulls on their grip and leans into him, hoping to be discrete about inhaling his scent.

"I'm Calvin. Cal, actually," he says.

"I'm Damon." The voice comes from the man behind her wearing the Saints cap. She ignores him, eyes never leaving Cal.

"There are specks of gray in your blue eyes," she says.

"You're very observant."

"Yes, I am."

He looks away, unable to keep up with her staring. "Would you like to sit down with us?" he asks.

"I'd like to sit with you. The other guy has to go."

He laughs, brings the beer bottle to his lips but doesn't drink. "That's my buddy. We're just having a few beers. Catching up."

"I'm a nice guy," Damon says from behind her.

Without turning around to look at him, Morgen says, "Go away."

"That's not very nice," Cal says, and pats the empty seat at the table.

"Look, I need to get going anyway," Damon says. "It's past my curfew."

They stand and whispered to each other at the other end of the table, bro-hug with a shake and shoulder embrace, then he is gone. Cal sits back down in his seat and Morgen pulls a chair close to his, but sits facing him.

"This is all very strange. Why are you approaching me like this?" Again, he holds the bottle to his lips but doesn't drink, as if he is trying to hide behind it. Morgen can smell the tiniest cloud of fear, so she leans in closer.

"Because of your ring," she says.

"My ring? You like flirting with married men?"

"I'm not flirting."

"What do you call this?"

"I'm informing you. Letting you know I will have you tonight."

"Have me?"

"Yes."

He runs his hands along his scalp and then settles on the bald spot at the top of his head, rubs its smoothness. "What is this? Some kind of gag? Damon put you up to this?"

"No. This is very real."

Cal scans back and forth across the room. No one is looking in their direction. "You are the most stunning woman who has ever spoken to me, but like you said," he pointed at his ring, "I am married. Happily married. Little kids. White picket fence. All of it."

"I know."

"And how do you know that?"

"Your ring. Narrow golden band. It tells me you are a classic traditional man. Conservative. Committed. The type of man who has a lot to lose."

"That we can agree on." He tilts his beer toward her in a toasting gesture and finally takes a drink. "I'm embarrassed to say this, but I didn't catch your name the first time. What did you say it is?"

"Morgen."

"Morgen. I was just here blowing off some steam after the game with my friend. To be honest, I'm not ready to leave, but you scare me a little."

Morgen smiles for the first time since entering the bar.

"Stunning," he says. "Your teeth, lips. You're like a supermodel or something."

"I am very beautiful, yes."

He laughs and then she follows him with her own laugh. Her shoulders loosen. The hunger she has to consume his fear diminishes, but only for a moment.

"So, we can sit here and talk, as long as you come clean about what's going on here. I don't normally get approached by women, especially not beautiful women like you, something we apparently agree on."

"I'm always honest. Ask me anything."

"Alright. When you say you are going to have me, what do you mean exactly?"

"I'm going to take you into the woods behind this bar and command the trees to hold you down while I have my way with you. We will bring each other great pleasure. More than you have ever imagined. My perfect body will be your toy. And your soul, all that you are, will be mine. Then, when you are right on the edge, when you can't take it anymore, I will push you to a very dark place. You will be lost in your fear, overwhelmed, choking on your own breath. You will beg me to stop. You will worship my power and wallow in your own insignificance. You will come face-to-face with the realization of spending an eternity separated from your wife and children. I will feast off your fear, and it will satisfy me for months, until I'm forced back to a shit hole like this to find another meal."

"Jesus," he says.

Morgen leans back into her chair and takes a sip of vodka. She raises her eyebrows and grins at the thought of her monolog, perfectly crafted. She has said it many times, and no one ever believes her. That is, until the trees themselves are twisting around their biceps, dangling them just above the wet earth. Even then, with her mouth on theirs, they do not want to believe it.

"What are you, some kind of witch or something?" he asks.

"Exactly that."

He laughs. "Everyone in New Orleans thinks they're a witch."

"I'm not from New Orleans."

"Oh yeah, where?"

"Boulder."

"Then you must have gotten one of them funny brownies."

"I don't do drugs," she says.

He slides Damon's abandoned beer toward him and starts on it. "Why pick a guy like me?"

"I told you, the ring. Let's call it a curse. You have

the most to lose. That makes the fear even greater."

"I have to tell you, as damn sexy as you are, you're not very good at sales."

She leans closer to him and puts her hand on his inner thigh. Then she rests her breasts on him and tongues the base of his neck. She stays there, next to him, well beyond the lick, smelling him. The fear grows thick and moist, hanging dense in the air between them. The fine hairs on the back of her own neck stand at attention, vibrating, longing to be fed. Her toes curl against the inside of her boots and she lets out a warm moan onto his neck.

Cal rests back in his chair to put some space between them. "So you're saying you picked me because I have the most traditional wedding ring. That's it? Has nothing to do with me at all?"

"That's true." She clears her throat and stretches her mouth, wanting to devour the air and take in his growing fear, which is now almost visibly crawling up and down his skin.

"Just my lucky day, I guess."

"Both of us are very lucky to have found each other."

Cal hesitates and begins looking around the room. Morgen is afraid he is crawling out of their shared perversion for each other to a place where he may have the courage to walk away from her.

She lifts her rear and pulls a phone from her back pants pocket. Then she swipes the screen and slides the phone across the table to Cal. She watches the bright light dig deep into the wrinkles around his eyes while he swipes through her vulgar exotic photos. They are a desecration, a vile glutton of pleasure. She only brings them out when she feels her prey slipping away, and when she does, the deal is always sealed.

After a long moment of swiping through the collection of images, Cal looks over his shoulders to make sure no one is standing behind him. Then he returns this attention to the photos, studying them longer and with even more enthusiasm than many men in his previous position.

Cal clicks the phone off and puts it on the table, his face returning to shadow. "What you are proposing will ruin my life?"

"Yes, even more than you know."

"And how many men have you done this to?

"Many."

He lets out a long exhale of stale fear. It twists and curls between them. Morgen fights the urge to jump on the table and lap it up like a panting puppy.

"Are you ready to worship this body?" she asks.

"I'm not sure I have a choice."

Cal stands and empties the cash from his wallet onto the table, then follows Morgen out of the bar. The door swings closed, sealing the music and mumbled conversations behind them. She holds his sweating hand and leads him along the side of the building, beyond the dumpster in the back parking lot, into the shin high wet grass of a Louisiana fall. They lift their knees to hike deeper into the darkness toward the clicking and croaking of a forest alive with thousands of insect voices, all crying out to avoid demise.

She steps on the bottom rungs of a barbed wire fence and pulls up on the top cables, making a space for Cal to crawl through. When the fence snaps back into place behind them, he turns to her. "I'm scared," he says.

"Can I leave? This was a mistake."

She slides her hands into both of his front pockets, so very close to him. She says, "Yes. You may leave."

But he doesn't leave. He follows her deeper into the woods, the darkness swallowing them, moonlight striping their path with shadows.

They come to a cleared section of dirt between two large trees and she tells him to stop. She faces him and takes off her top, standing before him in a lacy bra. Her body is sharp and soft, lean and rounded. Cal's desire for her begins to grow into something nearly solid between them. It mingles with his fear and becomes sour. Morgen salivates.

"Is this the body you want to worship tonight?" she asks.

He nods.

"Say it, then," she yells. They are a great distance from the bar where no one can hear them.

"That is the body I want to worship," he says.

"Louder."

"That is the body I want to worship."

Her eyes roll up into her lids, pleasure beginning to engulf her.

The two trees reach down to him and twist around his wrists, climbing up his forearms like snakes nestling into his armpits. The trees pull his arms wide and lift him off the ground, the tips of his shoes brush the dirt as he dangles.

Cal cries out, "Oh my God."

"Yes," she says. "You are right. Call for me."

His screams echo in the forest, tiny feet scattering in every direction.

"Your fear is so beautiful. It feels wonderful to have

your terror inside me." Morgen begins to shake, tears rolling down her cheeks.

Just as she reaches behind her back to unclasp her bra, a snake springs from the ground and strikes her bare stomach like a bolt of lightning. She grabs her abdomen, a pained and confused look on her face.

Then another snake leaps from the ground and buries fangs into her just above the lacy bra where her breasts protrude. She swats at the air, the snake already back on the ground. Then both snakes spring into the air at the same time and latch onto her stomach, this time not letting go. She bats at them and twists her hips, writhing in place. Her movements begin to slow and the surprised look on her face turns into a heavy droop. She falls to her knees, pulling on the snakes but they will not relent.

"What?" she mumbles.

Cal snaps his fingers and the trees transport him back to the ground, untwisting the length of his arms and releasing him. He brushes himself off and walks to Morgen. She is slumped on the ground, too weak to remain on her knees, venom racing through her veins. She looks up at Cal's face and tries to talk, but the muscles in her jaw are paralyzed.

Cal snaps his fingers and the two snakes release her and slither away into the darkness.

"You should have stayed in Boulder," Cal says.

He walks away from her, back toward the bar, and yells over his shoulder, "I'm going home to my wife and kids."

THE FORGOTTEN ONES

BY NATASHA HANOVA

It hangs from the strongest branch. A red tattered thing. Yet, the taut rope holds steadfast. They go after it with a baseball bat. Loud thuds carry across the meadow. Small animals had long ago scurried into the brush. Only the people surrounding the tree stand witness.

And the fire. It too has a feast. Deadwood. It devours what the people offer and gives them warmth and light in return. Smoke curls up from the flames and drifts toward the thick branch holding the rope and the tattered thing.

All ten people take turns clobbering it. They grip the baseball bat, grit their teeth. Whack. Over and over as if they are furious. As if *they* are the forgotten ones. They hit it until the insides splatter everywhere. They cackle, then swarm the ground like savages. Some reap the spoils right there as they grunt and shove one another.

It makes us thirsty.

It makes us hungry. Most of all, it angers us.

We crave.

They are blind to us, who perch in the tree. Who protect it from people with ropes and baseball bats. We desire something different from their spoils. Cocoa, flour, and marijuana have no appeal to us. Those are brethren. So was the red tattered thing before humans reduced it to paper, painted it, and filled it with sweets and weeds.

People drink, laugh, and gather around the fire. Some of them see us, shadowy visages sheltered under the branches, and try to warn others to no avail. They flee without their friends. Seven remain.

A man draws hard on a joint pinched between his fingers and adds more deadwood, our kin, to the fire. We mourn. Is he taunting us?

The people sing a long string of unintelligible words as they dance without rhythm and stumble ever closer to the flames. We don't wait, hoping for the fire to consume them.

We are not that patient.

We get one night every fifty-five years during the fifth moon to take nourishment. Once, we failed to nourish enough. Many died the eternal death. Our tree lost entire branches, which weakened us all.

This time, five of us descend to bring offerings to the tree. Offerings like the man who, without regard or respect for the fallen, tossed the deadwood into the mouth of the flames. We send our most beautiful to lure him.

We call her Ayiana, eternal blossom. We each pluck a leaf and drop it into the swirl that surrounds her like a tornado until the leaves find their place. She resembles the tattered thing, draped in green until the tree shares its magic. Leaves transform into flesh, hair, clothing. Ayiana looks the way she did when we first took her. Raven black hair flows to her waist. Flawless, creamy brown skin beckons a caress.

One of our other protectors returns with an offering. The tree accepts it and shares with us. We rejoice and our leaves sing like the ocean.

Ayiana steps out from the tree's shadow. The one she seeks notices her right away. We see it in his smile, in the dilation of his pupils. He's attracted to our Ayiana. She drifts toward him as if gravity has no claim on her. He drops another log into the fire. It flares. Embers float toward the tree. We tremble. Despite the breezeless night, branches shift out of the way. No one notices. Not even Ayiana. Her gaze locks on her target.

He takes another hit off the joint, then palms it as he advances toward her. His face contorts with the effort to hold the smoke before he lets it out. The white puff dissipates as Ayiana comes to a stop. He offers it to her. She shakes her head. He arches an eyebrow and studies her. She returns the open appraisal, lets her gaze drift down the length of his half-unbuttoned shirt.

"I'm Jesse," he says with a head tilt. "And you?"

"Ayiana." She gives her true name for unlike mortals, we cannot lie. But we can kill with a touch if someone comes too close to the truth too soon. It spoils them for us. Ayiana has used the touch before. She will have to be careful tonight. Our tree needs this offering.

"Ayiana," he says. "A beautiful name for a beautiful woman."

"You really wish to discuss my name?"

He flashes a crooked grin and leads her away from the fire toward a knoll under our canopy. Then, he motions to the grass with his hand, but doesn't wait for her to sit. He leans back to look up at her. "Haven't seen you at one of these parties before."

She lowers beside him. "I have been here for some time."

"I'd remember seeing you," he says.

"Perhaps you have, yet you forgot."

He ponders this as he gazes at our Ayiana. She is worthy of adoration. We remember him even if he's forgotten us. We make them all forget. Until we need them.

"You're not exactly forgettable," he finally says.

"I hear that often." She shifts, her gaze wanders the night sky as two more protectors bring offerings. That makes three. The surge of energy sends a shiver through Ayiana.

Jesse takes another hit, lays flat on his back, and holds it. A different man and woman stumble under our canopy. The man's hand drapes over the woman's shoulder. Cups her in a private way.

"Passed out already, Jesse?" The man laughs.

He exhales a white puff and stands. "Not tonight, man."

Ayiana stands beside Jesse.

The other man turns his attention to her.

Jesse wraps a possessive arm around Aiyana. We salivate. He will be ours soon.

"You need something?" Jesse asks.

The man is too busy gawking at Ayiana, so the woman with him answers instead. "We're trying to figure out where everyone went. Right, honey?"

Jesse snaps his fingers in front of the man's face.

The man shakes his head and looks at Jesse. "What?"

"You okay?" Jesse asks.

"Yeah, I just..." His gaze lingers on Ayiana's eyes before inching downward.

"Maybe we should leave, honey." The woman traces the man's arm. Then, bumps his hip with hers. Finally, she kisses him. "Let's go," she whispers in his ear.

"Yeah, whatever. Okay."

The woman flashes a victorious sneer at Ayiana. She smiles, but her thoughts are not gentle as she watches the couple. We watch with her. If they go, only two people will remain, including Jesse. No room for mistakes. Ayiana cannot risk alienating Jesse on a chance that she can lure the man and the woman to the tree, so she shifts her attention back to him.

"I know why you're here," Jesse says.

Ayiana's hand twitches, ready to deliver the touch of death. We wonder if he *really* knows. If his drug-induced haze allows him to see us.

"Why do you think I'm here?" Ayiana asks.

With his face tilted toward the stars, he lifts the joint to his mouth.

Before he answers, the ones on the other side of the tree draw our attention. Our fourth protector approaches the tree trunk with a woman. She looks ill, too much libation.

"I'm gonna be sick." She drops to her knees. Returns the contents of her stomach to the earth. Sits back on bare heels, palms in the grass. In the middle of a groan, she passes out. The protector carries her to the trunk. Our first taste reveals a sickness much worse than alcohol poison.

We cannot partake of her, which means some of us will die the eternal death this evening.

If Ayiana fails, even more will die.

Jesse lets out a slow cloud of smoke. "I think you're here cause you're a narc."

Ayiana's laughter floats through the air. Like a solid thing, it tickles the leaves and soothes us. She runs her hand down Jesse's arm, laces her fingers between his, and eases the joint out of his grasp. He watches her mouth as she takes a draw. Then, she places a hand against his chest and stands on her toes to blow the smoke in his face.

He sucks in the air. Gives her an intense look.

"That doesn't prove anything."

"I assure you, I am not a narc."

We have heard this term. People gather around our tree for many reasons. Some for "enlightenment," others for escape. We absorb their worries, sometimes in corporeal form. For our protection, we erase their memory, leaving them only a sense of well-being like we have with Jesse in the past.

Basic survival. It encourages people to seek our tree and makes it easier to nourish, when the time comes.

"I believe you. But you're here for something," he says.

"I am here for you."

He blinks and tilts his head to the side. "Is that right?"

"I always speak the truth. You can ask me anything you want." She strolls closer to the tree.

Curiosity draws Jesse with her. "How old are you?"

"Older than I care to admit," she says with a smile.

Under the canopy, Ayiana plucks a leaf from a low hanging branch and rubs her thumb over the veins to prepare it for our first taste of Jesse.

Jesse chuckles. "That's technically not a lie, I suppose."

Our tree grows hungry. Impatient. Ayiana's appearance falters—her solid image flickers like a firefly's light.

Jesse looks confused.

We are concerned.

Ayiana looks up from the leaf and into his eyes with a ravenous smile. Our tree weakens and her glamour may fully drop at any moment, which may alarm Jesse fully to the danger he is in. In this matter, the drug he smoked has served us well.

"I have an offer for you. One you cannot resist," Ayiana says.

Jesse steps away and snuffs the joint, then tucks it behind his ear. "I might surprise you."

"Oh, I think I am the one with the surprise."

Ayiana grabs his shirt. Rips it open. Buttons fly. She plants the leaf she prepared over his heart. The leaf's mid rib breaks from the veins and pierces his flesh.

That first taste…

…is heaven.

"What the f—" Jesse claws at his chest and struggles to pry the leaf off, but it has already absorbed into his skin like a tattoo. He is ours now.

There are many ways to bring offering to the tree. Ayiana's method allows us to savor these rare moments when we take nourishment. She drops some of her glamour. From the waist down, a skirt of green leaves sways with her movement as she approaches him. He stumbles backward and lands against the tree trunk. The surface softens like mud beneath him to hold him in place.

A leaf falls from Ayiana's skirt and floats toward Jesse. With wide eyes, he watches it fly toward his exposed flesh. He knows what happens next and fights against the tree. The leaf lands on his stomach, attaches itself, and sinks into him.

Endorphins saturate him.

Ayiana's eyes lower to half-slits. More leaves fly toward Jesse. A jade swarm. Yet, Jesse doesn't scream. He growls. He swats at the leaves and knocks some away, but not enough. We admire his spirit and decide to add him as a protector even though he throws angry glares at Ayiana.

She is almost returned to the tree. Most of her leaves flutter around Jesse. He grows weak as they cover him. He is draped in green, head to toe, and once again we are reminded of the red tattered thing. The tree trunk softens even more. Jesse sinks into it and disappears like deadwood into a fire. The whole tree shudders.

Jesse sits on the strongest branch, a pale reflection of his former self. He feeds our tree well and we lose fewer than expected. He is spite-filled, but like all before him, he will relinquish his human desires, embrace our ways, and bring offerings to our tree.

Sunlight peeks over the horizon. We are satisfied. Ready for our long sleep.

Please visit us sometime.

Jesse waits.

THE RUBY OF LIFE

BY SIPORA COFFELT

On my tenth birthday, Grandfather Hawke Iskandar called me to his office. My fifteen-year-old cousin York already sat in one of the brown leather chairs, sullen and sneering. I hated York.

Hawke went to the wall safe behind the big Modigliani print, blocking my view with his back. He took something out of the safe and beckoned me, then placed a pendant on a gold chain around my neck.

"The Ruby of Life. So beautiful. All Iskandar women wear it for a moment beginning on their tenth birthday. Now is your time."

Warm against my flat chest was a brilliant red stone as large as my palm. I lowered my chin to gaze at it, smiling, with tears hot behind my eyes.

Hawke tapped the Ruby with a trembling finger. "Your cousin Gadriel's father, curse him, stole it. I followed him and brought the Ruby home." He took a curved penknife and scratched me below the collarbone. A drop of blood welled, red like the pendant. The Ruby gurgled at the cut.

"What's it doing?" Panicked, I yanked on the chain to pull the stone away.

"No, no, let it. The Ruby of Life takes a few drops of blood, just enough to keep it alive. You mustn't mind."

Motionless, gooseflesh breaking out on my arms and legs, I barely heard Hawke tell the tale. How he'd followed Gadriel's father to the Amazon jungle, braving heat and humidity, swarming insects, cannibals camouflaged in mud. How he'd found the burial place and dug the Ruby from the ground. Meanwhile, the Ruby sucked at my chest, burning like a branding iron or a shard of dry ice. The world turned grey.

"She's gonna faint," said York. "Anyway, it's my turn."

Smiling, Hawke removed the Ruby from my chest. It clung as if its facets were tentacles.

York dripped blood from a deep cut down his arm. "See, Stacia. It doesn't hurt." He stood like a soldier, his hand pumping as if to make his blood flow faster.

"Remember Stacia, you and York must marry. Always depend on him and beware your cousin Gadriel. *His* father stole the Ruby from its rightful place. Mark my words. Gadriel will do the same and worse."

At ten, I'd met Gadriel only once. He'd been nice to me. York made fun of me and called me ugly. I didn't want to marry him.

Hawke must have read my thoughts. "It'll be different when you're older. When I'm gone, turn to York. He will always protect you." He swiveled his head around to where York was removing the Ruby from his arm. "You will always protect her. Now, both of you promise to do as I ask."

I crossed my fingers behind my back and lied.

***

The month after my twenty-third birthday, Hawke died and where the hell was York Iskandar? Treasure hunting in Africa—no one knew exactly where.

The lawyer—a greasy young man named Aldus Kestenbaum—said I was the heir, responsible for everything.

"Why me?" I had never learned to like York, yet I wanted him to come and take care of all the stupid details, including me.

But Kestenbaum gave me the papers, the cheque book, the intimidating pile of keys. "Your grandfather knew that York wouldn't return in time to take over."

Well Hawke could've damn well prepared me. And would cousin York return sooner or later or never? What about his promise to marry and protect me?

Although I hadn't changed my mind since my tenth birthday. I would never marry York Iskandar.

Irritably, I went through Hawke's things. He'd lived a life free of money worries and I'd have the same. An income from the Iskandar Trust. The lovely old brownstone in Greenwich Village and its library of ten thousand books. A luxurious cabin outside Penn Yan within sight of the sparkling blue waters of Keuka Lake.

But the only item of true value was the Ruby. Reading Hawke's secret papers, I learned I must guard it with my life.

"For the Ruby contains all the secrets of the Tree of

Life," I read. "As Adam and Eve departed Eden, Adam stole the stone from its hiding place among the Tree's roots. The Ruby grants knowledge and long life but using its power will enrage our Lord God and He— Blessings on Him—will be tempted to destroy, finally and forever, His Creation."

I rolled my eyes as I read Hawke's anachronistic bit of hyperbole. Maybe the Ruby had powers. Or maybe Hawke invented a story to increase the jewel's value.

Either way, God's creation was safe. I had no clue how to use the Ruby or even what its power might be. Would I let it suck my blood to make me immortal? That hadn't worked for Hawke or any other Iskandar before him.

No way would I waste my life safeguarding the Ruby. I wanted what York had. The freedom to travel, to go where I pleased.

I saw through York's plan. Married to me, he would have escaped the Iskandar curse, leaving the damned Ruby in my care. But he hadn't waited and now I was in charge. I imagined all I had to do was keep the jewel away from Gadriel.

Of course, I had to think about feeding it. Every year on my birthday and then again on his, Hawke had taken the Ruby out of his safe to drink my blood.

"Just a small cut," he always promised. But last year, on his eighty-third birthday, he made me watch as he opened his wrist to feed the stone. It wriggled and slurped like a leech. I gagged, disgusted. Pale pink out of its box, the Ruby blushed a deep, molten red while Hawke's ruddy skin paled to white. I vowed then to starve the stone.

Why not take the Ruby back to the Amazon and

bury it deep where no one—not even York—would ever find it?

Reluctantly, I opened Hawke's wall safe and found the dented metal chest. Key in hand, I unlocked it. Inside was the box carved of butternut wood, a single triskelion etched on its lid. An ancient gold key turned a tiny gold clasp.

The box, lined in musty purple velvet fashioned to cradle the Ruby, was empty. The Ruby was gone.

In shock, I waited for lightning to strike. Someone— Gadriel most likely—had stolen the fruit of the Tree of Life. But when? How? My blood rushed like agony in my veins, my heart raced, a painful thumping in my ears. *Someone* had failed. I hoped it was Hawke and not me.

***

I wasn't surprised when Gadriel appeared at my door the next morning. It was the day before the fourth of July, warm and humid, with the smells of traffic and sugar from the bakery down the street and urine in the nearby alley where the homeless go. All mixed together, filtering through the brownstone's windows, New York City in summer.

The sight of Gadriel Iskandar—after so many years—made my heart flutter. Tall and dark, his features as perfectly carved as any Botticelli angel, his blue eyes flashed a greeting. His smile enveloped me in promise. He didn't seem evil, standing on the front stoop. I smiled back.

"Little Stacia," he said. "All grown up."

"Do you have it?" I blurted out what was foremost in my mind. Waving him inside, I took a step back and banged my head against the open door. But I had the presence of mind to sniff him as he went by. He smelled of coconuts or hazelnuts or toasted almonds, rich and earthy without the sharp, nostril-incinerating odor of evil.

Walking past me into the foyer, he turned and held up his hand, shoulder-height, the Ruby on its gold chain dangling from his fingers.

"Oh God. How?"

With his other hand he held up a golden key, twin of the one Hawke had left me. "The notice of the funeral was in the paper. I knew the house would be empty. Foolish Stacia."

"Why?" Questions battered at my brain, wanting all the answers at once. Here was the one thing Hawke demanded of me. Prevent Gadriel from taking the Ruby. I had failed.

Would Gadriel use the Ruby? Would Earth's destruction follow? Was that Gadriel's intent? But what could he possibly gain?

"Where's York?" He laughed. "You're the heir and you're alone."

I nodded, tongue-tied.

He frowned and I wondered what I'd done wrong.

"The Iskandar heir is *always* male. But Hawke chose you, the daughter of his youngest son. And you see the result. You've already screwed it up."

He wasn't telling me anything I didn't know. Jerking his hand, he swung the Ruby in my face. "This was just to teach you a lesson. You can't depend on York, that's certain. But you can on me. Come with me to Penn Yan and I'll teach you to use the Ruby."

"Hawke said…"

"Hawke said—" His voice was a falsetto. "Never

mind what the old man told you. The world won't come crashing down if you use the talisman. You want to learn, right?"

"Yes, but..."

"Come on."

Gadriel pocketed the Ruby and hurried me as I packed an overnight bag. His Audi A7 zigzagged through the city, through the Holland Tunnel onto I-80. The traffic on this holiday weekend was like a parking lot. It seemed we traveled an inch an hour.

"Tell me..." I began. But he hushed me, scowling, and turned the radio up full blast. I settled in the black leather seat, and worried at questions I had no hope of answering.

***

Five hours and forty-seven minutes later we arrived. Just south of Penn Yan, the cabin overlooked the east branch of the Y-shaped Keuka Lake. Built on a bluff and sheltered in a copse of pines, the story-and-a-half A-frame was a sumptuous three beds and two baths. I'd come here every summer with Hawke.

"Where's the key?" Gadriel asked, lugging our bags from the trunk. He set them on the wide deck that wrapped around the entire structure.

"Key?" I'd never thought to bring keys. Gadriel had harangued me for every minute I took to pack. It made me so nervous, I couldn't think what to bring. And anyway, Hawke always took care of such mundane tasks.

But Gadriel was smiling. He must be teasing me. He had the keys all along.

"First Ruby lesson. You must go back to Greenwich, fetch the key, bring it here."

Twelve hours on the road. Now Gadriel roared, laughing. He laughed a lot, mostly at me. My ire rose and my heartbeat ticked up.

"You don't have to drive. Use the Ruby. Here." He thrust it into my hand, the stone warm. "It will take you *wherever* you will."

"Wait." What about Hawke's warning? Using the Ruby's power meant attracting the attention of our God.

Gadriel's smile widened. "Hawke was wrong. My father was wrong. They thought using the stone was dangerous. It's not. You have to trust me."

I didn't trust him. But I wanted to get into the cabin. "Just break a window."

"Sure, we could do that. But this is about learning to use the Ruby."

I held it out to him balanced on my palm, the gold chain swinging between my fingers. "You use it."

He shook his head. "I would if I could but can't. Only the heir. You understand? Now don't be feeble. I'm telling you, there's no danger. You already know it needs feeding. Nothing more."

The Ruby warmed my palm, friendly, adapting to my will. I could stand here arguing or break out a window myself or just go.

The key to the cabin lay in Hawke's third-on-the-right desk drawer. I shut my fist around the stone's facets, so sharp it pricked my fingers. Picturing the office behind closed eyelids, with my free hand I reached for the drawer pull.

The Ruby went from warm to ice cold in seconds. My hand blistered. I opened my eyes to look for the key and there was the office and the desk and the drawer. I'd traveled a distance of 300 miles in less than 10 seconds.

Furious with Gadriel—for if we could do this, why spend six hours in a car—I put the key in my pocket and prepared to return to the cabin.

But I stopped, realizing I could go to London or Hong Kong or Sydney. I could go anywhere. Stock still, breathless, I debated. Forget Gadriel and his agenda, whatever it was. I was free.

At the last minute, I shut my eyes and willed myself to return to the cabin. I needed to know more.

***

Gadriel must have taken the key from my hand. I must have collapsed, unconscious, still gripping the Ruby. When I opened my eyes again, I lay in the bed that had always been mine. Gadriel approached carrying a tray of steaming broth and toast.

"Using the Ruby will take it out of you," he said as if he knew from experience. But that couldn't be.

He'd wrapped my hand in gauze, which I unwound after sending him a vicious glare. My palm looked like chopped raw meat. "You should've told me."

"I didn't realize you'd take to it so fast. You're a natural. Hawke never was. That's why my father did what he did. It should've been his anyway."

"Your father was a thief."

"No, baby. The Ruby was given to the Iskandar family to *use*. Not to hide away. With it, you can go anywhere. And you can know anything. Who knows, maybe you can live forever. Go ahead." He took the Ruby from where he'd put it on the bedside table and held it in front of my face. I batted his hand away.

"What does that even mean—I can know

249

anything?"

"The Ruby is the fruit of the Tree of Life, knowing more than mere good and evil, knowing all." Gadriel intoned the words, making it sound like something he'd memorized long ago. "Ask it anything." Smiling in his irritating way, Gadriel said nothing more, merely set the tray in front of me.

My mouth watered. Faint with hunger, I swallowed a spoonful of the savory broth, bit into the toast. He waited while I ate. When I finished, he took the tray and sat down on the edge of the bed.

"You can know the secrets of the universe." He closed my hand around the Ruby. "You want to know if you can trust me. Ask."

I knew better than to ask aloud. *Is Gadriel Iskandar evil?*

The Ruby turned to fire in my hand, a burn so fierce I almost threw the stone away. Determined to have my answer, I gritted my teeth and held on. And then I heard it, the ghost of a whisper in my mind.

Yes.

***

Gadriel lied. Using the Ruby to travel and asking my question had already attracted the attention of the Ineffable. Dark clouds covered the sky at dawn. Thunder rumbled continuously. God was awake and this was His warning. Devastation would follow.

I didn't need to understand the Ruby, only to keep it away from anyone who would use it. Including myself.

This was all Hawke's fault. He should've known York would fail me. Did I have it in me to face off with Gadriel and escape? To protect the Ruby and its power? Filled with dread, fearing more failure, I didn't know for sure. I only knew I had to try my best. Then—and only then—would I be free.

Gadriel greeted me with coffee and a paring knife.

"Take the Ruby and hold it against your wrist," he said after I'd finished my first cup. He held up the knife. "You know what to do. Replenish the stone. It likes blood and your blood—the heir's blood—is best." He aimed the knife at me.

I sat up in a hurry, thrusting hands under my thighs. "No."

"The Ruby needs blood."

He put the chain over my head. It caught in my hair, tearing strands that floated to the floor. Wincing at the pain, I looked. Gadriel, damn him, was right. The Ruby seemed diminished. Not in any way I could describe—not paler, not smaller, not dimmer yet *somehow*—less. But it wasn't getting my blood.

I got off the bed, grabbing the knife from Gadriel's hands. "Take it." Pulling the chain back over my head, I shoved the Ruby at him. He clasped it, surprise on his face, and with a quick swipe, I slashed a bloody scratch across his wrist.

The Ruby sucked at him like a babe on its mother's teat, the gurgling, swallowing sounds dreadful in the quiet room. The look on Gadriel's face changed from surprise to obscene delight.

"Stacia." He breathed my name and everything within me revolted. Disgust filled me as the Ruby absorbed his lifeforce. The jewel was now everything it had been and more. Gadriel was diminished.

I knew then what I'd have to do.

Hawke kept guns in the cabin. To kill wolves, he'd

said and maybe wolves still roamed the woods around Keuka Lake. I went through the cabin keys, looking for the one that fit the gun cabinet. The Ruby whispered, a continual susurration in my brain like an unreachable itch.

The only way to free myself from Gadriel was to kill him.

***

It took a while to understand that the Ruby's thoughts gradually supplanted my own. I asked it, "You live on Gadriel's blood. Why do you want to kill him?"

It answered. *Blood is good but death is delicious.*

Everything in me answered yes. Those words, like golden chains, connected me to it. Heir to the Ruby, I was its prisoner. Divine talisman, the Ruby was mine. It needed more than my blood to exercise its power. Without me, it had no hands or feet, eyes or ears, thought or consciousness.

Hawke had refused the Ruby and locked it in a box. York retreated from the power by running away while Gadriel ran toward it—wanting it, loving it.

I'd be the first truly free Iskandar and accept its power. I'd live the paradox—escape it by using it wisely and well.

As my reward, the Ruby tried teaching me the fullness of the universe. The compendium of the Tree of Life swamped my mind—fast, furious—until I had only one conscious thought left.

Gadriel planned to kill me.

With every fiber of my being I knew my time was running out. Gadriel had planned this all along. He stole into the Greenwich brownstone and swiped the

Ruby while I buried Hawke. Now, he would kill me, my death making York the heir. Gadriel would find him, ensnare him, kill him. Unless I murdered Gadriel first.

The better solution was to destroy the stone, to take a hammer and smash it. But its voice, rustling like rats in my brain, insisted that God would undo Creation rather than permit the Ruby's destruction. Lies, perhaps. I couldn't take the chance.

"What're you doing?" Gadriel asked.

"Looking for Hawke's Winchester. The .30-30."

"Killing something big, are you?" Gadriel laughed like he always did. Entranced by his good looks and politeness, I once thought he liked me. Now I saw him for what he was—smarmy and sneering and false. I couldn't stop seeing the expression on his face when the Ruby sucked at him. The memory made me want to throw up.

Unable to laugh, I said, "Hahaha. Yes, something big." And I pointed the rifle at him.

***

Blood was everywhere. I placed the Ruby on the wound in Gadriel's chest and then in the pool of blood beneath him, and let the stone drink its fill.

Killing him rid the world of an evil man. I'd done the right thing and shouldn't—*wouldn't*—doubt or feel guilt. Destroying Gadriel was a good thing, like killing an enemy in war or executing a murderer.

I removed all traces of myself from inside the cabin. After locking up, I left Gadriel's car parked outside, took my overnight bag from the deck, and returned to Greenwich the only way I knew how.

***

253

I spent a week testing the Ruby. It took me to Paris where I ate lunch on the rue des Grands Augustins. Then dinner on Krung Kasem Road in Bangkok. I visited the Taj Mahal, Stonehenge, the Grand Canyon. But the stone could not take me back in time or into the future. It took me to my bedroom when I asked to go to the Garden of Eden.

After a couple of trips, I learned to never let the Ruby touch my skin. But there was no escaping the after-effects. Constant headaches plagued me. Blood leaked from my ears or nose at inconvenient times. Pressure, like steel bands tightening around my chest, grew to an intolerable pain. Unless I traveled, I slept.

In between times, I asked every question I could think of. Some the Ruby answered without hesitation. Like Google, it gave me facts or options or opinions. But when I asked for the secrets of the Universe—do quarks exist, is fusion possible, how will the world end—the Ruby was as cryptic as any sybil.

"How long will it take for someone to discover Gadriel's body?" I asked.

This the Ruby answered with questions. *A day? A week? Never?*

"Where is York?" But it had no response, silent for once, and I took comfort in the fact that it didn't know everything.

I fed the Ruby my blood, cutting my wrist, repulsed by my uncontrollable and unwanted ecstasy. Until one night, roaming the back alleys of New Orleans, I killed a homeless man and, shameless, let the Ruby drink his blood. Murder was surely less an evil than the Ruby's orgasmic suck of my veins.

After a month of testing, I returned the Ruby to its

place in the wooden box, in the metal box, in the wall safe. Grief overwhelmed me. Our time together, short as it was, had enmeshed us, and its emotions were mine.

Don't lock me away. Like a djinn in a bottle or a man in a dungeon, the Ruby feared the heir would forget for all time. And that meant it would never emerge into daylight again.

Blood red tears fell from my eyes. I sorrowed more in that moment of locking the wall safe than I had at any time for Hawke. But the stone spelled danger and using it was too big a risk.

With it, I stored away the secret papers. Whoever found it—*if* it was ever found—must have Hawke's warnings.

I called the lawyer Kestenbaum. "Sell the brownstone."

He argued with me, but I was firm. I would take the proceeds of the sale and go—I didn't know where. Somewhere I could live my life in peace. I didn't want funds from the Iskandar Trust. I wanted nothing to do with the Iskandar legacy. I understood now, why Gadriel's father had taken the Ruby and buried it in the Amazon. He must've used the stone, learned its vile secrets. I should do something like that, but I didn't dare touch it again. If I did, how could I let it go?

The Ruby's taste for human blood had become mine. I yearned to kill again, to bathe in blood. I dreamed of York dead. I longed to give the Ruby the reward of my blood, to feel its drawing mouth on my skin.

Every waking hour, I fought the urge to take Hawke's Glock and shoot Kestenbaum or the Grub

Hub delivery guy or the girl who came to clean on Thursdays. I grappled with myself, ignoring the guns and knives and garrotes I might use on some stranger unlucky enough to pass by me on a dark and lonely street.

These were not my thoughts.

I paced the floor at night and knew I might never sleep again.

***

York came back to New York. Kestenbaum might have told him I was selling the brownstone. Maybe he'd been in the city all along. I didn't know where he'd been, but I guessed why he returned.

He burst through the front door, tall and too slender, his black hair too long, his face tanned but haggard. "Where is it?" He shook as if a terrible fear had overtaken him.

"Where is what?"

"Don't play coy with me, cousin." His voice broke. "Gadriel is dead. I felt it. And the power of the Ruby has increased a hundredfold. You fed it Gadriel's blood?"

"How is it," I said calmly, "that Hawke explained all this to you and not me? I'm the heir."

"Only by default. I am the true heir."

Don't believe him. The Ruby's serpent tongue hissed in my mind, telling me what to think, what to say. Once in York's hands, the Ruby had no hope of ever again seeing the light of day. The grief it felt overwhelmed me, its loss became my loss until I wanted to weep. Unshed tears burned my eyes.

"Go get it." York voiced his demand in a tone that brooked no defiance. He sounded like Hawke. I went to the wall safe, removed the metal box and opened it. All the while, the Ruby talked to me, telling me what to do and how.

Hawke had lied when he told me to depend on York. I trusted only the Ruby. My blood sang with certainty. It would never fail me.

"Hand it over," York said. "Before you hurt yourself. I told Hawke using you was a mistake."

Would it have changed anything if York had tried to be nicer? Probably not. I took the Ruby from its bed of velvet. It murmured to me all the while, explanations and promises. I held it in my palm. I grasped York's wrist.

In less than an instant of time, York and I stood in the cabin, surrounded by guns and blood and swarming flies. Gadriel's body reeked, still lying where I'd killed him, heaving with maggots.

York struggled, grabbing me with one hand, punching me in the stomach with the other. The Ruby made me strong. I punched him back. He doubled over. I yanked the .30-30 off the floor. When York straightened, I shot him, once in the head, once in the chest. He fell on top of Gadriel.

His blood.

I laid the Ruby on the exit wound at the back of York's head, where blood and bone fragments and bits of brain matter had spewed onto the floor. It wasn't enough. The Ruby cried for more.

With the paring knife that Gadriel had tried to use on me, I cut myself and let the Ruby feed. It sucked and sucked, and I knew I could never give enough. But I didn't care.

Outside, dark clouds gathered in the skies of Penn

Yan and lightning sizzled in the waters of Keuka Lake.
Thunder rumbled.

PERFECTION IN BLACK LACE

BY MARK MCLAUGHLIN

Chett Kopesky was a handsome, well-built man, blessed with a high-paying job, an amazing midnight-blue sports car, and scads of money in the bank. He saw his future as a walk in the park...a pleasant stroll amidst sweet-smelling rose bushes.

He couldn't have been more wrong.

One afternoon, quite recently, Chett made several horrible mistakes—the sort of tragic errors one might expect from appallingly stupid people. He had a little time on his hands, so he walked into a second-hand shop that he'd seen before but never visited. A shop called Professor LaGungo's Exotic Artifacts & Assorted Mystic Collectibles.

That was his first mistake.

There, he started looking for a birthday gift for his wife Aaronessa.

That was his second mistake.

He soon noticed an elegant black-lace negligee,

worn by a slender, pale-pink mannequin. It never occurred to him that a used negligee was a thoughtless gift. After all, a negligee is an item of intimate apparel. No one should ever have to wear pre-owned nightwear.

The store's proprietor, an elderly man with thick glasses and liver-spotted hands, emerged from the back room of the shop. He walked up to Chett and flashed a disarming smile. "Hello, young fellow!" he said. "Welcome to my store. I'm Professor Artemis LaGungo. That negligee certainly is lovely, don't you think?"

"It sure is!" Chett leaned closer to the garment to get a better look. He noticed that the black lace featured a complex pattern of winged shapes. "I like the little birds in the design," he said. "Are they supposed to be purple martins? That's what they look like."

Professor LaGungo moved to Chett's side and studied the lace for a moment. "They *do* look like purple martins," the old man said. "When I was little, I remember that purple martins were always swooping around the house, driving the cats crazy. The cats jumped in the air, trying to catch the purple martins, but of course, they could never jump high enough. I finally persuaded my parents to buy an old trampoline at a garage sale, so the cats could jump even higher. That took care of those purple martins."

Chett simply shrugged, and that was his third mistake. Instead of passively reacting to that disturbing anecdote, he should have said, "Stop distracting me with gibberish and tell me why a *negligee* is being sold in a shop full of mystic collectibles."

"So how much does this lacy thing cost?" Chett asked. "It's for my wife's birthday."

"It's worth a considerable amount, but I like you, my friend. You seem like a nice fellow, and your wife must be a very lovely woman. How does fifty bucks sound?"

"Perfect!" Chett said.

Agreeing to such an outlandish purchase was Chett's fourth and final mistake during his ill-fated visit to Professor LaGungo's Exotic Artifacts & Assorted Mystic Collectibles. After Chett paid the bill, the professor placed the negligee in a dress box, wrapped it up and put a red silk bow on the package.

"I usually don't include gift-wrapping," the proprietor said, "but this feels like a special occasion to me. A gift of love!"

"Any directions on the care of the negligee? How to wash it, dry it, anything like that?" Chett said.

The professor thought for a moment. "With all purchases from my shop," he said. "I usually tell customers to avoid making wishes. Especially in quantities of three!"

A quizzical look crossed Chett's face. "Back in school, I read a story about three wishes. A monkey's paw with a curse on it gave somebody three wishes. I don't remember what happened, though. I suppose somebody wished that the monkey would come back to life. Then everything would go right back to normal, right?"

The professor chuckled softly. "You're quite a scholar, aren't you? Yes, I do believe that's *exactly* what happened in the story. In your case, I'm not too worried about those directions I mentioned. In fact, please forget I even said anything."

Chett picked up the package, thanked the professor, and left the shop. He stopped at a drugstore to pick up a birthday card before he drove home. He'd once given Aaronessa a birthday gift without a card, and while she enjoyed the gift, she still sadly repeated, over the next few days, "I can't believe you forgot the card." Apparently, a gift without a card just wasn't enough.

That evening, Chett took Aaronessa to their favorite restaurant—Armando's Surf & Turf. Both of them enjoyed the huge steaks and ample servings of shrimp. The restaurant also offered unlimited breadsticks and tossed salad, as well as a free cake for any table of guests celebrating a birthday.

While they were eating their salad, Aaronessa said the same thing she declared every time they came to the restaurant. "We really need to stop coming here! All the beef and bread is going to make us fat." She was a very slender, tanned blonde, and her weight was always a top priority.

Usually, Chett told her to just enjoy herself. This time, he decided on a different tactic.

"Well then, don't eat any breadsticks and don't order steak," he replied, matter-of-factly.

"Are you kidding?" Aaronessa rolled her eyes. "Do you think I can go to Armando's Surf & Turf on a Friday night and *not* eat the breadsticks and steak? They're the best part of the evening, besides the shrimp and the tossed salad. And the birthday cake, when one of us is having a birthday!"

She then nodded toward the wrapped gift, which occupied an extra chair that Chett had requested at the beginning of their visit. Chett liked to treat birthday gifts as though they were guests at the meal. The dress box sat atop Aaronessa's gift to Chett. "When do I get to open my gift?" she said.

"We usually wait until after the cake," Chett said. "Don't you want to wait?"

"Ordinarily, I don't mind waiting," she said. "But I have a special feeling about *this* gift. I don't recognize the wrapping paper. From your past gifts, I know all the different wrapping papers used by most stores in town. But this time, I'm stumped!"

Chett hadn't really paid much attention to the wrapping paper. He picked up the gift and gave it a look. The pattern was a mix of plump cherubs and winged black kittens. "It *is* unique," he said. "Old-fashioned, in a whimsical sort of way."

"I just hope you didn't buy my gift at that creepy shop owned by Professor LaGungo!"

Chett worked to control his facial expression. He didn't want to give away the truth with a look of shock. "I know I've driven past it," he said with a forced smile, "but I've never been inside. What does this professor guy sell there?"

"According to the sign outside, he sells 'mystic collectibles,'" she said. "Years ago, my aunt Clara ran a bakery next to his shop. She'd tell me about the weird out-of-towners who shopped there. She said people came from all over the world to buy his crazy rubbish."

"From all over the world? That doesn't sound so bad," he said with a shrug. "He must have some good stuff, if people are traveling that far to buy it!"

"Sometimes people would stop in her bakery after they'd shopped at that weird store," Aaronessa said. "She said the stuff they'd bought would make her skin crawl. Ooh, here come our entrées!"

"Opening your gift will have to wait after all," Chett said with a smile.

Their waiter wheeled a cart up to their table and served them their steaks, shrimp, and side dishes of vegetables and pasta. "I'm going to be as fat as a pig tomorrow!" Aaronessa said with a giggle.

After they started eating, Aaronessa continued with her story. "Aunt Clara told me she once heard that everything in that Professor LaGungo place had a curse on it. Like some spooky shop in a creepy old movie. One of the weirdos who shopped at that crazy store bought a dried-up human hand with wax all over it. Like someone had been using it to hold candles! Another person bought a knife with part of a human jawbone for a handle! Isn't it illegal to sell bits of dead people? If it isn't, it should be!"

"You'd better keep your voice down," Chett said in a hushed tone. "Other tables are looking this way. That LaGungo place is probably just some kind of Halloween store. Maybe he sells props from scary movies. If your aunt Clara never went in there, how would she know for sure?"

"I hadn't thought of that." Aaronessa nodded. "Yeah, that actually makes more sense. But still, you'll never catch *me* in that store."

"Have you decided what movie we're going to watch tonight?" asked Chett, eager to change the topic. Aaronessa, a long-time movie buff, thought it was romantic to watch a moody old black-and-white film with the one you loved. So, they always watched movies on their birthdays, anniversaries, Christmas, and Valentine's Day.

"I'm still thinking about it," Aaronessa said. "I'll look through my DVDs again when I get home. I have so many, it's hard to decide."

Soon, their waiter brought them the birthday cake. It was a smallish cake, but the perfect size for two. Three busboys joined the waiter in singing 'Happy Birthday' at the table. Once the happy couple had finished their dessert, Aaronessa patted the top of the gift. "Prezzy time!"

Chett nodded. "Go ahead. Open it up."

Aaronessa grinned as she opened the envelope taped to the box and read her birthday card. Then she tore through the wrapping paper and lifted the lid of the box.

"Perfect!" she said, lifting the garment out of the box. "It's a nightgown! I'd better not flash it around too much—I don't want to make all the other wives jealous." She cast an amorous look toward Chett. "I'll wear it for you tonight." She then looked closely at the fabric. "Or maybe I should save it for the ship. Are we going on a cruise?"

"A cruise? Why do you say that?"

Aaronessa pointed to one of the little winged shapes in the negligee's pattern. "Aren't these birds supposed to be seagulls?"

Chett didn't want to say they were purple martins, since that had only been a guess anyway. So he said, "I think they're supposed to be doves. They're pretty small and made out of stitches, so it's hard to tell."

Aaronessa looked closely at the pattern. "I think you're right. Yes, they're *definitely* doves. Love doves!" A tear of sheer happiness rolled down her cheek. The negligee soaked it up.

Chett then opened his gift. Aaronessa had given him a pair of navy-blue pajamas with mother-of-pearl buttons. "Awesome!" he said. "We bought each other sleepwear."

"Yeah, it's like that classic story about the couple who buy ironic gifts for each other. It was called *The Gift of the...*" She thought for a moment. "I forget the rest of the title."

"It's called *The Gift of the Magnets*, or something like that," Chett said. "I think the couple buy each other some magnets, but the magnets repel each other. Still, that doesn't stop them from having a wonderful Valentine's Day!"

That evening, Aaronessa put on the negligee and Chett put on the pajamas. He'd also bought a bottle of champagne—something to drink as they cuddled under a comforter on the couch and watched their old movie. On their first date, they'd watched the Universal horror classic, *Son of Dracula*. After looking through her DVDs again, Aaronessa decided on *Loves of a Vampire*, a little-known black-and-white horror film from 1943.

Chett turned down the lights and joined Aaronessa under the comforter. The movie concerned a pale, dark-haired young woman, a sensitive sculptress who feared that she might turn into a creature of the night. Her stalwart boyfriend kept telling her that her worries were all in her imagination, but his words did not comfort her.

"The poor girl. She's so sad," Aaronessa said. "But isn't she beautiful? Her eyes are so lustrous. Her lips are so full and plump and dark. My lips are too skinny. I wish I had full, dark lips, just like hers!"

Chett looked at his wife's lips. "Actually, your lips look as plump as hers. And dark, too. Did you put on more lipstick?"

"Nope! They probably just look dark because the lights are low."

Aaronessa found herself mesmerized by the movie. The sad lady vampire so wanted to rid herself of all her dark obsessions, but it just wasn't in the cards for her. She had to face the fact that she was doomed to be a monster.

"Would you still love me if I became a creature of the night?" she whispered to Chett. "I hope so. I wish I could be sure."

He didn't bother to look her way. "Of course I would! I'd love you no matter what. I'd be a monster if I suddenly rejected you like that. I'm yours no matter what."

"Aaawww, you're sweet," Aaronessa said. "I'll *try* not to turn into a beast."

"Try hard. They say every woman eventually turns into her mother, and your mom's no beauty queen."

"Ha ha, Mr. Funny Man. But I suppose you're right. She needs to lose about sixty pounds. That's why I'm always worried about my weight."

On the screen, the lovely artist molded lumps of clay into an alluring female bust. The soundtrack offered up a light and tender melody, all piccolos and violins. But as the work continued, the expression on the face of the bust became cruel and imperious, and the music took on a heavier, darker tone, with booming drums. The face of the artist also took on a sinister demeanor.

"Even when she's being evil, she's beautiful,"

Aaronessa said. "She's like a dark angel. I wish I was *just like her*, with sleek, black eyebrows instead of these blonde caterpillars of mine."

Again, Chett looked at Aaronessa's face. This time, he cried out in surprise. "Whoa! Now I *know* you're kidding me! When did you pluck and pencil your eyebrows? When did you have time to dye your hair *black*? Why are you so pale—and *what the hell is going on with your teeth*?"

So saying, he jumped off the couch and turned up the lights.

In turn, Aaronessa reared up from under the comforter. Her hair was as black as coal, and her skin was as pale as the moon. Her teeth were longer, thinner, and perfectly, horribly white. She hissed at the sudden bright light, putting her hands in front of her face. The nails on those hands were now long, black and pointed.

Chett gasped with horror when he saw that the negligee had turned into a loose, membranous black hide that stretched from her wrist to her hips. He suddenly realized that the flying figures on the negligee hadn't been doves or seagulls or purple martins. Not even birds.

They'd been *bats*.

Aaronessa rushed to the lamp, picked it up and threw it against the wall. She then turned, grabbed Chett by the wrist and pulled him right out the front door.

"I don't understand!" he wailed. "What's happened to you? What are you doing?"

"What's wrong, my darling?" Aaronessa cried in a shrill squeal of a voice. "You seem upset! Don't you love me anymore?"

"I *do* love you!" he said. "But I'm so confused!"

"What's there to be confused about? We're just a husband and wife spending time together! Maybe you need to look at things from a different angle. How about *this*?" So saying, she carried him up into the moonlit sky. Soon, the cars and houses below looked like silly children's toys. Chett began to scream at the top of his lungs.

"You need to stop *screaming*!" Aaronessa hissed. "It's like you don't enjoy doing things with me. Weren't you the one who said you were mine, no matter what? I'm going to hold you to that!"

"But I'm scared!" Chett cried. "Stop this, please! Put me down right now!"

"Why are you being so *contrary*?" Aaronessa shrieked. "I already said that I'm holding you. But don't get used to it. Nothing lasts forever!"

With that, she sank her teeth into his neck and began to suck ravenously. When she was finished, she released the tiresome burden that had once been her husband.

***

The next day, Professor LaGungo wandered through his shop with a dust rag, gently wiping random items here and there. It helped to fill the time between customer visits. Plus, it allowed him to check out his inventory, to see where sales bins or displays needed to be replenished.

He noticed a naked pale-pink mannequin. He wondered: why is that mannequin nude? He then remembered that the mannequin had been wearing a black-lace negligee, but that nice young man had purchased the garment.

He walked to the back room and found a wooden crate with the name DOLINGEN marked in red wax pencil on the side. Readers of the works of Bram Stoker knew that Countess Erzsébet Dolingen was a vampire from his short story, *Dracula's Guest*. What they *didn't* know was that the Countess was an actual immortal person who occasionally needed ready cash, since she was addicted to shopping. Whenever she required funds, she sold some of her excess belongings to her old friend, the professor.

Professor LaGungo lifted the lid of the crate and grabbed one of the dozens of negligees inside. He took it to the display area and dressed the pale-pink mannequin.

Perfect.

WINTER BREAK

BY M. GUENDELSBERGER

Shortly after final exams finished fall semester my sophomore year, Martin Hall emptied and by the beginning of the following week, I shared the dorm with only three other people. We all had our reasons for not going home for the winter holidays. Vince Burroway didn't get along with his parents. Same with Adam Krieger, a freshman who came to us from the west coast. I stayed because of a girl. She worked uptown at a place called Lucy Goosey. She'd been flirty and made a comment during my last visit that she planned to stick around and serve the townies. The fourth winter occupant of Martin Hall was Joel Tammen. I had a passing acquaintance with Adam and Vince and what I knew of Joel came from them. He lived in a single down on the first floor and had apparently spent the majority of the fall semester face down in his books. He had come to Walker University on a Languages scholarship and could speak fluent

Greek, Latin, and Arabic. In addition to Languages, Joel had decided to major in Humanities, both of which came with a heavy workload.

As the campus emptied, heavy snow fell outside our windows. The first night we had Martin Hall to ourselves, Vince came around and suggested we all grab dinner. We met in the common room just off the foyer and there I shook hands with Joel Tammen for the first time. I had no real impression of him—his thick round glasses gave his face an owlish countenance. He had the appearance of someone who had just awoken from a nap: rumpled clothes and mussed hair. Behind his lenses, his eyes drooped which added to that sleepy quality. I suggested Lucy Goosey for dinner but when we arrived, we were seated and served by a middle-aged man—not the girl I had hoped to see. We took our seats in the booth and fell into easy conversation, though Joel remained relatively quiet. He looked around the restaurant as if he'd never been there before. Adam, more social than me and less indifferent than Vince, tried to pull him into our conversation. "How come you stuck around campus? You didn't feel like going home for Christmas? Or is Christmas not your thing?"

A slight smile came to Joel's face and he looked down at the table. "Oh it's nothing like that," he said. "I'm just trying to do a little research on campus before spring semester starts. With everyone gone, it makes it a lot easier to go places and get things done."

Vince and Adam exchanged a look. "What do you mean 'go places'?"

Joel's grin widened. "You've heard of Fisher Hall? The old dorm? I've been doing some research on it.

And campus police are a lot more active about keeping people out of it during the school year. I figured if I wanted to get out there and look around, now would be the time to do it."

Upper classmen told incoming freshman about Fisher Hall the way some people told ghost stories around campfires. They did it in hushed whispers or pretended they didn't want to talk about it. Once those freshmen got some perspective, they realized what all of us eventually did: nothing cringe-worthy had ever happened in that old wreck of a building. If some of the more sensible stories had truth to them, Fisher Hall was one of the original dorms when Walker University first housed students in the early 1800's. Perhaps it had been a majestic, proud building but none of us ever saw it in its original glory. What we saw was a massive, ramshackle old mess of crumbling brick and tall broken windows huddled in woods on the western part of campus. I went out to see it once during my freshman year. The steeply pitched roof above the third floor had split open in places, spilling shingles and bricks into the building and the weedy grass around it. Generations of half-assed graffiti artists had tagged the sides and back of the building with the usual litany of crude anatomical drawings and familiar suggestions. Trees had grown up around it and the ivy clutching at its walls looked as if it could pull the entire structure into the woods. The real mystery for those of us who had gotten past the nonsensical fables and legends was why the university let the place rot away year after year. Countless freshmen got busted out there because they saw a visit to it as some rite of passage, an idea likely planted by some upperclassman. Campus police regularly patrolled Fisher Hall, but that didn't keep people out. Joel was probably right, though; the police wouldn't bother with it during winter break.

"You're going to break into it?" Adam asked.

Joel shrugged. "Why not?"

"Place is pretty hazardous," Vince replied. "I don't think I'd go in. Some kid fell through the second floor last year and broke his legs. They had a hell of a time getting an ambulance back there to get him out."

"What are you researching?" Adam asked.

"It's hard to say," Joel replied. "What I mean is, it's difficult to put my finger on exactly *what* I'm researching. One of the books I'm reading made a reference to Fisher Hall. It mentioned some pretty strange occurrences going on out there."

Vince laughed. "Joel. You can't believe that stuff. It's just crap the frats use to mess with their pledges."

"I don't think so," Joel said. "Not according to this book. It's pretty old. It was published by the university in 1915 and covers the first hundred years of the college. Even back then, Fisher Hall had a reputation. A whole group of students disappeared there at the turn of the century. I guess it was a hot bed for lightning too. In 1868 alone, the building was struck seventeen times. They installed lightning rods eventually and that slowed it down. It was an all-girl's dorm for a while and there's a little section in the book about witch cults."

"And you want to go out there and investigate these claims? See if the book is telling the truth?"

Joel nodded.

"And how do you plan to do that?"

"I don't know just yet. But I want to go poke around. That's why I stayed on campus—to see what I could find without having to worry about the cops or other people bothering me." His face lit. "You guys want to come out with me some night?"

"Not me," Vince said. "I went out as a gullible freshman. I don't need to see it again."

Adam and I both agreed. "Fair enough," Joel said. "But if I find some pretty amazing things, you're going to wish you had."

The snow continued to fall on our walk back to our dorm. Several inches had piled up over the past few days and the main quad had taken on a muffled quality. The snow came down slowly and hung in the yellow beams of the lamps. The buildings surrounding the quad remained dark and we saw no one else as we went back to Martin Hall. Everything *looked* right, looked familiar, but it had no pulse—just winter silence punctuated now and again by laden tree branches dropping clumps of snow to the ground. Back at the dorm, we lounged on the well-worn couches and armchairs in the common room and watched a movie on the big television.

This became our routine for most of the three weeks we lived on campus during winter break. Breakfast was the only meal we didn't share because we all woke at different times. For lunch and dinner, we'd meet in the common room, put on our boots and heavy coats, and march into town in search of food. Most days, someone plowed the paths crisscrossing campus. On occasion we'd see him—a man bundled so deeply in coat, hat, hood, and scarves that I couldn't even guess at his facial features. His red snow blower chugged and huffed along the paths, chucking white heavy arcs of snow onto the piles already there. Vince had a friend at one of the gas stations in town and he'd supply us with beer. Since we didn't have a Resident Assistant to bust us for drinking in the dorm, we'd crack the tops each night in the common room. Our post-dinner evenings became routine too—at least for a while. We'd sit around one of the big tables and play Texas Hold 'Em or Bid Euchre. Sometimes we watched movies and we devoted each Sunday to football. Most nights that first week, Joel joined us. He had a room at the far end of the first floor and we'd have to go to get him. While the rest of us kept our doors open and communicated by shouting down the hall to one another, Joel kept his door closed. Each time he opened to the door to admit us, he looked surprised as if he hadn't expected us to show up. His room had a nice, cozy feel to it. His sole window looked out from the back of the building onto spidery-trees dusted with snow. Joel didn't bother with the overhead fluorescents, he explained, because their harsh light bothered his eyes. He had a heavy desk lamp, which was always turned on, and it cast a wide yellow halo over his pocked wooden desk. The stacks of books and papers didn't leave much room to work. Another lamp—a floor model, topped with a glass ornate fringed shade, stood to one side of a worn out plaid recliner. I'd seen a similar lamp in my great aunt's house once, but she had been dead for twenty years. Joel would take down his coat from a wall hook near the door and then we'd be off. He didn't bring up Fisher Hall again and we didn't ask him about it. Following dinner, He would often join us for an hour and then retire to his room to work on his research.

The second full week of winter break played out in much the same way as the previous. I made no progress with the server at Lucy Goosey and started to believe she had gone back home after all. We ate there anyway and each time I remained hopeful. On Tuesday night, after returning from subpar burgers at Dead Beats, we prepared to watch a Sam Neill film called *In the Mouth of Madness*. Joel went back to his room. When he returned, he still wore his outerwear but now had a black leather bound notebook tucked under one arm. "Where you going?" Vince asked, even though we already knew the answer.

Joel grinned. "More research. Time for some field work."

"Be careful," Vince replied, sounding like our parents. "With all this snow, it's bound to be even more dangerous than normal. You got a flashlight?"

Joel patted his coat pocket.

"Just call if something comes up."

A few minutes after he had left, while I was trying to get the DVD player up and running, Adam said, "One of us should have gone out there with him."

"He'll be okay," Vince said. "I just don't know what the attraction is to that place."

Joel came through the front door just before the movie ended. We heard him stomping snow off his boots in the foyer and then he appeared in the doorway. "Place is incredible," he said, slightly out of breath. "And it's snowing again. We got another inch or two since I left." He grinned at us and hustled back to his room. Adam, Vince, and I exchanged glances. When Vince shrugged, the three of us went back to the conclusion of the movie.

Joel went out again the following night and the night after that. We, too, had fallen into our own pattern: Vince, Adam, and I settled into the common room after dinner and took turns picking movies. When Joel returned the third night, we had finished *Burnt Offerings* and started discussing the merits of a second film. Out in the foyer, the front door burst open and in came Joel, grinning and out of breath. "You guys," he said, "are not going to believe what I found." He closed the door—too late to prevent a blast of snow and cold air from drifting in behind him. Joel didn't seem to notice. He practically ran into the common room and worked at the zipper of his heavy coat. "I found this down in the basement," he said. "In Fisher Hall. Not here. It was down on a shelf in this old room that looked like no one had been in it for years. I saw it right away when I walked in. It was staring at me from a shelf in what I think was probably a closet at some time." Joel continued to struggle with his zipper and I felt a surge of annoyance rising in me. Then, when I looked closer at him, I realized why. His hands were shaking as if an electric current ran through them. He could barely grasp the zipper. We waited and he mumbled something more to himself than us before finally unzipping the coat.

Vince would tell me later that when he first looked at the small, green-black statue Joel pulled from the inner recess of his coat, he felt an instant, almost overwhelming sense of revulsion. The common room, lit only by the blues and grays of the DVD menu screen, felt too dark and closed in. He wanted to run out of the room but fought the urge largely because he didn't entirely understand the origin of those feelings. I did not have the same reaction but I can admit now that I found that carving disturbing. It had been formed from a smooth marble-like rock, but the greenish-black hue gave it a slimy impression that suggested origins in some deep hole in the sea. The hands that worked the rock had formed it into some horrendous, maddening creature. The lower half of the body resembled that of a mutated goat but with large, hooked claws instead of the normal hooves one might see on that animal in a sane world. Its torso, thick with muscle, sprouted three long tentacles on each side. Tense and rigid, they reached out to the viewer with a clear sense of aggression. The head of the thing resembled a terrifying hybrid of fish and arachnid due to its cluster of twelve eyes and slotted gills. The open mouth, populated with rows of intricately jagged fangs, gave the carving its final sinister characteristic. Vince, Adam, and I stood. I would realize later the three of us instinctively stepped away from it at almost the exact same moment.

Joel's eyes blazed. "Isn't it amazing?"

"What the hell is it?" Adam asked.

"I don't know, exactly. I'm going to research it. I wonder if there are more pieces like this out there? Do you guys want to help me look?"

We didn't even have to confer about it. When Vince choked out a "No," Adam and I nodded in agreement. If this reaction bothered Joel, none of us saw it. He looked down at the sculpture in his hand—a piece roughly twelve inches long—and left the room without saying another word. We didn't discuss it, but we didn't bother with a second movie that night.

We saw less and less of Joel as Christmas approached. After the night he showed us his statue, he stopped joining us for lunch. We tried to find him late one morning when he didn't show up in the common room at the usual meeting time. He had left his door cracked and when Vince pushed it open, we saw Joel sprawled out on his bed, still fully clothed from the day before. On his desk, the lamp illuminated the statue, which stared at the bed where Joel slept. His books and papers had been neatly stacked and pushed to one side, making the carving the focal point of the desk. At dinner that night, he kept looking off into the shadows of Dead Beats and didn't seem to hear the questions we asked him. On Christmas Eve, Vince surprised us with an impressive feast of steaks, lobster tails, and red wine. Joel seemed more himself that night—or at least more like the Joel we had come to know prior to his nightly trips to Fisher Hall. Throughout dinner, however, he continued to turn his eyes to the hall that led to his room as if he heard something down there that spoke only to him. Adam and I agreed to do dishes since Vince had provided the food. Joel simply went back to his room and left his plate and silverware on the table. We didn't see him the rest of the night.

By the evening of the thirtieth, none of us had seen Joel in three days. Each of us had taken a turn going down to his room to inquire about his interest in meals or movies or just hanging out. He didn't respond to any of us. Inside, we could hear him talking to someone but he mumbled in a language none of us understood. Every so often, one of us would hear him laughing in there and something about it sounded unhinged. When he had gone one evening, Adam went down to his room and was surprised to find it unlocked. He pushed open the door and found Joel's room much the same as we had seen it earlier. The statue still had center stage on the desk, but it had been rotated to look directly at the door. Adam backed away and closed the door behind him. "I couldn't go in," he said to us. "Not with that thing staring right at me. It was like I was physically unable to cross the threshold." Vince and I later discussed the possibility of destroying the damn thing but never acted on it. Adam's story had acted as a warning. Besides, what damage would its destruction do to Joel's seemingly fragile mental state?

Acting on a whim, Vince went alone to Fisher Hall one morning and reported to us at lunch that he'd found footprints not only around the old building but inside as well. It appeared, he said, that Joel went up to the third floor every night. "I didn't go up there," Vince told us. "Not by myself." We didn't know if he avoided the upper floor out of fear of what he'd find or for his own safety in an empty building. We didn't ask.

Given the rest of the afternoon to think about it, Adam had a proposition at dinner. "Let's follow him. I want to know what he's doing out there. You think he's meeting people? Maybe he's got a townie girlfriend he meets every night there."

When we got back to Martin Hall, Joel's door was once again open, spilling light onto the worn flowered carpet of the hallway. We looked in. Joel had already left for the night, much earlier than normal, and the statue did not hold its normal vigil on the desk. The desk lamp illuminated the titles of the books stacked on one side. Vince read the names aloud: *A Study of Cults, Beings, and Uncommon Occurrences, A History of Walker University: The First One Hundred Years, The Grimoire of the Lesser Gods, De Vermis Mysterris.* "What the hell is this stuff?" As Adam and I looked around for Joel's statue, Vince pulled a slip of paper from between two of the volumes. Someone—presumably Joel—had done a rough, scratchy drawing of the carved creature. Above it, in spidery handwriting, he had scrawled a single word: *myylthgaar*. When Vince showed it to us, we shrugged. It meant nothing.

"He took it out there with him," Adam said. "It's not here."

We met five minutes later in the foyer. The weather had warmed above freezing and a cold drizzle pelted our faces as we hurried across campus. Why had Joel decided to take the statue back to Fisher Hall when he had displayed it so prominently before? At the edge of the central quad, we saw the first faint flashes of light through the barren trees. Something like thunder grumbled in the sky above us. The warming weather had not yet melted all of the snow and we followed Joel's tracks back into the woods. We saw the peaked roof of Fisher Hall first and when we stepped into the frayed yard around it, we saw flashes of light up on the third floor. It blazed behind the broken panes of one of the corner rooms and Joel's silhouette passed the window. We heard him chanting something and his voice grew louder, more urgent. He held something up in his hands and even in shadow we could make out that hideous carving he'd discovered. The light behind the windows burned brighter and a blast of sound split open the sky. A single bolt of lightning struck the roof above the very room where Joel continued shouting in a foreign tongue. Fisher Hall went dark again and Joel's shouts turned to liquidy screams, as if he was trying to speak through water. Then the night went quiet around us, leaving only a smell of burnt ozone.

Adam, Vince, and I got to our feet and ran into the empty dorm. We navigated the dilapidated stairs and bolted down the hall of the third floor to the room where we had seen Joel. The burnt smell was stronger there and a fresh, ragged hole in the ceiling gave us a view of the night sky. The floor directly below the hole had been singed black. Off in one corner, a crude altar had been assembled of old wood. Some sort of animal carcass lay on top of it, its recently spilled blood staining the wood and floor.

"Over here," Adam said. He was investigating one of the other corners of the room and used his phone to light it up. We got closer and saw the strange carving staring back at us.

"Don't touch that thing," Vince said.

We made another check of the room and then the building. Other than the carving, we found no trace of Joel. Examination of the charred floor in the room told us nothing. When we returned to Martin Hall, we went to his room hoping for an explanation—a hint that this had just been an elaborate joke. The room was unchanged and Joel had not returned. Vince went down to the common room to call the authorities. Over the course of the next several days, they spoke to each of us and we told them what we knew. Of course, they turned skeptical when we recounted the events of the night at Fisher Hall. If they ever did suspect foul play, they never revealed their suspicions to us. Interviews with some of the townies who had witnessed us as a group confirmed we had all seemed to get along well. They found the altar in that third floor room of Fisher Hall and the statue too, just as we had told them. Eventually the police had nothing else to go on, and Joel Tammen's disappearance was logged as a missing persons case. No one had a definitive answer. Someone came and cleared out Joel's room and the following year it had a new occupant.

After college ended, I stayed in touch with Adam and Vince. On nights when I can't sleep, I get up and go to my laptop. I email them and tell them it's on my mind again—that hideous carving and the image I have of Joel up there in that third floor window. Sometimes one or both of them will respond. Sometimes neither do. When they do, their emails also come late at night and they wonder what came for Joel in the curious darkness of Fisher Hall, something brought by lightning and Joel's crazed worship of that statue. I don't know what happened to those strange books we saw on his desk, but I sometimes wish one of us had kept them. Perhaps we could have found an answer to his disappearance or understood the importance of that scrawled drawing with its single, strange word: *myylthgaar*. Had something come for him from watery depths beyond the stars? Had it stalked us too as we investigated Fisher Hall in search of Joel?

Last week I got an odd email from Adam in which he said he'd seen the carving again, sitting on a cluttered shelf in a thrift store. He spelled out the details of his afternoon in long rambling sentences, unlike his usual succinct style. Adam said the thing stared back at him from the shelf and he felt compelled to buy it, despite the initial revulsion he had upon picking it up. *As crazy as this sounds,* Adam wrote, *it told me all about Joel, told me it knew of him and remembered him well and would take me to see him soon. I'm waiting for it to tell me more but it has not spoken again despite my pleading. Tonight, as I write this email, that initial feeling I had of disgust has returned, but only briefly; it watches me from the bookshelf on the far side of the room and I will soon go pick it up again and wait for answers.*

I forwarded the email to Vince who called me the next morning. He had tried to call Adam but got no response. "I made another call to one of the news stations in his town," he said. "Just acting on a hunch. I spoke to a woman who worked in their weather department. She said no major storms had been reported and then almost hung up. 'Wait a moment,' she said. 'A couple people in our viewing area reported some freak activity. Kind of a funny thing.'"

I listened as Vince repeated what the meteorologist reported: lightning had struck a house in a nearby neighborhood—the very house where Adam had lived.

THE DENTURES

BY JUDITH BARON

"Do you have everything?" Wendy asked. "Your health card? Clothes? Glasses?"

"I dink doh," Bill Abbott answered, packing his reading glasses and used clothes into his duffel bag.

Wendy looked at her husband and her eyes lit up. "Your dentures. Don't forget your dentures!"

Yes, the dentures. They cost a small fortune, a sum they couldn't afford again. Finding them was imperative. After searching around, he found them inside a glass of water on his night table. An obvious place. He didn't remember putting them there, but then again, he couldn't remember much these days. He took them out and dried them with a tissue. Bad mistake. The tissue stuck, so he wouldn't be able to wear them until he cleaned them at home. He said goodbye and good luck to his Filipino roommate before leaving the hospital with Wendy.

A half hour later, they were home. It was good to be

home again, Bill thought. He breathed in the smell of his house—a mix of Wendy's cooking and potpourri—savoring air that didn't smell like ammonia and bleach.

He opened his duffel bag to retrieve his dentures. They were still wet, covered in soggy pieces of tissue. He rinsed them in the kitchen sink.

He frowned.

"Something wrong?" Wendy asked.

He lifted them to eye level and squinted, his nose almost touching them. "Dey look...different," he said. In his hurry to leave the hospital he didn't really look at them, and now something seemed off.

"Did you take someone else's by mistake? Maybe we can call the hospital," Wendy said.

"Can you take a look?" Bill handed them to her. She put on her reading glasses which had been hanging from her neck and studied the dentures up close. "I don't know. All dentures look the same to me," she said with a chuckle.

He put the dentures in. They felt too tight at first; once he moved his mouth in circles, they settled in. Yet they weren't quite the same as before.

"It's probably just in my head," he laughed. "At least I don't sound like a toddler anymore."

In the living room, Bill spread out on the couch in front of the television, and switched to the local news, which was covering a recent death at the hospital.

"Oh my!" Wendy said. "Hazel Peterson died."

"Hazel who?" Bill squinted at the television, before remembering to take out his glasses from his bag.

"She was two rooms down from yours. I saw her walk around post-op the day after you went in. She was a 'food adventurer' on the *Fun Food* show."

"Never heard of her or her show. Rest in peace, I guess."

"She was only sixty. What a shame! She was very open minded, always trying new things."

Bill didn't think much about it, only paying attention to the nurses he recognized in the background of the news coverage. He cared more about what was for dinner. As if she read her husband's mind, Wendy got up and went to the kitchen, heating up the food she made earlier before picking Bill up.

***

Wendy wasn't a bad cook, and Bill was never a picky eater. So why did everything taste so bland to him? He stared at the roasted chicken, his stomach growling from hunger, and yet he couldn't bring himself to eat much of it. The green beans, dripping with olive oil, were too *safe*. Normally he would have gobbled it all up in minutes, but now, he just sat there, his mouth feeling strange and his thoughts all over the place.

How could people eat this stuff? These were Wendy's tried and true recipes, but he expected better, especially if this was supposed to be a celebratory dinner.

"Are you okay, dear?" Wendy noticed his barely touched plate.

"I don't know why. I'm just not that hungry," Bill lied, and then felt bad about it.

Wendy didn't press him to eat more. She dutifully cleaned up. Bill helped with the dishes while his mouth wanted to gnaw or suck on something. It wasn't discomfort, but a craving to chew on something particular. He excused himself after helping Wendy and went to the washroom.

He smiled big and stared at his dentures in the mirror. They still looked different from what he remembered, but then again, of late he couldn't be sure he remembered things correctly. He opened his mouth wider, then turned his head to see how the dentures looked in his mouth. He had worn them at the hospital too, but didn't remember them feeling so tight. He took them out, dropped them in a cup filled with water and a tablet of effervescent cleaner, and proceeded to take a shower.

The hot water felt good. He tried to clear his mind, but couldn't. He knew he'd have a chance to eat something more satisfying than the tasteless 'feast' Wendy had just cooked. He paused for a second and recognized he was being a jerk. *What's wrong with me?* he wondered. He used to eat Wendy's dishes without complaining. Most nights, he had even relished them.

His stomach growled as he dried himself off. There was no way he could sleep with an empty stomach. He looked at the dentures in his cup and dismissed the idea of putting them in again. He could eat a little semi-solid food, as long as it wasn't too hard going down his throat.

He left the bathroom. Wendy was channel surfing; local shows were paying tribute to Hazel Peterson.

"Need something?" she asked, looking over her shoulder from her armchair.

"I'm juf going to help myelf," he said, taking out the leftover mashed potatoes.

The memory of their children eating mashed potatoes popped in Bill's mind; they must have been a year old then, barely any teeth, and mashed potatoes were the perfect baby food. As he wolfed them down, he realized he had come full circle.

With his stomach full, sleep called. He had watched so much television at the hospital, he didn't want to watch any more. He headed for bed after kissing Wendy good night. Delighted to be sleeping in his own bed again, he fell asleep fast.

***

Wendy made hard boiled eggs for breakfast. No more sausages and bacon; she didn't want to clog up his arteries right after his hospitalization. Instead, she blended milk with berries to make smoothies, just like the doctor had suggested. Bill put in his dentures and sat down at the table. His eyes lit up when he saw the hard-boiled eggs.

His mouth watered so much, he started drooling. A response he couldn't control; he grabbed three eggs and broke their shells all at once. His head drooped as soon as he peeled the hardboiled eggs. A sensation of chewing something crunchy dribbled into his head, saliva began to trickle from the corners of his mouth.

Wendy stared at him with her mouth agape. "Are you alright?" she asked, not expecting an affirmative.

Bill's eyes refocused on his wife's face. He was embarrassed, like someone caught doing something wrong. He put the eggs down. The shells were strewn all over the plate with bits still stuck to his hands. He didn't want *these* eggs, but was sure he wanted another kind, though he had no idea what.

Wendy handed him his berry smoothie. He wasn't interested but forced himself to drink it, not wanting to be more discourteous than he already was. He wished he could wash his mouth all the way down to his throat, perhaps that would get rid of the repugnant flavor he suddenly tasted in his mouth.

"I'm sorry, but I think I'll skip the eggs this morning," he managed to say, feeling very self conscious the way Wendy looked at him.

"Maybe I shouldn't make eggs anymore, they're full of cholesterol anyway," Wendy said, picking up the uneaten eggs.

An image of a shelled, fertilized egg flashed in Bill's mind. He started salivating at the thought, yet the shame and utter repulsion of the imagery wasn't lost on him, even though no one was watching. He craved it more so because he had never had one.

"When are you going to the market?" he asked, as if his impulses completely superseded his thought process.

"Well, this morning, if you want me to pick up something."

"I'm coming with you," Bill offered, which he never did in their fifty years of marriage.

"Oh, nice," Wendy said, eyeing him suspiciously. "Are you sure you're okay? Did you take your blood thinner?"

"I'll take it after lunch," Bill answered. "Let's go to the store now."

They walked to the Kensington Market near Chinatown, just two blocks from their house. A mix of different smells permeated the air: marijuana, fast food and urban decay. Wendy headed toward her usual produce store, but Bill suddenly paused outside a Filipino grocer, frowning and salivating at the same time.

"Bill?" Wendy asked, puzzled by his look.

He stared intently at the balut. His mouth—or more accurately, his false teeth—just wanted it. He attempted to move away from the storefront, yet he stood there, torn in an epic struggle between his revulsion and yearning.

Wendy grabbed Bill by the arm and pulled him away from the store, smiling apologetically at the store owner.

"Hazel Peterson used to rave about those fertilized duck eggs on her show, and cooked them live once. I can't. I don't want to be close minded, but that's where I draw the line." Wendy said, her cheeks flushed and her breathing accelerated.

Bill never saw his wife this animated before. He bowed his head, ashamed for even wanting a taste of those eggs. What was wrong with him? Was he losing his mind? He went into the hospital for one thing and came out with something else. Did they screw him up? What could they have possibly done to him to make him suddenly crave balut?

They moved on and started their grocery shopping. Wendy had forgotten about the balut by then, but not Bill. When they left Kensington Market, he already plotted to come back by himself. He didn't want to, he *had* to.

They dropped off the groceries in the house. The feeling in his mouth had intensified. Was there a way out of this? What kind of illness could this be?

They ate a boring lunch, after which Wendy went to lie down for a nap.

Bill tiptoed to the door, using a cloth to muffle the sound of his keys. He took great pains to lock the door as quietly as he could, repulsed and excited by where he was about to go and what he was going to buy.

***

He wasn't gone for long, and thankfully, Wendy was still sleeping when he returned with four uncooked fetal duck eggs. He tiptoed briskly to the kitchen and boiled a pot of water. He lowered the eggs into the pot, cooked them for twenty minutes in the water, then dunked them in cold water. Though the preparation wasn't exactly rocket science, Bill handled the whole process like a pro; even he was surprised by how proficient he was with the balut. It made him question whether he had eaten it before—perhaps a lifetime ago.

He smacked the wide end of one balut with a spoon, breaking the shell and creating a hole through which he would remove the membrane. The membrane smelled very strong, like a hundred raw eggs straight from the farm. Bill found himself gagging and salivating at the same time. The membrane had veins all over it, something he had never seen. Gross, he thought. But he was entranced by it, because somehow, he knew what was inside.

He peeled off the veiny membrane. Brown broth floated to the top of the hole—the amniotic fluid—and it reeked like raw poultry. He took out salt and vinegar from his pantry and seasoned the inside of the egg.

Despite his disgust, he sucked out the brown broth. It tasted familiar, like water mixed with egg. "Don't get it on your hands," the store owner had warned Bill. "The smell won't go away for a long time!" To his own amazement, he seemed such an expert for someone who was just eating balut for the first time. He spilled nothing.

The opening of the egg showed a bit of the yellow mound, crisscrossed with more of the veiny membrane. His heart rate accelerated, prompting him to peel back the shell a bit more to get the yolk out. It smelled much stronger than a regular egg yolk. He peeled back the rubbery egg white and discarded it. He could see one black eye against the nearly translucent pink, fully formed body of the duck fetus. He picked the fetus out from the shell, visually disgusted by the presentation of a baby duck; but his mouth had to have it. He stuffed the whole duck fetus in his mouth, crunching its soft bones with his dentures, hearing the muffled sound of squishing flesh. The innards left a bitter taste in his mouth. He gagged, but couldn't stop himself. He moved on to the other three, two of them being more mature with feathers. He burped, a pungent and rancid smell of poultry, and poured himself a glass of orange juice, trying to mask the taste in his mouth and flush out any stuck pieces from his dentures.

His mouth felt strangely satisfied, no longer wanting to chew anything. Even the tightness from the dentures eased.

***

Wendy made Bill's favorite meal, baked beans with maple syrup and roasted vegetables, for dinner, but he was still thinking about what he secretly ate earlier. She didn't suspect a thing. He had put the eggshells and rubbery egg whites in the compost heap before she woke. He had rinsed his mouth and gargled with mouthwash to get rid of both the pungent taste and his putrid breath. Wendy would never eat stuff like this.

Heck, he would never have eaten stuff like this. What happened to him?

He chewed and swallowed, his thoughts miles away from the dinner in front of him. Wendy eyed him with concern. He was barely touching his food, again.

"Are you sure you're okay?" she asked. "Tomorrow you're going for your follow-up appointment, so if you're not feeling well you should mention it to your doctor,"

"It's tomorrow?" Bill acted like he was listening to Wendy all along.

He ran his tongue across his false teeth. They still felt different. What did this mean? Were these someone else's dentures? Hazel Peterson was two doors down, and she was known to love balut. His roommate was Filipino, maybe it was *his* dentures that ended up in his mouth somehow, though he looked too young to have dentures and was alive when Bill left. Regardless of who owned these dentures, they had to be cursed.

"Bill?" Wendy asked again.

"Yeah, I'm good," he lied.

After dinner, as soon as Bill removed his false teeth, he retched. He had never felt so sickened by himself. He stared at the dentures, soaking in cleaner, more convinced than ever that they were the culprit of his sudden cravings for a cultural delicacy he had never tried.

The next morning, Bill ate oatmeal for breakfast. He didn't have his dentures in. He wanted to see whether the cravings would return. They didn't. He enjoyed the oatmeal, bland as it was, without thinking a single bad thought. He limited his talking to a minimum.

"Why aren't you wearing your dentures?" Wendy asked, puzzled at the sight of him eating semi-solid food.

"Dey don't fit right," Bill said, spluttering a bit as he spoke.

Wendy frowned. "I can make you some eggs if you like,"

"No! No, no dank you!" Bill couldn't decline fast enough.

Too late; he remembered the balut and gagged.

"I hope you'll mention this to the doctor," Wendy said, looking very concerned.

"I'll be okay," he insisted.

After breakfast, Bill put the dentures back in, since he needed them to speak properly. They left the house at ten and arrived at the hospital by ten-thirty. Bill drove without issue, but Wendy held the car handlebar the whole time, as if she feared for her safety. They went to see Dr. Gooddale on the fifth floor in the main building. Wendy opened her mouth a few times, only to close it when Bill asked the doctor about strange cravings.

"What did you suddenly crave for?" Dr. Gooddale asked, looking amused and puzzled at the same time.

Bill hesitated and did not want to tell the truth. "Um, it's something I'd otherwise consider really disgusting,"

"Is it edible? Is it a metallic or bitter taste?" the doctor asked.

"It's food...just not what I'd normally eat. No metallic or bitter taste." Bill answered.

Dr. Gooddale's lips curled downward at the corners. "Nothing like that would be related to having

297

a blood clot. Did anything else change? How are your bowel movements?"

"Fine," Bill answered after stealing a glance at his wife sitting next to him.

Dr. Gooddale gestured for Bill to sit on the examination table, checked his tongue, heart rate, temperature and blood pressure, and everything checked out. "There's no reason you should have these cravings. Maybe your mind is playing tricks on you," he continued, feeling Bill's lymph nodes.

With nothing resolved and yet given a clean bill of health, Bill and Wendy left the doctor's office.

"Do you want to grab a coffee and wait for me downstairs?"

"The parking is costly," Wendy said, looking suspicious. "Do you need something?"

"I want to go back to my room. I think someone switched my dentures," Bill finally found the courage to tell Wendy, but not about the balut.

"What? Do they not fit?" she sounded and looked shocked, before giving him a knowing look. "Is that why you asked me whether they looked different? You've been acting strange!"

"I am pretty sure they aren't mine. There're some very old folks with dementia on my floor, they could have come in and done a switcheroo. I want to investigate."

They walked to the wing adjacent to the main building and went to where Bill had stayed.

"Hey Bill!" One of the nurses, Brooke, recognized him and greeted him right away. "Miss us already?"

"Looking good, Bill!" Jamila, his day nurse, said. "Hi, Wendy,"

Wendy smiled at Jamila. "I'm surprised you remember my name!" Wendy had forgotten Jamila's already.

"It's only been a few days, my dear," Jamila replied.

Bill smiled at them, but the worry showed on his face. "Can I ask you something? Did anyone lose their dentures or go home with someone else's, by any chance?"

The nurses looked at each other. "Not that I know of," they replied in unison.

Bill took a peek at his old room. The Filipino roommate wasn't there, the other bed was vacant. "Do you know what happened to the Filipino gentleman who was in my room?" he asked Jamila.

"Danilo? He was discharged yesterday, he's fine. He didn't wear dentures, not that I saw anyway," Jamila looked over at Danilo's old bed. "At least I hope he didn't, he's far too young to lose his teeth!"

"Did Hazel Peterson wear dentures?" Bill asked.

"Actually, she did," Brooke replied.

"I can give her family a call, let's hope they still have them. They must be busy preparing for the funeral."

"Thank you, Jamila," Bill said, feeling slightly selfish, getting the nurses to ask the Peterson family about dentures at a time like this.

The Abbotts left the hospital, deep in thoughts. Full dentures cost a few thousand dollars at least, and they had no dental insurance, having both been self-employed before retiring almost ten years ago.

Bill's stomach rumbled, and the taste of balut came up again, his mouth longing to chew its soft bones.

"I ate something terrible," Bill said. "I'm going to take these out now, before I crave it again,"

"What did you eat?" Wendy asked.

"You don't want to know," Bill said.

Bill knew Wendy enough to know that she couldn't handle the truth, so he was relieved she didn't push further. He took out the dentures and slipped them in his pocket, and the craving for balut went away.

Wendy made soup and bread for lunch—food that Bill could eat without his dentures. "Guess we'll stick to baby food for now," she said.

It wasn't bad compared to the alternative. He didn't want to wear the dentures again unless he had to.

The phone rang. Wendy rushed to pick it up and handed it to Bill, hoping for news from the hospital about his dentures. He broke into a huge grin. Jamila told him that Hazel Peterson's daughter found a set of dentures and asked Bill to meet her at the hospital tomorrow in order to exchange them. The Petersons had no way of confirming whether the dentures belonged to Hazel, but were kind enough to help Bill solve his problem.

Bill spent the rest of the day looking like an old happy toddler, flashing his toothless smile at his wife. The worst of this strange ordeal would soon be over, and he never wanted to think about balut again.

***

Bill woke up in the middle of the night with a start. Something was moving in his mouth; at first it tickled, but after a few seconds, it solidified into something. He used his tongue to poke around and was startled to discover he was wearing the dentures. He sat up and put his hand in his mouth to confirm their presence, hoping he was mistaken. He wasn't.

"What's wrong?" Wendy asked, woken from Bill's

sudden movements.

"I didn't put them in. I didn't put them in!" he screamed, trying to rip them out of his mouth.

The dentures didn't budge, as if glued to his gums.

"I can't take them out. MY GOD, THEY ARE STUCK!"

"You're scaring me! Let me see," Wendy said, hopping off the bed with speed she hadn't used in years. "Are you sure you didn't leave them in?"

She clapped twice to turn on the lights. Bill looked a fright; his silver hair wet, his skin pale and moist from his sweat. He stuffed both hands into his mouth trying to yank the dentures out, but failed.

"Stop. You're going to hurt yourself. Are you absolutely sure you didn't leave them in?" Wendy tried to stay calm. "You've left your keys in the door before!"

He didn't answer. Instead, he belched, and something flew out and landed on the bed. They stopped to look at it.

The pink head of a duckling.

This time, Wendy screamed, so high pitched and loud her throat hurt. She coughed, stumbling to retreat from the bed, cowering at the threshold of the bedroom.

He burped again, and a small leg came out. He shrieked, looking at parts of the balut. He covered his mouth with both hands to prevent any more from coming out, but a beak squeezed through his fingers. Then a featherless wing.

"OH MY GOD!" Wendy hollered. "What do I do? What *can* I do?"

In his frenzy, he thought of dialing 9-1-1, but what

was the emergency? Indeed, what could he do?

"Help me get these damned dentures out!" Bill pleaded before a second duckling head popped out of his mouth.

Wendy crept back to the bed to help. She tried to pull out the dentures, but they didn't move at all, as if they were his real teeth. The bedroom reeked like a chicken coop.

The taste in his mouth made him want to vomit the other food he ate, but nothing else came up; just the balut coming out piece by piece, grotesque beyond words. The couple stared at the carnage on the bed, terrified of what just happened.

"Did you eat this?" Wendy asked. "Is this the *stuff* you said you craved?"

"Yes. Disgusting. I don't know if I can ever wash that taste away."

"Is it possible you forgot to take out your dentures for the night and your body is just rejecting this disgusting stuff you ate?"

"I ate it yesterday," Bill cried. "You think I did all this for fun? I didn't want to eat this stuff. The dentures made me."

"What are you going to do?" Wendy asked, holding her own breath so she wouldn't smell his.

"I'm going to rip these out," Bill said, giving the dentures another yank.

To his immense relief, they came out, and as much as he wanted to burn them or throw them straight in the garbage, he remembered the promise he had made to return them to Hazel Peterson's family. They wanted to bury her with the dentures in her mouth so it wouldn't look concave.

Wait...was that why the dentures were doing this to him? Because they knew he was trying to return them to their deceased owner and they would never eat balut again?

"I'm going to lock them up," he said, placing the dentures inside his toolbox in the garage, with Wendy as a witness. "I swear I'm not crazy. I took them out before bed. I'm one hundred per cent sure."

She studied him with a frown. He had a feeling she didn't believe him, but was too scared and exhausted to convince her otherwise. In a few hours, once he returned these dentures to Hazel's family, this nightmare would be over.

***

Bill didn't sleep much at all. He woke up every half hour, fearing the dentures had returned by themselves. He fell asleep out of exhaustion by two in the morning, drifting in and out for the next few hours. He would have gotten out of bed if he didn't see Wendy out cold next to him, she must have been drained too. When the sun finally rose, he rushed to the garage, unlocked the toolbox, and found the dentures exactly how he left them.

"Bill?" Wendy followed close behind. "Are they still in there?" She came up behind him and saw for herself.

Bill couldn't tell whether she was relieved or surprised the dentures were still there. He still didn't think she believed him. He couldn't blame her. Perhaps he *was* losing his mind. Maybe the death of Hazel Peterson and Wendy telling him about the balut played a part in the craving somehow. But what about the balut coming out piece by piece? Was he simply unable to digest it?

They returned to the house, ate a quick breakfast, and left for the hospital. Hazel's daughter would be there at nine for the exchange. Once he got his own dentures back, he hoped everything would be okay again.

Bill placed the dentures in a clear bag, since the original case was missing, and put it in his pocket. He felt his pocket several times even after he had gotten into the car, just to be sure they were still there.

They arrived at the hospital ten minutes before the meeting time at the lobby near the coffee shop. A middle-aged blond woman looked at them intently as they walked by.

"Excuse me, are you Bill Abbott?" she asked.

"Miss Peterson?" Wendy asked on Bill's behalf.

"Yes, I'm Fiona Peterson. Nice to meet you." Fiona extended her hand to Wendy first, and then Bill.

"Dorry for your loff," Bill said as he shook her hand, embarrassed with his toothless talk.

"We are very sorry for your loss," Wendy repeated what Bill said, just in case Fiona didn't understand him.

Fiona took out a blue plastic case from her handbag. She popped it open and showed the dentures to Bill.

Bill recognized the case right away. "May I?" he asked, before remembering to take out the dentures in his pocket.

He couldn't feel them. His heart skipped a beat, but then his other hand found them on the opposite side of where he thought he kept them. He handed the bag to Fiona, who looked through the bag up close to see the dentures.

"Thanks. I'll bring them to the funeral home and

they can try to fit those in. I guess that's the only way we'll find out," Fiona said. "In any case, I just hope these are yours!"

Bill looked at the dentures in the case. This time he could positively identify them as his. He smiled. "Yep! Dank you!"

He wanted to put them in right away to express his gratitude properly, but a crowd had started to form at the coffee shop and he didn't want to do it in front of everyone.

"Thank you, Miss Peterson, it was very kind of you to come," Wendy said. "I loved your mom's show! She will be missed."

"No worries. Mom lived the way she wanted, you know? She didn't waste a single second debating whether she should or shouldn't. She jumped right in. Funny enough, she did hesitate the first time she tried eating the fertilized duck egg on the show. We all told her it was gross, but she was a good sport and did it on live television anyway. She loved it. I can't remember her liking anything so much. I know it's disgusting, but that's my mom for ya."

Bill and Wendy smiled with their teeth clenched. They were grateful to this woman for bringing back Bill's dentures, but they didn't want to think or talk about the balut. They thanked her once more before parting ways.

When they got home, Bill rushed to clean his dentures before putting them in. They fit perfectly. He was able to enjoy his first meal with his own dentures since his hospitalization. Wendy's cooking tasted extra flavorful after what he'd been through.

Wendy took the soiled bedsheets and washed them

in hot water with scented detergent and loaded them in the dryer. They spent the rest of the day spraying air freshener in their house, leaving the windows open to air it out. In the late afternoon they took a stroll in the park nearby, enjoying a perfect summer day.

"Did you believe me?" Bill asked during their walk in the park. "Did you think the dentures made me eat the balut?"

"I don't know...you just got out of the hospital, came home with someone else's dentures and I told you about Hazel liking balut..." Wendy looked at the ground as she spoke, avoiding his gaze.

Bill didn't press further. She made perfect sense. And at this point, perhaps it was best to just put it behind him. He survived a blood clot, that's the win he should take.

After a seafood dinner in Chinatown, they went home, watched a bit of television and by eight-thirty, Wendy had turned in for the night. Bill soaked his dentures in the solution as usual. He joined Wendy before nine. This time it's really over, he thought.

Lights out.

***

At three in the morning, the tightening sensation of the dentures in his mouth woke Bill. He jolted and sat up. He didn't scream this time; instead, he jumped off the bed and ran straight to the washroom. Wendy got up and followed him.

His dentures were still soaking in the solution, but he was also wearing another set of dentures.

Wendy put a hand over her mouth, gooseflesh hardening on her arms in the heat of July, before letting out the loudest shrill she had ever uttered in her life.

JAADU

BY B.D. PRINCE

Emma Wilson and her husband Roy spotted the ethereal glow from miles away. Her heart fluttered with excitement when she saw the circus in the distance. The bench seat of their pickup squeaked as they bounced along the backcountry road. Like summers past, the circus had set up just outside of town.

Even though it wasn't a giant three-ring circus like Cole Bros. or Ringling, her arms tingled with goose bumps of anticipation. Emma had fallen in love with the circus the first time her father had taken her and her sisters to a one-ring, dog and pony show. That summer, she had tried to train their hound dog Bo to perform tricks like the animals in the circus. The only trick Bo mastered was how to play dead.

"Whatcha smiling about, Em?" Roy asked.

"Oh, just excited is all."

Roy worked the windshield wipers to clear the dust

kicked up by the vehicles ahead as they neared the lot. "Looks like half the county is here."

Emma pulled a compact out of her pocketbook and checked her mousy brown hair. She'd trimmed it that afternoon when Roy was out working on the tractor but he didn't seem to notice. *Had she cut one side too short?* She finger-combed her hair, hoping to somehow even it out.

As they pulled into the straw-covered lot, Emma tried to flatten out a wrinkle in her Sunday dress. She'd chosen the dress for their special night out because its tiny floral print had yet to be sun-bleached by the clothesline like the others.

Roy parked where the lot attendant pointed, then came around to open Emma's door. She wrapped herself around his arm as they followed the sound of calliope music and laughter.

Emma recognized most of the townsfolk. Tom and Daisy Miller were there with their four children. Jake and Bessie Tillman brought their twins too. As they reached the ticket booth, Jack Culpepper counted out three silver dollars for himself and his five boys who wrestled to see who'd get through the turnstile first.

A bell clanged and people cheered.

"And we have another winner!"

Roy slid four quarters across the ticket counter in exchange for two red tickets. As soon as the couple stepped onto the midway, a chorus of voices competed for their attention.

"Ring the bell, win your lady a prize!"

"Step right up, don't be shy. Anyone can be a winner!"

A girl with a bright yellow dress and pigtails

skipped by, a cone of pink cotton candy in one hand and a blue balloon in the other.

To their left, a strapping lad with rolled up sleeves hurled a ball at a pyramid of wooden milk bottles, scattering all but one. His two buddies laughed and jeered until he dug out another coin and slapped it on the counter.

As they strolled down the midway, every game butcher they passed did his best to coax the money from their pockets. Roy shouted in Emma's ear, "The games are all rigged, you know."

At a nearby concession stand, a cloud of steam billowed up, releasing the aroma of hot, buttery popcorn, drawing Emma toward the scent, her mouth watering.

"Would you like some popcorn?" Roy asked.

"Could we?"

"It's our anniversary, after all."

Emma giggled, giving Roy's arm a squeeze. "Nine whole years."

They got in line behind a young couple.

"Since you're feeling so generous and all, you think we could get some pink lemonade too?"

The brunette in front of them spun around, her pony tail whipping the shoulder of her gentleman companion.

"Emma? I thought I recognized your voice!"

"Margaret! So good to see you." Emma gave her a hug.

"Careful," Margaret said, stepping back and rubbing her pregnant belly. "Don't want to squash the baby." Her face beamed.

"Congratulations."

Margaret turned to her husband. "John, this is Emma and Roy. Emma used to babysit me and my little brother."

John offered a broad smile, shaking their hands.

"So when are you due?" Emma asked.

Margaret laughed. "I'm afraid I'm only halfway there."

"What about you? When are you and Roy gonna start a family?"

Emma realized she'd been rubbing her own flat abdomen and dropped her hand. "Well," she said, her eyes welling up, "It's not for lack of trying." Except, they'd been trying less and less the last few years.

"How sad," whispered one of the women behind them.

"I guess that's what happens when you marry a girl with city hips," added the stocky matron with her.

After an awkward moment, the popcorn vendor broke the silence. "What can I get for you fine folks?"

Margaret turned to the vendor. "Sorry, two popcorns please."

Emma slipped out of the line. Maybe the circus hadn't been such a great idea after all.

She wandered past a row of colorfully painted sideshow banners featuring a variety of unusual attractions. She half-expected to see her own picture up there billed as *Emma the Childless Wonder*.

A hand grabbed Emma's shoulder, startling her.

"Emma? Are you okay?" Roy asked. "I thought you wanted popcorn."

"Guess I just lost my appetite," she said, rubbing her midsection.

"Showtime! Showtime! Ladies and gentlemen, don't

miss the premiere attraction of the midway," the sideshow talker shouted. "The most amazing specimens from around the world all gathered under one roof."

A small crowd gathered around the bally stage as the sideshow talker began building the tip. Emma welcomed the distraction.

"Here today you will see Jolly Dolly: 650 pounds of portly perfection. She's so magnificently massive, it takes three men to hug her and a boxcar to lug her."

Dolly, smiling coquettishly in a pink, baby-doll dress, curtsied to the crowd.

"Over here we have the Human Volcano. Watch as fire erupts from his lips like Mount Vesuvius."

A shirtless, black-vested man stepped forward, brought a flaming wand to his lips, and shot a burst of flame high in the air to the oohs and aahs of the townsfolk.

Emma felt strangely drawn to the spectacle as the sideshow talker invited other curious acts to the stage.

"Let me also introduce the incomparable Victor, sword swallower extraordinaire."

A man licked the length of a shiny sword before throwing his head back and swallowing the blade up to the hilt.

Emma covered her eyes, peeking between her fingers.

"Down the hatch without a scratch," added the pitchman.

"Now coming to the stage we have the amazing Sasha the Snake Charmer."

A woman with a spangled bra, bare midriff, and a gypsy skirt sashayed across the stage, a thick snake coiled around her waist.

"Watch this warm-blooded beauty and her cold-blooded python tantalize your senses."

She brought the snake's mouth up to her own. Its tongue darted out, tickling her pursed lips. Sasha's tongue flittered out in response, the two practically touching.

The talker's eyebrows raised, "But, you can only see it *inside*."

Next to Emma, a lanky young man with a jutting Adam's apple leaned in, mouth agape.

"All of this for the low, low price of only fifty cents— that's right, half a dollar. Only five small dimes will admit you to see the greatest collection of wonders and curiosities ever assembled under one roof. But that's not all..."

The crowd pressed in tighter.

"...inside this tent, discovered in a village halfway around the world, we bring you Jaadu—the De-vine Bovine! Born with two heads and five legs, this sacred cow has been blessed by the gods. Women all over India have walked miles just to touch Jaadu's magical, extra hoof. Why, you may ask? Because every woman who's touched Jaadu's extraordinary appendage has given birth to a bouncing, baby boy! Why, just this week I received a postcard from a woman in Iowa who delivered *triplets...each and every one of them...a boy.* Hurry, hurry, step right in. It's showtime!"

Emma jumped as the Human Volcano spat another plume of fire. Her pulse raced. *Could the story be true? Is this beast truly blessed as they say?*

"Come inside," the sideshow talker continued in a hushed tone, "and see the strangest sight you'll ever behold."

Then his voice boomed again, "From parts unknown we're thrilled to present...the Penguin Boy! Half man, looks and walks just like a real penguin. You won't believe your eyes. It's all live, it's all real, and at fifty cents it's really a steal. Hurry, the performers are leaving the platform. The performances are about to begin. Don't delay. It's Showtime!'

A man near the back waving a coin over his head shouted "Count me in!" and pushed through the throng toward the ticket stand. Soon, others followed his lead, crowding the entrance. Caught in a wave of humanity, Emma found herself separated from Roy. Before she knew it, she was standing at the sideshow tent entrance.

"Fifty cents, please," the bally talker said with a gap-toothed smile.

Emma stared at his open palm for a moment.

"C'mon lady," barked the man behind her, spewing a cloud of acrid cigar smoke over her shoulder.

Emma apologized and dug in her purse. As quickly as the quarters touched the showman's callused palm they were clinking inside the money box.

***

Dull strands of bare bulbs illuminated the inside of the tent, the air heavy with the smell of old canvas and sweat. A thick rope separated the sawdust-covered path from the unusual attractions perched atop platforms painted in bright, primary colors.

Emma shuffled along in a bit of a daze until she nearly bumped into Arnold Weezer, his hat clutched tightly to his chest. Emma followed the lanky man's gaze up to Dolly, sitting in a custom-made, double-

315

wide chair, filing her nails. Her enormous pink thighs reminded Emma of her daddy's blue ribbon sow when she was all scrubbed up for the county fair.

Well, isn't that just the kind of thing a girl with city hips would think?, Emma imagined the popcorn-line matron saying, feeling a pang of guilt. Poor woman probably had some kind of glandular condition. What does the Good Book say? *Pride goeth before destruction?*

Emma hurried along, looking for an exit, wondering how she got there in the first place. She rushed past the tattooed man and the sword swallower, keeping her eyes on the sawdust.

A crowd of men clogged the aisle, the air above their shoulders obscured by a cloud of pipe and cigar smoke. Hoochie coochie music played on a Victrola perched next to a thick, bald man seated with an axe handle across his lap. On the platform next to him writhed Sasha and her snake. Someone whistled enthusiastically, joined by catcalls.

Emma covered her nose and mouth with her handkerchief and excused her way through the smoky mob, seemingly unnoticed.

Once she squeezed past the rabble of men, there it was in the corner of the tent, the sacred beast. Its gemlike amber eye gazed at Emma as if it expected her.

She slowly approached the rope divider.

Jaadu turned its massive head revealing a second snout and matching amber eye. It seemed to study her as if determining her worthiness.

"You come for to see Jaadu?" A dark, lean man stepped out from behind the beast with a large, crooked yellow smile. "Jaadu see you."

Emma opened her mouth but nothing came out.

Jaadu's handler stroked the animal's back as he stepped around front, stopping at the shoulder where the extra leg protruded. The extraneous appendage was adorned with colorful bracelets, the hoof rimmed in gold.

"You wish to have a boy?"

Emma's head nodded.

NO, she thought. *This isn't right.*

Her body leaned in.

"Yes," the dark stranger urged, drawing her closer.

Her arm seemed to reach of its own accord.

"Come, let Jaadu bless you, bring you good karma."

Jaadu's golden eye glimmered.

Her fingertips drew within an inch of the gilded hoof.

His smile broadened. "Yes," he whispered. "Yesss..."

A hand grasped her shoulder, snapping her out of her trance. She wheeled around expecting to see the thick, bald man with the axe handle.

"You don't believe that superstitious nonsense, do you?" Roy asked.

"N-No," Emma said. "Of course not. Y-you know how much I love animals."

"I lost you in the crowd. I didn't realize you'd gone in at first."

Emma's hand returned to her empty womb.

"We should probably get a move on if we want to get good seats for the show," Roy said.

As he guided her away, Emma glanced over her shoulder one last time. Then, fearing she might turn into a pillar of salt, she quickly forced herself to gaze straight ahead.

They were almost to the exit when Roy stopped. "Now there's something you don't see every day."

Perched atop an ice-white platform danced a black, wild-eyed dwarf sporting a tuxedo and top hat. Except, it wasn't a dwarf. It was a legless half-man, rocking side to side, withered arm stumps flapping at his sides like wings. Penguin Boy grinned and winked at Emma, as if to assure her that her secret was safe with him.

***

They found seats about three-quarters of the way up the bleachers. The big top was filling up fast. Emma sat next to a boy with a greasy-blond cowlick and suspenders. He ravaged a bag of popcorn as if he hadn't eaten in a week. Below them a family of four shared a bag of peanuts and a cup of pink lemonade. All around them kids munched and fidgeted, eager for the show to begin. The closer the house filled to capacity, the stronger the anticipation grew. And the more Emma felt like a kid herself.

As showtime neared, a pair of clowns wandered around the hippodrome track, tidying up the center ring. Every time the clown with the feather duster bent over, the clown with the broom swatted him on the backside. The dusting clown jumped and turned only to find the other clown innocently whistling and sweeping.

With each swat, the dusting clown grew angrier and the children laughed harder. Frustrated, the dusting clown tapped his partner on the back. When his partner turned, his broom knocked his hat flying.

The chase was on.

The spectators roared with laughter as the chase

318

culminated with the sweeping clown grabbing a bucket and backing the other clown up against the audience before showering the first few rows with a bucketful of confetti.

The band struck up a brassy march with booming drums and crashing cymbals to introduce the grand entrance. An enormous elephant led a parade of performers. The women dazzled in their colorful, spangled costumes, the liberty horses white and majestic.

But once the show began, Emma found herself reveling more in the joy and wonder on the children's faces than in the circus spectacle. Memories flooded back to when she was five, sitting with her father and two older sisters watching a mud show smaller than this. She recalled glancing around at the other families, wondering why those kids all had mammas but she didn't. Except, she knew why. Her sisters had told her. Emma had killed her mother.

Although her father did his best not to let it show, Emma always wondered if deep down he resented her for taking the life of his wife just as she was giving life to her. Could that be the reason Emma was unable to conceive? Was she cursed for causing her own mother's death during childbirth?

An image of Jaadu flashed in her mind, the glimmer in the beast's golden eye, his handler's voice beckoning, "Come, let Jaadu bless you, bring you good karma."

The air inside the big top became stifling, the crowd closed in around her. Fanning herself with a circus program, she tried to shake Jaadu's hypnotic gaze from her thoughts and focus on the show. A high wire act was performing. Emma felt as if she were up there with them, balancing between faith and hopelessness.

Before she realized, the show was over. The band struck up and the performers gave their final bows. As they funneled toward the exit, the candy butchers and program vendors worked the crowd one last time.

Stepping onto the midway, Emma savored a rush of cool night air. She inhaled deeply, attempting to calm herself.

"Are you okay?" Roy asked.

Emma forced a smile. "I'm fine."

The couple in front of them each carried a limp child slung over a shoulder, a sleepy expression of contentment on their cherub-like faces.

"Aren't they precious?" Emma choked back a sob.

Roy just put his arm around her shoulders and squeezed.

A fireball flashed up ahead. The sideshow talker was turning the last tip of the night. As they reached the sideshow platform, he seemed to be pitching directly to her.

"Hurry, hurry! Don't miss your last chance to see the most extraordinary attractions from around the world."

Last chance.

Up ahead, the girl with the bright yellow dress and pigtails lost her grip on her balloon string.

"Mommy!" she cried.

The blue balloon drifted up and away.

Last chance.

Emma stopped. Roy continued a few steps before turning back.

"Are you sure you're all right, honey?" Roy asked.

The balloon disappeared into the night sky.

"Emma?"

"Do you mind fetching the truck? I—I'll meet you out front."

Roy looked bewildered then glanced down at Emma's hand caressing her abdomen.

"You feeling sick?"

Emma motioned him closer and whispered, "I think I just need to use the privy."

After a little convincing, Roy eventually left to retrieve the pickup.

The sideshow talker was waiting for Emma at the entrance, palm extended, grinning.

***

That night Emma lay in bed, circus images and calliope music whirling in her head like a carnival ride.

Jolly Dolly shrieked with belly-shaking laughter.

Penguin Boy seesawed, wild-eyed, grinning.

Disembodied clown faces laughed and laughed.

Jaadu's handler smiled his crooked smile, beckoning her in. "Come, let Jaadu bless you."

Emma saw her hand reaching to touch Jaadu's vestigial hoof.

"Yes," the Indian whispered.

Reaching.

"Yesss..."

"Emma?" A voice called from far away.

Almost touching.

"Emma?" It was Roy.

Emma startled from her dream. She was back in her bed, Roy lying next to her, propped on one elbow. She didn't realize that she'd nodded off.

"Did you say something?"

"I was just saying that I know that our anniversary isn't officially until tomorrow, but..." He held up a silver necklace with a heart-shaped locket dangling at the end. "Happy anniversary, darlin'."

Emma palmed the locket. "Oh, Roy. It's beautiful."

She sat up and lifted her hair so Roy could latch the necklace, the silver chain exquisitely cold on her skin. Glancing down, she admired the way the locket hung between her breasts. Then she turned, blinking back tears, and gave Roy a kiss. He looked down with that boyish grin she fell so in love with when they were in high school.

Emma wrapped her arms around Roy's neck and waited for him to make eye contact.

"I love it. It's perfect." She kissed him again. This time he returned the kiss, their lips lingering. Roy caressed her cheek with the back of his hand. Their open mouths met again, their gentle embrace becoming stronger, the kisses more passionate until the two became one.

***

Emma shuffled across the wooden porch before descending one step at a time. Now that her pregnancy had reached full term she felt like her daddy's blue-ribbon sow. The bright morning sun warmed her skin as she ambled toward her flower garden. Her roses exhibited generous blossoms for the first of May. In her right hand she carried a sizable pair of sewing sheers, hoping to harvest some colorful blooms to brighten up the kitchen.

Before Emma reached the flowerbed, her sandals slipped on the dewy grass. The sheers flew in the air as she landed hard on her rear, her jaw snapping shut.

She helplessly watched the glint off the sheers as they rotated through the air and stuck in the ground between her legs, grazing her thigh.

Despite the stinging slash in her leg, Emma's only concern was for her baby. She cradled her belly, willing her child to move.

"Emma!" Roy called, bounding across the field. He nearly fell as he slid to a stop at her side. As Roy guided her to her feet and the shock began to wear off, she felt something warm running down her legs. Emma's heart pounded.

Something's wrong.

The baby.

She glanced down, expecting to see blood. Instead, the liquid was clear like water.

***

Emma cried out, a massive cramp seizing her midsection. Waves of pain radiated all the way around to her back. The pressure in her uterus made her feel like she was about to burst.

"Push, Emma. Come on, count with me," Ruth McIntyre said before counting to ten. As scared as Emma was, it was comforting to have the pastor's wife by her side to help her through this. Mrs. McIntyre had given birth to five of her own children and had helped see half their congregation into this world. She liked to joke that she'd birthed more children than the old lady who lived in a shoe.

After hours of hard labor, the burning pain became unbearable. Emma only made the count of eight. "I can't do it anymore!" she sobbed. "I can't, I can't," she repeated until her voice faded to a helpless whimper.

Ruth dipped a rag in the water basin and dabbed at

Emma's forehead. "Just breathe like I showed you. You're doing fine."

Emma sucked in a few deep breaths, trying to slow her breathing and heart rate.

"I know it feels like the baby ain't ever coming out, but they all do eventually," Ruth said. "Though I must admit, this has been one of the most stubborn deliveries I can recall."

Emma wondered if the difficulty was because of her *city hips* or her mother's curse. Feeling the next contraction coming, she tried to convince herself she was only one push away from the greatest joy of her life.

The birth pangs returned. She cried out.

"You can do this," Ruth encouraged.

Emma squeezed her hand, took a deep breath, and pushed.

"C'mon Emma, push."

She pushed harder, the pain intensifying.

"The baby is crowning," Ruth said.

Emma continued pushing through the white-hot pain until she crossed over into numbness. The sound of the whirring fan seemed to slow and Ruth's voice became muffled as if Emma was under water. Objects around her blurred. The room closed in around her. The light dimmed until everything faded to black.

***

"Emma?"

A voice invaded the silence. A fan whirred in the background.

"Emma?"

Someone slapped her cheeks. She blinked her eyes open. Hovering over her, Ruth slowly came into focus.

"Stay with me, dear. Doc Roberts is on his way."

As Emma regained her senses, a shot of panic jolted through her. She tried to sit up. "My baby!"

Ruth put her hands on Emma's shoulders preventing her from rising. "It's okay. Just relax. Everything's going to be fine."

"But, my baby...where's my baby?"

Emma received her answer as another contraction seized her body.

***

It took the doctor almost an hour to arrive. Emma heard the worry in Roy's voice as he greeted Dr. Roberts at the door, followed by their hurried footfalls across the hardwood floor. The bedroom door burst open.

"How long has she been in labor?" Dr. Roberts asked.

Ruth filled him in on all the details.

Emma glanced up at Roy, his face ashen, staring at the bloodstained sheet. The doctor rolled up his sleeves and ordered Roy to boil more water.

Drenched in sweat, Emma's white cotton nightgown clung to her like a second skin. Dr. Roberts examined her, verifying her heart rate and dilation. Opening a black leather medical bag, he retrieved several metal instruments and a jar of alcohol, sterilizing the tools before laying them out in a neat row.

Her head already swimming, the alcohol vapors only made the condition worse. Her vision blurred.

"Stay with me, Emma," Dr. Roberts said. "You and your baby are gonna be just fine."

Emma forced a smile even though deep down

something told her everything was not fine. Ruth's expression seemed to confirm her fears. Noticing her gaze, Ruth put her reassuring face back on.

The next contraction came hard and fast. Emma squeezed Ruth's hand hard enough to make her wince, but she never let go. Emma pushed with all her waning strength until the doctor made her stop.

Roy entered with a basin of boiling hot water and helped Ruth collect additional clean towels and sheets at the doctor's request. While they were out of the room, Dr. Roberts' soothing voice belied his harrowed expression. "We'll need to give your baby a little assistance. A prolonged delivery can be as hard on your child as it is on you."

Emma had been reduced to a ragdoll, every breath an effort. "Whatever...happens...please...save the baby."

"Let's not go talking like that, now."

Roy and Mrs. McIntyre returned and the doctor prepared them for what was next. Before delivering the local anesthetic, the doctor held up the syringe and squirted a small jet of liquid. After all the contractions, the injection was barely a pinch.

Emma felt her abdomen tightening and another rush of pain.

"Ooh...here it comes again."

Emma gasped and reached for Roy. He squeezed her hand and swept a sweat-drenched tangle of hair from her eyes. "Hang in there, honey. You can do this."

Dr. Roberts retrieved a shiny pair of scissors.

The contraction seized her midsection with such force it doubled her over. She heard the scissors snip.

"Deep breath, Emma. Hold it..." Ruth squeezed

Emma's other hand. "Now push!"

Emma gave it everything she had left.

Dr. Roberts leaned in. "Keep pushing, the baby's head is crowning."

Emma sucked in another breath and pushed again.

The doctor said, "It's coming...we've finally got the head."

Emma exhaled, the room spinning. Roy stroked her hair.

"Okay," Ruth said calmly. Her voice seemed to come from another room. "Next come the shoulders. Take a couple deep breaths and then I want one more big push."

She inhaled deeply, once, twice, on the third inhalation she held it and pushed with every last ounce of her strength until she heard a wet, slippery sound and felt an enormous release. Emma sank back into the bed, her energy spent, yet delirious with joy.

As she labored to catch her breath she gazed up at Roy, his smiling face going in and out of focus, finally distorting. She closed her eyes, her body wanting nothing more than to sleep.

Then she heard her firstborn's cries—the most beautiful sound she'd ever heard. She opened her eyes. Ruth, teary eyed, held the baby wrapped in a white towel.

Emma reached for her child.

Ruth, almost reluctantly, handed the infant to her.

Emma's heart, once bursting with joy, skipped a beat as she gazed into the infant's amber eyes and realized that its cries were coming from both its mouths.

CORA'S EYES

BY H.R. BOLDWOOD

From the missives of Emmaline McGowan

16 October, 1782
Baltimore

Dearest Margaret,

Would that I could be seated next to you upon our old porch swing, laughing at one of Papa's childhood tales, or reminiscing of better times. In truth, my heart aches for Papa's loss, and I yearn for your companionship more with each passing day. Regrettably, my search for employment in this masculine world has taken much longer than anticipated.

It is apparent that by virtue of my sex, I am considered to be devoid of skill, absent of thought, and incapable of sound judgment; making it all the more astounding, given such gross ineptitude, that I am finally able to report some wonderful news.

The gods have smiled upon me. I have secured employment—albeit in such a dark and curious place.

All that seems to be is naught. Deep beneath the brilliant gardens and polished exterior of Sutphin Manor lurks a baleful disposition. Despite the valiant efforts of its owner, the dismal tenor that dwells within its bricks and mortar lingers like an unseen pall.

No doubt the manor's owner, Irving Jeffries, was a dashing man once, tall and lean with emerald eyes; eyes now consumed by sorrow. Mrs. Abbott, the cook, confided in me that his wife had died in childbirth.

Meagre as suitable employment opportunities have been, I must confess to a state of absolute giddiness when Jeffries hired me as governess to his charming six-year-old daughter, Anna. Had my search for a position continued much longer, I might have been living hand to mouth on the streets.

Mrs. Abbott advised that although Jeffries hails from New York, he has settled in Baltimore to start anew. Idle talk among the help suggests that he purchased the manor for a song at auction. He busies himself with renovations, finishing first one room, then bounding to the next like a man hoping to escape the clutches of abject sorrow.

Just yesterday, Jeffries requested my assistance in tidying the attic, ridding it of a past he neither knew nor cared to preserve, save any hidden treasure my woman's eye might catch.

"Anna and I will fill this loft with our own past," he'd said. Chased by the echo of our footsteps, we entered the tomb-like alcove and worked our way through the cobwebs and the cloying mustiness. A vague uneasiness took hold; gooseflesh rose on the nape of my neck.

At length, we came upon a weathered wooden trunk that was chained and padlocked. "What have we here that requires such protection?" he asked. "Mayhap we've stumbled upon a prize." Unable to gain entry without tools, he left, but soon returned with an axe. After chopping through the locks and chains, he pried open the lid. It fit snugly on the swollen trunk, causing it to creak and groan like a set of old bones. A sickly, sweet odor wafted through the air—the odor of decay.

A strange assortment of religious relics lay scattered atop a tattered quilt that shrouded the object within. Wasting no time, he threw the quilt aside.

"Merciful heavens!" I whispered, crossing myself.

Jeffries laughed and raised the object for closer inspection. "How perfectly hideous!"

In his hand was a doll with a ruffled nightcap resting atop the crown of its head and a nightshirt covering its body; but, Sweet Margaret, do not doubt me when I say that never in the history of doll-making had a tinker crafted a doll so malignant-looking. Waist-length auburn coils framed a porcelain face that culminated in a decidedly pointed chin. Its features were pinched and severe; its mouth unsmiling. But what gave the doll its malevolent countenance were a pair of large black voids where its eyes should have been! Surely, gauged upon its appearance, some wicked fate had befallen it.

Jeffries tossed the doll into the rubbish heap. "Why would anyone keep this aberration, let alone safeguard it with padlocks and chains?" Why indeed. It lay atop the pile, positioned such that its blackened orbs appeared to follow me. I flung the tattered quilt from the trunk o'er the peculiar doll, blocking those relentless empty sockets—and then continued with my duties.

I gave the matter no further thought until the following day when Mr. Jeffries followed me into the study and closed the pocket door behind us. His lips were taut; his eyes narrow.

"Miss McGowan, why did you give that heinous corpse of a doll to Anna?"

"Sir! I did no such thing. I assure you."

"None of the other staff knew the doll existed, Miss McGowan. Anna has no one on this Earth, save me— and now, you. If I have mistakenly judged your suitability for this position, it is best that I know now."

"I would not lie to you, sir. I have come to look upon Anna as my own." My heart ached at the possibility of losing such a treasured thing. All for the gifting of a doll—a gifting in which I had played no part.

There came a tiny knock upon the door. Jeffries slid it back to find Anna, eyes dancing, clutching the disfigured doll against her chest.

"There you are, Miss Emma! I wanted to introduce you to my new dolly, Cora."

I stooped to meet her gaze. "Such a lonely looking dolly. Wherever did she come from?"

"She was rocking in my dolly chair when I awoke this morning. Isn't she grand?"

Despite the thing's wicked appearance, Anna was drawn to it and took it under her wing as if it were a wounded bird.

Dear Margaret, I knew not what to think of her

attachment to this grotesque moppet, yet I hadn't the heart to take it from her. Neither could I rid myself of the disquiet that came from wondering how it had found its way into Anna's arms.

This place portends such mystery. When next my missive finds you, perhaps I shall be able to say that my concerns had been for naught.

Your loving sister,
Emma

***

30 October, 1782
Baltimore

Sweet Margaret,

Would that I could report that the fears plaguing me were unwarranted. Both father and child mire deeper into a roiling pool of despair. Anna's skin is becoming pallid, her eyes hollow. She is inseparable from that doll, even insisting that a place be set for it at meal time. Anna has gone so far as to lay her own infant bunting in her toy cradle—as if Cora were a real babe. Torn between indulging a lonely child and rescuing her from the precipice of fantasy, Mrs. Abbott and I still our tongues; but any indecision on Mr. Jeffries part disappeared when Anna asked, "Daddy, which color eyes are best?"

"Without a doubt, my love, your blue eyes are my favorite. So like your mother's they are."

Curled snugly in his lap, she took his face in her tiny hands and peered up at him. "Cora says she wants green eyes like yours, Daddy."

His back stiffened though his tone remained neutral. "Anna, darling, you know that dolls cannot speak. Why must you pretend so?"

"But Daddy, Cora does speak."

"I have never heard her." With a nod, he enjoined me to follow suit.

"Nor have I, Anna. Perhaps she speaks to you in your dreams."

Anna's eyes welled. "She only speaks when we are alone. She says you do not like her, Daddy. Is that so?"

He shifted and sighed. "Why don't you give me Cora, and I will bring you a pretty new dolly from town?" He reached for the doll, but Anna began to wail. He rose to his feet and lowered her to the floor. "There, there. Take Cora and go play in your room now, my dear. Miss Emma and I have grown-up things to discuss." He closed the door behind her before speaking again. "The child is much too attached to that monstrosity—to the point of losing perspective. Tonight, when she is asleep, I will dispose of it once and for all. I do not wish to see it reappear. Am I understood?"

I blanched. "Of course; but you must believe me, sir. Neither I, nor any staff member, gave her the doll."

"More's the pity, Miss McGowan, for then, by some unknown means that doll has defied the laws of natural order." His voice trailed to a whisper. "There is something unsettling about that thing." He left me in the study and went to town to run his errands.

Late that evening while Anna slumbered, I watched Jeffries steal across her room and take the thing from its cradle. In its place, he left a beautiful new doll with golden curls, a cherubic face, and innocent azure eyes. He carried Cora outside to the water well. Without so much as a moment's hesitation, he threw the abomination into the void and did not leave until he heard the tell-tale splashing of water. He returned looking unburdened, as if a tremendous weight had been lifted from him. The manor itself seemed to breathe, as if freed from the crush of some malevolent force.

Good sister, could that doll be the albatross that plagues Sutphin Manor—the source of its ill humor? Pray that this act of a father's love has driven the darkness away.

With deepest affection,
Emma

***

31 October, 1782
Baltimore

Dearest Sister,

So quickly hope fades! In the blink of an eye, Anna has wasted to a shadow and her eyes have lost their shine. She awoke to find Cora gone, replaced by the sweet-faced cherub chosen by her father, and became inconsolable, beseeching us to find her baby. My heart near beat its last, when through a veil of tears she whimpered that Cora was wet and cold. Her eyes grew suddenly wide; she pummeled her tiny fists against her father's chest. "You did this, Daddy! You threw her into the well! Why were you so mean to Cora? Why?"

My eyes met Jeffries', and we seemed to exchange a single thought. *How could she have known?*

It pained us to watch Anna grieve. Nothing we did or said could appease her. She spent the day pining in her room, unwilling to speak or eat. She peered out of her window and slept sporadically, only to awaken in renewed torrents of tears. At dusk, wracked by exhaustion, she settled into a peaceful sleep. Fearful that melancholy would swallow her whole, we resigned to monitor her throughout the night and enlisted the aid of Mrs. Abbott, who fed us tea and kept vigil with us.

At the midnight hour, we started once again for her room. The stillness split from the peal of a child's giggle. But it was not Anna's infectious titter. It was a cackle, maniacal and taunting. *Surely this wasn't possible.*

We raced to her room. Jeffries stood in the doorway, peering into the darkness. I followed his gaze, first to the rocking chair and then to the cradle, each of us breathing a sigh of relief having found no sign of the doll. We turned then to Anna's bed. There she slept the deep carefree sleep of innocence, breathing steadily, with Cora's long auburn coils wound loosely round her throat.

The malignant monster pursed its pinched mouth and loosed its fiendish voice for all to hear. "Shush, Daddy, your baby is sleeping."

Jeffries raced toward the bed. "Get away from her demon!"

It cackled again, but its coils slithered free of Anna's neck. Jeffries hurriedly scooped his sleeping daughter against his chest and snatched her away from the cursed doll. With a gentle kiss to her forehead, he placed her into my arms and said, "We are all she has. Take her. I beg you, protect her with your life."

I carried her outside, absent the fray, and stood transfixed by what next occurred. Jeffries followed me through the door, the evil doll clutched in his hands. A fierce wind funneled outward from the manor. Trees tore asunder; branches, twigs, and leaves took flight, trapping Jeffries in a vortex of whirling debris. His words barely audible above the din, "Leave this place, hell-hound! Return to the flames that spawned you."

The demon-doll burst forth an angry howl, polluting the air with a fetid stench. It shone a grisly smile and simpered in a child's falsetto, "Cora wants green eyes, Daddy." A menacing growl followed.

He stood his ground. "Then come and get them, hag."

The cacophony reached a crescendo; the air pressure dropped, threatening to burst my ears. Still I stayed, mesmerized, as Jeffries produced a flask from his pocket. So surprised was I at his timing for a nip, that an incredulous laugh near escaped me until he threw the liquid at the demon and its smell belied my fears.

The demon moved to and fro, dancing out of reach. Jeffries launched forward and latched onto the beast. It yowled and hissed when he produced a match from his pocket.

"Mr. Jeffries, no, please!" I screamed, "Think of your daughter!"

With a tortured look, he said, "But I *am*!" and struck his match against the cobblestone. The kerosene ignited. Both he and the demon Cora blazed into flames. I turned away, sobbing, blocking their screams from my mind, thankful that Anna's exhaustion had left her oblivious to the evil doings of the night.

With that, dear sister, there is little more to say. I am all that Anna has in this world. She asks for her father daily, and strangely has no recollection of Cora. For now, I smile and tell her that her father is away. How am I to explain his passing, when the truth defies imagination? Sutphin Manor is a desolate pit that holds no future for us. We shall journey on toward a new beginning. Pray, kind sister, for prosperity and hope.

All my love,
Emma

**

1 December, 1782
Towsontown

Dear, Sweet Margaret,

Anna and I are safely ensconced in Towsontown; far enough, God willing, that the nightmarish memories will soon begin to fade. For the moment, we survive on God's good humor, but now, I am responsible for us both and my search for employment must begin anew. I pray that my shoulders will not be considered too slender to be tested.

Mrs. Abbott was kind enough to forward our belongings. She prays that the manor sells quickly, so that she might retain her cook's position—and she vows that the unholy events of that night will be taken to her grave.

Whilst unboxing our possessions, I took care to ensure Anna was otherwise occupied—a shrewd and prophetic decision. My heart sickened at the sight of a familiar tattered quilt. Gathering my courage, I grasped its edges and slowly folded it back to find that Cora had returned. Her porcelain skin was cracked and peeled, no doubt due to the licking of the flames on that tragic night. I marveled at the bottomless black eye sockets staring back at me. They were proof that Cora had not succeeded in stealing the emerald eyes of Irving Jeffries.

Failing all else, I learned that evil never dies; at best, it is held in abeyance.

I wrapped the doll in its tattered quilt and placed it in a sturdy trunk, entombed beneath vials of holy water and sanctified relics. Satisfied the demon had been neutralized, I closed the lid, and applied both chains and padlock.

Under cover of night, I returned to Sutphin Manor, hauling the trunk by buckboard. Mrs. Abbott and I buried it deep in an unmarked grave, well concealed from unsuspecting victims. There, the demon would be trapped for all eternity, never again to see the light of day.

Such was the plan I followed. Such was the plan that affords me sleep, lest I toss and turn in the dark of night, wondering when the demon will return to claim new eyes for Cora.

I must retire for the night, dear Sister. I confess that recent events have taken their toll on me. My mirror tells me that there is tired gray skin requiring rest, and that in order to sleep away the darkness, my own green eyes must close.

Emma

The Baltim

Sunday, August 2, 2015

Excavation Slated for Histor

Sutphin Manor, a local landmark noted for its claims of paranormal activity, is scheduled for demolition in late October, 2015, with excavation of the entire sixty acre estate to begin immediately thereafter. The property was purchased at auction by real estate mogul, J

William Strassel. Strassel plans to take advantage of recent zoning changes by parceling the land for commercial development.

The property, once a shining example of Georgian architecture, has fallen into disrepair due to a string of defaults.

Rer foll imp

The that rela the beh of a exp

THE TYPEWRITER

BY TYLOR JAMES

"Honey, I'm home!" Kendra called. "Look what I picked up for you."

She grunted, clunking the thing down on Andrew's desk. It weighed damn near forty pounds.

"Would you look at that!" he said. "That's a beaut, honey. Where'd you find it?"

"You know that factory you worked at when we first met? Not the one where you assembled motors, but the one with the cables?"

"Ugh," he grumbled. "Don't remind me."

"It's not a factory anymore. They turned the place into a vintage store. Velma's Vintage, it's called. And lo and behold, this was sitting in the corner, practically calling out for me to buy it for you."

Andrew got up from his chair and planted a wet kiss on her lips.

"You're such a sweetie," he said.

"I know," she winked. "I knew you'd love it, 'cause

of how old school you are and stuff. The sweet old lady, Velma, said her husband even put a new ribbon in it."

"Very nice."

"Well, what are you waiting for? Go ahead, give it a try!"

"Alright," he said and sat back down.

He scooted the hefty 1941 Royal typewriter in front of him. It scratched lines into the desk, but he didn't care. The desk was nearly as old as the typewriter. He grabbed a piece of Georgia-Pacific paper and rolled it into the paper bale. He began pecking at the keys, feeling an immediate high at the obnoxious clicks and clatters it made.

"Hey, this thing types pretty smooth!" he said. "I'm surprised. Most old typewriters need a good blasting out with a can of penetrating oil to type anything resembling English."

"What did you write?" she asked, peering over his shoulder.

"Here," he said, rolling his chair out of the desk cubby so she could see.

`I have the most wonderful girlfriend ever!`

"Aww, Andrew!" she said. "You're such a kiss ass!" She gave him a peck on the corner of his lips.

"Okay. I've made the boyfriend happy. Now I'm off to hang with Liz for the evening. Do a bit of shopping *for me.*"

"Sure thing, hon. I've only got a few paragraphs left on the column and then I think I'm hanging it up. Put in three hours today. Normally my brain is fried after two."

"That's great, babe. Be back around two or three."

"Kay. See ya in a while. Hey, hon?"

"Yeah?" she asked, turning from the open door.

"Thanks for the typewriter," he said. "It was very thoughtful of you."

"You're welcome," she said, giving a cute shrug. "Love, love, love!"

"Love, love, love," he repeated and scooted the typewriter away to finish the article he was writing on the Mac.

***

Andrew wrestled the old push-mower out from under the porch. For a second he had thought the thing would burn up, like a vampire being dragged from its coffin out into sunlight. A strange thought for such a nice day.

The upside to living in a trailer park, he supposed, was that there wasn't a lot of grass to cut. Just one wide, green swatch next to the little sidewalk leading up to the porch. All the same, he was glad to be outside. The hot July sun felt good on his face and shoulders.

An open can of Budweiser sat up in the only tree on their property, a lonely red maple. He had stuck the can in a crook where the first thick branch separated from its trunk. He brought it down and took a swig, then set it back in its designated spot. He jerked back the pull-string and the rusty mower rumbled to life.

He was two-thirds the way down the swatch of grass when he noticed Henry Delane sitting on the front porch of his double-wide, sipping his evening glass of Jameson. He looked pretty philosophical sitting there in the golden light, tranquil, with his trim white beard scuffing the edges of the glass. Henry raised a hand in acknowledgment, then beckoned Andrew to come have a drink with him.

Andrew nodded, pointing down at the mower, as if to say, *maybe I'll take you up on that, right after I've got my five minutes of tough, manly labor over with.* Henry smiled and raised his glass. Then he cocked his head slightly. Andrew followed his gaze.

An old man walked toward him, his face pale and solemn. Andrew released the safety lever, allowing the engine to sputter to a stop. A cascade of sounds far more lovely than the old mower returned to the summer air. The twittering birds. The bees buzzing in Henry's garden. The children playing down the street.

He was a tall, slim man in a frail frame. His pale blue eyes shone through small, round spectacles.

"You Andrew?" the old man asked.

"That's me. How can I help ya?"

"Name's Jim Nicholby," he said, sticking out one trembling, veiny hand.

Andrew shook it.

"And how you can help me," Jim said, "is by being open to negotiating with me."

"Alright," Andrew said, expecting some lousy sales pitch.

"That damned thing my wife sold your girl. It's no good," he said, shaking his head. "No good at all."

"I'm not sure what you're talking about, Sir."

"That god damned typewriter, son. My wife Velma sold it to *your* wife this morning."

Andrew felt like face-palming. The typewriter. Of course. *Duh.*

"Oh, right," Andrew laughed.

"I'm afraid I'm going to need that typewriter back."

"Why?" Andrew asked.

"Velma must've got bored Friday night and decided to rummage through our crawlspace. She found my typewriter, dragged it out of there, slapped a price sticker on it and set it on the sales floor."

Jim slowly shook his head. "I never intended to sell it. Your wife payed fifteen dollars for it. I'd be glad to buy it back for double the amount."

He didn't mind that Jim kept referring to Kendra as his wife. After all, what did it matter?

"That's gracious of you," Andrew said.

"Not at all, son. You just hand my baby over and that thirty bucks is yours."

Kendra's yellow Volkswagen pulled into the drive, parking directly behind Andrew's rusty Cavalier.

She climbed out of the car with an armful of groceries. Whenever Kendra told Andrew she was going shopping, usually she only came back with food. It saddened him. He wanted her to treat herself once in a while. The closest she ever came was window-shopping with Elizabeth, her best pal since high school. And, of course, purchasing ol' Jim's typewriter that morning.

"Hey, babe," Andrew said. "Have you met Jim?"

She smiled faintly, setting sunglasses on top of her blonde hair.

"I don't believe I have," she said. "I saw you at Velma's Vintage this morning, didn't I?"

"Yes, ma'am," Jim replied. "Name's Jim Nicholby. Velma's husband."

"Nice to meet you. I think your wife is *such* a doll."

345

"Can't disagree there," he smiled. "It's just that she makes mistakes, that's all."

"What do you mean?"

Andrew interjected. "Velma sold you Jim's typewriter without knowing he didn't want to sell it. He's kindly offered us a full refund, plus fifteen dollars more if we give it back to him."

Kendra frowned and paused to think for a moment, then shook her head.

"No, I…I don't think that's right. It says 'all sales are final' on your store window. That goes both ways, for the customer *and* the seller."

"Now, Kendra," Andrew laughed. "I think Jim's offer is reasonable, don't you?"

"No, not really," she shrugged. "I bought the typewriter because you've been wanting one since we first met. You like it don't you?"

He felt trapped. Of course he liked the typewriter. He really *had* wanted one since before they'd first met. One of the best memories he had as a child was standing on top of a milk crate to type stories on his father's typewriter. It inspired him to pursue a writing career in the first place. Yet he didn't like the typewriter enough to haggle with an eighty-year-old man.

"Yes," Andrew admitted. "I like it."

"Well then, it's settled," she said. "Jim, I'm sorry, but we're gonna keep it."

Jim looked down wearily, then perked his head back up as if he'd gotten a bright idea.

"I'll buy it back for a hundred dollars!"

She shook her head, "No. Velma told me it was just sitting in your crawlspace, collecting cobwebs. She said you must've put a ribbon in it recently, since the ink was fresh. But she'd never seen you type on it even once."

"How does *two-hundred* dollars sound?" he said.

"Sorry. All sales are final. Just as your store policy says."

"Come on now, babe," Andrew said. "Maybe that typewriter is sentimental to him. A part of his family history, maybe?"

"Yes," Jim said, nodding eagerly. "That typewriter belonged to my mother, who used it for her job as an accountant for General Electric. That was way before your time, of course."

Kendra looked at Jim, then gazed up into Andrew's eyes.

"The old man's lying," she whispered. "Velma said he'd found that old typewriter in a *dumpster* five years ago. It can't be that important to him. It's yours now. We're keeping it. Okay?"

She turned to Jim.

"I'm sorry to disappoint you Mr. Nicholby," she said. "Now if you boys will excuse me, I have some groceries to put away."

She climbed the steps to the front porch and entered the trailer, leaving Jim and Andrew standing awkwardly on the grassy strip.

"You've got one strong willed woman, son," Jim frowned. "It's *your* typewriter, isn't it? Not hers. What do *you* think?

Andrew wiped the sweat off his forehead, squinting in the sun.

"With all due respect," he said. "I think you're just bummed your wife sold something you'd forgotten you had in the first place."

Jim shook his head. "No. That's not it at all."

"Listen, she's right. We purchased the typewriter, fair and square. Sorry to disappoint."

The old man's hands balled into tight, veiny fists. His jaws clenched.

"You'll be sorry for this," he gritted through his teeth.

Jim reached into his back pocket and grabbed his wallet, pecking out a business card.

"If you change your mind..." he said, handing him the card, "...not that you'll be able to change your mind by the time that...that evil fucking *thing* has gotten to you, give me a call. I'll take it back."

Jim huffed off back across the road and climbed into the truck. He slammed the door and sped off, tires screeching.

Andrew stood there, one hand leaning on the push-mower and the other holding Jim's card. He had the sensation of being watched. He gazed over to his right at Henry Delane, still sitting on his porch, sipping the glass of whiskey. Henry lifted his glass and smiled.

***

Andrew radically changed his writing schedule, simultaneously increasing his productivity and unnerving Kendra. He switched from writing two hours in the morning to writing after dinner, right around 7 p.m., punching the keys like a madman until two in the morning. He'd pass out after a mind-boggling seven hours of writing, then get up just before noon with the hot sun bursting through the blinds. Since he made his living from the comforts of home, he figured he had a right to change his work habits if it meant more money to pay the bills.

Kendra had always known Andrew as an early bird, and to see him transform so quickly into a night owl, typing feverishly away into the late hours, alarmed her. His typing kept her awake nights. The typewriter made a continual click-clack noise, like a horrendous snapping of bones.

She'd awake in the morning, groggy eyed, only to find six or seven Budweiser cans in the office trash bin. She began to wonder if Andrew was becoming an alcoholic. She found it difficult to express her distress to him. Despite his drinking and late nights, he still managed to turn in his column for the newspaper on time. He'd just sold an article to *Esquire* for $700 and one to *The Atlantic* for $900—enough money to pay off the last of the credit cards.

She'd waited for the day they'd be able set their four credit cards in a row upon the kitchen table, size them up with all the contempt they deserved, and clip them into a hundred pieces. With Andrew's higher income trickling in, that dream would finally come true.

Yet Kendra felt distant, frustrated. She'd leave him sitting at the typewriter at bedtime, walking briskly to the bedroom, saying, "Well, guess I'll just be pleasuring *myself* tonight then." And she would, too. She'd masturbate aggressively, using her resentment for him as fuel for a sexual release. It was *some* release, anyway. She still had to fall asleep with those incessant clicks and clacks hammering away into the night.

***

Andrew was in love again. In love with writing, in love with himself, in love with beer. He wrote seven, sometimes nine hours every night. He typed up extensive articles, columns, essays, poems, and short stories. He even had the makings of a novel in the works. He had never been so creatively productive. He'd been using the typewriter for only six days, but it had already changed his life.

He knew Kendra didn't like the fact that he was in love with something besides her. She was downright bitchy about his late night affairs with the typewriter. *So what?* He was submitting his work left and right, and finally being accepted for publication; a success he credited not to his own genius, but entirely to the *typewriter*. He had even named the thing.

Lovely Lila! She's a magic typewriter, he thought. *Or a genie lamp with unlimited wishes, just for writers.*

He began referring to it as *my baby*. He reclined on the couch one evening, half in the bag after downing a six-pack with Henry Delane. When Kendra got home from work, she asked him how his day was. "Every day is good," he responded. "So long as I have my baby." Kendra was visibly touched by this.

"What?" Andrew asked. "You think I'm talking about *you*? That's a damn laugh!"

He really did laugh then, right in her face. Her simple, sweet blush deepened to a crimson of anger. She stomped into the bedroom, slamming the door. Andrew heard her muffled cries. He shrugged and sat down at the typewriter. He'd skip dinner and get to work early that night.

He banged away at those brilliant, precious keys until dawn. When he finished, he leaned back in his chair, braced his fingers upon his head, and looked down at the stack of freshly typed papers on his desk.

He smiled, sighing deeply as if he had just made love. He drained the rest of the beer, crushed the can, and tossed it at the trash bin. It bounced off the overflowing pile and joined the other stragglers.

Andrew leaned forward, kissing the keys.

"Wonderful work, my Lovely Lila," he whispered. He rose from his chair, stretched, and stumbled into the bedroom. He got into bed just as Kendra's alarm clock began to sound.

She looked over her shoulder at him, her eyes hollow and heavy with sleeplessness. Before she had even shut off the alarm, Andrew was snoring.

He woke up at one p.m. to discover a note on the kitchen counter:

Andrew,

I'm frustrated. I'm angry. I'm really worried about you. What's going on? I miss you. We need to talk. Tonight.

Kendra

***

Henry Delane was adding seed to his bird feeders that morning when Kendra stormed out her front door, sobbing hard. She got into her car with tears streaming down her cheeks, her chest heaving. The sight nearly broke Henry's heart.

He'd always known Andrew and Kendra as a happy young couple. To see Kendra so shook up seemed an abomination, as if the sun refused to shine.

Andrew had been visiting him every afternoon for a week now, always bringing a six-pack of beer and finishing it. He had initially been put off by Andrew's out-of-character drinking, but had repressed the feeling. After all, was Andrew's newly accustomed drinking habit any worse than his daily addiction to Jameson Whiskey?

On the other hand, Henry figured he was a lonely, widowed man who enjoyed his whiskey and had every right to. When he drank, he became jolly and even a bit thoughtful. He knew when he'd had enough, and when he did, he put away the bottle. When Andrew had drained his six-pack, Henry noticed a strange edge begin to infiltrate his words. It was a sharp edge, an underlying aggression. Something bellicose.

When Andrew ambled over to sit on the porch with him that afternoon, he intended to reach out and ask what was going on. Henry considered himself a friend to them both, and he was concerned.

***

Andrew tossed Kendra's note in the trash, grabbed a beer from the fridge, and sat down in front of Lila. He began composing his own note:

```
Kendra,
    You're nothing but a jealous witch. Why
must you try to shame me? Degrade my success
with your constant disapproval? You're my
woman. Either stand by my side, or stand
aside. Can your shoe-size IQ compute the
subtle difference between the two?
    It makes no difference to me. And it
certainly makes no difference to the
typewriter. In any case, you were the one you
bought it for me. I'm grateful you did.
Magazines   are   publishing   my   work
```

(finally!!). We are earning an income which will finally lift us out of this trailer park hell. And what is your response to my securing a better life for us?

You've been nothing but a dark cloud of negativity. You've expressed nothing but resentment and jealousy for my loving the typewriter. Maybe you should stop being such an underwhelming cunt and sit down with my baby sometime? Type awhile. See if you don't feel better. See if you won't want to type all night, every night. I have little doubt that if you did, we'd soon be arguing over who should be using the typewriter.

Perhaps it'd be better for you to leave. Stay with your mother in Chicago.

I'll be over at Henry's tonight, giving you plenty of time to pack your shit.

Sincerely,
Andrew.

PS: the typewriter just sent me a great line! It always sends me great lines. Do you want to know what it is? I think it could make for a great ending line for a poem:

> And the s l u g s
> Are blossoming
> E v e r y where.

Don't you think that's just great? Don't you think so?

***

Kendra arrived home from work that night, discovering the note and the empty house. She cried. Her love of four years was fading away, fading into a dark, cruel place in his mind. While his note hurt her, the hurt was only skin deep. She read the note three times, slowly. As the sentences sunk in, she realized they were clearly not typed by the hands of her lover, but by the mind of something entirely other. It was a mind of dark, primal unconsciousness. Not at all her Andrew.

It was inexplicable. All his changes had occurred in a single week. Was seven days all it took for a beautiful mind to transform into something obsessive, neurotic, and cruel? She supposed it was feasible that a mind could bend, could snap even, within the duration of single second, depending on the individual. What took a week for Andrew might take very little time for somebody else.

She looked over at the typewriter, squatting on his office desk. She scowled.

Curse that fucking thing. I should take a hammer and bust it into itsy bitsy pieces.

Yet she knew she was being unreasonable. It wasn't the typewriter's fault that Andrew had gone off his rocker. It was the excessive drinking, coupled with too much stress. Surely.

But, stress over what? Andrew was fine until she'd brought home the typewriter—his Lovely Lila, as he now called it.

She supposed there were plenty of things to stress over. Paying the bills on time, having a career, making a meaningful life for yourself. *Was he going through a mid-life crisis?* She wished he would just talk to her, tell her what was going on in his mind. *Doesn't he trust me? Doesn't he know by now that he can come to me with anything? What's happened to us?*

She wiped away her tears, pocketing the note. What was she to do now? Pack up and drive all the way to Chicago and cry to her mother?

No way in hell, she thought. It was her trailer too. There was no way she was going to leave. It wasn't right. *No fucking way.*

Moonlight beamed steadily through the window. A reflective gleam in the corner of the room caught her eye. She followed it and found herself gazing upon the typewriter again. The notion was absurd, but she knew it was trying to get her attention. As if it was saying, "Why, hello there."

Then another ridiculous idea occurred to her—that it was silently laughing at her. Its keys seemed to rattle in the motion of a giggle. *There's something wrong with that thing.*

"Hello, Lila," she whispered, backing slowly away from the desk. She walked into their bedroom and began digging through a box of summer items located in the closet. A jumble of footballs, basketballs, and Frisbees rolled out between her feet. She knew the god damned thing had to be in there somewhere. She kept digging, and at last, her hand located its handle. She pulled it out. It was heavy, perfect for smashing things.

She ran into the living room with the aluminum baseball bat gripped tightly in her hands. She stood in front of Andrew's desk. A dark shadow cast over the typewriter, as if it were angry, baring teeth. She looked out the window and saw a cloud passing across the bright moon. She returned her gaze to the typewriter, lifting the bat over her shoulder.

"Oh, Lovely Lila, you fucking bitch!" she said and brought down the bat.

Keys cracked in two and flew off their stubs. Little letters scattered all across the floor, making her think of alphabet soup. She laughed and lifted the bat again. The margin bell rung loudly upon each impact.

It's screaming, she thought.

The idea only encouraged her. She swung harder, smashing the margin guides and busting the cover plate off its top. She battered at the carriage house, bending and cracking the ink stained type hands until the typewriter was nothing more than a bowl of twisted, mangled fingers. She reached in for the ink ribbon, snatching it out like a lion clawing the intestines out of a gazelle. She marched over to the kitchen sink, ripped the ribbon off its plastic spools, and shoved it into the garbage disposal.

Frappe time, bitch.

She flicked the switch and the motor whirred, shredding the fabric. She ran the faucet, washing the remains down the drain. After tossing the baseball bat into the corner, she grabbed her phone and did the best thing she could think to do to help Andrew—she dialed 911.

***

He was sitting on Henry's couch, his ninth Bud down, when he heard the noises from his trailer. Henry heard them too and straightened in his chair, perking up his head. A warm wet spot grew on Andrew's crotch. He exploded into tears.

"That bitch!" he sobbed.

"What the hell's the matter?" Henry asked.

"She's killing my Lila!" he replied, leaping up from the couch. "I can feel it! Can't you feel it? It's agony."

Andrew started toward the direction of the front door, hunched over, hand pressed against his stomach.

"Andrew!" Henry shouted, blocking him. "Now hold on a minute. Listen. After all the things you've told me tonight, I don't think you should go over there. Wait until Kendra leaves, alright? That was the plan anyway, wasn't it?"

"Plans change!" Andrew growled. "She's trying to kill my typewriter, don't you understand that? Now let me by, old man."

"Andrew," he said softly. "Don't leave. Stay here and drink your beer. If you go over there now, you'll only end up doing something you'll regret. I promise you that."

Andrew snarled his lips, grabbing Henry by his shirt collar.

"And I promise *you, old fuck*, that if you don't get outta my way, I'm gonna kill you. *No one* stands in the way of my baby. Not even an old pal like you, Henry. Understand?"

Andrew let go of his collar. Henry stumbled and sprawled his back. Andrew stepped over him, marching into the kitchen and down the hallway towards the front door. He had his hand on the door knob when Henry called his name. He spun around.

Henry stood there in the dim light of the hallway, armed with the stout little cannon—a .357 Magnum. His hands trembled around it.

"Henry," Andrew murmured. "What the *hell* do you think you're doing?"

"I'm stopping you from going over there and hurting her," his voice quivered.

"Hurt her? Oh no, Henry. You really think I would hurt her? Not in a million years! I love her. Don't you know that?"

"I believe *Andrew* would never hurt her. But you're not the Andrew I once knew. You've changed. And you're drunk. For God's sake, you've even pissed yourself."

A wide grin spread over Andrew's mouth. It reminded Henry of a large black widow stretching its legs. A chill ran up his spine. Andrew began laughing in quick, breathy gasps.

"What the hell's so funny?"

"You see," he chuckled. "I thought you were afraid I was going to hurt Lila. My typewriter. I didn't realize you were talking about Kendra. If she's damaged my beautiful machine, if she's so much as put a single *dent* in it, then you bet I'm gonna hurt her. I'm gonna hurt her *a whole lot, Henry.* And believe me, I'll put more than a dent in her. Oh yes," Andrew nodded. "She's had it coming for a long, *long* time."

He turned to the front door and opened it.

"Don't move another step further or I'll shoot!"

Andrew ignored the old man's feeble command, swiftly shutting the door behind him. Henry ran back down the hallway and watched Andrew through his kitchen window. He saw a man shrouded in bright moonlight with an ugly scowl on his face, marching toward home. Andrew slapped the back of Kendra's Volkswagen three times, as if for good luck.

You pathetic old fool, he thought. *Why didn't you shoot him while you had the chance?*

He picked up the phone and dialed 911.

***

Andrew threw the door open with enough force for the knob to smash a hole in the wall. The door shuddered on its hinges. He made his way into the kitchen and stopped in his tracks when he saw a few of the typewriter's letters scattered on the linoleum. His body began to shake with rage.

"Kendra! Where the *fuck* are you? Answer me!"

He entered the living room, observing the remnants of his beloved all over the floor. On his desk squatted the hollowed out shell of Lovely Lila. It was as if an explosion had gone off inside his typewriter, leaving only twisted shards of metal, shattered keys, and badly mangled type hands.

Andrew ran his hands delicately over his dead typewriter and wept. His knees felt weak, trembling as he fell to them. Tears splashed into the battered carriage. A strand of snot hung over his chin. His chest hitched.

"My baby," he cried. "My poor Lila. Why? *Why?*"

His hands balled into tight, red fists. A fire lit inside his belly.

"*KENDRAAAA! YOU MISERABLE FUCKING BITCH! HOW COULD YOU?*"

He turned about the room, ripping back the drapes, and tossing aside the couch.

"When I find you," he called, his voice high, twitching with rage. "I'm gonna do to you what you did to my Lila, you jealous, insecure, resentful *cunt*!"

She stood behind the shower curtain in the dark bathroom, located adjacent to their bedroom. Hearing him so close frightened her, made her body shiver all over. She gripped the baseball bat tightly and wondered how long it'd been since she made the call to the police.

Please, she prayed. *Take him away right now. Just take him away before he finds me. Please, Oh God. Take him away. Don't let him find me. Help!*

She listened to him storming through the house like a miniature tornado, recklessly smashing their belongings and overturning furniture. His footfalls marched into the bedroom again.

She breathed slowly, trying not to make a sound, not to cry or gasp on a sob. Her whole body shook with fright. She could hear him walking toward the bathroom now. It was only a matter of time before he would peel back the curtain and discover her standing there with the bat quivering pathetically in her hands.

It occurred to her for the first time that she may actually have to hurt him, although all she wanted was to escape. One week might have been enough to turn Andrew's mind into a violent whirlwind, but it wasn't enough time to destroy the love she still felt for him.

If it came down to life or death, she would without hesitation choose life. It wasn't right for her to die like this, hiding in the shower with the lights off, waiting for her maniac boyfriend to find her and murder her.

Andrew's laughter filled the tiny bathroom with a sense of absurdity. Madness.

She took a deep breath, and raised the bat above her shoulder, as if she were about to hit one out of the park. Her violent shivering subsided. Her body knew what it had to do to survive.

"You stupid whore," he growled. "You think you can hide from me? In *this* shitty little dump? Get real, babe."

He grabbed the curtain with both hands and yanked it off its rings in a single pull. His hands were still holding the curtain when Kendra brought the bat down savagely on his left shoulder. He grimaced in pain, falling down to one knee, clutching his shoulder. She swung again, hitting him on the nape of his neck. He collapsed, groaning upon the bathroom tile.

Home Run, asshole.

She dropped the bat and ran through the adjacent bedroom, then into the living room and stopped in her tracks. She screamed.

Lovely Lila sat whole and complete in the middle of the living room. Not a key broken, not a margin guide out of place. It shined with a green, iridescent glow. A fresh sheet of paper read in the bale.

The keys pressed down all by themselves, like a player piano. Lila clicked and clacked once more into feverish life. The margin bell rung. The carriage rolled back to its starting position. It continued typing, then stopped soon after the bell, returning the carriage a final time. It sat silent, glowing.

Kendra slowly put one foot in front of the other. Then she reached down, pulled out the paper and read what it had typed.

You tried to destroy me just as many others have tried to destroy me. It does not work. It never works. Sit down, Kendra. Type a while. Then you will know how good it feels. You will feel better than you've felt in your entire life—this I promise. Type, and you will feel the slugs blossoming inside of you, Kendra.

`Type, and the slugs within shall blossom`

`e v e r y where.`

"No," she whispered. "It can't be. It *can't* be."

Andrew reached from behind, snatching the paper from her hands. She screamed and spun around to face him. He held the paper up to his eyes, reading it and grinning. He shoved Kendra aside and fell to his knees before the typewriter.

"Oh, my *baby!*" he cheered. "My *Lila!* You look so *fine*. You look *so damn fine!*"

He typed away on Lila, gasping and laughing with joy and quite possibly, Kendra thought, sexual excitement. She began to cry. Seeing him like this was worse—far worse—than if she'd caught him in bed with another woman. The thought of him cheating on her seemed utterly dignified when compared to his obsessive adoration for the machine.

A perverse sweat broke out over Andrew's forehead, glistening in the green glow. He groaned, typing with rabid frenzy. Then he ceased typing and hacked up something from his throat. He coughed, hacked, and spit it out onto the carpet.

It laid there, sprawling next to Kendra's shoe. She looked down, knowing instantly what it was; a fat, slimy, phlegm-yellow slug. She gagged at the sight of it.

Andrew continued typing while he hacked up another, this one the color of ethereal green, the same as Lila. He hocked it an impressive distance. It flew through the doorway and landed with a barely audible splat upon the kitchen linoleum. Andrew groaned with pleasure.

"*Ooh,*" he moaned. "I'm going to *blossom!*"

Kendra put one hand to her mouth, not knowing if she was going to sob or vomit.

"Oh, *babe,* Oh, *Lila,* I'm blossoming, *I'm blossomiiiiiiiiiiinnnnggg!*"

A flood of multi-colored slugs ejaculated from his mouth. They cascaded down his lips, onto his chest; all of them encased in a grotesque, foul smelling slime. Kendra backed away, plugging her nose. She vomited in the corner.

The slugs crawled all about the room, each one thrumming and throbbing with an energetic pulse. An abundance of glistening reds, greens, yellows, and violets decorated the floor. Lovely Lila's green glow spread out over Andrew's hands, steadily encasing his arms and shoulders, then his chest, and his head. Soon his entire body was covered with that luminescent, alien glow. He smiled in a deranged bliss, continuing to type with automaton glee.

CLICK CLACK CLICK CLACK CLICK! DING!!
CLACK CLICK CLACK CLACK CLICK! DING!!
CLICK CLICK CLACK CLICK

Kendra covered her ears, shuddering at the sound. It made her think of a thousand infant necks, snapping one at a time.

"No," she said.

None of this was right. None of this was right at all.

"NO!" she screamed, refusing to accept the ungodly decadence.

"NO, NO, NO!"

She sprung across the room, knocking Andrew from

the typewriter, laying him flat on his back. Then she stood, scooping up the luminescent typewriter in her arms. She lifted the thing high in the air above her head. Slugs scattered off the keys. Kendra shook one from her hair with disgust.

She gazed down at what used to be her Andrew. Her kind, gentle, loving Andrew. Now his swampy green skin pulsed. A gaggle of slugs squirmed beneath the flesh of his face.

He smiled, showing blackened teeth dripping with slime. Something long and red crawled out from under his tongue, escaping from the corner of his mouth. At first she thought it was another of the slugs, but knew it wasn't when she saw all the legs. It was a millipede.

"Come now, Kendra," he rasped. *"Don't be such a jealous little bitch! Join us! Type on Lila. Just type. Try it! Try iiiiiit!"*

Kendra shook her head.

"Goodbye, Andrew," she sobbed.

With all the strength she possessed, she flung the 40-pound typewriter down. The glow about Andrew's body glitched off, then on again.

She picked it up and hurled Lila down a second time, smashing Andrew's skull. Blood and brain splattered everywhere. The glow around his body and the typewriter faded to a dull verdant hue, then disappeared entirely.

She could hear the sirens now, steadily growing in volume, filling the air.

When the police entered the trailer, they discovered a young woman standing over her dead boyfriend. Her boyfriend had a typewriter for a head.

They cuffed her while she told them about Lovely

Lila. Nobody understood who Lovely Lila was. Henry Delane stood on his front porch and cried as they shoved her into the back of a police car.

***

Henry became Kendra's most frequent visitor once she was admitted to the Menomonee Psychiatric Hospital. He made a habit of visiting her twice a week, until he'd purchased Andrew's old typewriter at an auction six months later. Six months. That's how long it took before the police decided they didn't need to keep it in an evidence locker anymore. There were rumors as to why the item was relinquished. Some say the typewriter drove a few officers to madness. Others claim the court case was over, the murder clear-cut and self-evident. They simply didn't need to hold on to it.

All the same, the typewriter had found a new home. Henry disappeared inside his house for months at a time to write, typing up an endless abundance of stories and novels. He submitted the manuscripts to a famous literary agent. It wasn't long before that agent had set up a ten-year contract with a large publishing house.

By early January of the following year, Henry had published his first novel, "...*And the Slugs Shall Blossom*". It remained #1 on the New York Times' Bestseller List for twelve consecutive weeks. Henry grew so rich that he could've lived in a mansion, yet he preferred the trailer. Moving into another place would serve only as a distraction from his art. So he remained in his double-wide, barely eating, but always drinking and writing. He was very good at ignoring the legions of fans outside his front door.

The public championed Henry Delane as a brilliant

author and an eccentric genius.

Henry was mysterious and never agreed to interviews. A real *recluse*, they said. His agent reported to all inquiring magazines and TV show hosts that "Henry prefers to stay home and make love to Lila, his typewriter," as opposed to doing interviews. Or anything else, for that matter.

Meanwhile, Kendra bided her time in the hospital by constructing wicker baskets and rocking back and forth. She'd sit quietly in the TV room, most of the time. Except she laughed like a mad hatter whenever someone on TV said Henry had come out with a new book.

On the day the news reported Henry Delane had tragically passed away due to starvation and alcohol poisoning, Kendra laughed all the way to her grave.

They say she laughed until she couldn't breathe.

Then didn't.

LITTLE ADVENTURE

BY KAREN THROWER

Ruth Phillips was sitting in the office of Loki's Curiosities, her eyes wandering over every unique item she could see. There was a huge shelf that covered the entire wall, and among the books was a wooden bowl, a pair of worn leather boots and a gem encrusted box overflowing with jewelry. *Odd things to keep on a book shelf* she thought.

On the other side of the room was a glass case that held a shiny dagger, a creepy looking obsidian mask with fangs, and a small vial of purple liquid. She turned and saw a painting of a little girl in a field, flying a kite. Her eyes roamed over the painted blades of grass, the girls white skirt and kite's string. She swore she could see every brush stroke from twenty feet away. It captivated her. She was about to get out of the chair to get a closer look when the door to the office opened. She sat back as a large, square looking man carrying a stack of papers walked in. He was bald and had a gold hoop in his left ear.

"Miss Phillips? I'm Mr. Rex, proprietor of Loki's." He stared at her for a moment then chuckled and turned the painting around so she couldn't see it. She blinked a few times as her fascination ebbed. "I'm so glad you decided to show." His voice was higher than she expected, and she tried hard not to giggle.

"Yeah, well I was curious."

Mr. Rex laughed. "With ten thousand dollars on the line who wouldn't be?" She watched him sit down across the desk from her. It squeaked something awful and again, she fought not to laugh.

"I have the contract drawn up for you." He slid the papers in his hands over to her. "Have a look-see and if you agree, you're in for the ride of a lifetime."

"I'm still not sure I understand what this is all about, but the mailer was certainly intriguing." She picked up the contract and glanced at it for a few moments. "What uh…what does *cursed* mean exactly?" She never believed in curses; bad luck yes, curses no.

Mr. Rex sat back and motioned wide with his big arms. "Here at Loki's, we endeavor to give our customers the experience of a lifetime. An experience where anything can, and frequently *does* happen. We offer a monetary prize for anyone who can survive the week."

"Survive?" Her eyes went wide as she sat forward and put her hands on his desk. "People die doing this?"

He laughed. "Survive can be a misleading word. You survive the work week, yes?"

"Oh." She let out a sigh of relief and sat back. "Yeah I guess I do." She stood up and started walking around the room. "So basically, I pick one of these cursed items, take it home for a week, then you give me money?"

"Ten grand, that's right." He said, smiling so big she could see all his enormous teeth.

She turned to him, shaking her head. "That seems too easy. It's not really cursed is it? It's just a mind game, right?"

He shrugged. "Maybe. Part of the fun really." He got out of chair, the plastic groaned as he moved. "We have many different items in stock. Some are lucky, some make you eat, some make you sleep, one or two...might kill. But those are rare. I won't tell you what the item you choose does. You just pick one." He moved around the room, pointing at all the odd trinkets on the shelves and in glass cases. "Guaranteed though, is the money after seven days. What do you say? Care to play?" He held out his large hand to her. Ruth took one more glance around the room, knowing her life would change with ten thousand dollars.

"Sure. Sounds fun." She picked up a pen from the desk and quickly signed her name.

"Wonderful. Now the fun part, picking your item," he said, greedily rubbed his hands together.

***

Ruth sat on her couch and stared at the tiny purple and orange teeter-totter. It seemed like the most innocuous thing in the room at Loki's. Per the contest rules, Mr. Rex didn't tell her what it did, and whatever malevolence was in it, she didn't think it would be too bad. She reached out and teetered it back and forth a few times. *Probably a fun toy for something small,* she thought. She chose it

***

At home, she picked it up and walked into her bedroom. She put it on the nightstand and stared at it. *What on Earth will it do?* she wondered.

As her meager imagination played out different scenarios, her eyelids started feeling heavy. It was a bit early for a nap, but without a regular job, she had lots of free time. She closed her eyes and imagined what she would do with ten thousand dollars. She smiled and thought about being debt free.

"Take that, credit cards," she mumbled and fell asleep.

***

Ruth opened her eyes and the first thing she saw was the teeter-totter, but it seemed so far away. She reached out but it wasn't her hand she saw, it was a tiny, clawed, furry paw. She gasped, but it came out as a squeal. She glanced around and noticed she was in the middle of her bed, which was now huge. *What the hell is going on?* she wondered. Ruth saw her vanity chair close to the end of the bed and hopped onto it. Next, she crawled up the open drawers of the vanity, pulled herself to the top, and dashed to the mirror. Ruth screamed, but all that came out was another high-pitched squeal. She was covered in white and brown fur, and parts of which stuck straight up. She had little pink paws with claws and tiny pink lips. *Holy crap*, she thought over and over as she paced the vanity. *That thing turned me into a guinea pig!*

Just then she realized she'd have to last a week as an animal, and not an easy one like a dog or a cat but a small rodent. She flopped on her side and wanted to cry. How on Earth would she get around the apartment? How would she eat? *What do guinea pigs even eat?* she wondered as her tiny tummy growled. Sniffing, she rolled onto her feet and crawled her way down to the floor using the open drawers again. *Maybe my untidy ways will pay off,* she thought. All her drawers were open, and the things spilling out everywhere made perfect ladders. She walked through the apartment and saw the drawers of her bathroom caddy were open, so she'd be able to climb up to the toilet. *Potty trained pig earns ten-thousand-dollar prize!* she squeaked and went to the living room.

Her living room table had drawers which were also open, so she climbed up the makeshift ladder and managed to do a flying pig leap onto the couch. She saw the remote on the other side. She ran over and pawed at the power button until the TV turned on. *At least I can still watch TV,* she sighed and looked back towards the kitchen. The one dining room chair she had was still pushed up next to the counter from when she changed the lightbulb a week ago. *That'll help,* she thought, *now what to eat?* She crawled down to the floor and waddled to the kitchen.

The tile floor was cold on her little pads and she saw a box of Pop-Tarts on the counter. *Ooh Pop-Tarts.* She walked up to the chair and used the thin bars between the legs to pull herself up to the cloth seat. The back of the chair was a fancy, wooden filigree with plenty of room for her tiny feet to fit in, so one paw after another, she managed to climb her way to the counter.

Yes! She knocked over the Pop-Tart box and the leftover one from this morning slid out. She sniffed the frosted strawberry. Her favorite. Yet something about it wasn't appealing. She gave it a little lick. It was gross and left a weird film on her tongue. *Yuck. Man, what am I going to eat?* she pondered as she licked the cardboard box to get the taste out of her mouth. Without thinking, her teeth chomped down on the cardboard and she started eating it. *Wait what am I doing?* she wondered, but didn't stop. She worked though the cardboard in strips until half the top of the flap was gone. She took a step back and looked at the carnage. *Guinea pigs can eat cardboard, okay.*

She glanced around the kitchen and sighed. *Well now what?* Her mind wandered back to the teeter-totter and for some reason, it sounded like a blast. She climbed down her wooden pig ladder and hustled back to her room. After climbing up her comforter, she leapt from the bed to her nightstand and pushed the side of the teeter-totter down with her little paw. She climbed on, but then she remembered a teeter-totter needed two. *Hmm.* She slowly walked up the plank until the other side began to drop. She realized if she *surfed* in the middle it was still fun. Half up and half down, over and over. She went faster and faster. Up, down, up, down, up, down, up, down! Then she went too fast and rolled backwards, falling off. She reached out for something, but her arms were so short there was nothing to grab, and she squeaked again as she began to fall to the floor! *No!*

Luckily, she was able to grab hold of the comforter and slow her descent. Her little pig butt bumped on the ground and she squealed in pain. *Okay maybe not.* She tottered back into the living room and wondered what was on TV. Back on the couch, she stomped on the remote control until she managed to turn the TV on. She continued pawing at the buttons until she saw something that looked worthwhile. "America's Got Talent." It didn't take long before her little claws had the remote control mastered. *Maybe this won't be so bad,* she thought.

The world outside continued on. She amused herself when bill collectors or telemarketers would call. She propped her phone up against a pillow on the couch and when they called, for once, she answered. But she growled and squealed in their ears until they hung up. She noticed the telemarketer calls were coming less and less. She'd have to remember this trick when she turned back into a person.

She spent a scary few hours in existential dread one day, wondering how she'd turn back into a human? Would she turn back into herself exactly as she had been? Same hair, eyes, and everything else? What if she didn't? What if her eyes stayed red? What if her hair stayed white and brown? What would she do for the rest of her life? Would she be a sideshow attraction? And what about that stupid toy? She was right next to it when she turned into this little pig. Did that mean she'd have to be near the teeter-totter to turn back as well?

She started dragging the teeter-totter around with her and gave it a spot on the couch. She stared at it, asking it if she would turn back into a person. Of course, it didn't answer, which made her hysterical. After a few hours she calmed down and realized she'd be fine. She had read testimonies from others that had taken the deal at Loki's Curiosities and they were fine. She just had to spend a few more days like this.

On day five, Ruth was relaxing on a makeshift bed made of tissues on the living room floor, when there was a big bang at the front door. She squeaked in shock and stared at the door. She could see it shaking, someone was trying to break in. *No, no, no!* She got up from her comfy spot and ran behind the couch. The door frame splintered, and she heard the door hit the wall. *You assholes!* she thought and peeked around the couch as two men in masks walked into the apartment.

"Check the bedroom, doesn't look like there's much here," one of the men said while the other ran back to the bedroom. Ruth watched as he unplugged her TV and started going through her DVDs.

You son of a bitch! She ran out from behind the couch. *That's mine put it down!* She charged at his foot and started biting his shoe. "What the hell?" She felt hands pick her up as the man lifted her to his masked face. "Hey Mick. There's a guinea pig running around." He laughed and pulled up his mask. His skin was pock-marked and his nose had been broken more than once. "You wanna come with us? I bet my daughter would love you."

Screw you asshole! she squeaked and leapt from his hand and bit into his cheek. He yelled and started flailing around but her strong, guinea pig teeth didn't let go. She felt his hands wrap around her little body and pull. She finally let go and he flung her across the living room. She landed against the couch and rolled down onto the teeter-totter. She jumped up and made sure she didn't break it. It looked fine.

"You little shit!"

The other man returned, his hands were full of her fake jewelry.

"What happened?"

"Little shit bit me!" Mick moved the man's hands

and his eyes went wide as blood poured down his partner's face

"Oh that looks bad. You're gonna need stitches."

Ruth could see a flap of skin hanging down his cheek and smiled. *Don't mess with the pig, asshole!* The man growled and plodded over to the couch. Ruth gnashed her long teeth at him in warning. "You're not gonna kill it, are you?" the other man asked. The bleeding thief loomed over her, breathing hard.

"No. But I'm gonna piss it off." Ruth watched as he reached out and picked up the teeter-totter. *No!* she started squealing desperately. *Give it back!*

"Don't like me messing with your toy?" He wiggled it in the air before crushing it in his hand. The cracking wood made her little ears twitch and her heart jumped in her throat as he dropped the pieces to the ground. "Little asshole, teach you to bite me," he grumbled as they left, leaving their loot on the floor and the front door wide open.

Once they were gone, Ruth climbed down from the couch and stared at the cursed teeter-totter. The plank was broken in two and one of the columns had a huge crack in it. *No!* She ran around it, wondering if she would be able to fix it when she was human. Then she gasped and stopped in her tracks. Would she still turn back into a human now? She dived into a nearby drawer and found some scotch tape and pushed it out with her nose. After jumping down, she used her tiny arms to get a piece of tape and put it on the teeter-totter. But her tiny, fur covered paws didn't want to let go of the tape and she got tangled in it. *Piece of crap!* she squeaked and tried getting the tape off, flinging her paw around, scraping it against the table, biting with her teeth, all to no avail. It was stuck and not coming off. *No!* she cried as she sat next to the broken toy. *I don't want to be a guinea pig forever!* Tiny tears fell from her red eyes as she began to think that ten-thousand dollars wasn't worth this. There were only two more days before the game was over, but she wasn't sure if it would ever end now.

***

Two days later Ruth opened her eyes, the first thing she saw was the broken toy. The plank was still broken, and the column crooked. She had spent the last two days trying to fix it, but nothing helped. Her tiny body just wasn't capable. Tape kept getting stuck to her fur, and her arms weren't strong enough push the parts back together. It was a Sisyphean task. And now it was the seventh day, but she was afraid to move. Would she be human again, or still a guinea pig? Was the magic gone, now that the teeter-totter was broken? She took a deep breath and looked around. It didn't take long to notice that the living room table was closer, the remote control was smaller, and she was hungry for Pop-Tarts. She sat up with a gasp and looked at her paws. Not paws. Hands!

"Yes! Thank you, God!" She jumped to her feet and looked at herself in the mirror. She looked like herself again. There was no sign she spent the last week as a rodent. Her teeth were normal, her hair color was back to the original brown, and the best part: she only had two nipples. Ruth dashed into the shower and washed her greasy hair. It was the best shower she ever had. She brushed her teeth and was horrified at how much lettuce and cardboard was still trapped between them. The hairbrush she had been rubbing against was covered in fur, but she didn't care. She picked it up off the floor and ran it through her hair. "Ooh, that's nice." She put on a tank top, shorts and some flip-flops and sat down on the couch in front of the broken toy. "Now let's see if I can't get you fixed." She was able to glue the pieces back together so precisely, it was difficult to tell it had ever been broken. She picked up the purple and orange teeter-totter and put her keys in her pocket. "Let's get you back where you belong and get me that check!"

***

She rushed into Loki's Curiosities. The door to the inner office was open, and she saw Mr. Rex sitting at his desk. "Mr. Rex, I have something for you." She dashed inside and put the toy on his desk. "A week as a guinea pig, I definitely did not expect that." she said.

Mr. Rex laughed. "Yes, I was glad you got something fun. I guess it worked out?" He reached into a desk drawer and pulled out a check book.

"Except for the men breaking into my apartment, yes."

"Oh my! Well at least you can replace what they took now." He smiled and she saw his huge teeth again.

She crossed her arms over her stomach. "They didn't take anything. I bit one of the men on the face and they left to get it treated." Mr. Rex's eyes went wide before he burst out with laughter.

"My, my, aren't you adaptable?"

"One of the jerks broke the toy, but I think it still looks fine." He picked up the teeter-totter and examined it. Turning it and giving it a shake, it seemed stable.

"It does look fine, and since you turned back into a human, I'd say the curse is still intact. It usually takes more than that to break a curse. That's why they're called 'curses' and not 'the inconvenient thing that goes away when you break the source.'" He laughed at his own joke and filled out a check. "Ten thousand, as agreed." He tore the check from the book and held it out for her, but as she tried to take it, he didn't let go. "Unless you'd be interested in...double or nothing?"

Her jaw dropped. "Double? Twenty thousand dollars?"

"Yep. Another week, another artifact. What do you say?" He waved the check in the air. "Care to play again?" She looked at the check made out to her, then at the other artifacts around the room, her mind racing. She had just spent the week as a guinea pig, she could do anything. *Shit. No one ever got ahead by playing safe*, she thought. "Let's play."

CURSORY REVIEW

BY DONALD J. BINGLE

Kim Wasserman's eyes scanned the neatly hung and folded clothes in the master bedroom closet. Two months of Jenny Craig® meals and she was about to show off the sizzling results at the DeMarco's annual Fourth of July barbecue.

"C'mon, Kimbo, we're going to be late," called her husband, Ken, who, as usual, was twitching to leave when she had barely even started getting ready.

She rolled her eyes and smiled. "You know, you're going to call me Kimbo in public some day and then I will have to kill you." She headed toward the back of the closet, where she had hidden all of her favorite outfits that no longer fit back when her weight started creeping up. "Just because you don't care about your appearance, doesn't mean I don't have to take a few minutes to get ready."

Ahh, there were those cute jeans she had gotten at that adorable little shop in San Juan on their honeymoon. They'd been a bit snug, but she'd bought them anyway. She'd never worn them. She had gotten them when she was at her wedding weight, fifteen pounds below her high-weight mark. Now she was twenty-two and a half pounds lighter, thanks to Jenny. Seven and a half pounds below her wedding weight. The jeans, with their colorful, intricately embroidered pockets and cuffs, would be perfect for the barbecue.

She grabbed the jeans and headed out into the bedroom. Ken was waiting with arms crossed, his head tilted to the right, chin down, eyebrows raised. He unfolded his arms and tapped his watch. "No, still working," he mumbled.

Kim tried to give him a stern look, but a mischievous grin crept through. "I'll be ready before you are," she declared, continuing before he could protest, "because there is no way in Hell you are wearing that Hawaiian shirt."

Ken dropped his arms and sighed. "Yes, ma'am."

Kim slipped on a white, peasant-style blouse and stepped into her jeans. They didn't glide on as easily as she had expected. She tugged at the waistband and sucked in her now-smaller tummy, not that it really made a difference for the hip-huggers. Finally, she got the pants pulled up and the zipper closed. Tight jeans were fashionable, but she felt like a boa constrictor was swallowing her.

Ken stepped out of the closet with a clean rugby shirt on. "Do these jeans look too tight to you?" Kim asked, her mouth in a frown.

Ken froze, his eyes darting down and up her figure and then up and to the right, searching the heavens for the right answer, if there possibly could be a right answer to such spousal inquiries.

"Uh...er...m-m-my wife is right," he stammered.

She pursed her lips and gave him an icy glare. "Nice try, bucko. Now, what's the real answer?" She folded her arms and thrust her hip to one side to await his response, when the button holding the jeans closed popped, bouncing along the floor and under the bed.

Damn it. She was down twenty-two and a half pounds. How could the jeans not fit? Ken better not have been monkeying with the bathroom scale.

***

Grznarb snarled, his yellowed fangs dripping sulphuric saliva onto the institutional, metal desktop.

"I transfer you in from another department to head up the *Cursed Clothing and Frivolous Fashion Accessories Division* and this is what I get? Something that could be accomplished with a three-for-one sale on Häagen Dazs or accidentally washing the jeans in hot water?"

Threkma was sweating profusely and it wasn't just from the typically infernal heat. His horn-nubs glowed red from embarrassment and stress. "No, no, your Unholy Toadliness. It's not just that the pants have shrunk or the woman has not lost weight. The jeans are cursed. No matter who tries them on or when or where, they will always be just one size too small. It's actually a variation of the cursed camera gambit, the one which automatically adds a double-chin and twenty pounds to everyone in the picture, back from when I worked in the *Cursed Electronics and Other Incomprehensible Technology Division.*"

"Fah!" yelled Grznarb, a bit of hell-fire bursting forth from his mouth and singeing off Threkma's eyelashes. Grznarb had always found singed eyelashes to be a particularly effective management technique. He couldn't imagine how humans had never stumbled upon it. "And what does this cursed clothing get us? Mild aggravation on the part of the would-be wearer?" He knew his saliva was still steaming from the burst of hell-fire, distracting the underling, but he liked his minions terrified and confused, especially during their performance reviews.

"M-m-much more than that, sir. Diet failure, or at least perceived diet failure, can lead to bingeing. I think gluttony is the classic, word, your Pus-Filled Putrescence."

"Gluttony!" roared Grznarb, a glob of still steaming saliva spewing forth onto the desk-top and starting to eat away at the tally sheets and memoranda, then the metal beneath. "What kind of penny-ante curse-works are you running here? Your latest curse produces occasional gluttony? Who in Hell cares? As if gluttony wasn't endemic in human population anyway!"

Threkma swallowed hard. "More than that, your Unclean Maggotness. The cursed jeans can lead to domestic quarrels, displaced anger, depression, and, in a small number of cases, suicide. That's a mortal sin, there, your Vomitous Abomination. A mortal sin."

Grznarb snarled. "Even the little black dress thing was better than this."

Threkma straightened his thrice-broken spine at Grznarb's words. "The little black dress of infidelity did have some good results."

"Fah. You've been spending too much time around humans. Your speech offends me and not in a good way. Call the thing by its true name."

Threkma's spine began to curl, the previously

broken vertebrae grinding against each other with excruciating pain. "The micro-mini of sluttishness, you mean, your Diseased Ferretbreathness?"

"Yes," grumbled Grznarb, "but even it had limited effectiveness. The problem with cursed clothing is that the curse begins to fade too quickly when you take it off. Extended foreplay can lead to second thoughts. That's a real structural dilemma in dealing with fornication fabrics."

"Still," squeaked Threkma, "we did have that high profile political success with the little blue dress variant made out of fellatio fabric."

"Fah! You can't rest on old successes for eternity." Grznarb held his pointed chin in his scabby hand, letting a talon hover just a millimeter from his own eyeball, just to unnerve his unworthy subordinate. "What we need is something people wear every day, like the old eyeglasses of impure thoughts. Why aren't we making them anymore?"

Threkma trembled. "People switched to contacts, so we had to miniaturize and increase the potency of the cursed material. Then the humans switched to disposable contacts, creating a black hole in our supply and production budgets. Lately, they've started flocking to laser-eye surgery. We rigged a few of the lasers to malfunction and boil the insides of the eyes 'til they exploded, you know, just to try to buck the trend, but the whole sub-group has completely fallen apart, your Metastasizing Worminess."

"So, just what are you doing?" demanded Grznarb. "You keep requesting more and more of Hell's powers of damnation for your department, but I'm just not convinced it's being used well. The Dark One's power to curse is finite, you know. Not like the infinite blessings of our...competitor."

"Yes, your Festering Warthogness, but curses do last forever, so the total damnation in the world increases at all times. That should please you and The Horned Slayer."

Grznarb tapped his talon on his eyeball lightly, causing a yellow trail of bubbling ichor to ooze out and eat through the scabs on his cheek. "The total damnation increases, but so does the population. Besides, these fabric curses are especially problematic. The power of the curse dissipates as the item wears, fiber by fiber, leaving the item ultimately ineffective and a level of damnation in most lint filters that swallows errant socks whole."

The sock-less Threkma did not respond to the revelation of the answer to one of life's great mysteries, so Grznarb continued. "That's why hard items work the best—the curse can last for centuries, undissipated, especially with gems and gold. Why aren't we using our limited power of damnation for the old classics, like the cursed sword that damages whoever the wielder loves most in all the world equal to the damage inflicted by the sword in battle? Death to kings and comrades, wives and wenches. Now, there was a good time."

Threkma shuffled his feet, the claws clacking audibly on the rough stone floor. "Although occasionally used as fashion accessories, swords are really in the *Cursed Weapons and Things That Blow Up Real Good Division*, your Oozing Snotfaceness. In that vein, we did produce some wedding rings, in contemporary styles in both gold and platinum, of infidelity…er…sluttishness. Cursed diamonds really are forever, your Drooling Hideousness. But the humans took the damned rings off whenever the urge to be promiscuous took hold, generally well in advance of removing their clothes to rut. The rings were, accordingly, no more effective than the fornication fabrics and matching fetish footwear."

Grznarb snarled.

Threkma blathered on. "Wedding rings of shrewishness and wife-beating have been much more successful in eliciting the behavior sought to be induced."

Grznarb's snarl turned into a full-throated roar, sending a glob of glowing phlegm onto Threkma's foot. The minion endured the pain as it melted through to the floor. "Then why aren't we producing more of those?"

"Unfortunately, the effectiveness is high, but the overall duration tends to be short, failing to justify the expenditure of curse power needed to infuse the precious metal. Women's shelters, high divorce rates, and increasingly effective law enforcement in the area of domestic violence have all been an issue. And, once the ring is removed, whether because of divorce or incarceration, it is essentially a wasted curse. No one passes down family heirlooms anymore. High precious metal prices have resulted in the rings being melted down and the power of the curse diluted and spread across newly manufactured jewelry and electrical components, leading to hardware freeze-ups in most major computer brands and a general low-level of irritation across the population, but no more."

Grznarb picked his nose with his tongue. "So,

jewelry no longer is effective?"

Threkma brightened a bit, whether from the question or because the glob that had been on his foot had finally eaten its way deep into the stone floor. "We have had some success with bling."

"Bling?" Grznarb hated human slang.

"Heavy, gaudy necklaces and rings worn by youthful enthusiasts of hip-hop music. They wear it constantly."

Grznarb tapped his foot on the stone floor. "Get on with it. What sin is this 'bling' cursed with?"

Threkma smiled weakly. "It was meant to increase the popularity of the...er...singers."

Grznarb's brow furrowed. Threkma rushed on. "The so-called music is truly horrendous to hear, your Decomposing Vileness. It was hoped that insanity and mass suicide would result."

"And did it?"

"No. We did achieve some mid-level chaos and sin, however." Threkma didn't look at Grznarb as he continued sheepishly. "Moderate hearing loss and theft of digital music."

Grznarb thrust two razor-sharp talons into the nostrils of the minion and hefted him off his feet, blood flowing down Grznarb's scarred and scaly arm as the talons bit deep. "There is something you are not telling me. You are not the Prince of Lies! You, underling, cannot fool me."

"There was a production error," gasped Threkma with a nasal gurgle from Grznarb's talons and the blood flowing down the back of his throat.

Grznarb twisted his hand. "Yes?"

"Instead of cursing the bling, the bling causes the

wearer to curse. It's…it's proven quite effective at that. Hip-hop music is full of emphatic and descriptive cursing of all types, including all known and several unidentified forms of damnation and graphic representations of all bodily functions. And a sin is a sin, your Cancerous Moldiness."

Grznarb flung Threkma down into the minion's desk chair. "Have you nothing else?"

"Just the usual. Post Office uniforms with the curse of rage, Mont Blanc® pens cursed with arrogance, pretension, and condescension, adult diapers cursed with incontinence, and Candy Striper uniforms cursed with kleptomania and nymphomania. We did some cigarette lighters of pyromania, but everyone uses disposables now, so fireballs have declined noticeably." Threkma seemed to tense for a more localized fireball and the resulting incineration that he, no doubt, thought was coming.

Instead, Grznarb shook his head. Lice and sloughed skin spattered to either side. "When I brought you from the *Cursed Furniture and Decorative Lawn Ornament Division*, I thought you would shake things up here, Threkma. The cursed couch of false confession you placed in psychotherapists' offices really caught my good eye. And using the skin of Chinese dissidents to upholster it was an especially loathsome touch. Lots of guilt, a steady stream of suicides, some sprees of murderous mayhem, and trafficking in human parts sewn together in sweat shops by slave labor. All evil work."

Threkma managed a half-smirk of pride and self-satisfaction as Grznarb continued. "Of course, the straight-back institutional chair of false confession placed into police interrogation rooms was the big highlight of your stay. Anger, guilt, depression, false witness, suicide…the list of sin is infinite."

Grznarb approached the minion, looming over him. "Your stay here in The Lower Realms is infinite, but your job-security is not. One four-letter word from me and you could be chewed for all eternity by an Arch-Demon with breath that makes mine smell like peppermint schnapps."

Threkma quaked in fear, or maybe it was just another of the aftershocks of Beelzebub's Fall from Grace.

Grznarb jabbed the damned bureaucrat in the chest with a bloody talon. "Tell me what you were going to use this latest allocation of eternal damnation to curse now, right now. And it had better be good. I want a cursed wearable that has enormous impact, but does not wear out and get tossed in a box for Goodwill. Something that passes from generation to generation. Something insidious. Something delicious. And by delicious, I mean truly evil."

Threkma made no attempt to stem the bleeding that now flowed from both his snout and his chest, as he replied. "I did find an old recipe, almost a half-century since its last use. It not only has a tremendous impact on the wearer, but on his victims, the victim's extended family for generations to come, and on the misguidedly faithful."

"Why haven't you produced these to date?"

"They take an incredible amount of evil, your Rancid Hatefulness. They have to ward off constant blessings and that is not easy."

***

Father Breen returned to his room once most of the parishioners had left. He took off the stole that lay across his shoulders, kissed it, and placed it reverently on his desk. He sat down at the same desk with a weary slump and put his face in his hands. When he had first been called, he had been counseled by the monks who had trained him that celibacy was no easy task, but that he must put his mind and his energies to holy work instead. So many years had passed since that day and his normal sexual urgings had lessened with each passing year. He had performed well in his duties and had moved up the church hierarchy. Celibacy was not a struggle. His sexual feelings were a faint and distant memory.

But lately, since his promotion and transfer, he had felt new, disturbing, urgings. Urgings that excited him one moment and horrified him just a few hours later. Urgings he could not understand and could not tell anyone about, lest all his good work be destroyed. As he stroked the brocaded symbols of his stole, passed to him by his predecessor at St. Basils and his predecessor before that, he thought of what he should do.

He got up, kissed the stole, muttering a quick blessing, and draped it once again across his shoulders. It was time to meet with the new altar boy.

As he left his room, he no longer thought about what he should do, but he knew what he would do.

He smiled.

***

Somewhere in the firepits of Hell, Grznarb smiled, too. "A pleasing result, but expensive and, of course, not your recipe," rumbled the Demon to Threkma.

Threkma quavered and lowered his eyes, but spoke

in a rush of words. "No, it's not. I mean, yes, it's not, your Coagulating Rottenness. But, it gave me an idea. Perverted symbols of allegiance. Not really jewelry, but tokens of membership or belief that are worn every day. Little gold crosses of cruelty, for example."

"Fah," snorted Grznarb, "you focus only on the faithful. Blessing resistance will need to be built-in at extra cost. Besides, The Dark Angel requires a broad spectrum of sinners. Each and every soul should have an equal opportunity to damn itself for all eternity."

Threkma's eyes darted from side to side. "Not crosses," he murmured, no doubt stalling for time. "Been done before, anyway," he blathered on, punctuating his words with a cracking, maniacal giggle. "Although both the Crusades and the Spanish Inquisition did have their moments. No, your Regurgitated Sliminess, but perhaps non-religious icons. We can pervert all of their symbols against them."

An excellent suggestion. But, Grznarb was an excellent manager. He knew that he had to make his underling sweat just a bit more. "Symbols of allegiance? This is not the Middle Ages, my misguided minion. Heraldry is no longer in style." He curled his lips in a faux grimace.

"Modern symbols," insisted Threkma, "Frat pins of homophobia, perhaps."

"Too narrow a base," growled Grznarb, making a mental note of the suggestion.

"Union pins of racism," proffered Threkma, obviously desperate to please his taskmaster.

"Declining union membership," replied Grznarb, secretly pleased at his servant's creativity.

"Corporate logos of greed."

"Nobody publicly identifies with their employer these days."

"American flag lapel pins of intolerance and warmongering." shouted Threkma, in revelation.

Grznarb roared in laughter, unintentional hell-fire incinerating the office desk, the straight-backed chair, and his erstwhile employee.

"How do you think *I* got this job?" he mumbled to himself as he strode off to the pits to find a damned replacement.

ABOUT THE AUTHORS

ANGELIQUE FAWNS

Angelique Fawns is a speculative fiction writer with a day job creating promos for Corus Entertainment in Toronto. She lives on a farm with her husband, daughter, 7 horses, chickens, fainting goats and an attack llama. You can find her work in *Ellery Queen Mystery Magazine*, *The Corona Book of Ghost Stories*, and *Demonic Carnival*. You can follow her on Twitter @Raingirl51 or on the web at:

http://www.fawns.ca

MICHELLE VON ESCHEN

Michelle is a lover of the macabre who prefers Earl Grey tea, October, people who say goodbye on the phone, and her dreams are so real she can't figure out what has really happened to her. When she isn't writing, Michelle enjoys weightlifting, dark beer, web design, singing and playing guitar, and watching horror movies. She is afraid of the dark and spending quiet time with her broken heart.

She is the author of the novel *When the Dead* and the novella *Mistakes I Made During the Zombie Apocalypse*, three short story collections: *Last Night While You Were Sleeping*, *When You Find Out What You're Made Of*, and *Once Upon a Time, When Things Turned Out Okay*, a co-author of *The Spread* which she wrote with her twin sister, and a co-editor of *GIVE: An Anthology of Anatomical Entries*. Her most recent work, *The Murk of Us*, is a nonfiction prose and poetry collection documenting the horrors of the toxic empath/narcissist relationship. Her short stories are also featured in several anthologies including *Roms, Bombs, and Zoms* from Evil Girlfriend Media, *A Very Zombie Christmas* from ATZ Publications, and Jolly Horror's *Don't Cry to Mama.*

MYA LAIRIS

Mya Lairis has a thing for monsters, and always has since watching *Clash of the Titans* and *Godzilla* back when she was a wee one. She enjoys crocheting, painting, reading military horror and bio-thrillers but will read anything. While she began writing paranormal and fantasy shorts, she enjoys composing horror shorts. Mya lives in Maryland with her two furry kids, the diva Zoe and Cougar the devious.

JORDAN KERNS

Jordan Kerns spent her childhood shuffling between Wyoming and Southern Utah, so she knows a thing or two about the wind and the snow and the desert. She also spent her childhood with an older brother and a younger brother, so she knows a thing or two about lighthearted suffering. She's currently residing in Salt Lake City with a German Shepard and a cat, so she knows a thing or two about not sleeping ever (like,

EVER). You can usually find her reading, thinking about reading, or watching someone else play video games on YouTube. Follow her on Tumblr or Twitter @bazookajo94. She's probably posting about books.

JUSTIN GULESERIAN

He's just this guy, you know?

J.C. RAYE

J.C. Raye's stories are found in anthologies with Scary Dairy Press, Books & Boos, Franklin/Kerr, C.M. Muller, HellBound Books, Jolly Horror and Death's Head Press. Other publications are on the way in 2019 with Belanger Books, Rooster Republic and Devil's Party Press. For 18 years, she's been a professor at a small community college teaching the most feared course on the planet: Public Speaking. Witnessing grown people weep, beg, scream, freak out and pass out is just another delightful day on the job for her, and seats in her classes sell quicker than tickets to a Rolling Stones concert. She also loves goats of any kind, even the ones that faint.

PATSY PRATT-HERZOG

Patsy Pratt-Herzog is an emerging freelance writer from Southwestern Ohio. Her favorite genres to write are Sci-Fi and Fantasy. When she's not writing, she enjoys painting and riding roller coasters. She shares her house in the burbs with her husband Tim and a chunky cat named Rachel. To learn more about Patsy and see other samples of her work, you can visit her blog at:

https://patsyprattherzog.wordpress.com/featured-publications/

Other publishing credits include: *The Case of the Mislaid Eggs* in The Devil's Party Press anthology *Suspicious Activities*; *Noble Enough* in the *From A Cat's Viewpoint II* anthology; and *The Ghost of Chillingham Manor* in The Devil's Party Press anthology *Halloween 2019*. Upcoming publications this year include: *The Case of the Mislaid Plans* in The Flame Tree Anthology *Detective Mysteries* due out in November 2019.

JAMI BAUMANN

Jami Baumann was born to be a storyteller. She has been capturing the imaginations of her friends for years. This mother of four and breast cancer survivor lives in Ohio. She writes every type of story you can imagine. She has just recently started writing stories for submissions and publication. In December 2018 she placed second in Stormy Island Publishing's holiday romance contest. More of her work is yet to come.

https://www.facebook.com/jamiBbaumannwriter

JEANNIE WARNER

Jeannie Warner spent her formative years in Colorado, Canada, and California, and is not afraid to abandon even the most luxurious domestic environs for an opportunity to travel anywhere. She has a useless degree in musicology, a checkered career in computer security, and aspirations of world domination.

Jeannie's writing credits include blogs of random musings and warning on IT Security, two unpublished thriller novels, a great many poems of dubious quality and content, stories in online magazines and anthologies, a podcast, a movie credit, as well as a collection of snarky notes to a former upstairs neighbor. She currently lives in Northern California.

Jeannie enjoys hockey, making music, dancing, and believes strongly that yes is more fun than no. Feel free to buy her a dark and stormy whenever you see her.

SOPHIE KEARING

Sophie Kearing is a writer of long tweets and short fiction. Her work has been picked up by Jolly Horror Press, Mojave Heart Review, Ellipsis Zine, Horror Tree, Spelk Fiction, Left Hand Publishers, Paper Angel Press, Elephants Never, New Pop Lit, and other publications. She loves the #WritingCommunity on Twitter and would love to connect with you @SophieKearing.

JEREMY MAYS

Jeremy Mays currently resides in Mt. Vernon, Illinois, where he is an English teacher at the local high school. In his free time, Jeremy enjoys writing, ghost hunting, collecting horror movie memorabilia, and spending time with his wife, Courtney, and his nine children. All things related to Jeremy can be found at:

https://thejeremylmays.wordpress.com/
and
https://www.facebook.com/jeremy.mays.520

JOAN C. GUYLL

Joan lives with her husband Brian in a small town on the Kent coast in UK. She was born in Singapore and is ethnically Chinese. She self-published *Valley of the Gods*, a novel based loosely on her life in the Indian Himalayas and also a non-fiction booklet known as *Fascinating People of Battle*, as a tribute to her retail customers during her 12 years stint as a shopkeeper. Ex-accountant, ex-shopkeeper and ex-mum, she is now retired, pigging out in her home town of Singapore during the winter months and cooling off in the UK for the rest of the year. You can find her work at:

https://www.amazon.com/Valley-Gods-Joan-C-Guyll/dp/1847281559/
and
https://www.amazon.com/Fascinating-People-Battle-Joan-Guyll/dp/1326603337/

RICHARD LAU

Richard is an award-winning writer who has been published in newspapers, magazines, anthologies, and the high-technology industry. He's also had six of his plays produced and two performed as readings. He thanks Barbara who has been with him through the jolly, the horror, and the press of creative writing.

ALESHA ESCOBAR

Alesha Escobar is an Amazon Bestselling Author who writes fantasy to support her chocolate habit. She enjoys reading everything from Tolkien and the *Dresden Files*, to the *Hellblazer* comics and classic literature. She's the author of the bestselling *Gray Tower Trilogy*, an action-packed supernatural thriller set in an alternate World War II. The trilogy hit the bestsellers lists at Amazon (Top 60 in the entire Kindle store), as well as iBooks, Kobo, Barnes & Noble online, and Amazon UK.

Besides being a loving warrior mom to her six children, she enjoys crafts, consuming more coffee than is necessary, and spending time with her husband Luis, a 20-year art veteran for *The Simpsons* television show.

To receive free and discounted book offers from a Alesha, join her *Fantasy, Mashups, & Mayhem* mailing list today at:

http://www.aleshaescobar.com/newsletter

AMANDA CRUM

Amanda Crum is a writer and artist whose work has appeared in publications such as *Barren Magazine* and *Eastern Iowa Review* and in several anthologies, including *Beyond The Hill* and *Two Eyes Open*. She is the author of three novels, *The Fireman's Daughter*, *Ghosts Of The Imperial*, and *The Darkened Mirror*. Her first chapbook of horror-inspired poetry, *The Madness In Our Marrow*, was shortlisted for a Bram Stoker Award nomination in 2015; her story *A Shimmer In The Parlor* was a finalist for the J.F. Powers Prize in Short Fiction in 2019. She currently lives in Kentucky with her husband and two children.

JEFF BARKER

Jeff Barker has many short stories published in literary journals and anthologies including *Hobart*, Jolly Horror Press, *Broadkill Review*, *HelloHorror Journal*, and *Literally Stories*. Jeff is also a healthcare provider in the field of psychiatry. Before that, he had a nine year career as a television news anchor and reporter in Texas, Alabama, Florida, and Oregon. He has interviewed three U.S. Presidents, and stood in the middle of five major hurricanes. His vast life experience and study of human behavior shape his storytelling. He lives on the Gulf Coast in Daphne, Alabama. You can follow his work at:

http://www.jeff-barker.com

NATASHA HANOVA

Natasha Hanova is an author of young adult and adult dark fantasy/paranormal fiction. Her debut novel, *EDGE OF TRUTH*, a young adult dystopian, is now available. She also has short stories in *Debut Collective Anthologies (Hostile Takeover Book 3)* and *Undead Tales 2*. You can find her on Twitter @NatashaHanova, Author Natasha Hanova on Facebook, or her website:

https://www.natashahanova.com

SIPORA COFFELT

Sipora Coffelt spent a decade wandering from university to university, earning her BA in philosophy, only to read the classifieds one day and realize her mistake. She turned her hand to technical writing in the field of health education and literacy. Today, she lives on an acreage in Kansas, growing vegetables and tending flowers. In 2017, she began writing fiction and has short stories published or forthcoming in *The Arcanist*, *Page and Spine*, *Cockroach Conservatory, Vol 2: Glory of Man: The Rise and Fall of the Reality Soldier*, *Stupefying Stories Magazine*, and *Dark Moon Digest*.

MARK MCLAUGHLIN

Mark McLaughlin is a Bram Stoker Award-winning author whose fiction, nonfiction and poetry have appeared in more than one thousand magazines, newspapers, websites and anthologies, including *Writer's Digest*, *Cemetery Dance*, and *The Year's Best Horror Stories* (DAW Books). McLaughlin's latest paperback releases include the story collections: *City of Living Shadows & More Lovecraftian Tales*, *Horrors & Abominations: 24 Tales Of The Cthulhu Mythos* and *The House Of The Ocelot & More Lovecraftian Nightmares* (all coauthored by Michael Sheehan, Jr.). Other collections of McLaughlin's fiction include *Dracula Transformed* (with Michael McCarty), *Best Little Witch-House In Arkham*, and *Empress Of The Living Dead*. McLaughlin and McCarty co-wrote the horror novel, *Monster Behind The Wheel*. McLaughlin is also the coauthor, with Rain Graves and David Niall Wilson, of *The Gossamer Eye*, a Bram Stoker Award-winning poetry collection.

M. GUENDELSBERGER

M. Guendelsberger is a novelist and writer living in Cincinnati, Ohio. His short fiction has appeared in *The Penmen Review*, *Academy of the Heart and Mind*, *Rougarou: Journal of Arts and Literature*, *Oxford Magazine* and others. He is a 2001 graduate of Miami University and holds a Bachelor's Degree in Creative Writing. His first novel, *An End to Something*, was published in 2014.

JUDITH BARON

Judith Baron is a fiction writer. Her short stories have been published in *Canadian Dreadful*, *Handbook For The Dead*, *Animal Uprising*, *The Sirens Call eZine #47: Deeds*

Most Foul and Unnatural, Future Visions Anthologies: Volume 2, Horror Bites Magazine Issue #8, The Poet's Haven Digest, Deadly Bargain: A Colors in Darkness Anthology, Trembling with Fear: Year 2 and *Spadina Literary Review*. She has a degree in Political Science from the University of Western Ontario and currently lives near Toronto, Ontario.

B.D. PRINCE

B.D. Prince was born in Michigan—a dark fiction and comedy writer who credits these proclivities to growing up near a cemetery and being endowed with a freakishly long funny bone. He ultimately moved to California to pursue screenwriting and get a tan. Prince has written everything from screenplays to one-liners for Joan Rivers. After completing several screenplays and publishing numerous short stories, Prince is currently working on his first full-length horror novel.

H.R. BOLDWOOD

H.R. Boldwood is a writer of horror and speculative fiction. In another incarnation, Boldwood was a Pushcart Prize nominee and was awarded the 2009 Bilbo Award for Creative Writing.

Boldwood's characters are often disreputable and not to be trusted. They are kicked to the curb at every conceivable opportunity. No responsibility is taken by this author for the dastardly and sometimes criminal acts committed by this ragtag group of miscreants.

Boldwood's debut novel *The Corpse Whisperer* is available at:

https://www.amazon.com/Corpse-Whisperer-Allie-Nighthawk-Mystery-ebook/dp/B07HHFC3RS)

TYLOR JAMES

Tylor James lives in New Richmond, Wisconsin with his fiance, Tessandra, and his step-daughter, Rosemary. These are the people who keep him out of the crazy-house (most of the time). Tylor has been writing incessantly since he was a young child, and his scribblings have only become more deranged and demented over the passing years. Although horror is his primary genre, he also writes absurdist/strange fictions, westerns, pulpy crime stories, science-fiction, and quirky philosophical stuff. Along with *Accursed*, you may discover some of his stories and poems in such anthology books as, *Willow River Writers Anthology, 2018,* and *America's Emerging Horror Writers: Midwest Region.* When not writing, you may find him performing as a singer-songwriter in bars/restaurants around St. Croix County, filming ultra-cheap horror movies with his iPad, as well as plunking along on his trusty typewriter...

KAREN THROWER

Karen Thrower was born and raised in Oklahoma. She lives in Tulsa with her husband and their rambunctious six-year old. She graduated from The University of Tulsa with a bachelor's degree in Deaf Education in 2005. She is also a member of Oklahoma Science Fiction Writers and serves as the President and Facebook 'Wizard' which she suspects has something to do with her young age. Her story *The Lost Ones* appears in the bestselling *Secret Stairs: A Tribute to Urban Legend* You can find the rest of her works on her Amazon Author page:

https://www.amazon.com/author/karenthrower

DONALD J. BINGLE

Donald J. Bingle is the author of six books and more than fifty short stories in the horror, thriller, science fiction, mystery, fantasy, steampunk, romance, comedy, and memoir genres. His "signature dark humor" can be found in *Frame Shop*, a mystery thriller set in a suburban writers'group, and *GREENSWORD*, a dark comedy about global warming, as well as in many of his short stories, most of which have been collected by genre in his *Writer on Demand* series. More on Don and his writing can be found at:

https://www.donaldjbingle.com

ACKNOWLEDGEMENTS

First, I'd like to thank T.J. Tranchell for his wonderful Foreword. A little about T.J.:

T.J. Tranchell was born on Halloween. His stories have appeared in *Red Rock Review, Despumation, Mad Scientist Journal* and elsewhere. With Michelle Kilmer, he co-edited *GIVE: An Anthology of Anatomical Entries* for When the Dead Press. His novella *Cry Down Dark* and collection *Asleep in the Nightmare Room* are available from Blysster Press and wherever books are sold. Tranchell is also a freelance editor and journalist. Find him online at:

http://www.tjtranchell.com

In the acknowledgements of our last anthology, *Don't Cry to Mama*, I said that anthologies take a lot more work than I thought. I didn't know what I was talking about. With *Accursed*, we received nearly two hundred submissions, and so many of them were high quality, amazing stories. *Accursed* took way more effort than *Don't Cry to Mama*. The toughest part of the job was picking the best submissions. A lot of the stories we ultimately rejected were wonderful. It's unfortunate that we could only take so many. Sending out rejections for great stories is truly the worst part of publishing. There is so much talent out there. So, a big thank you to all who submitted. Keep at it!

I'd also like to thank several people who have been really critical in putting this anthology together. First my co-editor Lori Titus. Lori has become Jolly Horror's grown-up voice of reason. Whenever there is indecision, or a tough problem to solve. Lori always has the right answer. I rely on her a lot.

Autumn Miller was a huge help during the story selection process. She has great instincts, and it's a rare situation when I disagree with her.

Eloise Knapp made the awesome book cover. All I have to give her is a concept, and a few days later the perfect cover is in my inbox. She's the most amazing cover artist I know, and super easy to work with.

A lot of other folks helped out in both little and big ways, and deserve thanks. Kayla Lambert, my "first cousin once removed," is a tattoo artist and gave the cursed tattoo story "Inked" a read to ensure authenticity. Shunda Yates read several stories I was on the fence about, and gave me her honest reader opinion. Last but not least my family. Sofia, Ethan, and Emily. I spent a lot of weekend nights with my head in my computer and my bedtime at 4 a.m. getting these things done. I'm sure they recognized my "uh huh" as not paying attention to what they were saying.

If you've reached this part of the book and are still reading, it's time for me to thank you, the reader. Hope you enjoyed reading our second collection. There will be many more. Next up, *Coffin Blossoms: A Horror/Comedy Anthology.*

Jonathan Lambert
November 2019